TRAIN TRACKS

TRAIN TRACKS

. . . can death, deceit, disruption save them?

PETER ALDERMAN

FCP

Dedicated to all the children who are or
were victims of abuse.

In his new novel, Train Tracks, Alderman brilliantly tackles the trials and challenges inherent in the human condition. Alderman's gentle and thoughtful tone brings to light the unique differences in our individual realities. In a melting pot of beliefs and traditions, Train Tracks shows us that diversity and contrast are tools that help us expand our awareness of our interconnectedness.

—H.T. Manogue, Award-Winning Author
www.shortsleeves.net

A modern day epic, a snapshot of America's past, and a generational tale for the ages. Peter Alderman has given us a precious and unforgettable gift with TRAIN TRACKS. Buckle up, and enjoy the ride! (Can't wait to see this movie!)

—Howard A. Klausner
Screenwriter, Director, and Producer

Howard Klausner is a writer, director and producer of films such as "Space Cowboys", starring Oscar winner Clint Eastwood, "The Identical" starring Golden Globe nominated Ray Liotta, "Hoovey" starring Alyson Stoner, "The Last Ride", "The Secret Handshake" and "The Grace Card".

CHAPTER 1 - THE RITUAL . . . 1980

"Inside each of us, there is the seed of both good and evil.
It's a constant struggle as to which one will win.
And one cannot exist without the other." Eric Burdon

. . . .

In the sleepy, middle Tennessee town of Caldron, twenty or so miles south of Nashville where nothing happens, . . . except behind closed doors, a small bowl sailed by a young woman's head missing her face by inches and smashing against the wall. It shattered into pieces as glass fell to the ground like egg shells. The girl named Grace stood quivering with fear not noticing the hole in the wall left by the missile that Billy, her husband, had just hurled at her. "I'm out of chips, and now you broke the bowl," he yelled. Obviously, Grace knew she didn't break the bowl but made no attempt to contradict him. She was in a stranglehold of fear. Her defense mechanisms had been stripped several years ago as well as her ability to stand up for what was right. She was a hostage in her own house. Her weak,

fragile, guilty state of mind made her a prime target for manipulation, and Billy did just that, manipulate and . . . terrorize.

"I'm out of beer, you bitch! You should have gotten some
on the way home from work!"

"I'm sorry, Billy," squeaked Grace. Billy just glared at her,
teeth bared. Shaking Grace continued, "I'll get it right now."
She pivoted to leave when her eyes noticed the hole in the wall
and the glass scattered on the floor. "I'll clean that up later,
Billy." Billy groaned his response as Grace grabbed winter gear
to put on to protect her from the cold night.

A light wind swept the leaves from the sidewalk as Grace
shuffled her way to the store. She dragged her feet giving her
a maximum amount of time to be away from him. Her black
knit cap sat on top of her head defying the cold. She had on a
heavy, brown jacket which concealed most of the gray uniform
she wore at her factory job. Her gray pants covered her skinny
limbs and overlapped her scuffed, bruised work boots. Grace's
delicate nose was dripping and red from the cold. She scolded
herself for not picking up his beer on the way home from work.
She dreaded this nightly ritual and, more so, the aftermath. She
was almost there. A few more steps.

The crescent moon made vain attempts to break through
the thick clouds but was only able to manage a few brief ap-
pearances until it was consumed by the darkness. The light from
lampposts guided Grace as she wrapped her scarf tighter around
her neck to ward off the chill of the late, fall night. She reached
her destination, Donnelly's, a small mom and pop operation
owned by Mike Donnelly and his wife, Lynnda. Grace's family
had been coming here for years during happier times and had

formed a strong bond with the couple. She struggled to push open the heavy oak door and was greeted with a sad smile from Lynnda who was sweeping an area in front of the stools by the counter.

Mike was clearing off the only table they had for customers to gather. However, there were no other customers on this raw, cold night. Just Grace. Though only twenty-two, she was burdened by the hardships of one who had lived an entire life. Her once comely face now was etched with the lines of worry...or even fear. Strands of her dark hair dangled recklessly over her face with some extending down over her cheeks and hanging to her neck. It was a peek-a-boo look which would usually convey a cuteness, an innocence for most girls who were twenty-two. Not with Grace. Her dark, hallow, lonely eyes now only drew one in trying to understand what happened to this pathetic creature.

Mike was gripped with sorrow upon seeing Grace but tried his best to greet her with an element of cheeriness. She was special to the Donnelly's, and they hated to see that she had eroded to this level of wreckage. "Hi, Grace. We've got to fix that old door or at least grease the hinges. How are you doing on this cold evening?"

"I'm OK," which was Grace's usual response. A weak attempt to conceal the misery that weighed on her every day, every hour, every minute. She was now limited to curt, laconic responses and reluctant to engage in conversation. Why should she burden folks with her problems? It wasn't right. She was just going to perform her mission and depart.

"The usual," Lynnda offered.

"Yes," said Grace quivering, still trying to shake off the chill.

Lynnda turned and reached into the cooler for a six-pack of Bud Light. She placed the cans into a bag and handed it to Grace. Grace quietly thanked her, grabbed the bag, turned and walked out the door. Lynnda watched her slip out into the night. She sighed softly as Mike approached and stood by her side. The door closed. They watched through the store window as Grace's silhouette shuffled slowly down the sidewalk back to her house.

. . . .

Grace was not always enveloped in gloom. There was a time her eyes sparkled with innocence and hope. She was a happy girl growing up. Having lost her dad to a tragic accident at an early age didn't darken her spirit. Her mom, Pam, worked at a local factory and Grace joined her soon after her Pops, as she called him, died. She had dropped out of school to help pay the bills, and mom and daughter had become a team dealing with the adversity that life had sold them.

They would walk together to work at the textile factory located down the street and around the block from their home. They would tell jokes, play tag, and discuss the going on's at the factory. It was a bonding time between mother and daughter. Who knew that going to work could be so much fun. And they would repeat the same antics on their way home, a home that Pam Keenan and her husband, Clark, had purchased. Oh, it wasn't a castle, but it was their castle.

Time and neglect had been hard on the structure: it needed some serious attention; major remodeling. Clark was more than up to the task. He would return home from work, grab his tools and immediately would begin restoring parts of the old, weathered home. When Pam got home from her shift, she would join Clark in the refurbishing projects. They became a dynamic duo happily working together shaping up their castle. In time, he and his wife had refinished the floors, painted the walls, fixed the leaks on the roof and patched and nailed and sanded their shack into a home: a loving home for their family.

It was at this home where Grace had been born. She grew up surrounded by laughter and love. Her parents didn't coddle her but were protective and caring. Their means were limited, so being a spoiled little girl was never in the picture. Having a roof over their heads and food on the table were always acknowledged and appreciated at their dinner prayers. They took nothing for granted and, ironically, these limitations actually made them happy. They were grateful for what they had and didn't envy what they didn't have. To them, they had it all; shelter, food, and each other as well as Lily, their rescued mutt who seemed quite content in the dog house in the back yard that Clark had built for her.

. . . .

However, now Grace trudged reluctantly to her house: it was not a home anymore. At least not in the way she had at one time experienced or perceived.

Her legs seemed heavy as she got closer to the structure.

The cottage that was once the envy of the neighborhood was now deteriorating much like Grace's spirit. The paint was peeling, shingles had been ripped off the roof by ruthless winds, and overgrown shrubs shoved their way against the house and up, underneath the clapboards Leaves scattered the lawn, broken branches from a maple tree that her dad had planted shed twigs and limbs everywhere. A broken porch swing on one hinge swung precariously in the breeze. No, it was not the same house that Grace grew up in.

She stopped briefly before climbing the three steps to the porch, took a deep breath and forced her way up to the front door. She pushed it gently as it groaned opening up into a small foyer. To her right, a picture hung on the wall of her parents. They were seated in the swing on the front porch during happier days holding hands and grinning. A brief smile creased Grace's face then quickly faded.

As she ventured further into the living room, the TV glared back at her with some game that was being played. She didn't know which one. Most likely the Tennessee Vols against another SEC team. She didn't care. The room she had cleaned before she had left in the morning was now cluttered, disorderly. It was strewn with papers, empty beer cans, and a dirty, orange sweatshirt that was draped over the couch. Pieces of glass from the bowl Billy had chucked at her were scattered on the floor. "Hello! I'm back," she managed.

"What took you so long?" barked the irritated voice from the living room. Billy hadn't moved an inch. Grace was disgusted but, again, tried to conceal her contempt.

"Well, I ...I..."

"I what? I slave all day working around this dump, and you drag your ass to get me my beer," Billy growled. "What a cheap excuse you are for a wife."

Grace hung her head. "I'm sorry. I'll be faster next time," all along knowing that he did nothing while in the house except drink, watch TV, and scowl.

"You better be," as he grabbed the beer from Grace, slipped one out and popped open the can. His eyes returned to the screen. Grace walked to the kitchen and glanced at the dirty dishes in the sink. This morning it was glistening clean. Now, it was a mess; as was her life. "What's for dinner?" Billy snapped from his sofa seat. Grace jumped a little, but she had become numb to such outbursts.

"I cooked up some beef stew last night. I thought it would help in this cold weather. I'll reheat it, and then we'll be ready to eat," she said shaking her head when Billy couldn't see her.

"Good! You did something right."

Grace and Billy sat down at the kitchen table to eat. They'd peek up between spoonfuls of stew. Billy would glare at Grace whereas Grace would try to avoid eye contact. The only conversation was limited to idle talk about the weather, work, or whatever game Billy had watched that day. Serious discussion and compatibility eroded years ago.

Grace missed the ole days when the family would express their appreciation at dinner for what they had. She missed the time when Billy was infatuated with the young girl who was....happy, innocent, and grateful. And she missed the young Billy who grinned easily and had a quick sense of humor, smart ass as it was. He was free and easy and loving. Yes, she missed it. All of it.

As she got up to clear the table to put the dishes in the sink, she glanced out the kitchen window. She saw Lily's dog house in the back yard littered with discarded plastic cups, paper plates, and beer cans. Although Lily had died years ago, Grace still considered it Lily's dog house. She had been very fond of Lily for she was special even though she was just a mongrel. Her dad and Grace had found Lily emaciated along the tracks. Grace had pleaded with her father to allow her to bring the mutt home. He was hesitant but acquiesced and carried their new family member back to their home. They all took turns caring for the sores that Lily had endured in her previous life. Grace especially had taken great care to nurse her back to health. However, now Lily's dog house was occupied by another.

"Did you feed Caleb?" Grace asked.

"No!" Billy blurted. " . . . And I'm not going to. It's too damn cold out there." He turned to look at Grace to see what she was going to say next as he took a swig of his beer.

She looked back at him and said, "Well, Caleb must be cold too as well as hungry."

"He'll be fine. Quit fussing over him. I think you love him more than me."

Grace tried to conceal the magnitude of truth in his words as she reached for some leftover stew and put it in a plastic dog bowl.

"I'm going to see how he's doing and bring him some stew," she said.

"Fine!" Billy snarled as he guzzled some more of his beer.

Grace had to put on her shawl. It seemed cooler than it did when she had gone to the store earlier that evening. She opened the door as a chill cut through her clothing, and closed it with her foot. Grace then gazed out at the dog house as she shivered warmed only by the bowl of hot stew that she cradled in her hands.

There was no movement in Lily's dog house. The night was silent except for a train on the tracks in the distance and the whistling of the wind.   Grace stared at the opening of the dog house. With every step she took, she kept her focus on the entrance. Her breathing became increasingly labored as she got closer to the dog house. Her eyes pooled with moisture. She knelt down by the opening, peered into the pile of blankets and said, "Caleb, I got something for you, sweetie." Nothing. "Caleb, are you OK, little buddy." The clatter of the train rumbled in darkness. Grace could feel the stab of Billy's piercing eyes on her back as he gazed out of the kitchen window. "Caleb......" Grace laid the bowl in the front entrance, stood up, concerned and afraid. She headed back to the rear door with hurried steps and turned to look one more time at the dog house.

A shaking, small hand reached out from the opening, grabbed the bowl of stew, and pulled it into the bedding. Small eyes peered back at Grace. A weak, trembling voice called out "I love you, mommy." The train rumbled by shaking the ground with a loud clacking, wailing into the night swallowing the words. A single tear trickled down Grace's cheek.

Grace shuttered with shame and sadness and .... fear. She mouthed the words, "I love you, too, Caleb." Buried in weakness, she turned, opened the door, afraid to go back inside her house, but, none-the-less, did.

CHAPTER 2 - TWELVE YEARS EARLIER - 1968

"Where there is love there is life." Mahatma Gandhi

Pam had worked on their garden earlier that day, and it was abundant with tomatoes, cucumbers, and an array of flowers. Clark had cut the lawn, picked up twigs, and prepared the back yard for a family cookout. Lily, the dog, was busy chasing after the ball that Grace, who recently turned ten, had tossed to her. Now Clark was grilling hamburgers, and Pam sat in an old wooden lawn chair with contentment painted on her face. The radio softly played Glenn Campbell's newest song, "Wichita Lineman." Music was always a part of their lives as Clark's guitar leaned against the outside wall of the house as he cooked. Grammy, Clark's mom whose name was Barbara, was seated next to her with a wide grin, tapping her foot while watching her granddaughter frolicking with Lily and knowing her daughter's home was alive with happiness. It was a perfect family setting. Grammy was grateful for this turn of events for she remembers a more tragic time in the past.

The romance between Pam and Clark was the offshoot of a tragedy that happened in Kalamazoo, Michigan. Clark Keenan and his mom and dad lived there in a modest home just outside of the city. Clark's mom worked as a nursery school teacher, and his father had a job at the local college, Western Michigan University, doing maintenance work.

Clark liked to play the guitar and write music but was realistic that that would never materialize into a career, so he began taking classes at WMU. It was on one of those days when Clark was taking classes, and his mom was working at the nursery that it happened. Barbara's husband was busy doing an electrical project in the attic of their home when a blaze started in the kitchen unbeknownst to him. The house went up like a tinder box and crumbled to the ground along with Clark's father's ashes.

Preacher Jennings and his family took them in and tried to comfort them during this horrendous time. Clark and his mom would attend his sermons while sitting with the preacher's family.

Preacher Jennings was black and spoke with a power and energy that made one feel he had a personal connection with the lord. His message of love, acceptance, and doing good were met with "Amens" and "Hallelujahs," but all his prayers couldn't seem to shed the despair that the mother and son were draped in for their life was shredded into ashes along with the man they loved.

Clark and his mom were grateful for the Jennings' kindness but were devastated by the loss of his Clark's dad, his mother's husband. They were torn apart with misery and had to distance themselves from their torment.

Barbara Keenan took the insurance, what little there was, and she and her son moved to Nashville to escape the misery and the cold, harsh winters of Michigan. It was in Nashville where Clark meant Pam. He was singing and playing his guitar at a songwriters' night at Douglas Corner in Nashville. It was love at first sight for both of them. Pam's long, dark brown hair cascading down her shoulders and framing her shy, sweet face netted Clark's attention immediately. She was drawn to him because of his voice, charm, and, oh yeah, his good looks. Their love for music simply created even more of a bond between them. The radio was always playing and, on occasions, Clark would strum on his guitar and sing.

Yes! This was undoubtedly happier times for them all. The brutal summer heat hadn't crept in yet, and the coolish breeze gently brushed against one's skin to enhance the comfort of the day. When the burgers were done, Clark summoned the clan to the old, but doable, picnic table. "OK! What do you want on your burgers, folks?"

"I'll have just ketchup on mine," smiled Pam. "What would you like, mom?"

"I'll have the works: tomatoes, onions, lettuce, and ketchup. How's that?"

"Will just onions do? Our tomatoes haven't ripened yet," said Clark.

"What kind of a restaurant you running here? I guess that will have to do," chided Grammy who liked to egg Clark on.

Clark looked at his ten-year-old daughter, Grace. Sweet Grace, who was the apple of his eye. "And you, Grace."

"I'll have the works," she grinned.

"You've been hanging around Grammy too much," said Pam.

"Ketchup will be fine," Grace chuckled.

After dinner, Pops and Grace headed for their walking ritual along the side of the train tracks to the lake about a fourth of a mile away. Clark loved this time with Grace which he often referred to as his Grace time. The tracks were sandwiched between two extended berms with houses shielded by a berm on one side and a forest nudging the other. It was a tranquil setting absent of cars, people, and congestion. It was perfect for a dad and his daughter to share some ... well, some Grace time without the world intruding.

They just talked about simple stuff such as Grace's school friends, classes, how beautiful the day was. They observed the flights of birds and the scurrying of squirrels, and chipmunks darting between the spaces in the tracks. Often times they wouldn't chat at all and just soaked in the calm, the sounds, and the beautiful natural setting surrounding them. They enjoyed their walks, but it was their private spot by the lake that they cherished the most. Today the water was as still as glass with an occasional fish leaping out of the water for a fly, disturbing the calm. The croaking of frogs, the chirping of birds, and a myriad of other forest sounds blended into a harmony of nature. They loved this special place.

Pops would talk to Grace about his youth and how his dad always would encourage him to try his hardest in everything. His dad would say things such as "Do your best, or it ain't worth doin'," and "Treat others as you would like to be treated." He would also tell Grace corny jokes that she thought were hilarious. After a fish would jump, he would lean over and say, "Do you know why fish are so smart?" Grace would shrug her shoulders, and he answered, "because they're always in schools." They would both burst out laughing even though they heard it a million times. It was part of their ritual.

One of Pops' favorite moments was sharing lessons with Grace while at the lake. One time he was observing the pasture adjacent to the lake. He watched the variety of cows, horses, a few sheep and, on this day, even a deer was grazing amongst them all.

Looking at the field, he said to Grace, "Honey, that is how society should be," as he pointed in the direction where the animals were scattered in the field.

"What do you mean?" She responded looking curiously up at her Pops.

Clark's mind was heavy with the recent assassination of Martin Luther King. Robert Kennedy had been mortally wounded by some guy named Sirhan Sirhan, and protests in the Vietnam War were erupting in violence throughout cities in America. He didn't want his beloved daughter to grow up in a world of hate. He didn't talk overtly about his concerns but attempted to massage Grace into a place of goodness through life lessons. "Grace, tell me what you see in the pasture."

Her eyes gazed out at the field at the animals. "Well, I see four black Angus cows, two brown Jersey cows, three black and white Holstein cows, ... " She looked up at her dad.

"Wow! You sure know you're cows. I'm impressed. Keep going," he smiled.

Encouraged, she continued her task, " . . . two brown Salerno horses, one white Lipizzaner horse, two sheep, and one young deer. How's that?"

"That's good, Grace," he grinned. "How do you know the names of all these cows and horses?

"I was interested in them when we came out before, so I looked them up." Now she desired to get to the core of why her dad wanted her to notice the animals. "So what's your point, Pops ... I mean about 'society?'"

"Well, there are all sorts of animals out there, Grace: horses, cows, sheep, and even a deer. How are they behaving out in the field?"

Grace looked back at the assortment of animals. "They're just hanging out having a nice time together."

"Now . . . on to my society analogy. There all different kinds of people in the world." She nodded her head in agreement acknowledging where he was going with this. "People should accept each other, value each other, enjoy each other just like all those animals grazing in the pasture." They both looked out and soaked in the tranquility of the scene in the meadow. Even though she was only ten, she was aware of the troubles in America. She didn't focus on the news, but she did pick up tidbits when watching TV or listening to the radio. Her Pops was right. Why can't people just value, enjoy, and accept each other? She thought.

When the sun began to set, they headed back home walking hand in hand. Again, they didn't talk much but, instead, were consumed in the wonderment of the moment ... reflecting on nature, corny jokes, the sun glistening off the water, lessons learned, and the warmth and love of a father/daughter relationship. They capped off the hike as they did all of their walks by singing the chorus of Ol' Man River, Pops' favorite song. Why was it his favorite song? Because he always said that life goes on no matter how good or how bad things got like Ol' Man River . . . Ol' man, that Ol' Man River. He must know some pin', but he don't say nothing. He just keep rollin', he keeps on rollin' along.

CHAPTER 3 - IN A MOMENT

"Things change. And friends leave. Life doesn't stop for anybody."

Stephen Chbosky

Four years had passed, and Grace was now a gangly four-teen-year-old teenager. Her brown hair dangled over her eyes in the front and was pulled into a ponytail in the back. She walked home from school with a group of her neighborhood buddies; her ponytail bobbed up and down with every step.

The pack consisted of four girls, Angie, Stephanie, and Ninette as well as Grace and one boy, Jay, who they nicknamed Jaybird. The girls loved to tease Jaybird, and he would take all the harmless ribbing with a smirk. He was the first to break off from the group to head home waving goodbye accompanied by his perpetual grin. The others trotted off to their houses until Grace and Angie were the last of the group.

When Grace got to her front walk, she turned and waved goodbye to her friend, Angie. Her father smiled from the swing as she trotted up to the house. Grace was happy to see her Pops on the porch. His guitar was leaning against the house. He must have been playing it as he often did waiting for her to come home from school. She jumped up the steps, skipped over to him and gave her Pops a peck on the cheek. Her dad was swaying on the porch swing as he always did when waiting for Grace. She took the seat beside him, and they swung together.

He put his arms around Grace and asked, "How was school, sweetheart?"

"Fine! Did you know that everything is made of molecules?" she chirped enthusiastically. "And that there are three states of matter; solids, liquids, and gases."

"Wow! It seems like you were listening pretty good in school, Grace. I'm proud of you. The more you know, the more interesting life becomes," as he pulled her in for a little hug. "Tell me more."

For the next fifteen minutes, Grace talked about various aspects of each state of matter. She would have gone on for a half an hour having such an attentive listener in Pops, but her expression changed., Her face saddened. "What's wrong dear," Clark asked.

"Are black people stupid?"

Clark bolted back in shock and stared into Grace's eyes. "No, Grace! Not in the least. Why would you say such a thing."

"Well, some of the kids in school were saying that black people were dumb and didn't deserve to be with white folks."

Clark's thoughts immediately drifted to the Jennings family in Kalamazoo. He remembered their kindness, their guidance, and their general goodness in his and his mother's time of grief. "Honey, they just don't know them. Unfortunately, some people are cruel to folks who are not like them."

Just then Pam opened the front door and asked if they would like to join Lily and her in the back yard. They hopped off from the swing and followed Pam through the house. Grace paused to take a quick look at the picture in the hallway of her parents sitting in the same swing on the front porch that she and her Pops just used. She loved that picture and all that it represented. Grace loved seeing her parents so close with genuine smiles of happiness. She wondered to herself if she would be that happy when she got married. She sure hoped so.

Outback, Lily was jumping around flinging a twig from her teeth into the air. Pam walked to her garden where she was planting some more vegetables. She had taken the radio outside with Billy Joel was singing "Piano Man." She hummed along. The garden, though small, was surprisingly productive. Tomatoes, cucumbers, green beans, and yellow squash were the main crops which they used almost every night. "Do you want to eat soon," Pam inquired, "or do you want to go for your Grace Time walk?" Pam knew how important their ritual was to both of them. It was their special time together, and she was happy to facilitate the memory for them.

"How about we go for our walk and build up our appetites?" Clark asked as he looked at his daughter. "Does that sound good to you, Grace?"

"Sure does!" she smiled. She strolled to her father's side and grabbed his hand. Clark looked down at her and smiled back as both turned and waved to Pam, and then they started off for their ritual trek. Pam watched them fade as they walked down the tracks; her tall husband with his messy hair and clothes to match holding sweet, little Grace's hand, her ponytail bobbing behind her. She loved seeing them together, and she loved Clark for his devotion to his daughter. Pam thought about how fortunate Grace was to have a Pops like Clark. She bent down and put some tomatoes and cucumbers in her basket for a garden salad to go with their dinner as they drifted out of sight.

The Eagles were now singing their hit, "Peaceful Easy Feeling," on the radio. Pam sang along as she delicately pulled a cucumber off its stalk and placed it with the other vegetables.

. . . .

Clark was upset by Grace's friends' comments and decided to use this walk as a lesson in racism. Attentively, she listened while walking along the tracks as her Pops launched into a commentary about Jesse Owens, the Olympic Track hero. He spoke quietly and solemnly, "Jesse crashed into track history when at Ohio State. Owens won a record of eight individual NCAA championships. Though Owens had incredible athletic success, he had to live off campus with other African-American athletes. When the team traveled, Owens was restricted to ordering carry-out or eating at "blacks only restaurants. He also could only stay at "blacks only" hotels. For all his athletic success at Ohio State, Jesse did not receive a scholarship and had to work part time to pay for school." Grace's face contorted with annoyance about the way Jesse was treated as her father talked on lost in thought. She didn't interrupt him even though she wanted to express her disgust. She managed to just listen.

"In a Big Ten track meet in 1935 sometime in May, Jesse set three world records and tied a fourth in a matter of 45 minutes. The next year, Owens was invited to the 1936 Olympics where he won four gold medals."

"Wow, he was a great athlete. Right, Pops?"

"He certainly was. However, you'd think he'd be treated like a hero when he got to the America. He was not. After the games had ended, Owens returned home from the 1936

Olympics with four gold medals and international fame, but racism was a part of life in the United States, and he had difficulty finding work. He took on menial jobs as a gas station attendant, playground janitor, and manager of a dry cleaning firm. He also raced against amateurs and horses for cash." Clark then quoted the Olympic champion with a deep voice, "'People say that it was degrading for an Olympic champion to run against a horse, but what was I supposed to do? I had four gold medals, but you can't eat four gold medals.'"

Grace wanted to smile at her father's imitation of Mr. Owens, but the seriousness of the subject kept her in check. Her father continued talking about the lack of opportunities for blacks. "There was no television, no big advertising, no endorsements then. Not for a black man, anyway. In the reception to honor his Olympic success, Owens was not permitted to enter through the main doors of the Waldorf Historia New York but instead forced to travel up to the event in a freight elevator. "

"Why not?" asked a horrified Grace.

Her father searched for the right words. "Because some people don't realize the goodness in others if they are different from themselves.

"Here is another example of racism about the first black Academy Award recipient, Hattie MacDonald, who was not permitted to attend the premiere of *Gone with the Wind* because Georgia was racially segregated." Grace felt squeamish with these stories and wanted to move on to lighter subjects. However, her father was on a roll and she just listened. " At the Oscars ceremony in Los Angeles, she was required to sit at a segregated table at the far wall of the room; the hotel had a strict no-blacks policy, but allowed McDaniel in as a favor."

"But, Pops. That just isn't right."

"I agree," said Clark as he stared down the tracks. "Unfortunately, racism still exists today. That's why you hear . . . " he paused, ". . . mean talk like that in school."

It was difficult for Grace to understand. It was just so unfair. She tried to grasp why people would be so cruel to another just because they were of a different color. Her mind wandered to the image of the animals in the field. Pops was right. Why can't people just value, enjoy, and accept each other?

He could have gone on about hangings, the KKK, and more but wanted to spare his daughter from the gory details of racism. "Let's change the subject," said Clark.

That was fine with Grace since she felt uncomfortable with all this talk of cruelty. Since she was still hyped about what she had learned in school, she thought this would be a good time to pick up on the discussion about the three states of matter. And she did just that. Grace went on to explain that in solids the molecules were closer together. However, depending on the solid, like iron, the molecules were real close and with wood, the molecules were further apart.

Pops just absorbed everything that she was saying as well as her enthusiasm, rosy cheeks, bouncing ponytail and the gangly way she walked. He cherished his daughter, and she adored him for his thoughtfulness, goodness, and for loving her.

By the time Grace got to the topic of gases and that air was made up of molecules too, the sound of a train approaching in the distance seeped into the air. Pops reached for Grace's hand

and placed it on the tracks. "Do you feel that vibration?" Grace nodded. "Well, that is from the train." That is from the molecules in the tracks bumping into each other all the way down to here from where the train is now. In fact, we better step back out of the way. It isn't that far in the distance."

Suddenly, they heard screaming about a hundred yards down the tracks. "Help me! Please, help me!" bellowed a boy or was it a young man. Hard to tell from that distance.

"Stay here, Grace, out of the way," her dad demanded and off he ran toward the panicked boy. The rumble of the train grew louder: Clark ran faster. He was almost at the boy's side when the train roared past Grace. Her eyes were tearing with alarm. Her Pops was twisting the boy around whose foot was wedged between the tracks and a railroad spike, and now the train obstructed Grace's view. She couldn't see anything except massive, streaming steel in front of her. The blaring of the train horn muffled her screams of terror. The boy appeared from in front of the train, leaped out of harm's way and scurried into the woods. The train's screeching wheels were heard all the way from town. Grace's shrieks continued long after the train came to a stop.

CHAPTER 4 - NOW THERE ARE TWO

"Absolute silence leads to sadness. It is the image of death."

Jean-Jacques Rousseau

St. Mary's church depicted the traditional appearance of Catholic Churches around the country. Catholic churches in the south were scarce, but all aspects of the church structure, inside and out, reflected scenes from the Old Testament and from the life of Christ were impressive. The sacred art took many forms: statues, reliefs, paintings, murals, mosaics, icons, and stained glass made all who entered feel the sense of heaven, of God. The soaring heights of the spaces spoke to the attendees of reaching toward heaven, of transcendence — bringing the Heavenly Jerusalem down to them through the medium of the church building. Well, that was what it was intended to accomplish.

The church had a vast treasury of sacred art and a wonderful tradition to follow. St. Mary's was a place that accommodated not only public liturgy, but also public devotions such as Holy Hours, processions, May crownings, and Stations of the Cross as well as private devotions such as Eucharistic adoration, the Rosary, and other intercessory prayers to Mary and the saints. The shrines, statues, relics, vigil candles, and the like were essential to the Catholic church building. On this day, the church, however, was for the funeral of Clark Keenan. The statues, shrines, candles, and architecture were all non-existent to many for the loss of a loved one was almost too much to endure and blinded them of tactile objects.

St. Mary's Church was crowded with people from the Keenan's neighborhood and many of the factory workers as well as family members. Grace's little group of friends consisting of Angie, Stephanie, Ninette as well as Jason were joined by two of Grace's other school buddies, Chris and Shaun. They took up the pew at the rear of the church awkwardly trying to control their emotions with sniffling noses and wiping tears from their eyes.

Stunning stain glass windows flanked the walls on each side of the church casting a multitude of colors on the mourners. The stained glass served a two-fold purpose in the church. One was to create a "heavenly light" that symbolized the presence of God in the church, and the other was to serve as a "Poor man's Bible" to teach Biblical stories to those who were illiterate. Both of those goals were attained on this day for many of those sitting in the pews were seeking understanding, and a few others were actually illiterate. Good people but not well educated. All were devastated by the loss of Clark Keenan.

They weren't the only ones. Clark was regarded as a good man who always reached out to others to lend a hand. He loved his family and adored his daughter, Grace, and loved his wife, Pam. Everyone knew that Pam and Grace adored him as well and wondered . . . no . . . worried how they would cope with the loss of his support, goodness, and love.

Barbara, Clark's mother, Grace's grammy, sat in the front with the rest of the family with a hollow feeling. Her Clark, her only child, was gone in such an unexpected, horrific manner.

Her chest heaved with the weight of their loss as Grace buried her head in her shaking hands and just cried; her body convulsed with sadness. Pam tried to be stoic. She took deep breaths as she draped her arm around Grace and patted her back. All eyes were on them, and a shared sense of extreme loss engulfed the church.

The ceremony was short. Father Mark welcomed everyone to the church and expressed how their presence honored Clark's life. The crucifix loomed majestically in the sanctuary behind the altar. In keeping with Catholic tradition, the crucifix sought to include the corpus of Jesus suffering on the cross. This visible suffering was to help followers better connect with Jesus' sacrifice on the cross. The only suffering at this moment was one of loss for Pam and Grace. It will take time for them to transition or connect the pain to Christ's suffering.

When he had finished, a representative of the factory spoke of the integrity of the man in the coffin and how he made everyone around him better by his kindness. Several uncles talked about the brotherhood they felt toward Clark and how he was always there to help them.

Now, it was Grace's turn to talk from the pulpit. She rose slowly from the pew. Pam gave her a reassuring smile and patted her arm as she left her seat. Her daughter's emotions were raw, and she trembled as she struggled to the altar.

When Grace reached the pulpit, she clenched the sides for support. She didn't say anything for several agonizing minutes. She slowly raised her head and stared out at those gathering to mourn her dad. Her eyes were glassy with moisture, and the people seated appeared as a blur. She was able to make out her friends in the back. A subtle ping of comfort ran through her being. She took a heavy breath trying to find the strength to force out her words. The church was totally silent with an occasional cough breaking into the air. Grace didn't know what she wanted to say or how to say it. But the words snuck out in a whisper and were picked up by the mic.

She fought back tears and began, "My father was a special dad, a great son to my grammy, and a wonderful husband to my mom, Pam, and a friend to everyone he met." She paused, took a deep breath and forged on, "He was a hard worker and always provided for us. He made mom, grammy, and me laugh and was always there for us . . ." Cracking sobs broke her continuity and then she continued. "Pops would always find time for me as we would take our ritual walk. " Another deep, deep breath. "It was on our walk....our last walk...that he made his journey to God. During that last moment of his life . . . " a short pause, another breath . . ." he ended his life as he lived his life . . . helping another." She closed as she began . . . with a whisper, "We will miss you, Pops, but you will always live within our hearts."

As she struggled to find her way to her pew, the attendees began to mourn collectively: tears rolling down cheeks, sobbing, and hushed whispers of sadness.

. . . .

The short ride to the graveyard seemed like hours for Grace, Pam, and Grammy. The car was quiet except for an occasional gasp or a painful sigh as each of them was trapped in the memories of their lost one: of a son who was always there for his

mother; of a husband who showered his wife with love and support; of a father who never stopped being a person of goodness,
of kindness, of hope. Now he was gone.

The sun peeked out from gently rolling clouds. A soft
wind caressed the faces of those assembled at the gravesite. It
was a perfect day except for the heat, but, nonetheless, dark and
sad for the Keenan family. Father Mark gave the final message
of Clark's poignant journey to God's world, a world where he
would flourish and watch down upon all his loved ones here on
earth. Though the words were meant to be comforting, nothing
could crack the wall of pain that Clark's loved ones were hovering behind.

As the casket was lowered, Grace looked up with teary eyes
to take one last glimpse at her Pops. Her vision was blurred
again with moisture. She scanned the surroundings: her mother
and grammy draped in black, friends and neighbors peering
down at the casket, as well as strangers to her from the factory
and . . . What was that?   Something caught her eye in the distance near a drooping tree. Who is it or what is it? Her blurred
eyes struggled to focus. It was the form of a boy or was it? She
wiped her eyes and looked up again. Nothing. It must have been
her mind just playing tricks with this emotional roller coaster
she was riding. She returned her attention to the lowering casket. A few minutes passed, and Grace was then gently escorted
away by her mother and her Grammy to begin life without Pops.

. . . .

Days had passed, and the loss of Clark had taken a toll on

all of them. The three women made an effort to put their lives back into place, but it was especially hard on Grammy. Losing her only son was too devastating for her. It was just two months after Clark had passed away that Pam and Grace were attending, yet, another funeral.

CHAPTER 5 - PUTTING THE PIECES BACK TOGETHER

"The soul always knows what to do to heal itself.
The challenge is to silence the mind." **Caroline Myss**

It is said that time heals everything. That is not always exactly true. Time may move the pain and the misery to the back of one's mind, but they are still lurking there, in the darkness with a dull throbbing that manifests itself on those weak, nostalgic occasions when one is least expecting them. However, the art of diversion can stave off the hurt, the loss, and the sadness. Grace and her mother chose the detour to cushion their despair. They embraced the fond memories of their loved one and focused on the present and each other rather than being consumed with self-pity. The pangs of reality tend to shove aside the pains of a loss. The mundane necessities of living coerce one to address life rather than dwelling on death.

While folks in the community were engaged in talk about the findings of the Watergate Scandal and Richard Nixon becoming the first US president forced to resign from office, the Keenan women could care less. The loss of Clark's income bolted them back into reality as another loss was looming, the loss of their home. Pam picked up more hours at the factory, and Grace had to drop out of school before her junior year eventually. The high school administration was sympathetic with her decision but was also opposed to her leaving. She was a good

TRAIN TRACKS - 31

student and well liked among the staff and her peers. She was destined for graduation and even college and success after that, but the current monetary burdens outweighed any future securities. So Grace did the only thing she could do: she dropped out of school leaving her teachers, her classmates, her books, and . . . her promising future in those halls of education.

Grace and her mom now walked to the factory together. They immersed themselves in conversation which often entertained the funny times with Clark. They didn't wallow in the sorrow of his absence but thrived in the goodness and joy of his life. They also talked about the work at the factory and their coworkers. They would discuss items at home that needed to be addressed such as repairs to the porch, feeding Lily, working on the garden, and paying the bills. They were going to survive without Clark no matter what. Grace was getting an education not available in school and maturing very quickly. She was becoming a comely sixteen-year-old teenager. Her light, blue eyes were bright and lively. Her long, brown hair flirted with blond high lights compliments of the Tennessee sun. Gone was the little girl bounce in her walk as she now moved gracefully. And with their time together, mother and daughter bonded, and their closeness helped mitigate the pain of their loss and hardship.

After work, they would stop by Donnelly's, the neighborhood mom and pop store. The heavy oak door groaned as they entered, and the wide pine floors squeaked when they walked on them. Lynyrd Skynyrd's new, hit song, "Sweet Home Alabama," floated out from the speakers. When Mike saw them, he greeted them with his usual welcoming smile. Lynnda waved from behind the counter as other customers enjoyed the comfort of the cozy atmosphere munching on their burgers and French fries.

Pam and Grace sat on the stools at the counter and ordered their usual treats. Pam got her favorite: a vanilla coke, and Grace purchased her favorite: a scope of chocolate chip ice cream on a waffle cone. One of the cute mysteries they would ponder while at the counter was why were there only three stools instead of four? Four would allow two couples to sit up at the counter whereas three would create limitations. They asked Mike about that, and he chuckled, "It's a secret."

"Is it really?" Grace asked.

"Not really," said Mike. "We have a spare stool in the back for exceptional occasions." Grace seemed a bit disappointed.

"What type of an occasion would that be? Inquired Pam.

Mike grinned and said, "That, my dear, would be when more people came."

"Oh, Mr. Mike!!!" they laughed.

The other customers were a group of four teenagers who sat in the booth, two boys and two girls. They were not from the area. It was easy to tell from the boys' polo shirts and neatly pressed pants. The girls had their hair neatly coifed, and they wore skirts accompanied by lettergram sweaters. No! They were not from this area and posed quite a contrast from the dirty work uniforms that frequented Donnelly's. When they spoke, they were "elegant" in speech as Pam would say. They weren't arrogant, but there was an air about them that made one feel less than them.

When they got up to leave, they all were giggling and chuckling at some "inside" joke. The foursome pretty much ignored everyone else in the shop keeping their conversation and attention to their little group. However, when they walked by the counter, one of the boys, the quiet one, smiled when he passed by Grace. The teenagers pulled the door open and began to walk outside. The quiet boy hesitated at the door and glanced back at Grace one more time before he left. The old, heavy door groaned to a close behind them.

"Who are they?" asked Pam as Mike was wiping off the table at the booth.

"I really don't know" replied Mike. "Once in a while, they come in here from over yonder." He pointed in the direction where stately homes far across the tracks sat on huge plots of land. "I guess they just want to see how the other side lives."

Lynnda chimed in from behind the counter laughing, "And we live pretty good." And they did. They all did. The simplicity of their lives surrounded by friends and family provided just enough of the life that they needed or even wanted. None of them had an urgency for more. Well, maybe a little more...but, other than that, they were beyond content.

"You're darn right," said Mike. Pam and Grace nodded their heads in approval. They could hear the engine of a car roar to life. They looked out the store window at the kids climbing into a shiny, blue Cadillac, a rarity in this neighborhood. They pulled out of their parking space and drove slowly by the shop as a boy in the front passenger side of the car, turned to take one, last, quick look at Donnellys.

CHAPTER 6 - THE MANSION

"There is an empty place within me where my heart once was."

George R. R. Martin

The blue Cadillac with its teenage passengers rolled away past the old storefronts, over the tracks with the factory parallel to them. Shuffling out of doors, tired but joking workers were heading home in their dirty uniforms glad that their shift was over and that they would soon be with their families.

"Look at them!" snorted one of the female passengers. "What do they have to laugh about? They have shitty jobs and wear shitty, dirty uniforms."

"Yeah, Judy!" chuckled the other girl. "I wouldn't be caught dead in those rags they're wearing."

"Well, the stuff they're wearing isn't any worse than what you have on." Judy snickered followed by a bellowing laugh. The others in the car erupted with laughter . . . except Dora, who was the target of the comment. Judy was like the ring leader. She was articulate and smart, but those qualities were dwarfed by her cruelty and manipulation. She was the queen of back-stabbing. No one wanted to mess with her because they didn't want to be her next victim. She was relentless in her criticism of others behind their backs or, for that matter, even to their faces. Nobody was exempt. Because of that, her peers always treated her with wary respect. She really only had a few chums, and they were sycophants to her whims. Others tried to avoid her when possible or just agreed with her.

Ann tried to mirror Judy's behavior to keep on her right side and to create a veneer of strength. She was tenacious in one sense but not strong enough not to be sucked into Judy's wicked world.

Alex, the driver, was just a pain in the ass. He was absent of empathy and got his kicks out of seeing others being made fun of. The other boy was just a lost soul searching for an identity, any identity, and this crew drew him in with their manipulation, deception, and appearance of confidence.

On their journey back home, they made fun of the neighborhood they had just left: the tired buildings, the curling smoke from the factory, the cracked roads. All were now blurs in the review mirror. The idyllic countryside of green pastures, horses grazing in the fields, and grand houses cradled in the depths of meadows was now their visual entertainment. "How could anyone live back there in that crappy environment," cracked Judy."

Dora quipped, "They love being peasants to the elite. Us!!!" A cacophony of laughter burst out among the them.

"And did you see the metals of crap they were driving; rusted Corvairs, old Impalas, and dented trucks," Alex cruelly added.

Grins and nodding reacted to his statement. They couldn't wait to get back to their source of ridicule in the future. Another trip for another time. The anticipation of their return to Donnellys fueled their sense of superiority. Judy leaned over and turned on the radio. "Sundown" by Gordon Lightfoot filled the air. The girls tried singing along. The boys cringed as they listened to Judy's and Dora's screeching. These girls couldn't carry a note in a bucket.

After the "concert," the conversation moved onto other subjects such as their material lives consisting of new TV's, cars, vacations that were planned in the future, beaches in Florida, sun and surf in the Virgin Islands. Shit. They were living the life.

The blue Cadillac cruised by manicured lawns and elaborate landscaping surrounding massive homes. They slowed down and took a right into a long horseshoe driveway that led to a residence of what could only be called a mansion. Nothing about it suggested humility. Four pillars rose stoically on the front porch like soldiers guarding the palace. Six floor to ceiling windows expanded across the front of the house. The double door entrance way was adorned on either side with planters that were overflowing with pink mini orchids, fragrant gardenias, blue calla lilies, pink and yellow roses, white azaleas, Hawaiian hibiscuses, and hopping purple hydrangeas. Everything was in sharp contrast to the homes across the tracks.

The car jolted to a stop, "OK, Billy! You're home," said Alex.

Billy opened the passenger door, slid out of the car as Judy got out to take his place in the front. "See ya later, he said."

"Yeah. See you later, Billy. We'll see you at school. Maybe we can plan our next trip to our exquisite restaurant, Donnelly's, in study hall," smirked Judy.

Can't wait," as Billy gave them all a listless wave.

The shiny, blue car reflected the sun off its hood and drove out the other side of the horseshoe driveway. "What a dip-shit he is," groaned Judy.

"You're not kidding," said Dora. "I don't even know why we let him hang around with us."

"Because he has a swimming pool and other crap like that, . . . you dip-shit," blasted Alex. They all howled with laughter. "The Bitch is Back" by Billy Joel blasted over the radio speakers. The Cadillac sped down the road flying past horses, cows, rolling hills and mansions.

. . . .

Billy was just stepping up to the front door of his house. He turned to watch the blue vehicle disappear behind the trees to a backdrop of picturesque pastures. A placid frown crept across his face. Yes! He was at his house. He turned the brass handle and pushed open the door which unveiled a mammoth foyer with a triple wide spiral staircase directly in front of Billy which seemed to soar into the clouds. The floors were shiny oak protected with spotless oriental area rugs dispersed in exactly in the right places. High-end furniture rested in exactly the right placcs were also . . . spotless. Everything shined, glistened, and exuded affluence and a decorator's touch of perfection.

In a vain effort to arouse a reaction, Billy called out, "I'm home. Is anybody here? I'm home. " No response as expected. Billy moved to the back of the house to the kitchen which was massive and, yes, . . . spotless. The kitchen was in want of nothing for it had everything. The refrigerator had double doors on either side. The bright, white stove had six burners and a wide grilling area which would be the envy of Julia Child. The oak cabinets lined the walls with enough storage space to house all the dining sets used at the Ritz. Billy glanced out the kitchen window and scanned the pool area which was a beckoning oasis with plantings, pristine, outdoor furniture and more. He spotted a figure laying on the chaise lounge with a bottle of French wine sitting on the tile paired with an empty, stemmed glass.

Billy opened the rear door and approached the woman who appeared to be sleeping. He walked toward her. "Brown Eyed Girl" was drifting from the radio. When he got next to her, he reached down for the volume and silenced Van Morrison's music "Hi, mother. I'm home."

His mother looked up shielding her eyes with her hand from the sun or was it the son. "So, you are, my dear. Could you do me a favor and refresh my glass. This glare is exhausting me."

"Sure, mother." Billy leaned down, grabbed the bottle and poured wine halfway into the glass."

His mother peeked from behind her hand. "You can do better than that, Billy," she smiled. Billy filled the glass nearly to the top and handed it to her. "Thank you, dear. How was your day with your friends?"

"It was good. We just hung around and ...."

"Oh, good!" she interrupted. "I'm glad you had a good time." His mother took another sip of her wine, laid down on the chaise and went back to sunning herself.

Billy just looked at her as his mother's eyes closed like a dark cloud blocking the sun. However, the sun was still shining as his mother drifted off to wherever. He looked around at the expansive property. Trees dotted the green land which was crowded by a thick forest way in the back. There was a swing set, a reflection of earlier days. The barn, which was not really a barn, stood to the right side of the lot. That was where his father kept at least seven of his cars and where Billy had his own vehicle, a bright red Bronco as well as a motorized scooter, and several golf carts. Oh, yes! There was a nine-hole pitch and putt golf course in the back as well, a tennis court, a basketball court and a horseshoe pit complete with two bars, one at each pit.

There was also an overdone pool house with one-third of it used for storing pool equipment such as chemicals, leaf filters, and more. On the other two-thirds was a guest cottage with its own entrance. It was a studio complete with a kitchenette, a full bathroom, a double window at the back end with panoramic views of the property, and even a bed for overflow guests. Billy's father had high hopes that all of these "toys" would keep little Billy busy . . . or, as he would put it, . . . out of his hair.

Billy took off his shoes and socks, rolled up his pants, and sat at the edge of the pool with his feet dangling in the water. He was not thinking of all of his toys. His mind floated back to the mom and pop store . . . to the scruffy girl sitting on the stool by the counter licking the chocolate chip ice cream off of her waffle cone. No! He was not thinking of his toys.

CHAPTER 7 - FRIENDS, MEMORIES, AND BURGERS

"All days will pass, all moments will last,
each friend will part, it's a journey too fast."
Senora Roy

The garden was still producing, and the soil was a little damp from recent rain. However, today was dry enough to allow Pam and Grace to work in their garden. They were diligent about weeding and not disturbing the growth of vegetables and flowers. Their knees were wet with mud stains and their hands dirty from the soil. They loved the smell of earth and the feeling of going back in time producing the food they needed. It also was a pleasant opportunity for them to be together, sharing in their mutual love of watching plants grow.

Grace always wanted to know about everything. She missed school for that very reason and anytime she saw a chance to learn something new, she jumped at it. "Mom, why do you always plant marigolds around the perimeter of the garden?"

Pam lifted her head and looked at the marigolds that surrounded the area in a colorful rectangular splash of orange and yellow. She smiled for she was happy that Grace shared her love of gardening. "Well, Grace, there are several reasons." Grace was attentive. "They attract bees, are easy to care for, and they have a pungent aroma that keeps pests and possibly even bunnies and deer at bay."

"I had heard about the strong odor, but do they really keep bunnies and deer away?"

"Well, that's the rumor. Have you seen any deer in our garden?"

"Oh, mom!" Grace chuckled. "The only deer around here are possibly in the woods by the train tracks.

"I was just kidding about the deer here in our garden. Although, it is rumored to work on them." All of a sudden, they heard talking coming from the front of the house. The voices got louder as they got nearer and rounded the corner to the back yard.

"Hi, Mrs. Clark. Hi, Grace," said Angie in a cheery voice. Ninette and Stephanie followed her and offered similar, pleasant greetings. Pam looked up and smiled whereas Grace hopped up from her kneeling position and ran to hug,...a group hug,...her three friends. Being back with her buddies was a reincarnation of normalcy for Grace. She had seen her friends rarely since dropping out of school and working at the factory. Her friends had been consumed with their school activities and often time did not cooperate for everyone to get together. This was a special treat for all of them.

"Would you like to stay for lunch? " said Pam. "We can throw on some burgers."

"Oh, we don't want to trouble you. We just want to see Grace and you."

"Perfect! I'll get the grill going, and we can all chat." Pam climbed the back steps to their home to get the meat while the girls all gave each other another group hug.

"I missed you, you goofballs," said Grace, a bit misty-eyed.

"We missed you, too, Grace," Stephanie replied. "It's so good to see you again."

The girls and Pam spent the afternoon talking about old times, how school was going, new music that they liked. "Annie's Song" by John Denver, they all agreed, was their favorite. The also talked about how their friends, Chris, Shaun, and Jaybird, were doing and what antics they were up too. The Vietnam War was still going on, and the girls were concerned that the boys might be drafted, but for the most part, they stuck to lighter subjects.

Under a clear sky with an occasional, puffy cloud drifting above, the smell of hamburgers and laughter filled the air. The joy of friendship embraced the afternoon. It was a recipe for the healing for both Grace and Pam and probably for Grace's friends as well. Not having Clark sitting in his chair, cracking corny jokes and watching the girls having fun, caused a churning in all of their hearts. Especially for Grace.

The day was slipping by way too quickly for Grace and her friends. It was dinner time for everyone. They continue their conversations and catching up while eating. Afterward, everyone said their goodbyes. When the girls had departed, Grace turned to her mom and said, "Mom, can you do me a BIG favor?"

"Anything, sweetheart."

"Can you walk with me along the . . . train tra . . ." Grace stammered ". . . the train tracks," followed by a deep breath. The words tumbled from her mouth in pieces. It was not an easy request for her, but it was now time to face those demons that had haunted her since her Pop's death.

"Yes, I can do that!" said Mom. Tears began to well in her eyes. She pulled Grace toward her and held her tightly. Softly she repeated, "I can do that!"

. . . .

As they walked along the tracks that Grace and Pops had walked so many times before, memories flowed through Grace's mind. Visions of birds in flight, chipmunks scurrying over the tracks, and a slight breeze swaying the leaves all remained. It was the same journey, the same sights, the same feeling that rushed through Grace's mind. She smiled to herself about those precious moments with her Pops. There was only one thing different: he was not with her.. Pam said nothing for nothing needed to be said. She just looked at her daughter who was gazing at the surroundings; lost in the memories with her Pops.

They eventually reached the destination where it happened: where Clark had died. A small cross supported by a mound of railroad gravel had been placed near the site by someone in memory of Clark. Pam and Grace stopped and paused to say a prayer. Everything seemed to take a break as well: birds weren't in flight; little critters sat up from their positions; the breeze dwindled. A dense but beautiful calm wrapped Pam and Grace with mixed feelings of family, of love, of life, . . . and of death.

They continued their walk until they got to the lake. They climbed up over the berm to the place that was Grace's and Pops' "special" place. Grace looked over at the pasture. The cows and horses were still there grazing listlessly. No deer this time, but the lesson again rang in Grace's mind about Pops' wish for society.

She then turned her attention to the lake. The water was as still as glass with an occasional ripple touching upon the serenity. Grace gazed out and smiled. She turned to her mom and said, "Mom, do you know why fish are so smart?" She shook her head "No" with a curious grin. " . . . because they are always in schools."

"Oh, Grace, I love you."

CHAPTER 8 - SPLASH

"Fortune is like glass - the brighter the glitter, the more easily broken."
Publius Syrus

The oppressive humidity coupled with the Tennessee summer heat seemed to melt the wax off of the candles at Billy's house. Cows and horses in the pastures huddled under the shade of the stretched out tree branches to escape the sweltering sun. The rising hot air rippled above the tarred roads. Even turtles skipped sunning themselves and dug a cool bed into the muddy shorelines of the pond. Most people sheltered themselves in the comfort of their air-conditioned homes. Not at the Cromwell house.

Judy and Dora were in one, fleeting, golf cart with their hair trailing behind them tossing wildly in the wind. Billy and Alex were in the another sailing cart leaning forward attempting to pick of speed. They sped across the green terrain, up and down rolling mounds, through sand traps, and even driving over greens was fair game. They did wheelies, were airborne at times, and left tire tracks everywhere. All of their faces were gritted with determination as they raced across the acres of Billy's back yard. Whoops and hollers rattled the air as they sped up to the fence by the pool and slammed on the breaks. "We won!!!!" Judy screamed with Dora pumping her fist in the sky for victory.

"Yeah, you did," scorned Alex. ". . . but you cut us off at the pond."

"Who cares?" grunted Judy. "We won, and that is all that matters." She turned to her driving companion. "Now let's go for a victory swim, Dora. You losers get us some beers. Actually, we prefer wine," she demanded.

The crew dismounted their vehicles, and the girls shed their clothing with the exception of their undergarments ready to jump into the pool. The boys sulked and walked to the house to fetch the drinks. Alex, without even turning around, flipped the girls the bird keeping in line with the finesse in which they all communicated.

When the boys returned to the pool, the girls had turned up the radio and were dancing to Steppenwolf's "Born to be Wild". Their moves exceeded wild and were downright raunchy. Judy reached out to Billy trying to grab his hand and had him dance with her. He put his beer down and did a few jigs. Alex joined Dora on the tiled dance floor and then suddenly pushed her into the pool. Billy caught Alex's move from the corner of his eye and shoved Judy in as well. The boys then danced at the edge of the pool looking down at the girls singing at the top of their lungs "Born to be Wild."

In an afternoon of belittling their teachers and making fun of their school mates, they polished off two bottles of Billy's mom's treasured French wine. The boys consumed two plus six-packs of beer and, why not? Billy's mother was playing bridge at the golf course all day and partying with her bridge mates in the evening. Billy's father, Mr. Dickhead, as Judy and Dora fondly called him, was flying to who knows where for one meeting or another. No one was there to watch them, to reprimand them, or to show that they cared.

As the day began to sink into darkness, Alex, Judy, and Dora got in the blue, shiny Cadillac and rolled away. Inside the trio waved to Billy and bellowed in unison, "Bye, Dip-shit," out of his hearing range. Billy watched the car disappear behind the trees. He then went back to the pool area. Bottles, beer cans, and pizza packaging littered the area. Someone will pick them up....not him nor his mom. It would be Nellie, the maid. She cleaned up all sorts of crap, this being the least of her chores.

Billy sat on the chaise lounge and examined what was before him as he guzzled another beer. He looked at the mess at his feet; the pool with blowups floating casually, the elaborate pool house, the golf carts parked recklessly by the fence, the barn in the distance and the land, the woods, the golf course. He had it all. He had it all. ......or did he?

CHAPTER 9 - RETURN 1975

The days soon manufactured a comforting routine for Pam and Grace. They walked to work together and occupied similar jobs at the factory. When their shift was over, they walked out of the doors mingled with the rest of the employees. On their way home, they stopped at Donnelly's for their treats: a vanilla coke and one scope of chocolate chip ice cream on a waffle cone. They would chat with Mike and Lynnda who always made their day more pleasant by being so welcoming.

When they got home, they would go out back to the dog house and play with Lily. Sometimes the girls, Angie, Stephanie, and Ninette, would drop by, and they would all take a walk down the train tracks. Grace would keep her thoughts of Pops to herself, and the conversation would revolve around family or friends and, again, the antics of Shaun, Chris, and Jason which always made them chuckle.

Jaws, the movie, occupied much of their conversation. Even though there wasn't an ocean within hundreds of miles from them, they were petrified. They didn't even want to swim in Percy Priest Lake located near Nashville. The small lake they visited on the train tracks walk was even intimidating to them. They would stand several feet away from the shore and survey the water as if some aquatic monster would leap out after them. However, only a harmless ripple on the water from small fish posed the only danger they ever encounter. Now, snakes, that was a different story.

Sometimes Grace and her mom would walk the tracks. Just the two of them. These journeys became therapeutic and comforting. The healing process was getting better even though the loss of Pops would always leave a hole in Grace's heart. Sometimes Grace would take a solo hike along the tracks consumed with her thoughts of Pops so she could have private time with him. She would replay the conversations they had had. She would smile to herself, . . . alone, yet not alone . . . , as the sun glistened off the tracks.

. . . .

One day, after work, as was the routine, they stopped by Donnelly's for their treats. The usual harmonies of the shop welcomed them as the door groaned when it opened, and the floorboards squeaked as they walked. They assumed their traditional spots on the stools by the counter as Mike, who already had prepared Pam's vanilla coke and Grace's chocolate chip ice cream on a waffle cone, handed the treats to them with a smile. Lynnda poked her head up from behind a stack of shelves and waved from the rear of the store. Pam and Grace waved back happy to see her. An older couple was looking at the penny candy. Barry Manilow's "Mandy" floated out from the speakers.

While they were enjoying their favorite goodies, the door pushed open, and the four teenagers from awhile back sauntered in like they owned the place. They were cackling and loud and wrestled their way into the benches at the booth. Even

Barry Manilow couldn't bring the sooth back. Their demeanor was much more demanding than the previous time when they were at the shop. "Oh, waiter! Can we get some service here," Judy barked. The entourage snickered and giggled. "Oooh, waaaaiter," she said again tapping her finger on the table. Pam and Grace turned to take a quick peek and looked at each other with dismay and then went back to their munchies. The older couple appeared uncomfortable with the happenings. The gentleman quickly tucked the woman's arm under his, and they shuffled out the door never looking back.

Mike walked over to the booth and said courteously, "How can I help you?"

"How can I help you?" mocked Alex. The group started to giggle again. Mike kept his composure, masked his displeasure and continued with the task of serving them. After a series of wisecracks, Mike was able to acquire their order and serve them.

They jeered and joked with each other wolfing down their meals. Then their eyes caught Grace and Pam on their counter stools. They became the target of the group's taunts. Within earshot, they made fun of their stained, factory clothes, the clunky shoes they had on, and their disheveled hair. Grace and Pam just focused on downing their treats, trying to ignore the verbal assaults.

When the cluster of teenagers had finished eating, they got up to leave. They peered at Pam and Grace as they passed by them. Judy snickered, "Nice clothes, ladies." The group chuckled.

Dora got into the act by adding, "Yeah, where did you get

them? . . . At Goodwill?" Another belittling round of laughter followed.

Alex started, "Yeah, you girls look like.....'

Billy grabbed Alex, swung him around and growled in his face, "That's enough!"

"What's with you, Billy!!!"

"Nothing, let's just get out of here."

The mood of the group changed from taunting to disgruntled. They marched out of the store clacking at each other.

. . . .

The ride home was awkward. Billy sat quietly in the passenger seat staring out the window. The rest of the crew harassed him about his "behavior" at Donnelly's. Billy didn't respond and continued to gaze out the window blocking out their insults. His mind was back at the Donnelly's thinking of the quiet, ragged girl with the ice cream cone.

Alex, Judy, and Dora turned to other topics; being the usual ridiculing of their "friends" and people they knew. They dropped Billy off at his house and screeched down the driveway with a mocking wave and the parting "What a dip-shit!" comment.

Billy, once again, watched the blue Cadillac disappear behind the trees. Now he was alone. Really alone. He knew he had blown his ties with the trio. His mom didn't give a shit about him, and nor did his father give a crap. Yes! He was alone.

CHAPTER 10 - OH, OH!

Days had passed since the Donnelly incident with the teenage posse as Grace called them. After work, Pam and Grace positioned themselves at the counter relieved that they hadn't seen a trace the "posse" in weeks. Now they laughed about it with Mike and Lynnda who were also grateful for the same reason.

After talking with the Donnelly's, they slid off their stools, said their goodbyes, and departed for the home. When they walked out of the door, they noticed a truck of some kind parked diagonally across the street. It was occupied by one person, the driver, but it was hard to see who it was. Not that it really mattered. It was just that they hadn't seen the red truck parked in this area before.

When they got home, Stephanie and Angie were playing with Lily and, of all things, Shaun and Chris were there as well. Hugs were received all around. The girls chatted and caught up with what was happening in school and in the neighborhood. The boys played catch with a ball and tormented Lily who wanted to partake in the fun. It was good to see everyone. Then Jaybird flew in from around the corner followed by Ninette. Everyone started hootin' and hollering'. The old gang was back together again. Pam made a huge spaghetti dinner for them all, and they played their favorite card game, . . . spoons.

It was still early, so they all joined in on the walk along the train track except for mom who wanted Grace to have time to hang out with her friends. Pam cleaned the pots and pans and dishes from the meal. She then went out to the front living area to take a break. Something caught her eye when she walked by the window to sit down . . . a red car? . . . or truck? . . . parked down the street across from her home. She got up to get a better look when the red vehicle slowly crawled down the road and then slipped out of sight.

. . . .

Billy continued to drive with no destination in mind . . . just heading down the road, any road. While his red Bronco cruised forward, he couldn't seem to get the "peasant" girl out of his mind. Why was she so intriguing? She obviously lived in a dump by his standards. She wasn't gorgeous. She dressed in Walmart brand clothes. What was it? All he knew of her was her simple demeanor, overheard conversations with her mother about everyday things. She did smile a lot. She was cute, well, in a plain way. Her hair was scraggly, but, for some reason, it gave that appealing carefree impression. Why was he drawn to this simplistic girl from across the tracks?

CHAPTER 11- SERENDIPITY

It was relatively quiet at the Keenan house. None of Grace's friends were socializing in the back yard. Pam was busy preparing something for a dinner a guest that night, and Grace was outside doing something. Pam enjoyed cooking for everyone, but this time she had a look of concern. She opened the refrigerator searching for something; shuffled the frozen items around in the freezer. No! Not there. She shut the fridge, hurried to the back door and opened it. "Grace, can you do me a big favor?" her mom called out.

Grace, who was weeding the garden, popped her head up. "Sure, Mom. What do you need?" as Lily wagged her tail by Grace's side.

"It's a big one."

"Mom, I already said 'yes.' What is it?"

"Would you mind walking to the bakery across town and getting some sweet rolls for dinner tonight? I invited my good friend, Ashlie, over for dinner."

"Ashlie!!!" shouted Grace. "Oh, God! I haven't seen her for so long. Yes! Yes! Yes, I'll go." Ashlie was a good friend of the family that they hadn't seen since Clark passed away. She was fun...always fun. She spoke with a smile and welcomed you into her heart. Grace and Pam loved her, so for Grace to walk across town for some sweet rolls wasn't a chore. It was a delight. Grace ran up the back steps and headed for the front door. "I'll see you in a bit, mom."

"Wait, Grace! You need some money." Pam reached into her wallet and pulled out several dollars.

"Oh, right." She scooped the money out of her mom's hand, gave her a peck on the cheek and waltzed down the front steps. As she skipped down the sidewalk, she made a quick turn and waved to her mom. Her mom grinned and waved back. Pam couldn't help but think of Grace as the little girl waving goodbye on her way to school, but now she wasn't a little girl. However, to Pam, she would always be her little girl. She thought to herself as Grace drifted out of sight, there goes my baby.

Grace had to walk downtown, past the factory, across the tracks to get to Susan's Special Treats, the best bakery in town. Why was that? It was the only bakery in the town. A band of dark clouds began to form in the sky, and the wind picked up. She got to Susan's Treats and purchased the sweet rolls mom wanted. She shuffled down the street excited with the thought of Ashlie coming over for dinner. She picked up her pace as a light sprinkle began to fall. The rain drummed down a little harder. Grace started to run as other pedestrians did as well splashing with every step. When she turned the corner of a building, she bumped into a man and fell to the wet pavement. A hand reached down to help her up as his other hand held an umbrella to shield her from the rain. She noticed that the sweet rolls she had just purchased had been crushed under the weight of her petite body.

"Oh! No!" she exclaimed softly. She looked up at the man who had reached out to her, but it wasn't a man. He was a boy about the same age as her, maybe a bit older. She looked at the familiar face, but couldn't quite place it. "Thank you, . . . and I'm sorry I bumped into you."

"I'm not," quipped the boy.

Grace now got a good look at his face as rain trickled down her forehead. "Wait! You're the boy at Donnelly's with those...." she paused, ". . . those .other kids. I've gotta go....and thank you again...and sorry ..."

"Please, let me drive you to wherever you're going," coaxed the young man.

"I don't think that would be right." The cruelty of the incident at Donnelly's surfaced in her mind.

Sensing her alarm, Billy offered his perspective, "They were wrong. I didn't like what they were saying to you and to your mother."

Grace remembered how he pulled the other boy away and then asked, "How did you know she was my mother?"

He bowed his head a bit in embarrassment. "I was watching you and listening in to you both talking. I was....."

The rain started pelting the ground. Billy and Grace both hovered under the umbrella. She abruptly finished his sentence for him: "Eavesdropping!! I think I should go."

"You can't go, Grace. It's pouring."

She looked at him incredulously. "You know my name....?" she blurted.

"Again, I heard your conversations. Please, Grace. Let me take you home." She looked down at her crushed sweet rolls. "My name is Billy." He crouched down and picked up the soggy bag of pastries. "Let me buy you another bag, and then I can take

you home. Please, Grace. Let me make up for my friends....well,
I should say, my past friends' rudeness."

Her wet, matted, curly hair dangled down around her
shoulders. Grace looked up at him with rain licking her face.
Coyly, reluctantly she said, ". . . OK!"

. . . .

Billy escorted Grace to his car preventing the rain from
striking her by holding his umbrella over her head. He opened
the passenger side of the car, and she boarded the red Bronco
with her new, dry bag of pastries. She was glad that both she
and the pastries were now protected from the downpour. Billy
hustled around to the driver's side, closed his umbrella, and slid
into the seat as rain slanted in the door before he shut it. "Hi,"
he smiled. "Where do I go?" as if he didn't already know.

It was a short trip to the Keenan's house. The rain danced
off the windshield, and the wipers swiped at the drops providing
intermittent visibility. The red Ford Bronco turned onto Grace's
street and stopped in front of the Keenan house. The downpour
began to subside, and the sun seemed to be trying to peek out
from behind the dark clouds. Billy looked at his wet passenger,
"Well, we're at your house, Grace."

"Yes, we are. Billy, you have to come in and meet my
mother." Grace said flatly.

"I don't think so."

Without even looking at the house, "My mother is watching us right now."

. . . And she was. The curtain was pulled aside with her

mother's right hand. Concern was written all over her face. Pam recognized the red vehicle from earlier in the day. What was Grace doing in that truck or car or whatever it was and who the hell is that person driving it?

"Billy, you don't have a choice. If you don't come in and introduce yourself to my mom, all hel . . .. heck will break out," Grace said with a sense of urgency. "My mom is a good, reasonable person, but this not knowing what is going on will create unneeded anxiety for her. Just come in, say hi, and then get the heck out of here."

This was a side of the sweet, shy girl that Billy hadn't seen. Strong willed. But when it came to her mother, Grace was protective. "All right!" said Billy. He opened the driver side door, stepped out and walked to the passenger side. Grace was already out of the car clutching her bag of pastries while stepping aside to avoid a puddle. Her mother let go of the curtain, and it swung back into place. She marched to the front door, opened it and stared at the two teenagers as they walked up the steps to the porch.

"Grace!?!?" asserted Pam.

"I know, I know." They walked up the steps onto the porch landing. Pam glared at Billy. "Mom, this is Billy."

"I recognize him from Donnelly's. Why is he here .... with you?" she snapped. "Come inside, and you can explain."

They walked into the house and turned into the living room. Ashlie rose from the sofa and approached Grace. "Hi, sweetheart, so glad to see you." She gave Grace a gentle hug and a peck on the cheek. That was just what Grace needed to alleviate the tension.

"Ashlie, it is so good to see you."

"You too, my dear," Her attention turned to Billy. " . . . and whom do we have here?" Ashlie said as she smiled at the young man.

Pam picked up where she left off. "That's what I want to know!!!!"

"I'm Billy and I....."

"Well, have a seat here, Billy," Ashlie said patting the sofa. "We'll talk and get to know each other." Ashlie had a magical way of relaxing the mood with her sincere kindness.

Even though Ashlie was sort of taking over the situation, Pam didn't mind relinquishing the moment to her. She was detached from the incident at Donnelly's and didn't harbor any suspicions about Billy like Pam did. Pam was calming down now as well and much more receptive to a conversation as opposed to confrontation.

Billy sat down on one end of the sofa. Grace sat at the extreme end of the other side cramming herself tightly against the armrest. Pam and Ashlie sat in two chairs divided by a small table with some books, a small evergreen plant resting on top, and frame with a picture of Clark playing the guitar. They faced the teenagers. Ashlie smiled gently. Pam just stared, absent the scowl, at the Grace and Billy. The kids just looked uncomfortably at the two women.

"Mom, I can explain," said Grace nervously. Pam just nodded her head suspiciously and let her proceed.

. . . .

It was about eight that night. Grace and Billy covered the

entire story: the rain, bumping into each other outside of Susan's Bakery and Billy paying for the sweet rolls. The gem of the revelations to Pam was how remorseful Billy was about the incident at Donnelly's. Billy ended up staying over for dinner with friendly banter and talk flowing like water between fork loads of spaghetti. Ashlie was a receptive audience and interjected laughter and oh's when most appropriate. Pam's reservations about Billy were appeased the more he spoke and, again, by the apparent remorsefulness about the "incident." Grace retreated to her former, quiet self and just absorbed the social aspects of the dinner. Every once in a while she glanced at Billy trying to get a better read of the kid. She couldn't believe that she was warming up to this boy whom only hours ago she detested.

When it was time to go, Billy said his goodbyes to Ashlie and Pam. Grace walked him to the door when Pam spoke, "Billy, thank you for taking Grace home and out of the rain."

Billy smiled back, "I was glad to do it, and thank you so much for dinner." Pam nodded her response with a return smile. At the door, Billy looked into Grace's now sparkling eyes. "Thank you, too, Grace. Thank you for letting me meet your mom and Ashlie, and thank you for letting me get to know you better." Grace bowed her head politely and smiled. Billy walked out the door to his red Bronco, looked back as Grace gave him a tiny wave goodbye from the porch.

On the way home, Billy couldn't get over the evening. It was just a dinner with a plain girl and her mom and their friend. However, it was so much more to him than that. It was the first time in a long time that he had dinner with ... well,....a family.

It was the first time in a long time that he was in a room with friendly laughter, with acceptance, with people that he had just met and that he was beginning to care about. It was the first time he was with a girl he actually had feelings for. Apathy had been a fortress he had built to stave off the doubt, the insensitivity, the cruelty in his own life, and now the walls of the ramparts were cracking. Yes, cracking . . . but not demolished.

Billy arrived at the spacious mansion, opened the door and as usual shouted, "I'm home." He tried again, "Hello! I'm home." Silence. No answer . . . as expected.

CHAPTER 13 - INTERESTING

Pam and Grace seemed closer and happier in the days that followed. The dinner was special with Ashlie and having Billy, a stranger to their neighborhood and a stranger from their lifestyle, made for an exciting night; actually, a reach outside of their comfort zone. After work, the two women stopped by Donnelly's as usual. Lynnda greeted them as Mike was busy talking with a customer at the rear of the store. A vanilla coke was plunked on the counter for Pam, and Lynnda handed Grace her chocolate chip ice cream on a waffle cone. They had a fun exchange about the little things in life: the new movie, Jaws, and how scary it was, the weather, changes in the neighborhood, the presidential race next year with the possibility of Jimmy Carter and Gerald Ford facing off for the election, and, most importantly, how mature Grace was getting.

Lynnda gave a concerned glance toward the back of the store. She heard the conversation with Mike and the man grow louder. He was dressed in an upscale suit, flashy tie, and shiny shoes that reflected the fluorescent lights on the ceiling. He stood erect with confidence or, more appropriately, arrogance that oozed from him. Just then Grace had dropped her napkin, gotten off her stool to reach down to retrieve it. The man tossed a few rude words at Mike and turned to march out of the store He crashed into Pam knocking her over from her crouched position. He almost fell, righted himself and glared down at Pam. She nervously looked up at him. Evil radiated from his eyes when he growled, "Get out the way, you piece of shi.. . . .trash," barely preventing an obscenity from tumbling out of his mouth. He glared a moment longer at Grace, turned, marched out the door and slammed it behind him. The windows shook.

Mike scrambled over to help Grace up, "Are you OK, Grace?" Pam had slid off her stool and was by her side by now.

"I'm OK!" she sobbed as tears welled in her eyes. Grace didn't have any bruises or cuts. The hurt was more profound than that. The words, you piece of trash, echoed over and over in her head. She had doubts about herself, her life, and where she lived as it was, but those words just hammered home those self-doubts.

"Who was that guy?" said Pam with anger rattling her voice.

With a deep breath, Mike said, "He is the man who wants to buy our store."

"Buy your store!!!" Grace and Pam blurted collectively. Lynnda stared down at the floor with a hint of shame. "You can't sell your store!" Their eyes darted back and forth from Mike to Lynnda.

"We don't want to, but that man and his company are trying to buy up the properties in this part of town to make it upscale," Mike said. "If he is able to purchase the buildings around us and convert them to ... "

"To what? . . . Upscale arrogance!!!!" Grace shouted. Her mother glanced at her daughter surprised at her aggressive comment.

"Grace, this whole project is in its early stages. We're just trying to consider our options," said Lynnda desperately.

"Right now it is just an interesting scenario which is presenting itself to us," said Mike trying to calm the escalating tension.

"It goes beyond interesting. Donnelly's, you and Lynnda, are the heart of our community. Interesting, . . . it is not." The speakers were playing "Take the Money and Run" by the Steve Miller Band. How appropriate thought Grace. How damn appropriate.

. . . .

Pam and Grace were saddened over the possibility of Donnelly's closing. Even more so, they were fuming at the possible sale to that arrogant man in the slick suit. They were not mad at the Donnelly's but upset about potentially having a bit of their history, and their friends ripped away from them. The topic dominated their verbal exchange on the way home. Grace assumed the cooler, more tempered approach in an effort to calm her mother. It worked to some degree, but what worked better was the appearance of Ninette, Stephanie, and Angie who were joined with Jason and Shaun as well as another boy whom Grace did not recognize assembled on their front porch. The group's exuberance was like a switch that redirected Pam's and Grace's thoughts.

"Hi, Grace! Hi, Mrs. Keenan" they said in scattered greetings.

Pam smiled happily, glad to have her mind diverted, "Hi, y'all!" They hardly heard her as Grace melted into the group and conversation of teenage stuff filled the air. The girl's introduced the new boy, Charlie, to Grace whom she had seen around the neighborhood. They then all flowed to the back yard to play, to chat, and to catch up. Pam went inside the house to the kitchen to see what goodies she could bring out for Grace's friends. Chips, Cool Aid, and some cookies that she had made from the previous day were all she had. When she brought them out, the kids were grateful and gulped everything down within a few minutes.

The boys began throwing a ball around and, again, tormented Lily who wanted to partake in the game. The girls talked about school activities, jobs or colleges they were pursuing, and kids that Grace knew. She missed school. Grace missed everything about it: the bells, the walks in the halls between class, Mr. Buckley's science classes and his funny stories. She even missed the classes, the books, the learning. She thought about missing out on the possibility of going to college. Schools like the University of Tennessee, MTSU, and Lipscomb were being thrown around by her friends. She was embarrassed by her envy and tried to conceal it.

Eventually, her attention drifted. Every once in a while, Grace would look over at the boys playing with the ball. She had a curiosity about the new boy, Charlie. He looked back at the girls and on occasions. Grace's eyes would catch his. He responded with a smile and then went back to the game.

When it was time to say goodbye, the group thanked Mrs. Keenan, and the girls gave Grace a hug. Charlie made a special effort to thank Mrs. Keenan and Grace. Pam and Grace turned to each other as everyone was leaving. "That new boy seems nice," said Pam.

Grace said, "Yah! He did seem nice." Her eyes followed them all leave the back yard. She glanced at Charlie as he trailed the group, his long black hair bouncing on the back of his neck.

. . . .

The light faded into darkness as the evening seemed to sneak up on the Keenan home. The day had been a contrast of emotions between a low of the possibility of the Donnelly's selling their shop and the high of the mini-reunion with Grace's friends. Pam and Grace had finished their thankful prayers when the phone rang startling Pam and Grace who were seated at the kitchen table to have soup. Grace nearly dropped her spoon. Pam reached for the phone on the counter and picked it up. "Hello?" She paused a bit while the caller spoke. Then she looked at Grace, shrugged her shoulders and extended the phone out to her. "It's for you."

"Who is it? Grace whispered.

"It's Billy!" said Pam holding the phone away from her and shielding her lips with her free hand.

"What!?! What should I do?" she quietly stammered with a shocked look while Pam covered the mouthpiece.

"What you should do is talk to him," she said with feigned frustration.

Cautiously, hesitantly, Grace reached for the phone. With a tiny voice, she said, "Hello? Oh! Hello, Billy." Her eyes locked onto her mom's face while Billy talked. After a few moments, she muffles the phone with her hand, contorts her face, pulls her elbows into her body and says to her mom nervously, "He wants to go out with me to a pizza place on Friday."

"Well, what do want me to do?" replied mom. "He didn't ask your mother out. He asked you."

"What should I do???" The voice on the other end could be heard asking for Grace not sure if they had disconnected.

"Oh! For crying out loud," Pam said rolling her eyes. "Go out with him, but tell him you can't stay out late," she grinned. However, Pam was not wholly comfortable with Grace going out with this boy whom she hardly knew. She cautioned Grace to be careful. Grace agreed with her mom for she, too, was not entirely at ease with the boy in the red Bronco.

. . . .

In the mansion's living room, Billy held the phone by his side and stared out the window thinking about his phone call with Grace. "Who was that?" asked a brusque voice in the open entryway."

Billy was jolted from his thoughts, "Dad, what are you doing here?"

"I live here....on occasions."

"... but I thought you were away on business."

"Actually, I'm home on business. Now, who was that?" he demanded.

"It's just a friend."

"A friend that you're going out on a date with? Is it that nice girl, Judy, that I met a while back?

"No!" Billy quickly responded. Maybe a bit too quickly.

Billy couldn't believe his dad got sucked into the web of deceit that Judy threw out. She was a magician of manipulative charm and the queen of backstabbing. Judy would throw him or anyone else under the bus. The charm was a ploy to get people to do what she wanted and, then "wham" they became the victim.

"That's too bad. I liked Judy. Well, nice to see you, Billy. I have work to do," He turned to leave the room and then turned with a stern face, "... and when you get around to it, tell me who you were talking to!"

Billy watched his dad march out of the room to his office. "Nice to see you too, dad," he said softly.

CHAPTER 14 - PIZZA WITH THE WORKS

Billy gripped the steering wheel of his Ford Bronco a little tighter than usual. He was excited to be taking out this unusual, plain girl, and he didn't know why. She was distant, shy and, yet, at times, strong. She had a sweetness about her, a goodness that Billy couldn't detect in his circle of friends.

He was also a bit anxious at his father's brief but intense interrogation about the girl at the other end of the line. Billy didn't divulge much information other than that he had met a girl in whom he was interested and wanted to get to know better. His sparse release of facts raised his father's suspicions. His dad was a man who always needed to be in control and was. He didn't become President and CEO of one of the most significant real estate development firms in the country by being "the nice guy." If he had to cut you at the knees, he would. His firm hired cheap labor by skirting immigration laws. He would secure the services of sleazy lawyers to grease the hands of inspectors, and, more commonly, political figures. In his business dealings, he mixed with the likes of other business tycoons, politicians, mafia figures, and low life criminals. Billy gripped the steering wheel even tighter as he traveled through the countryside.

He pulled up and saw Grace and her mom on the porch swing. He grinned at the sight. It was a pure sense of happiness that overcame him. This girl did make him happy, and she had nothing but a dumpy house. She didn't even attend high school. Then why was he drawn to her? "Hi, Grace. Hi, Mrs. Keenan,"

Billy said as he popped out the car and jumped onto the porch steps.

"Hi, Billy," Pam said looking at him and then at Grace who was just smiling.

"We won't be gone late, Mrs. Keenan." Pam nodded her head in response.

Billy reached for Grace's hand to escort her off the porch. Pam took a deep breath. It was her baby going out with this . . . well, stranger. Was she doing the right thing by letting Grace go? "Be careful you two." Another deep breath, "I love you, Grace."

"Love you too, mom."

"We're just going out for pizza, Mrs. Keenan. We'll be back soon," Billy said reassuringly reading concern in Mrs. Keenan's facial expression. They hopped into his car and gave a quick wave to Pam as she stood alone on the porch waving back at them.

The Bronco rolled down the street. "I love you, Grace," she whispered to herself and thought as she often did when Grace walked away from their home; there goes my baby. The car then disappeared around the corner. There goes my baby.

. . . .

Billy looked across the table with the checkered cloth. "This is my favorite pizza place," Billy said. "They have great vegetable pizza. Of course, you don't have to have vegetable pizza . . ." he stammered. "You can have any pizza you want. Actually, you don't even have to have pizza. You can have spaghetti or lasagna . . . They have great lasagna or . . ."

"Vegetable pizza will be fine," smiled Grace finding humor in Billy's menu rambling.

"O.K. Then veggie pizza it will be," Billy proclaimed. "How Sweet It Is" by James Taylor played on the Juke Box while they talked about everything. Grace quietly asked Billy about his life. Billy thought this is pretty sweet. Here is someone who wants to know about me.

Billy told her what he liked to do in his spare time. "I love swimming in my pool and laying on floats just watching the clouds gliding in the sky. I enjoy driving one of the golf carts around our property on our mini golf course."

Grace's eyes widened. Golf course on his property. "Oh! That sounds like fun." She really was thinking that she was way out of her league.

"It is Grace. You will have to come over and see it some-time."

"Yes! That would be fun." The words slipped out of her mouth before she could stop them. She realized how trite and foolish she may have sounded.

He pushed on with his dialogue, "I really like going away on vacations to places like Bermuda, Cancun and such. I like playing golf, but I'm not really that good." He had to stick some humility in there.

Grace's eyes widened even more. The closest she ever came to exotic places like Bermuda and Cancun were in the pages of National Geographic. And as far as golf was concerned, she couldn't tell the difference between a golf tee and a tea leaf.

Grace fumbled with her words, "Oh, I don't play golf well either." She couldn't believe she said that. "I mean, I've never played golf." Her eyes dropped with embarrassment. She paused and then stuttered, " I, I mean . . . I've never been on a golf course."

Sensing her being uncomfortable, Billy thought he would try a little humor, "I really have an obsession with beer. All kinds of beer." Grace quickly drew back in her seat. Talking about being uncomfortable. He read the concern in her face and quickly smiled, "I'm only kidding." Realizing his error, he switched to talking about the landscaping, the fish in the pond, the deer at the edge of the woods hoping to disarm her with happy images and experiences. Although, he did like his beer.

Grace dismissed the "beer joke" as an awkward attempt by Billy at humor. She assumed a protective posture with her hands folded on her lap and continued listening. She had nothing to offer for she was in awe of his experiences and wealth. Even though he was elaborating on all his "stuff," it wasn't like he was bragging. That was just his life: a life far different than hers.

What she noticed most about Billy was that he rarely discussed his parents with the exception that his dad was a prominent real estate developer and that his mom played bridge. He never mentioned anything about family get-togethers, cookouts, or . . . any suggestion resembling togetherness. America's "Lonely People" kicked in on the Juke Box.

Billy asked her about her life. Grace felt insecure knowing her life paled to his. But she presented tidbits about her world; her friends, her and her mom's garden and such. Grace talked about her dog, Lily, and how the pup would make her laugh. She spoke about how she and her mom would take walks down the railroad tracks in memory of her dad. It was then that Billy began to stiffen, to become more attentive. He wanted to know more about the "incident" and seemed truly saddened to hear about her father's death. His reaction made Grace feel a little more comfortable and even more attracted to Billy, . . . his soft side. She talked about her friends and how her mom would have casual cookouts with them all. Billy listened intently, even with envy. He had so much material stuff, but he didn't have what Grace had . . . which he so wanted.

The dinner seemed to flew by. It was actually getting dark out, and Billy wanted to get Grace home at a decent time. He didn't want to cross the line with Mrs. Keenan and desired to keep on his right side.

Billy dropped a twenty dollar bill on the table, and they got up to leave. As they were walking toward the door, Grace looked out the pizza restaurant's window to check the sky's darkness. The store's neon light lit up the area. Those same lights also reflected off of the hood of a shiny, blue Cadillac across the street as it pulled out of a parking space.

. . . .

Billy stopped the car in front of Grace's house. They could see her mom in the chair by the window. A look of relief seemed to sweep across her face. They waved to her as Billy walked Grace to the front door. They stopped and turned to look at each other. "I had a nice time," Billy said.

"I did, too," Grace demurely answered.

"Can we do something like this again?

"We'll have to see, "Grace hesitated. "Well, I mean, I guess so."

They looked at each other when Billy reached down for Grace's hands. "Grace, I . . . "

The front door popped open. Billy dropped her hands, and they flopped by her side. "Hi, Grace. Hi, Billy" Pam said cheerfully. "I hope the pizza was good."

"Oh, it was, mom. We went to Pinky's Pizza which is Billy's favorite restaurant."

"That's nice, Billy."

Billy sensed in her voice that the evening was over, "Well, thank you for letting me take your daughter out. We had fun." Billy turned to Grace, "Bye, Grace. See you soon." He jumped down the front steps, hopped into his car and waved one last time as he drove off.

Pam looked at her daughter, "See you soon, huh?" Grace just glanced back with a meek smile. They both walked into the house closing the door behind them and shut off the porch light. In the darkness, a shiny, blue Cadillac pulled out from down the street and crept past the Keenan house with its headlights turned off.

CHAPTER 15 - FIREWORKS

"Anger dwells only in the bosom of fools" Albert Einstein

It was the fourth of July, and Pam thought it would be a nice idea to have Grace's friends over for a cookout. And why not, for she has welcomed them over for casual dinners on many occasions. Grace loved the idea. Grace and Billy had run into each other incidentally at times; or was it intentionally. After all, Billy had sort of stalked her when they first met. Never-the-less, Grace, although cautious, felt comfortable enough with him to invite Billy to the cookout as well.

Ashlie was helping Pam in the kitchen as she was making a large bowl of salad with tomatoes and cucumbers from Pam's garden. Ashlie marveled at Pam's green thumb. Some people envied other people's talents. Not Ashlie. She always admired the abilities of others. She was supportive, encouraging to friends and to strangers. Her positivity is what drew Pam to her. Ashlie made everyone around her a better person. "You certainly have a magical way with growing vegetables, Pam," she said.

"Thank you, Ashlie," responded Pam as she was patting hamburgers, "and thank you for bringing the hamburger meat over."

"Glad to help. I was impressed that the kids contributed to the party by bringing sodas, buns, and chips."

"Yeah. They're a good group."

Looking out the kitchen window, Ashlie watched the boys

playing with the ball, . . . tormenting poor Lily again. Billy was playing as well. When he chucked the ball, it was with a little more force than needed. Some of the boys struggled to catch his throws as the ball whizzed through their hands and bounced off their chests. Ashlie continued watching and then asked, "How do you like that boy, Billy? You mentioned that Pam invited him."

Pam looked up while still shaping the burgers, "The jury is still out. He seems nice enough, but..." Pam hesitated.

"But what?"

"He's just not like us; like our friends. I don't know. I don't know how to put it." Ashlie listened intently. "I don't want to be judgmental, but I . . . " She never finished her sentence as they both looked out the window at the boys playing. Both were silent now. Thinking. Wondering: wondering about . . . Billy.

The girls were sitting in a circle as the boys played. Again, their conversation revolved around each other's families, what each of them was going to do after graduation at the end of the year, bands they liked and so on. Angie enjoyed her long-haired music, and it wasn't Mozart. Guns 'N Roses, Aerosmith, and AC/DC. Stephanie did go for the classics. Chopin was her favorite. Not only did she listen to that long-haired music, but she also played it on the piano. Ninette went for the newer brands of music which most of the girls hadn't heard of, and Grace just listened to the girls. She didn't really have a favorite for she enjoyed them all.

The girls' conversation and attention drifted to the boys. Charlie was a relatively new addition to the Chris, Shaun, and Jason clan. He was pleasant, fun and, generally, a good guy.

What about Billy? The girls were unsure about him. When he first came to introduce himself, he seemed a bit too self-assured. He also was a bit out of place with his appearance: golf shirt, slick pants, and so on as well as the fact that he was the only one who drove his own car, the glossy, red Bronco. While watching the boys playing, it was apparent that Billy was trying to make an impression. He threw harder, talked louder, and he was out of place in this "family" environment where each member was viewed as equals: not adversaries to be outdone by the other.

"How do you like Billy?" asked Angie.

"Yeah, what about that Billy boy?" grinned Stephanie.

Grace shot them a funny look and said, "He seems nice. We went out for pizza the oth...."

"Holy cow!!! You went out on a date with him?" Ninette blurted. The girls leaned forward to listen to Grace's answer. They didn't want to miss a beat: her words, her inflections, her pauses. In girl language, all of that was a story within the message.

Grace continued, "Yes! We went out for a pizza. No big deal."

"What do you mean, 'No big deal?'" quizzed Ninette. "You never go out on dates alone with a boy. It's always with a group."

"Well, he asked. I went. We had fun." Grace was aware that Billy was not of her element but deflected any of his shortcomings. She was enthralled with the boy who took her out and wanted to give him a chance. "That's it," she smiled.

Their attention was diverted to a commotion with the boys. "Hey, Billy, quit throwing the ball so hard," Shaun snapped.

"You can't take it? Huh! Shaun?"

"Come on, Billy!!" said Jaybird. "We're just trying to have fun."

"OK! OK! Sorry, Shaun." Billy felt himself reverting to the old Billy. He knew he had to pull back.

Pam broke the tension when she slammed the back door open with a plate full of burgers and hot dogs followed by Ashlie cradling a bowl of salad. "We're just about to eat. Who wants what?" The flock of boys glanced quickly at each other shuffled toward the food slowly brushing their hostilities aside. Goodies had a calming effect on them. However, the girls flew from their spots and ascended on the two women. It was an orderly series of meal requests . . . , well, as uniformly as a bunch of hungry teenagers and a mutt could be.

After downing hamburgers and hot dogs and munching on a salad, the girls and the boys joined each other listening to Simon and Garfunkel music and talking about their favorite pro basketball and football players and their teams. Billy tried to bring up the topic of golf and his favorite players, but that topic fell flat with this crew.

The sun began to sink behind the trees. It was getting late. After thank you's and goodbyes, the kids started to disperse. Grace and some of the kids with Billy curled around the back of the house to the front where Billy's car was parked. "What the hell!!!" he yelled glaring at his Bronco. Grace and the others stopped abruptly and stared in the same direction. Billy's car was a mess. It had been egged. Egged mercilessly; especially the driver's side. "Who the $@&% egged my car?" Billy lost it. His impulsivity took over. "What a crappy neighborhood you guys live in," he blasted channeling his anger at Grace and her friends.

"Billy, stop it. Just stop it!" cried Grace with tears streaming down her face. She was thinking: why did she invite him? Why in the world did she invite this "stranger?"

He jumped in his car and floored the Bronco. The wheels spun, and burnt rubber polluted the air. He screeched by the kids and glared at Grace's friends as if they had been responsible.

Jaybird murmured quietly, but not so softly as not to be heard, "That car ain't so shiny anymore."

CHAPTER 16 - MAKING AMENDS

"The weak can never forgive. Forgiveness is the attribute of the strong."

Mahatma Gandhi

It had been weeks since Grace and Billy had talked. Pam, after hearing Billy's eloquent tirade outside in front of her house, just said, "She's not home," when Billy called. But that screening was nearly impossible in that Pam was not always home when Grace was. Inevitably, Billy was able to connect with Grace, and he began the process of appeasing her emotions. He was smooth when he wanted to be, and he sure wanted to be now; with this girl.

She was reluctant to even talk with him, but, eventually, submitted after he implored to her that he was "incredibly sorry" for his actions and words. He wanted to apologize to her face to face. She thought she interpreted sincerity in his voice and decided to meet him under one condition: that the meeting take place at Donnelly's and with her mother present. Billy was hesitant but realized he was not in the position to negotiate. So it was set. He would meet Grace at Donnelly's after work with her mother present the following Wednesday.

Wednesday came sooner than Billy had expected. When he got to Donnelly's, Pam and Grace had not yet arrived which was good. He didn't want to be late for their "meeting" so as not to have them imagine any doubts about his sincerity. This was indeed not the occasion to have a misstep in patching relations.

He sat on one of the stools by the counter sipping on a regular coke. For some reason, fountain sodas always tasted better. As usual, the speaker system was pushing out music. This time "Blue Eyes Cryin' in the Rain" by Willie Nelson was playing.

Lynnda was working the counter and had a small conversation with Billy while he waited for Grace and her mother to arrive. Lynnda shared with Billy that she was amazed that the cost of gasoline had gone up to 44 cents a gallon the previous year and had heard rumors that it was going to climb to 59 cents. Billy responded that it was a shame and that people wouldn't be able to pay such increases. In actuality, Billy didn't give a hoot. His family was loaded, and he thought very little of the cost of things. However, Billy wanted to keep on the same page as Lynnda knowing that the Donnelly's were good friends of the Keenan family. He would feed her or anybody any line to get what he wanted: and Billy wanted Grace. Yes, he was smooth.

Mike was talking with an elderly group at the booth. Laughter and smiles and gratefulness showered that area which usually happens with Mike around. He had that gift of making everyone feel valued as did Lynnda. Their establishment didn't just serve vanilla cokes and chocolate chip ice cream. One could wonder, was Lynnda a reflection of Mike or was it the other way around? Either way, they both made Donnelly's a special place and an escape from the toils of work and the world. Donnelly's was the Mom and Pop store of the neighborhood . . . but it is so much more than that.

Billy was getting that vibe. He sensed that Donnelly's was

something special and, actually, this community was something special. Billy got the same feeling when he was with Grace, but Billy was having a difficult time blending into this small community and with the people. They were simple folks and grasped onto the simple delicacies of life whereas he had just passed them by until recently....until he met Grace, her friends, her mom, Ashlie, and the Donnelly's. Why was he having such a struggle fitting in?

The door opened accompanied by the ringing of tiny chimes, a recent addition Mike thought would be nice. Grace and her mother walked in, smiled at Lynnda and gave a nod to Billy. Billy fidgeted in his seat like a toddler. He was nervous. He didn't want to blow this opportunity to make amends. Billy got off his stool to create a more welcoming gesture. When Grace and Pam had taken their seat, Grace sat next to him. Billy spoke first, "I hope you had a good day at work?" He went for a pleasant, safe tactic to break the ice.

"Oh, it was like any other day," said Pam. Grace just nodded in agreement.

After a few more general exchanges, Billy decided to face the concerns directly, "I want to apologize . . . for my rant outside your home." He was greeted with silence and stares waiting for more to unravel. Billy pressed on, "I was shocked to see my car destroyed like that . . . ," He paused realizing he was offering excuses rather remorsefulness. ". . . and I should not have talked that way." He lowered his head, "I should not have acted that way." He looked up at both of them with Lynnda wiping the counter within earshot. "You were so kind to invite me to your home, introduce me to your friends, and to feed me...," water began to collect in his eyes which even surprised him. "I just want to tell you that I'm sorry." Grace reached out to touch his hand as he slid himself off the stool. He looked at them again, ". . . I'm . . . I'm so sorry." Billy turned and walked out the door.

Grace and Pam exchanged confused looks when Pam quickly said, "Follow him! Talk to him!"

"But what should I say?" Grace pleaded.

"You will find the right words. Now go!" It wasn't that Pam wanted Billy in their lives that she coaxed Grace to talk to him, but, instead, she felt it was the right thing to do considering he had made such an effort to apologize. She was still not comfortable with him.

Grace seemed to dance to the door and pulled it open. The chimes rang behind her as she ran after Billy.

. . . .

Billy was plodding down the sidewalk. Grace quickened her pace to catch up with him.

"Billy! Billy! Please wait! "

Billy stopped and turned, "I just don't fit in, Grace. I want to, but I know I don't."

She looked him directly in the eyes displaying no shyness, no reservation. "Give it a try, Billy. Don't just leave," urged Grace.

"Are you saying you want to see me, to have me be a part of your life?" Billy changed his position of defeat and began to nurture a suggestion of hope.

"I'm saying don't run from what you want, and, yes, . . .

YES, ... I would like to see you again." The noise of traffic, shuffling feet, and curious eyes upon them filled the void of the stillness between them. They stared at each other for what seemed like an hour when suddenly Billy, without thought, pulled Grace into his arms, hugged her and kissed her softly. Grace did not resist. The cars drove on, some pedestrians looked at them without breaking their stride, and Pam glared from the doorway of Donnelly's. Oh shit! What did I do?

CHAPTER 17 - QUESTIONS

Billy and Grace spent more and more time with each other which bordered on "dating." Billy would come over and try to help around the house with chores, but this was a guy who had difficulty changing a light bulb. His help was restricted to carrying out the garbage, sweeping the porch or other menial tasks. He wanted desperately to get on Pam's good graces. He upped his game in politeness and expressed gratitude for everything to the extreme of thanking her for letting him vacuum the rugs. Billy surprised himself in doing these "crappy" jobs since he didn't lift a finger around his house except for pointing out to the maid a mess that needed to be cleaned up.

His efforts were succeeding. Pam appreciated his work and Grace thought it was sweet. They often had dinner together and got to know each other better. Things looked pretty good between them all. Sometimes Billy would be over at the house when Grace's friends stopped by to visit. However, he just couldn't seem to crack the wall of suspicion they all had. They refused to shed the memory of his tantrum. Besides, he was just not their kind of person. Billy, to them, was a bit too confident, too flashy, and too hung up on himself. They couldn't figure out why Grace was attracted to him, and, in honesty, nor could Grace at times. However, she did appreciate the attention he gave her and, also, his funny way of trying to help. Grace also liked his confidence which to the others was a detraction and more like cockiness. But to Grace, it was something she admired since she was so full of self-doubt and relatively shy.

Pam didn't share the same admiration for Billy. Her feelings coincided with Grace's friends. The thing that bothered Pam the most was that he always seemed to be trying too hard. His efforts didn't seem genuine. And, unlike Grace, she didn't view his work around the house as sweet, but, somewhat, manipulative. Pam kept a cautious eye on Billy and shuddered every time he tried to show affection to her baby, Grace: a hug, a pat, an exchange of giggles sent pangs of concern down her spine. No! Billy had undoubtedly not won over Pam.

. . . .

Back at Billy's house, his mom and dad relaxed by the pool. A rarity on three accounts: relaxing, with each other, and by the pool. They talked about Billy.

"Where the hell has Billy been lately," hissed Mr. Cromwell. He hasn't been around the house hardly at all." He took a sip of his cocktail.

"He hasn't been hanging with his old friends, Judy, Dora, and Alex either," said Dolly. "I wonder what he's been doing? Certainly not working on the chores at the mansion," she chuckled. Mr. Cromwell shot her an annoying glance.

Mr. and Mrs. Cromwell didn't really look at each other when talking. They gazed over the water with a drink in hand and engaged in conversation. Many times, when the other person was saying something, it did not register with their partner.

Other thoughts mired the message and only bits and pieces of whatever was said filtered through to the other spouse.

However, the topic here was of shared interest. The curiosity factor more than concern for Billy made their receptive abilities spike. All of a sudden, Billy's dad jolted up in his chaise lounge startling Dolly. He seemed to have had an epiphany. "I have an idea! I'm going to call that sweet girl, Judy, and see if she knows anything."

Dolly's eyes popped open. "That sounds like a grand idea, Norman," she said as she took a sip of her wine . . . maybe a little more than a sip. "Why don't you invite Judy and her friends over for a swim and snacks. Then we can have a "pow-wow" to get the full story about Billy. At least any portion of which they may be aware."

"Sometimes, Dolly, you amaze me," Norman called to Nellie, the maid, to get the phone. Nellie hustled out of the kitchen to the pool area, phone in hand, and gave it to Mr. Cromwell. He made the call and the connection. After talking to Judy for a few minutes, he grinned and turned to Dolly, "They're coming over in half an hour." He called out to the maid again, "Nellie, could you whip together some goodies? We're having guests arriving in about thirty minutes." He leaned back in his lounge chair as did Dolly. Like synchronized lounging, they both closed their eyes, sighed, and had smug smiles on their faces.

Dolly opened her eyes and inquired, "Should we have beer and wine for them?"

"Wow, Dolly! You're impressive. Another good idea. That may loosen them up." Norman, again, leaned back and the smug smile resurface. "We'll get to the bottom of this."

Dolly nodded in agreement even though Mr. Cromwell couldn't see her with his eyes closed. She took another swig of her wine, put her head back, and whispered, "The mystery will be solved and . . . " She drifted off in sleep.

CHAPTER 18 ～ REVELATIONS

The blue Cadillac eased to a stop with its three passengers giggling with excitement. The Tennessee sun hung high in the sky, and its rays beamed down with a warmth that exceeded being comfortable. A few hours in the pool was just what the doctor ordered, and these three patients were impatient. They wanted to dive in as soon as possible. They scrambled out of the car and shut the doors with a bang, bang, bang. When they got to the pool gate, Mr. Cromwell appeared pleased and said, "So glad you all were able to make it over. It's a good day to cool off."

"It sure is," said Judy as she took off her clothing to unveil her two-piece bathing suit. Mr. Cromwell's grin got even bigger. Dora did the same and, within minutes after arriving, all three were ready for sea world as the pool had floats of whales and boats gliding on the glistening water. Judy asked if she could turn on the radio and Norman replied positively. Judy then turned the dial to the rock station, increased the volume as Led Zeppelin belted out "Stairway to Heaven". "Let the party begin," she shouted. The trio jumped in and began frolicking in the pool, splashing the water at each other to start their session of party time.

An hour had slipped by, and the pool activities still prevailed. Dora dove off of the diving board just missing Judy who splashed her when she rose to the surface. Norman sat poolside with Alex, feet dangling in the pool. Both were gulping down

beers and yucking it up. Dolly seemed comatose on her chaise
lounge with a near empty bottle of wine resting on the tile beside her. Judy and Dora hoisted themselves up from the pool
next to Mr. Cromwell whom they now referred to as Norman.
Norman seemed to be enjoying the view while taking another
swig of his beer.

"Thanks for having us over, Mr. Cromwell," said Judy with
an alluring smile.

"Please, call me Norman. Remember?" he insisted while
checking out Judy's credentials.

"OK, Norman. Do you mind if I have another glass of
wine?

"Certainly not. Help yourself."

Judy pulled herself out of the pool as did Dora, and they
poured more wine into their empty glasses. They took a quick
sip and sat down in their chaise lounges. Mr. Cromwell and
Alex stood up and dripped their way to the folding lounge furniture while Mrs. Cromwell remained nearly motionless except
for some heavy breathing.

"This is the life. Thank you again for having us over," said
Judy.

"Yah, this is a blast," contributed Alex raising his beer in
approval.

"I'm glad you all were able to come and enjoy yourself,"
said Norman. His face turned serious. "I have a question to ask
you, and I am hoping you can help me." The three teenagers
were intrigued and focused their complete attention on Norman. "Billy hasn't been home a lot recently. Not that I have been
either, but when I am, I usually run into him. Not so much in

the past months. Do any of you know what he's been doing or where he has been going?"

The kids exchanged quick glances. Judy spoke first . . . of course, "Funny you should ask." Another quick glance between them, this time accompanied by curious grins. She continued, "Billy seems to have hooked up with a girl."

"Hooked up? What do you mean?" Mr. Cromwell questioned.

"He has been seeing a girl from the other side of town," said Judy. Her cohorts nodded their heads in agreement.

"What do you mean, the other side of town?" asked Mr. Cromwell.

"From across the tracks," answered Judy relishing in being the messenger of this spicy news. "25 or 6 to 4" by Chicago accompanied her delivery of this information.

Norman went silent. A severe look washed over his face, and his eyes seemed to flare. He didn't spend a lot of time with Billy, but he certainly had high expectations for his future that didn't include hanging around with a girl from across the tracks. This sort of companionship could derail his intentions for Billy. He had given that kid everything. Now the ungrateful brat was flushing it all down the drain for a piece of trash from the other side of town. The more he contemplated the scenario, the more he fumed. He had gotten the information he wanted from the three teenagers, and now he was just pissed. "All right! Get the hell out of here." He blasted.

Stunned, the three stood up, quickly gathered their clothing, and began walking toward the pool gate to exit.

"No! Wait!" They all stopped in their tracks and turned to

face Norman...or was it, Mr. Cromwell, now. "Who is the girl? Tell me more about her!"

The group returned to their seats and to their drinking eager to divulge what they knew. After an hour, Mr. Cromwell was filled in about the girl from across the tracks: the girl that worked in the factory, lived within walking distance from work, and who lived with her mother in a crappy house.

Mrs. Cromwell recovered from her dazed state clueless about what was happening. She had even forgotten that the kids were there. Mr. Cromwell's curiosity consumed him. He wanted to meet this girl, see her house and crush this relationship IMMEDIATELY. Mrs. Cromwell grabbed her glass and held it up, "Could you get me another glass of wine, dear."

"Get your own," Norman growled.

. . . .

That night Norman sat alone in his study clutching a beer. His face was gnarled with anger. He was making grunting noises without even knowing it. Nellie walked gingerly by the entrance of the study to see if he needed anything. Reading his body language, seeing the fire in his eyes, and noticing the half crushed, half full beer can in his hand, she made an abrupt about-face and steered for safer waters, her bedroom. Nellie had witnessed that level of rage before. She locked the door and rested her back against it while looking up at the ceiling releasing a gasp of air.

CHAPTER 19 - YIKES!

"Anger is useful only to a certain point.
After that, it becomes rage, and rage will make you careless."

Lauren Oliver, Pandemonium

It was late. Billy opened the door to his house as quietly as he could, clutched the sides, and then closed it delicately. He turned to head up the massive staircase to his room. "Billy?" His father rumbled with authority. Mr. Cromwell was sitting in his favorite chair in the living room. Billy had heard fury in his father's voice in the past when he trashed his neighbor's pool and when he put nails his mother's friend's tires on her Mercedes and on a few other dramatic occasions. However, this time the decibels, the intonations, the frustration seemed much more intense than all those other times. He looked at his father sitting in his massive chair. He swore he could steam rising above his head. He approached his father cautiously. Norman sprung up, strutted right toward Billy, and, without hesitation, slapped him across the face so hard that Billy fell back onto the floor. "Who the hell is this bitch you're seeing?" Norman hung over him like a crazed bear: gritted teeth and saliva dripping from his mouth. Billy didn't have time to answer when his father reached down, pulled him halfway up, and hit him again: this time even harder knocking him to the floor again. Blood began to drain from his nose and pain rifled through his body.

Billy put his hand to the side of his face and tried to crawl backward: away from this maniac; who was his dad. His father reached his arm back to hammer Billy one more time. As his fist was coming down, his father was hit full force by a diminutive body. "Noooooo!" screamed Billy's mom as she toppled Norman backward onto the floor. Billy laid on the oriental rug; dazed and confused. Billy's father was furious, ready to take on two victims as he gathered himself. His mom was in a heap on the angora rug looking up at her husband, fear in her eyes and rage in his.

Norman's chest heaved as he snorted like a bull. He drew a deep breath, glanced at the two of them and growled, "I have to catch an early flight in the morning. I'll take care of this matter later." He began to stomp out of the room. When he passed Billy, he glared at him, stopped, and gave him one last kick. Through gritted teeth, he hissed, "Stay away from that piece of trash."

Billy rolled in pain clutching his ribs. Billy's mom dropped to her knees by his side. "Billy, are you OK?"

"Yes, mother. I'm OK," he coughed as blood dripped from his mouth. But Billy wasn't OK. Aside from his broken nose and his cracked rib and, even more than his father's rage, he was mostly concerned about his relationship with Grace, and how his father's fury might derail it. He had finally found something in life beyond "stuff" that made him feel more of a person. He was afraid that this unusual sense of joy he was experiencing with Grace would be destroyed because of his father's unpredictable fury.

"Are you sure?" said Dolly softly brushing his hair to the

side and wiping the blood off his face with her robe. Billy looked up at his mother. This was one of the very few times that she had displayed pure, sincere concern for his welfare. She had put her own well-being in jeopardy to protect him. Was this the moment in his life that had been missing?

"Thank you, mother." Billy reached out to her, and she embraced him. Nellie kept her door locked.

. . . .

In his bedroom, Billy stared up at the ceiling with a myriad of thoughts rushing through his head. None of them good. He had feelings for Grace. He wasn't sure if he loved her. In fact, he wasn't sure he even knew what love was living in this bazaar home. He did know that Grace was kind to him. Something that was absent in his family until tonight . . . in an ironic contrast of anger, his dad, and love, his mother. And that same something did not exist among his group of "friends." He liked being with Grace. He did not like being around the mansion even though he enjoyed the perks: the pool, the golf course, the free food, maid service, and cars. Did that override his attraction for Grace? He wasn't sure. But he was sure that he wanted to see her again, and his father's crazy, brutal response to "that piece of trash" only enhanced Billy's determination to continue to see Grace. It was an incentive to get back at his father for not only this most recent incident but for many verbal and physical outbursts in the past. A grin spread across his face.

Another thought entered his mind, a pleasant one. His mother actually came to his defense and not in a casual way. She physically protected him from his father's anger. It was the first time he had ever been the recipient of her concern. Was this love or just an impulsive act of desperation? He didn't know, but he found himself having a speck of being grateful.

Meanwhile, his father was fuming alone in his bed. Dolly had her own room, her own bed to which she had quietly retreated. Norman had to catch a flight early, very early in the morning before anyone else awoke. He would have to deal with this matter in a few weeks when he returned. His boiling point began to simmer and, the more he thought, the calmer he got. Yes! He will deal with this matter when he returned; a grin spread across his face. Like father, like son.

CHAPTER 20 - THE PLAN

"Innocence is thought charming because it; offers delightful possibilities for exploitation." Mason Cooley

Grace hadn't seen Billy for a few days which was fine with her. She and, especially, her mom felt as though Billy was hovering. They both needed their space from him and found comfort in their everyday routines, simplistic as they were. Today they were both out weeding the garden and plucking some full, ripe tomatoes off the vine.

"Look at this one, mom," said Grace as though she had found a gem.

"Wow! That's a beauty. Bet that will taste great in our salad," Pam replied. Interrupting their conversation was the slight screeching of brakes in front of their house. They both jerked their heads up and then looked at each other. A muffled knocking at the front door made its way to the back yard. "I'll get it," said Pam. She wrestled to her feet and headed for the front door. When she opened it, Billy peered back with a wide grin. "Oh! Hi, Billy. What brings you this way?"

"I was in the neighborhood and thought I'd drop in to see you and Grace. Is she here?" He craned his head searching behind Pam to see if he could find Grace.

Reluctantly Pam said, "Yes! She is out back working on the garden."

"Oh, good," said Billy as he nudged the door open and walked past Mrs. Keenan forcing her to step aside.

I don't like that kid Pam thought to herself as she watched Billy saunter toward the kitchen and out the rear door. She shook her head as she walked into the kitchen. When Pam got to the sink, she watched the two from the window. To Pam, she wasn't being nosy: she was being protective.

Billy bounced down the back steps toward Grace. With a cheery voice, he said, "Hi, Grace. Looks like you're doing a great job."

Grace looked up surprised to see Billy. She responded politely, yet, tentatively, "Thank you, but it's really my mom who has a green thumb with a little help from me." Grace never took credit for work that someone else deserved. She wanted to earn the accolades not steal them. She tried to keep her composure. "Look at this tomato, Billy," holding it up. It was large, richly red, and represented the pride that she had in their home garden. "It's a real beauty."

Billy smiled and then said, "You're a real beauty, Grace." Grace's face turned flush with red a little lighter than the tomato. Her shoulders swayed gently back and forth and with her heard down looked up at Billy with those big eyes of hers. She did look beautiful; beautifully innocent. She wasn't expecting that and never had been the recipient of much praise about her appearance. Grace was not sure if she wanted such a compliment. Hovering . . . or was he being sincere?

Grace demurely responded, "Thank you," and began to weed more of the garden trying to deflect the compliment.

Billy dropped to his knees, "Let me help you weed," He began digging in the dirt and then proudly pulled up a dangling piece of vegetation,

"Billy!"

"What?" he chirped.

"That's a cucumber plant," grinned Grace. Pam watched from the kitchen window as Billy and Grace interacted with grins and laughter. But Pam was not smiling.

. . . .

Billy stayed for much longer than anticipated. Dropping by translated into three hours topped off with dinner. Billy was cordial, funny at times, and appeared to be genuinely grateful for the time he had had with them. And, actually, they seemed to enjoy their time with him as well. When Billy was leaving, he stopped at the front foyer with Grace. He looked into her brown eyes, touched the side of her arm and with a heartfelt smile said, 'Grace, I had a wonderful time with you and your mother."

Grace looked up and said, "We did too, Billy. We did too."

With that, Billy leaned over and gave her a peck on the cheek, turned, headed out the door, and skipped to his car. He hopped in his car as Grace waved from the porch. He waved back and thought to himself, I'm not much of a gardener, but the seed is planted.

CHAPTER 21 - I'M HOME

The jet soared through the patchy clouds high above the lakes, streams, and houses. The vegetation, plains, mountains, and water peeked through the vapor painting the landscape below with blues, greens, and oranges. Mr. Cromwell sat back in his first-class seat holding a martini and gazing out the window watching the world go by.

Mr. Cromwell's business trip had gone well. He was able to secure 5,000 acres of prime farmland with little money. The only thing he was going to plant there was cement. Those gently rolling plains, scattered ponds, and picturesque views only appeared as dollars to him. He was blind to the beauty of the land, the sweat of the farmers, the pain of loss to the families who for generations had toiled to make a life for themselves on that land. Hell, to him it was only dirt: Let the cows find another farm, let the deer search for another forest, let the farmers learn another trade. When he thought of the displaced birds in flight, he chuckled at the vision of one hundred dollar bills falling from the sky, as housing, roads, parking spaces, and malls replaced all that and more.

The pilot's announcement of the plane's imminent landing and instructions to keep seated and buckled in until the big bird had stopped broke his meditation. Norman now diverted his thoughts back to home: to Billy. His anger had been diluted by time and his anticipation of the windfall of money he was going to get. He was even happy and almost forgot what the argument was about. Then it all rushed back to him . . . "that piece of trash." No way was he going to let that relationship grow. He was no farmer, but he knew how to destroy the crops.

The landing was rough. A splash of Norman's martini landed on his lap. He was supposed to have given it to the stewardess when she came by to retrieve any debris in preparation for the landing. But he wanted the last few swigs and gripped the plastic container in his hand. Now he wished he had given it to her. The plane jerked to a stop. His mood had taken a leap from euphoric about the windfall he was about to make to being really pissed. His pants were wet with spilled wine. He was annoyed, and now furious about his son's reckless behavior and that piece of trash.

. . . .

Billy had transformed himself into a schmoozing machine. When he was at Grace's house, he interjected a plethora of pleases and thank you's. Billy jumped at the opportunity to help in any way: clearing the dishes, raking the lawn, and pulling weeds. He now was able to distinguish the weeds from the cucumbers and a whole lot more.

Billy encountered a few obstacles in his tasks. For example, it took him some time to learn how to turn on the vacuum, but eventually, he got the hang of it. Grace had to go over what he did because he would miss a few spots, but she still thought it was sweet of him. Billy had done more work in the few months that he had known Grace than he had done his entire life. He was even feeling a sense of accomplishment for one of the few times ever.

. . . .

The trio of Billy's former friends drove to the Cromwell estate looking forward to a fun day at the "retreat." They carried on with their usual demeaning banter of belittling everybody when Dora leaned forward from the back seat between Alex and Judy. "Do you think Mr. Cromwell will be happy?"

"Oh, Norman will be overjoyed," grinned Judy raising her hand with two fingers for the victory sign. A sparkling, gold bracelet slipped down toward her elbow.

"Hey, what's that?" blurted Dora. Alex took a quick peek to see what "that" was.

"It's a bracelet, you moron."

"Well, I know that. But you've never worn it before."

"I have plenty of jewelry I haven't worn before."

Alex turned into the horseshoe driveway and parked near the front door. They all got out and jaunted up to the house, excited, looking forward to their day in the sun. "We're here!"

The interest in the bracelet ceased for the time being, but questions still lurked in Dora's head for that was not just a bracelet. It was a gold bracelet, adorned with diamonds.

. . . .

Norman and Dolly were out by the pool. Norman was swinging a nine iron hitting golf balls over the chain link fence and into the mini-course. As usual, Dolly was relaxing and sipping on a glass of wine. Nellie, the maid, called out from the kitchen, "Mr. Cromwell, you have some people who would like to see you."

"Who is it?"

"It's those three friends of Billy's."

Norman smiled, "Let them in and bring us some beverages,"...which always meant beer and wine.

Judy, Dora, and Alex sauntered out of the kitchen toward the pool area entertaining broad smiles. "How'd it go?" asked Mr. Cromwell before they even got near him.

"Perfect! Just perfect," grinned Judy with the other two equally pleased. They stopped beside him. Alex had stepped on one of the golf balls burying it halfway into the ground. Norman noticed but didn't care. He was much more interested in the details they were about to divulge to him concerning their "field trip."

The trio enthusiastically went on and on about their surveillance of Billy and Grace. The beer and wine flowed smoothly amongst them. With every swallow, they became more emboldened with their revelations, and Norman became more pleased with them.

"Terrific," said Norman as he peeled off a hundred dollar bill for each of spies. "Enjoy yourselves by the pool for a while." And to himself, he muttered, "Terrific!" A confused Dolly just looked up from her chaise lounge. She knew better than to poke her nose into Norman's "business." She took another sip of her wine, undid the ties to her top piece and laid down on her stomach to resume tanning herself.

. . . .

Earlier that day, Billy was visiting Grace, yet again. He was invited over for dinner. Pam had cooked a special meal of corned beef and cabbage. Since it was a nice day, they sat in the back yard eating their meal. Lily was prancing around with a dog bone in her mouth. She would twist her head and somehow fling the bone into the air. Then Lily would hop over and grab it, run a little more, and toss it into the air again. Pam, Grace, and Billy got a kick out of her athletic endeavors. While eating their meal, they enjoyed the entertainment that Lily was providing. They talked about mundane things such as the weather, the garden, and Lily. The radio was gently playing Roberta Flack's song, "Killing Me Softly With His Love". Billy smiled thinking to himself: this is a good song. Hope it works for me. Amongst the conversation and music, they heard some tapping but couldn't discern from where it was coming.

"Someone must be working on some repairs," said Pam.

"Maybe we should send you over to help, Billy," kidded Grace, "since you're becoming such a handyman."

Billy looked at her. He hadn't seen this snarky side of Grace before. He kind of liked it. "Oh, funny! Real funny!"

"I'm just messin' with you, Billy," Grace smiled.

"I know. I love it," he grinned back.

Even Pam enjoyed the banter. They had had a nice, calm, pleasant dinner together. However, now the sun was sinking in the horizon. The three of them collected the dishes, brought them into the house, and placed them in the kitchen sink. Grace and her mom were getting tired. They had to work at the factory in the morning and had to get some rest. Billy had developed a sense of reading the women, and knew that it was time for him to head home.

"Well, thank you for dinner," Mrs. Keenan.

"You're welcome, Billy. I hope you enjoyed it?"

"I did. It was a pleasant surprise," Billy lied. Soggy cabbage and overdone salted meat didn't conform to his taste buds. "I never had corned beef and cabbage before." He looked at the clock on the kitchen wall. "I better leave now. It's getting late."

"You're not going now, are you? There's still time to visit," Pam jested. She was happy that Billy was leaving. Not that they had had a bad time, but fatigue was taking over, and she was ready to hit the sack.

"I'll walk you to the door, Billy," Grace said as he grabbed his hand. Pam cringed. Any sign of romantic interest by Grace toward Billy still made her uneasy. She didn't say anything but let it play out.

From the kitchen, Pam watched as Billy and Grace walked to the front door. Billy opened it. They talked some, and he stepped onto the porch toward his car. Billy pivoted at the bottom step to wave to Grace and then shuffled to his Bronco. Suddenly, he crouched down and clenched his fists. "What the hell!" he screamed. All the tires on his Bronco had been flattened. A nail had been hammered into each one. Billy was pissed, seems to run in his family, but he knew this had nothing to do with the neighborhood he was in. He tried to stifle his colorful language as best he could as he vented.

Pam had rushed out to the porch to join Grace. They both just stared with shock at the damaged tires and the disgruntled boy. Billy squelched his anger as best he could. He didn't want to stain the image he had worked so hard to develop with them. However, deep down inside Billy was mad to the point of bursting.

CHAPTER 22 - ROUND ONE

Several weeks had transpired since the tire incident. Now that the Bronco was drivable again, Billy decided to take Grace to Donnelly's to get her favorite treat; chocolate chip ice-cream nestled in a waffle cone. When they entered the mom and pop store, the chimes rang, the door groaned, and their steps made the floors squeak; part of the charm of Donnelly's. They were greeted with a smile from Lynnda who was wiping down the counter. The Allman Brothers were singing "Ramblin' Man" over the speakers. There were only a few people in the store. A middle-aged couple was seated at the booth eating lunch while a young mother and her daughter were eyeing the penny candy. It looked like a scene straight out of a Norman Rockwell painting.

"Hi, Mrs. Donnelly," said Grace. Billy nodded and smiled his greeting.

"Do you want the usual, Grace," said Lynnda happy to see them.

"That would be nice. Billy is treating me to my favorite." She looked up at Billy with grateful eyes.

Lynnda grinned at him, " That's good of you, Billy. And what would you like?"

"I'll have a beer." Lynnda looked shocked, and so did Grace. "I'm just kidding. I'd love a vanilla coke."

The two let out a breath of relief, Lynnda replied, "That's Pam's favorite drink.

"Beer?" Billy said jokingly.

"Now, Billy! You be nice," scolded Lynnda humorously. I'll be right with you."

The little girl at the penny candy counter had selected Necco Wafers. She peeked up at Lynnda and extended her tiny hand high to give her the money. Her mother smiled as she should have for the little girl was adorable. "Thank you, sweetie," said Lynnda. She looked down and handed the little girl the change.

She waved goodbye to the mother and daughter pair as they cheerfully walked away. The scene brought back memories of Pam with Grace when Grace was a little girl. She mixed Billy's coke with vanilla and slid it to him on the counter. "Sorry for the delay. Here's your beer," she chuckled.

Billy grinned, held up his glass, "Cheers!"

They then had a nice chat with Lynnda and, again, Billy was at the top of his game; being as charismatic and polite as ever. He was attempting to endear himself to most of Pam's and Grace's friends. It seemed to be churning out some success. Lynnda appeared to be more comfortable with him with each passing minute. Even Grace's childhood friends seemed to be warming up to Billy except for Chris who still was a bit distant with him. He thought Billy was too much like Wally from *Leave It to Beaver* but more conniving. Billy talked with Lynnda as Grace looked around the store. "Where's Mike?" she asked.

"Oh! He's out in the back office with . . . well . . . a client."

"Hopefully we'll see him before we leave," said Grace.

Within seconds the office door swung open. Mike appeared smiling as he allowed the client to go before him. Always the gentleman. The man was passing by the counter when he said, "Billy, what the hell are you doing here?"

"Dad, what are you doing here?" a surprised Billy asked.

"Is this the sweet girl you've been seeing?" looking at Grace. He wanted to say "piece of trash" but controlled himself not wanting to raise a ruckus. Not now.

"Yes!" said Billy, surprised again by his father. "Dad, this is Grace, and, Grace, this is my dad."

"Nice to meet you, sir." said Grace quietly, cautiously, not forgetting their last encounter.

"Well, I've got to go," Mr. Cromwell said with an air of urgency. He looked at the two teenagers and, just quiet enough for only Grace and Billy to hear, said, "You piece of trash."

He rambled out of the door. Billy was furious. He pivoted off of his stool ready to go after him, but Grace grabbed him by the arm. "No Billy! Let it go! Just let it go!" she insisted. Billy glared at his father's back as the door closed. He was steaming mad. However, he realized he had to convey restraint or the image he was trying to portray would be destroyed.

He climbed back onto the stool; took a couple of deep breaths; then turned to Grace: "Grace, I'm so sorry. I am so very, very sorry."

Grace looked back at him and smiled with understanding. But she wasn't understanding. Grace felt uncomfortable and questioned her relationship with the boy who lived in the mansion. She kept that to herself, but it lingered in the back of her mind, a dark little secret.

Norman got to his black Mercedes, settled into his seat and gripped the steering wheel. He felt his heart pounding, and his head was throbbing with anger. What a piss poor excuse I have for a son he thought. As he looked out the windshield at nothingness, a bird dropping splashed on the glass. "Shit!" He was beginning to have a meltdown. He took a few deep breaths and let them out slowly trying to compose himself. He turned the key, and the engine came alive. He pushed down on the gas pedal and laid rubber as the sleek car streaked down the road. He thought to himself: So that's the tramp Billy's been going out with lately. A flashing, blue light in his review mirror caught his eye and then the blast of a siren. "Crap! That little bitch!!!"

. . . .

It was a quiet ride when Billy and Grace drove back to her home with the exception of apologies exchanged both ways. Billy parked the car in front of Grace's house. He gazed at Grace and said, "It doesn't seem right that I'm seeing you: we are so different in so many ways. I just don't know Grace." His eyes began to tear up. Grace started to tear up as well for she knew Billy was right. Their worlds were galaxies apart and, yet, they were drawn to each other like some magnetic force. Neither could make sense of the attraction, but, none-the-less, it was there.

"Billy, maybe we should just create some distance between ourselves for a while."

"I know you're right, but I can't do that," he said with his voice trembling. Grace reached out to comfort him, and they embraced, both trying to fight back the tears.

"Grace, I think ....," Billy stuttered. "I think I love you. I can't believe I said that," as he wiped the moisture from his eyes.

"Neither can I," said Grace. "Neither can I." They embraced for a long time not knowing for how long. Pam peered out the window at the two figures in the car which seemed more like one. She let go of the curtain and let it fall into its natural position. She then inhaled deeply and let it out slowly with her head bowed. A tear trickled down her cheek and dropped to the floor.

CHAPTER 23 - REALLY?

The tension at Billy's house was so thick one could hardly breathe. Occupants maneuvered their way around the house on eggshells except for Norman. He was like a bull in a China shop. Stay out of his way or get trampled: the others did just that....avoided him at all costs. Billy, in particular, was the most evasive. For two reasons; he was pissed at his father, and his father was pissed at him. A conflict would be inevitable with those dynamics. Fortunately, or unfortunately, the house was so spacious that a person could die in one of the many rooms and would not be found for several weeks....except, possibly, by Nellie, who did the cleaning.

This was the day Billy had been anticipating for a long time. He heard his father step out the front entrance way, then motorized barn door open, and the Mercedes started up. The car purred down the driveway. Billy watched as the black Mercedes took a right onto the road and disappeared behind the trees. His father would be gone for a least another week wheeling and dealing somewhere in the U.S., eroding the landscape of America for . . . what? ...money; lots and lots of money. His mother would be leaving shortly as well for a bridge tournament in Las Vegas. He would be free for several days without the burden of his parents suffocating his every move. Only Nellie would be in the house, and Nellie was like a part of the decor: there but hardly visible.

. . . .

Billy smiled from ear to ear as he drove to Grace's home. His excitement was hardly containable. He tried to manage his emotions so that his eagerness would not manifest itself. It was a flawless day with blue skies and gentle breezes. But it could have been a hurricane, and Billy would still have been smiling. He finally got to the Keenan's home and parked in front. He checked out the porch to see if there was any sign of Grace. There was none. He hopped out of the car, jumped the steps and knocked on the door with vigor. Pam opened the door and curiously looked at Billy who was face glowed with glee.

"You seem awfully cheery today," she said.

"I am. I am. I am," Billy repeated foolishly. "Is Grace home?" He knew she was but went through the motions of asking anyway.

"Yes, she is. Why don't you come in?"

"Oh, thank you," he said courteously trying to reinforce his charm on her as if he had it at all.

Grace appeared in the living room, "Hi, Billy! What's up?"

"Grace, I thought I'd take you to see my house. You've never seen it, and this is a beautiful day for a ride," he said enthusiastically.

Grace turned to her mom. "Would that be OK, mom?"

Pam loved her daughter and was torn between protecting her or not disappointing her. Pam knew that Grace was growing up and that she shouldn't drown her with too much mothering. Grace needed to find her wings and make her own decisions. However, Pam was uncomfortable with this situation, but none-the-less said, "Have a good time and don't come back too late."

"Thanks, mom. I love you."

"I love you, too, Grace."

"We won't be too late, Mrs. Keenan, and thank you," Billy said politely.

They slid out the front door all smiles and walked to the car. They got into the red Bronco and drove off. Grace waved goodbye to her mom. Pam stood on the porch, waved back and wheezed softly, "There goes my baby."

. . . .

The day was absolutely beautiful in every way; A few cumulous clouds floated slowly in the blue sky, the trees branched out to form a canopy of green, and horses grazed listlessly in the fields with mansions in the distance serving as a backdrop. The stifling Tennessee humidity was forgiving on this day with a light breeze making it delightful. When they arrived at the driveway in front of Billy's house, Grace's eyes widened and her jaw dropped. She had never seen such a big home in her life except in movies. It looked more like a 5-star hotel rather than a...a house. She gasped, "Billy, you've got to be kidding. This can't be your house?"

He smiled, "Yes, it is Grace."

Billy parked the car in the driveway, turned off the engine and just studied Grace's reaction. Grace was in awe. Looking out the window from the passenger side, she couldn't keep her eyes of the massive building with ornate architecture surrounded by impeccable landscaping, perfectly shaped shrubs, and gorgeous flowers. She could hardly speak, "Oh, Billy, I've never in my life have seen anything like this up so close." There are many huge houses in the middle Tennessee area. They are as common as horses in this part of the country. However, the closer one gets to one of these incredible structures, the magnitude of their size becomes overwhelming, especially, when a person like Grace, who comes from a humble background, gets this intimate with proximity. "When you mentioned that you lived in a big house, I was not expecting anything like this."

Grace seemed frozen in her seat, unable to remove her eyes from the spectacle which Billy called home. Billy opened his door and walked around to open Grace's. She wasn't even aware that he had exited the car. She was entranced. Billy opened her door and said, "Would you like to come in and see the inside?" Grace was cemented in her seat just staring.

"Huh," Grace said absent-mindedly.

"I said, 'Would you like to come in....'"

"Yes! Oh, yes! I would. I'm sorry," Grace stammered while still staring at the beautiful home, not even sharing a glance at Billy.

Billy reached for her hand and gently guided her out of the car. Her head seemed like it was on a swivel; she looked up at the towering, corinthian pillars, down to the massive entrance way, to the sides at the incredible flowering planters, and out to the pristine, expansive acreage. Billy was finally able to steer her attention toward the door and ushered her into the house. When inside, they found Nellie vacuuming the rugs near the entryway. Walking by, Billy acknowledged her with a slight nod. Grace gave her a meek wave and smile. Nellie liked this girl already and smiled back.

Looking around, Grace just repeated the same words accompanied by sounds of astonishment, "Oh! Wow! This is amazing." Billy just smiled and continued to escort her through the living room, into the dining room, and then led her to the kitchen.

Finally, they made their way out to the pool area through the double doors of the den. Grace's eyes opened wide at the image before her: the pool, the landscaping, the golf course, the woods, the open space . . . everything rattled Grace's sense of reality. "Billy, I need to sit down," she said as her legs began to wobble. He helped her to one of the lawn chairs. "Billy," she gasped, "I don't belong here. I just don't . . . ," still gazing at the vision she was witnessing.

"Grace, you do belong here. You belong anywhere you go. Just relax." She looked up at him for the first time since they had arrived and shook her head lightly. She allowed herself to calm down a bit but was still stunned by the opulence that overwhelmed her. "Can I get you anything? Do you want something to drink?"

"That would be nice," she whispered. "Could I have some water?"

Billy pressed a button on a white table near where Grace was seated. "Yes, Mr. Billy," Nellie's voice said from a small speaker.

"Nellie, could you please bring us two glasses of ice water with cut lemons on the side." Grace then stared at the white table with the button, and thought to herself: Yikes! . . . Water with cut lemons on the side.

Soon they were sipping their water as the Tennessee sun radiated down. Billy talked and talked and talked about his house, the amenities, and his life. Grace was more than happy to listen to everything he had to say. She was fascinated by, well, by everything. Then Billy asked Grace, "Would you like to go swimming?" Without waiting for an answer, Billy shuffled off to the pool house to fetch a new, spare, swimming suit for Grace. She watched him walk away from her seated position questioning what she was doing there. He popped out of the door and jogged back to her holding two tiny pieces of cloth. "I hope this fits. If not you can look through a wardrobe of new suits that mom had purchased for guests in the pool house closet."

Grace looked at the two pieces and said, "Thank you, Billy. But I'll check out the other choices in the pool house. Can I change in there?"

"Sure! Unless you want to . . . "

"Don't go there, Billy," Grace said sternly. She was innocent to a degree, but she certainly was not foolish. She wanted to make sure that Billy knew that she had some control even though this was his domain.

"I'm sorry, Grace. I was just trying to be funny." Grace just gave a questionable smile, stood up from her seated position, and walked off to the pool house.

They spent the next hour splashing around in the pool; laughing and talking, and splashing some more. Afterward, the two got out and talked some more as the sun dried them. Billy was looking for more ways to make Grace's visit a unique and pleasant one as if it wasn't already that way. "Grace, would you like to go for a ride on the golf cart?" Billy asked.

"Sure!" smiled Grace enthusiastically. I've never been on one before."

They walked off and into the barn to get the golf cart. Again, Grace was blown away. She had never seen such beautiful vehicles. They were spotless, and the lights glistened off their shiny surfaces. Incredible! However, Grace was a bit disappointed that the barn was occupied only with machines rather than horses. She kept that to herself.

They boarded one of the two golf carts, and Billy carefully maneuvered it out of the barn. When they got outside, he floored it. Their heads jerked back. Grace shrieked, gripped the side of the cart, and off they went.

Billy slowed down and became the tour guide as they casually meandered around the property. The cart took them through the forest, to fields, to a hill with views that were majestic and then past a small stream down that led to a pond. Lily pads floated delicately on top with yellow flowers accenting their beauty. Frogs lightly croaked, and an occasional fish rippled the water. They dismounted the cart and walked out on the small dock. A rowboat was tied to one of the dock cleats attached to the wooden piling. "Do you want to go for a boat ride?" asked Billy.

"That would be fun," said Grace.

Billy held Grace's hand as she lowered herself into the boat. Billy carefully boarded the vessel, took the oars and rowed casually out into the pond. The views were amazing from the water. The back of the mansion seemed to go on forever. Beautiful, mature magnolia trees perfectly placed evenly in a row provided a picture much like a resort. The upstairs balconies had plants cascading over their railings with an array of colorful flowers. Magnificent! Grace was enthralled by it all.

Billy picked up the oars and let the boat drift on its own course. He gazed into Grace's eyes affectionately and then got down on one knee. The boat teetered a bit, and he had to grab a side as did Grace. She was nervous. Not about falling over but, instead, what Billy was about to do. Billy spoke softly, sincerely, "Grace, I've never met anyone like you. You bring me joy. You bring me peace. I know I'm not perfect, but I love you." Grace just held her breath afraid to move. She sensed what was coming and wasn't sure how to respond. He pulled a sparkling diamond ring out of his pocket: a ring he had taken from his mother's jewelry box. Dolly had been married twice previous to marrying Norman and jewelry from all the men in her life amounted to a treasure trove. She had so much bling; she'd never miss it. Holding the ring up, he continued, "Grace, will you marry me." Grace gulped, a lump caught in her throat, and pools of water filled her eyes. "Grace, will you please marry me?" Billy pleaded.

Grace was confused, dazed. This was not expected. She stared at the ring with a fixation. Not because it was so brilliant and astonishing, but, rather, what it represented: the commitment, the life, . . . everything. His eyes remained glued to hers awaiting the answer. Finally, Grace softly, hesitantly whispered, "Yes! . . . Yes, I will, Billy." Billy slid the ring onto her finger then grabbed her, pulled her up in a tight embrace as the boat tilted to the side sending Billy and Grace cascading overboard into the water.

CHAPTER 24 - WEDDING BELLS

Pam was beside herself. When Grace showed her the ring, her mother nearly barfed. Grace was too young, just turning eighteen, to get married, and Billy was too young as well. Also, Billy was just so different from them in so many ways. There were so many questions about the future and so many more about Billy: Where would they live? What would Billy do for a living? Would the marriage last?

Who was the real Billy for he presented so many personalities to them: he was kind, he was angry, he was helpful, he was a mystery. Would the real Billy please stand up for Pam didn't know who Grace was really marrying, and they both had so much growing up to do. In Pam's mind, the marriage was a recipe for disaster. Others close to Pam felt the same way; her group of friends, Ashlie, the Donnellys. Yes, a recipe for disaster.

However, Grace pleaded with her mom to accept Billy: to look beyond the questions, to view the good. For Pam, she just couldn't "view the good." She thought of it as an illusion that Grace was imagining as reality. But, the truth to Pam was that she didn't want to lose her little girl, so she ultimately acquiesced to Grace's pleas reluctantly, sadly, regrettably.

. . . .

A few months had gone by faster than anyone had expected. The church was occupied with just some uncles and aunts, Pam's friends and their families, and, of course, Ashlie and the Donnelly's. The only representation from Billy's side was his mother accompanied by Nellie. They were the only ones sitting on the groom's side of the aisle. Mr. Cromwell refused to go. In fact, he all but ostracized Billy from the family.

Mingling in the back of the church was the wedding party consisting of familiar faces. They were a motley crew: The ushers were dressed in their best suits or sports jackets or pants and shirts. The bridesmaids were all adorned in their favorite dresses. Ninette had on a garment adorned with a large floral pattern. Angie wore a simple black dress with white ruffles at the sleeves and collar, and Stephanie had on a bright green dress that she loved. Though none of the wedding party matched, they didn't care. They were not there for a fashion show. They were there for their good friend, Grace, who was dressed in a white pleated peasant dress. Her hair was pulled back and braided with a crown of delicate flowers, yes, from their garden, resting on her head. The simplicity of her attire magnified her beauty. She looked incredible. No! . . . She looked angelic and innocence, sincerity, and kindness radiated from her.

Chris was the best man which was ironic. Of all of Grace's friends, he was the one who was most suspicious of Billy. But Billy liked Chris, and, also, wanted to use this "assignment" to get on the better side of him. Shaun, Jason, and Charlie were the ushers. Their responsibilities were minimal since there were so few people attending, but they greeted people with enthusiasm and huge smiles. Stephanie was the maid of honor. There was no flower girl nor was there a ring bearer. Angie assumed the responsibilities of the flower girl carrying a bouquet of flowers that had been grown in the Keenan's garden. Jaybird served as the ring bearer: rings Billy had plucked from his mom's treasure trove, her jewelry box.

It was time. The wedding party started their procession to the altar. Shaun playfully hooked his arm and grinned at Pam as he escorted her down the aisle. He was proud of this role for he loved Pam as they all did. The ushers and bridesmaids smiled with their eyes searching the sparse crowd for friends and family members. The organist played the wedding march which, to Pam and many of those attending, sounded more like a dirge. Mr. Donnelly smiled at Grace as he hooked his arm for her to grab for them to walk down the aisle together. Grace extended her hand out and then suddenly pulled it back. She gazed down the aisle which seemed like a thousand miles to the altar. All her friends were gathered there with Father Mark looking back at her. She looked down at the floor. The music paused awaiting the appearance of the bride.

Grace took a deep breath, looked up and reached for Mr. Donnelly's arm. Her fingers clutched his arm, and her nails dug into his skin beneath his garments. The organ commenced playing again. They took several steps. Then Grace hesitated, locking her feet to the floor and pulling Mr. Donnelly's arm back. The music stopped again. He smiled at her and patted her arm to comfort her. "You know you don't have to go through with this, Grace," he said in a hushed voice.

"I know," Grace whispered looking at his kind face and clutching his arm.

"Do what you feel is best," he said softly as he smiled down at her.

She looked back down the aisle at the altar. Billy was standing there with Father Mark. The wedding party looked at Grace and Mr. Donnelly at the back of the church with quizzical expressions. Billy's eyebrows furrowed, his shoulders shrugged, and his hands opened palms up in front of him saying without speaking ... What's going on?

Grace pulled on Mr. Donnelly's arm, and they resumed the long walk down the aisle. The organ kicked in one more time for their short journey.

After an awkward exchange of vows. Pam cringed, and moisture invaded her eyes. The wedding march then blasted. A subtle clapping accompanied the newlyweds as they walked back down the aisle to the entrance of the church.

Three forms hovered out of site in the back row of the balcony in darkness. "Can you believe this shit?" Alex said with a heavy whisper.

"Hey, you're in church. Knock it off!" said Dora with the organ hitting the last notes of its melody.

"When did you become so religious?"

"Both of you, shut up!" Judy said pondering what just happened. She looked out at the altar and echoed Alex's sentiments, "Can you believe this shit?"

CHAPTER 25 - LET'S EAT

The wedding reception was held at Pam's house. Grace's friends' and their parents prepared food for a pot luck extravaganza: lasagna, a pot roast, chicken casserole dishes, mashed potatoes, sweet potatoes, green beans, peas, pasta salad, garden salad, fruit salad, and much more. For dessert, a table was loaded with homemade cookies, brownies, cupcakes, white fudge, dark fudge, and ice cream. There were all sorts of snacks to munch on dispersed on tables donated for the event from neighbors. Chairs, strategically placed, were also donated. Peanuts, M&M's, crackers, an array of cheeses, cut fruit, and on and on were everywhere. The entire feast was like the participants were in competition with each other. The truth was that they loved Pam and Grace and wanted to cushion the uneasiness of the event which everyone sensed.

The Donnelly's provided the drinks, paper plates and cups, napkins, plastic forks and spoons, decorations, and lighting. Flowers were placed all around even decorating Lily's dog house. The back yard had been transformed into a festival setting, and the weather had cooperated entirely with thin, cirrus clouds easing across the blue sky. A soft wind cooled the otherwise oppressive, Tennessee humidity. Everything was perfect, especially the wedding cake. Nellie had designed an incredibly beautiful cake consisting of three terraces each adorned with colorful flowers made of frosting: a cake that would challenge the best of bakeries. Even Susan from Susan's Special Treats was impressed.

The reception line looked like a high school homeroom picture. The wedding party wore their mismatched attire. Pam looked like the teacher, somewhat serious, and Mr. Donnelly, the friendly principal. Grace could have passed as the prom queen and Billy, the prom king. When folks finished congratulating the very young couple, they mingled with friends. The line moved quickly. With Nellie by her side, it was Mrs. Cromwell's turn to address the bride and groom. She hugged Billy and wished him good luck. She then shuffled over to Grace, held her by her hands, looked her in the eye's and said, "You've got quite a challenge, my dear. I truly wish you the best." Then she backed up to get a better view of Grace. "You really are a pretty girl. A nice dress, some makeup here and there, and a different hairstyle would do wonders for you."

Grace politely smiled and said, "Thank you." In her mind, she followed with . . . I think.

Mrs. Cromwell then reached for Grace's hands, held them up, and gazed at her fingers. "Beautiful ring, my dear, just beautiful." She then turned to Billy, smiled and went off to mingle.

Nellie had just congratulated Billy. She then stepped up to Grace. She hugged Grace and whispered in her ear, "You are too darn good for him, sweetheart." Nellie then backed away and gave Grace a reassuring smile.

Shaun began playing Clark's old guitar, and all of Grace's friends sang "I'll Have to Say I Love You in a Song" by Jim Groce. When they finished they all yelled out, "We Love You, Grace."

Grace lifted her shoulders, rocked back and forth and said, "I love you, too."

The live entertainment ended there, and music poured out

from the radio. Couples of all ages were showing off their best moves....and that is a gracious description. Dolly, after a few glasses of wine, wanted to show off her steps which were more like something from the Boom Boom Lounge. Billy lasted about twenty seconds with his mom, and Dolly's eyes searched for another victim. There were no takers as they tried to make the appearance of being occupied in deep conversation. Giving up, Dolly poured herself another glass of wine.

Charlie approached Grace and asked Billy if he could dance with her. One would think he was asking Billy for his first born, but he begrudgingly agreed to let Charlie dance with his new bride. They danced slowly and whispered to the song "My Love" by Paul McCartney. Billy was having a slow burn as he tried not to stare at them. When the song was over, Charlie gave Grace a gentle hug and escorted her back to Billy. Charlie said, "You have married a wonderful girl, Billy." Billy nodded in agreement. He did not smile.

The reception was coming to a close. Everyone chipped in on the cleaning details except for Dolly who was polishing off a bottle of wine. By this time she had forgone the use of a glass and just chugged the merlot from the bottle. When she was ready to leave, . . . in actuality she wasn't ready, she would have been content to spend the time draped over the folding chair, Nellie pulled her up and guided her wobbly legs to the car. Most of the guests were either concerned or shocked. Billy was not. It was an every other day occurrence in his life. Nellie, also, wasn't rattled as she hoisted, shoved, and pushed Mrs. Cromwell into the passenger seat. The only thing that really bothered Nellie was to have to drive the big Mercedes home. She knew that Mrs.

Cromwell would sleep most of the way. As Nellie jerked the car forward into drive, Mrs. Cromwell suddenly muttered between burps, "Those...rings sure...looked famil...iar."

CHAPTER 26 - A NEW BEGINNING

The newlyweds were starting off on the right foot with everybody in the family and neighborhood. They had forgone their honeymoon because financing did not exist for such luxury. Neither Billy nor Grace were phased by that omission in the usual wedding follow-up. They were staying at Pam's house in Pam's old room. Down the hall, Billy's mother-in-law spent her nights. Surprisingly, the three were getting along well. Billy seemed to have adjusted to the deprivation of opulence and was content in the VERY modest surroundings.

The day after the wedding, Pam, Grace, and Billy sat at the kitchen table opening up envelopes containing wedding cards expressing well wishes. Many of them included modest gifts of $5 to $20 which were very generous for folks in their community. They eventually came across an envelope that was bigger than the rest and had impeccable penmanship. Grace opened it and took out the beautiful, over-the-top card as Billy and Pam looked at her. Their mouths dropped open when one hundred dollar bills began slipping out. Grace and Pam stared motionless as Billy raked the bills up with his fingers from the table and picked a few that dropped onto the floor. There were ten of those bills altogether. Grace opened the card and read the personalized message.

Your wedding is like the bloom of a flower— beautiful and full of hope;

may your love and care for one another know no boundaries.

Love to you both, Dolly

Billy looked at the two women with water forming in his eyes. It was the second time that his mom had surprised him: the first being when she protected him physically from his father's assault and now this. Billy quietly whispered, almost to himself, . . . "Mom." He closed his eyes and flushed the moisture down his cheeks.

. . . .

On the following Monday, Billy jumped into the responsibility of being a new husband. He scoured the shops in the downtown area for work. He had not been very successful until he entered a local furniture store. Billy introduced himself to the man behind the desk who also happened to be the owner. He liked Billy right from the start. And why not? Billy was good looking, clean-cut, articulate, and had a knack for engaging others. The man was impressed and scooped up this young, ambitious salesman without hesitation. Sure Billy was limited in his hand/eye coordination, but the guy could talk. This job suited him well.

Grace and Pam continued working at the factory and enjoyed their time together without a third wheel tagging along. Not that Billy was a bother, but moms and daughters need mom and daughter time together. People get used to their ways of doing things and having the freedom to act on instincts without question. With another figure in the household, it did not lend itself to those freedoms. Now dinners, household chores, purchases, and, in general, their life had to consider the quirks of a third party.

Pam's cookouts with Grace and her friends helped Billy slowly become more accepted among them. He was trying not to force his opinions. He actually began to listen to the others without trying to dominate the conversation. Oh! He had his moments for sure, but he was at least trying and that was noticed and appreciated by everyone, especially Grace.

On weekends, Billy helped with menial chores around the house. He improved his vacuuming skills by not missing too many areas. When gardening, Billy did not confuse the vegetables with the weeds which really pleased Pam. He played with Lily and fed her on occasions which created a bond between the two. Billy enjoyed cutting the lawn. He even clipped the shrubs, but after being stung by a few hornets was reluctant to do that job again.

He had never lifted a finger at his own house. This was not just turning a new leaf. This was the emergence of a new plant. Needless to say, Billy was making an impression, a good one. And a boast to that impression was when Billy purchased some new furniture for the house combined with his employee discount and his mother's wedding gift.

This certainly was a great start. And occasionally, in the darkness of night, a blue Cadillac would crawl past their home.

CHAPTER 27 - THE WALK

"There is just so much hurt, disappointment, and oppression one can take...

The line between reason and madness grows thinner."
Rosa Parks

Grace would still take her every now-and-then walks along the railroad tracks. Often times, she was accompanied by one or two or all three of her girlfriends, Ninette, Stephanie, and/ or Angie. Sometimes her mother would accompany her. Many times she would ask Billy to walk with her, but he had always seemed to find something else that he had to do. Grace felt over time that he was more reluctant to join her rather than actually being occupied with tasks. One day she decided to be a little more persistent in trying to convince Billy to accompany her on her walk. She tried the soft approach this afternoon, "Hey Billy."

"Hi, Honey! What's up?" Billy asked as he threw the ball for Lily to fetch. The sun glistened brightly on the warm fall day.

"Mom isn't home, and I was hoping you would join me on the walk along the tracks."

"Really? Lily and I are having a moment here." He tossed the ball again.

"That's nice, but I would really like it if you could come along. It would be nice to have this time to talk and just enjoy this nice day together."

Billy looked at her, took a deep breath, and then let it out. "Do you really want me to go?" He seemed annoyed.

"Yes, I would, Billy," Grace smiled sensing that, although he was bothered, he was gravitating to her suggestion.

"OK! OK, Grace. You win." He tied Lily to her dog house on a long rope, turned and grabbed Grace's hand. "Let's go!"

"Oh, Billy. Thank you. This means a lot to me."

. . . .

It was tranquil along the tracks. The fall leaves were changing color, and an occasional orange or red maple leaf would wander away from its branch to float in the air. A feisty breeze would kick up every now and then to startle a flock of leaves to take flight. The heavily traveled rails glistened in the sun, and the crunch of crushed stone could be heard with each step. Billy and Grace walked silently both lost in their own thoughts, their own memories. Finally, Billy said, "It is beautiful out here, Grace."

"Grace looked up and smiled, "Yes, it is. There is a certain magic along these tracks. It reflects not only the passage of trains and of time but presents a serenity that allows one to drift off in....well, never-never-land."

"Holy cow, Grace, that's pretty deep."

"Once in a while, a gem slips out. I have no idea where I get it," she smiled.

A hawk glided high above, and the couple followed it with their eyes. The graceful bird floated as though it was studying the path of the tracks. It eventually merged with the forest then appeared soaring along the tracks at the height of the trees. Grace and Billy watched it fade away further down the tracks.

Billy then pulled up suddenly and said, "I think we should go back now."

"Why, Billy? We have just a little ways to go before we get to the lake."

"No! We should go!" he coaxed.

Now, Grace was perplexed. She looked him in the face and saw that his vision was drawn down to the side of the tracks in the direction of the lake. It was then she noticed what he was staring at: the small stack of rocks with the weathered cross leaning on top. "Billy! What's wrong? she said with concern."

Billy just looked away to where they had been walking. "We've got to go!" he blurted and
    began to head back to their home.

Grace watched him and then looked back at the mini-memorial. Then she ran up to Billy, grabbed him by the shoulder, swung him around forcefully, and said,
    "Billy, tell me what's going on."

He looked down at the pebbles at his feet. "Grace, I...I...can't. Let's just go!"

Grace stared into his eyes and then back to the memorial and then back to him. "Billy, it was you, wasn't it?" she implored.

"What do you mean, 'It was me?'" he muttered defensively.

"You were the boy. You were that boy that my father saved. You, . . . were that boy who ran into the woods," Grace shrieked with tears streaming down her face.

A response wasn't required. Billy's silence was all that she needed. The shame and guilt covered his face like a dark veil, and all he could do was stare back at her. Words couldn't construct the feelings, the pain, and the agony he was enduring, but the statue of despair that he presented did.

Grace turned her back to him and said, "Oh, Billy! Why didn't you just tell me." Then she swung around, stood on her toes, and glared directly into his eyes. "And you were the boy by the tree at the gravesite, weren't you?!!" She paused for a few painful seconds and blurted, "Did you marry out of pity, Billy?" She gasped as her tiny fists started to beat on his chest. "Answer me!!!" Tears rolled down her cheeks. He stood there motionless, confused, and defeated.

She drew a deep breath and collected herself. Grace then gasped: "Was that why you followed me? Is that why you ran into me in the rain, drove me home and all that other crap? It was all a ploy to get to 'the poor, little girl who lost her daddy,' a father who would still be here if he hadn't saved the boy on the tracks."

Grace ran awkwardly past Billy toward home. Her legs were flying in front of her, her arms flailing. Billy stared at her back, her hair bouncing behind her as she disappeared in the distance.

He slowly meandered back home . . . alone. Even though he was experiencing a whirlpool of emotions, Grace's question rankled in his mind, "Did you marry me out of pity, Billy?" The question kept pounding louder and louder with every step he took. The drum of doubt kept beating way beyond the time he finally reached the house.

. . . .

Pam popped in the front door a little later than she had expected to be home. She was visiting Ashlie who was not feeling well and brought her dinner. The home was relatively quiet except for the TV in the background. She announced her presence with a "hello," but no one answered. The further she walked into the home, she saw Billy sprawled in a chair watching TV clutching a can of beer. Several other cans rested by his feet. He looked up, gave her a nod, and went back to his blank stare at the screen.

When she got to the kitchen, she looked out the window and saw Grace sitting on the step, Lily resting beside her. This whole scene is not right she thought to herself. She carefully opened the door and cautiously approached Grace. Grace shifted around and abruptly yelled, "I don't want to talk about it!" A startled Pam jumped back, her eyes bulging. "Oh, it's you, mom." Grace jumped up, put her arms around her mom and held her tightly as tears made their way to Pam's shoulder.

"Honey, what's wrong?

"Everything, mom," said Grace with her head still on Pam's shoulder. Pam guided her to the step, and they both sat down. Lily looked up at them curiously from her resting position. Her head cocked to the side, and her ears perked upwards. Pam looked at Grace, her baby, and patted her back gently. After a delicate silence, Grace told her about the walk with Billy on the train tracks: the revelations about Billy being the boy Pops had saved as well as him being the boy at the funeral.

Pam held her daughter tightly, her mind processing the emotions and the possible impact of the walk.

A face peered out of the kitchen window at the backs of

the two women seated embracing on the step. It was a face racked with turmoil, with sadness and . . . with anger. This was not how it was supposed to be.

CHAPTER 28 - MYSTERIES

Nellie dragged the net along the top of the water in the pool collecting leaves and twigs that had found a home there. Clouds began to form in the sky in earnest. She wanted to get any debris out while she still had dry weather. As she went about her task, she noticed the door to the pool house was ajar. She set the net on the ground and walked over to shut the door. When she got closer, she realized that a light had been left on in the bathroom. Nellie then stepped in to shut off the light. It seemed as though the sheets in the bed had been disturbed. She straightened out the sheets, shut off the light, and backed out the door glancing around the room for one last, curious look.

In her bedroom, Dolly was just rolling out of the sack. She sat on the edge of her bed and steadied herself with her hands extended by her side and her feet planted on the floor about a foot apart. The dizziness had gotten worse. She attributed it to her wine consumption and dismissed any concerns. She was able to maneuver herself onto her feet. She wobbled to the window to check out the weather. She saw that Nellie was just coming out of the pool house who then picked up the pool net and started raking out the debris.

Dolly was fond of Nellie. She admired how she always took the initiative to address chores around the house without being directed to do so. Dolly also valued her steady, pleasant demeanor which was in sharp contrast to the men in the household. But mostly, she admired how Nellie watched over her, . . .

took care of her. Yes! Nellie was a good person with pure intentions, but what the hell was she doing in the pool house?

Dolly meandered around her bedroom observing trinkets Norman had bought her in the early, romantic stages of their relationship. The spacious room was meticulously decorated and maintained. Busts of Greek goddesses guarded either side of the fireplace. China vases purchased on their trip to, . . . well, China had an array of fresh flowers reaching out from them. Several Persian rugs placed perfectly covered areas of the hardwood floors. Pictures of Dolly and Norman and Billy at exotic resorts in Mexico, the Bahamas, and places around the world hung on the walls. Those were happier times, although she always felt as though something was missing. An intangible void she could not seem to have filled.

She wandered over to her makeup table which was more the size of a banker's desk. She reached into the drawer on the left-hand side of her "table" and pulled out her jewelry box. Dolly laid it on the top of the desk, opened the box and began to used her index finger to stir through the potpourri of diamond necklaces, gold rings, bangle bracelets, a variety of silver, gold, and diamond earrings. She stopped and thought for several seconds and then went back to the compartment with a multitude of rings. She stirred and stirred and then looked up into the mirror. Her eyes were slightly bloodshot and had hammocks under them. Her skin was pale, and creases stretched here and there. Dolly looked down again at the ring compartment, stirred one more time, and then peeked back up at the mirror . . . and smiled.

Norman rolled out of bed with a grunt, went to the bathroom, and splashed water on his face several times. He looked into the mirror. His hair was beginning to recede but still was relatively thick compared to most men his age. The grey shades made him look distinguished or at least he thought so. He stood straight up and held his stomach in and stuck out his chest. Yeah! He still had it. He wasn't done yet.

He showered, shaved and picked out another slick, black suit. He was ready to take on the world. Heck, the universe. He walked out of his bedroom and heard dishes rattling from way down in the kitchen. When he eventually got there, Nellie and Dolly were sitting down at the table having coffee. Nellie had prepared a first class breakfast for the Cromwell's consisting of poached eggs, bacon, cinnamon rolls, orange juice, coffee, and her incredible pecan, date, breakfast bread.

"Good morning, ladies," he said in an excellent mood and gave Dolly a peck on the cheek.

"What was that for?" she asked.

"Oh, I don't know? Just a good morning wake up call," he smiled. "And how are you doing, Nellie?"

"I'm doing fine, Mr. Cromwell. Just fine," she responded with a perplexed expression. This guy is never this happy.

Norman reached for Nellie's special breakfast bread and filled his traveling mug with coffee. "I've got to go. Some big business deals to wrap up." He grabbed his attaché case and strolled out of the kitchen, began to whistle, and made a beeline for the front door. "Adios!" he said as he slammed the door.

Dolly and Nellie looked at each other, chuckled and simultaneously giggled, "Adios?"

"What's with him, Miss Dolly?" asked Nellie.

"I have no idea," said Dolly as they got up to watch the black Mercedes weave out of the driveway and down the road.

CHAPTER 29 - CHEERS

Several weeks after Billy had revealed that he was that boy on the tracks during Grace's dad's death, things at the Keenan household had gone sour. Billy drank more and more. Grace slumped into a deep state of depression, and her mother's worst fears about the marriage and the impact on her daughter came to fruition. Billy went off to work, came home, and drowned himself in booze while wallowing in a world of silence and uselessness. The house began to fall into disrepair even though Pam tried to keep up with the chores. Grace chipped in but was in a different space. She, as well, had ventured off into a place of sadness. Grace wasn't much help, and Billy was worthless. In fact, he was the primary factor behind the litter, the overgrown lawn, and the clutter in the house.

One evening, when Pam and Grace came home from the factory, they spotted a faded blue Cadillac parked in front of their house. Grace didn't have to guess who it belonged to and started to haul in deeper breaths the closer they got to the vehicle and to their home. The Cadillac did not shine as it had in the past as time and use had taken its toll. When they walked by it, Pam peeked in the window and noticed an empty bottle of wine in the back seat. That observation did not sit well with her.

They could hear laughter inside the house, and one person stood out with her loud cackle. When they entered their home, Judy, Alex, and Dora were hanging out with Billy in the living room. The TV was on with dull conversation from the sitcom

All in the Family serving as background noise. Billy saw Grace and with slurred speech, said, "Hey, Honey. You remember Judy, Dora, and Alex. They're my buddies from the ole stomping grounds."

Grace just glared at him with a stern face, her coat half draped over her shoulders as she took it off. Pam looked suspiciously at the group. The girls saluted the mother and daughter with glasses full of wine, some of which splattered out. Billy and Alex were gripping cans of beer with grins on their faces. A half-eaten bowl of chips rested on the table; crumbs scattered over it and on the floor. The girls were wearing gleeful, clown smirks. Their taunting didn't have to be verbal. They knew that just their presence was doing the trick to dismantle Grace . . . and her mother.

Judy said, "Why don't you and ..."

"This is my mother, Pam," Grace said with the most cordiality she could muster.

"Hello, Pam," she said as she extended her hand out. "I'm Judy, a gooood friend of Billy's." She lingered on the good longer than necessary.

Pam didn't shake it but took off her coat instead. "Nice to meet you, Judy and..."

"Oh, this is Alex and Dora," Billy said. Alex gave Pam and Grace a quick wave. Dora curtsied. Nice touch. "Why don't you sit down with us and have a beer or a glass of wine."

" . . . Or mix them together," Judy chuckled. The others burst out laughing as they raised their cans or glasses to toast each other.

Pam told them that she was tired, and Grace echoed the

same excuse. The mother and daughter left the revelers to their partying and headed upstairs to escape. When the got to the top, they retreated to Pam's bedroom, sat on her bed, and spoke softly about the circumstances downstairs. Grace was crying. Pam tried to comfort her as she had done so many times in the last few months with Billy falling into his old world of selfishness and apathy. The raucous below didn't subside until late in the evening. Eventually, the loud slurring of voices cracked the night air outside as Judy, Dora, and Alex boarded the Cadillac. The car screeched out from the front of their house with its boisterous passengers. The engine's sound faded as the car rolled off into the night.

Billy could be heard banging around downstairs. He turned off the lights, the TV and sat in the dark . . . drinking.

. . . .

Two days later, Grace had gone out to feed Lily, but she wasn't in her dog house. She called out for her little buddy, but the panting and the thumping of her paws on the ground were not to be heard. She looked around the yard and thereby the garden in a heap was Lily. Her body was still, lifeless, her tongue hung out of the side of her mouth. Grace let out a howl. Visions of Lily playing with her friends, chasing the ball, and sitting by her feet on the back steps flashed through her mind. Pam rushed out alerted by Grace's cries of misery. Both women knelt by their friend in a duet of sobs as they patted the lifeless pooch. Billy was staring out of the kitchen window; a tear meandered down his cheek; he loved that dog. Possibly the only thing he had really loved in his life.

Lily had been the only constant in Billy's life. That puppy didn't judge: she accepted Billy as Billy, screwed up as he was. Lily wagged her tail every time Billy appeared and clumped beside him when he was watching TV. She didn't know despair, deceit, manipulation, or anything negative. Lily was a true friend and an incredible loss to everybody: especially Billy.

As Pam and Grace hovered over Lily, a shadow loomed over them. The two women turned and looked up: it was Billy. Tears were cradled in his eyes. He said nothing; nor did they. He knelt beside them and patted Lily's stiff carcass. Pam, Grace, and Billy now all had something in common: grief.

CHAPTER 30 - FRIENDS AND FOES

The following Sunday, after Lily's passing, Grace's friends came over for a cookout to not only mourn the death of Lily but also to celebrate her life. Ashlie was present as well and was helping Pam prepare the hamburgers and salad. Grace, Billy and Grace's friends were sitting outside in a crude, haphazard circle talking about their good times with Lily. They reflected about throwing the ball with Lily as she leaped after it, her tail wagging wildly. As if on cue, the guys all looked at the ball resting on the ground by Lily's dog house. Charlie, who was sitting next to Grace, gave her a gentle pat on her arm. Billy shot Charlie a sharp glance which was not picked up by him. Charlie simply continued to be caught up in the emotions of the group.

Pam heard a knocking at the door, looked out the window, and blurted, "Oh, shit!" Ashlie jerked her head up. She had never heard Pam use that language before.

When Pam opened the door, Billy's three "friends" were standing there with beers in hand.

Judy smiled and said, "We heard about your dog dying and thought we'd come by to pay our respects." The other two goofballs were behind her nodding and grinning in agreement.

With no other choice, Pam reluctantly let them into the house. She said, "I'll go let Billy know that you're here."

They wandered into the living room, each popped a beer open and giggled to each other. Ashlie peered in from the kitchen not knowing what to think. Billy came in from outside and said, "What the heck are y'all doing here?"

Judy spoke first as always, "We've come to mourn the dog's death, Billy boy." They giggled again and took swigs from the cans.

"How did you know about Lily?"

"Lily! Was that her name? Sounds kinda wimpy," Judy mocked. The trio laughed. Billy didn't. He began to scowl. Seeing his reaction, Judy coaxed him, "Come on, Billy. Sit down and have a beer." Judy patted the cushion beside her on the couch. The conversation drifted to other topics, and Billy's mind wandered away from thinking about Lily. They began sharing laughs together. Judy put her hand on Billy's thigh during much of the talk.

Eventually, the group made its way outside. Before Billy could make any introductions, Judy swept over to the group waved her hand up high and bellowed, "Howdy, folks. Sorry that the dog is dead."

. . . .

The house was empty now except for its three residents: Pam, Grace, and Billy. A cloud of doom hung in the air as thick as mud. No one talked to each other. There was a conscious effort to avoid eye contact and one another. Grace then headed out the back door and stomped down the rear steps. "Where are you going, Grace," shouted her mom.

"I'm just going for a walk along the tracks. I'm good. I just need some me time. Don't worry. I'll be back soon."

Pam watched her daughter walk away and then turned to Billy, "I don't want those, . . . those friends," avoiding using a stronger, more heated description, "of yours coming here again, Billy!" He simply nodded his head. "Do you understand!!!" she said firmly. He nodded in agreement and lifted his can of beer to his lips.

CHAPTER 31 - THE STRANGER

The train tracks were unusually quiet. Grace saw a sign notifying everyone about work being done on a portion of the tracks and that no trains would be using the rails for several days. The walk was not tranquil although there were the same sights and sounds of nature all around, birds chirping, squirrels scampering, clouds floating above . . . all of that. But Grace's mind was replaying the cackling of Judy's grating voice over and over. Grace kicked stones, shuffled her feet at the rerun from the most recent episodes that she found most offensive, which were many.

She forged on wandering down the tracks. Then she stopped when she saw the simple memorial for her dad with the weathered cross leaning on top of the small mound of crushed rocks. She knelt down and adjusted the cross to an upright position and added new gravel for support. New thoughts traveled through her mind: she saw the image of her father running down the tracks in an effort to save the boy; she saw the youngster skirting into the woods; she saw Billy standing before her in despair when he told her he was that boy. The reel played over and over again until it seemed to run out of tape.

Grace proceeded with her journey. She passed the spot where she and her dad found poor, little Lily hurt and abandoned. She relived them picking her up and cradling her gently, taking her home and bringing her back to life. The tracks brought back so many memories that flowed relentlessly in her mind. She heard her father singing "Ol' man, that Ol' Man River. He must know some pin', but he don't say nothing. He just keep rollin', he keeps on rollin' along."

Then Grace braked abruptly. She heard something, . . . or, rather, someone. It was singing. She held her breath and listened carefully trying to block out any other noise other than the song: that beautiful song from her dear past now being sung, "Ol' Man River." She shivered at the coincidence of her thoughts being reflected in real time. And it was being sung. It was truly being sung in a smooth, delicate baritone. She nervously, cautiously followed the notes up and over the berm near where she and her pops would sit by the lake.

. . . .

Small flames leaped from a fire surrounded by stones. A man, a black man, was sitting on a boulder resting by the side of the lake. In his hand, he held a branch that extended over the water with a string dangling from it. The lake was still. The air was still with the quiet being interrupted only by voices from another fire about a hundred yards down the tracks and from the deep baritone singing "Ol' Man River."

Grace approached the figure from behind. He was oblivious to her being there: immersed in his own world of fishing, singing, and escape. Grace said softly, "That's the same...."

The man jumped from his seat on the boulder. His makeshift fishing pool leaped from his hand, the string catching on a low lying branch. He spun around, his hand on his chest and saw the young girl before him. He coughed, "Oh, Lordy!

Sweetheart, y'all scared the bejesus out of me!" still gasping for breath.

"I'm sorry, sir," Grace said sincerely, politely. "I was just admiring your singing and especially that song you were singing."

"Oh, thank you, mam," the man said in a deep voice still seeming a little rattled from having his peace interrupted. He was about six feet tall with large hands. His skin was of a cocoa color. His pants were worn and had dirt stains matted on them. His white shirt was far from white as dirt and sweat patterns had transformed the color to more of a tan tone. He was quite an intimidating presence except that his face was gentle, kind. His mannerisms were humble and thoughtful.

"My dad used to sing that song when we used to take our walk along the tracks."

"Used ta???" the man questioned.

"Oh, yes!" she paused. Her voice softened, "My dad died several years ago on these very tracks."

"I's so sorry to hear dat," said the man bowing his head with sincerity. "My's name is Daniel, but mos folks calls me C.M.

"C.M.?" questioned Grace.

"Oh! C.M. stands for Cash Man cuz folks mess with me dat I save every pennies I's earn. However, I sends it all to my's family. They done don't know dat."

"Well, that's a good thing, and my name is Grace," she said with a small curtsy.

"Nice to meet y'all, Grace," he smiled.

"And nice to meet you, Daniel, or should I call you C.M."

"Boat name is fine wit me." Grace decided to stick with

Daniel. "Would y'all like to settle down here?" asked Daniel pointing to the fire. "Y'all can takes a load offs your feet." Grace nodded a yes and they both walked to the fire and sat.

They talked for some time. Grace was doing most of the chatting in the beginning with the glow of the flames lighting up their faces. She told him about the sadness in her life: her dad and what happened to him, her dog dying, and the trouble she had with Billy. She had to unload her pain on to someone to release the pressure building up inside her. This gentle stranger seemed more than willing to listen and appeared to be actually interested in her sorrow.

Then the conversation switched to Daniel. He spoke about his work with the railroad and that he lived somewhat of a no-madic life working on "fixin'" tracks all over the country.

In a lull in their interaction, voices from the direction of another fire could be heard from about a hundred yards away. Daniel explained that they were his coworkers on the job.

"Why are you not with them?" Grace asked.

A gentle smile crossed his face: "Grace, y'all are so sweet; like a bucket full of innocence. Look here ah my skin. I's a black man. They's whiteys."

"You're kidding me? You are not with them because they're racists?"

"No, I's not kiddin'. But I don't give dat no mind. I like my alone time. Is not dat those there boys don't like me. Is jus dat where they all done comes from; colors should be kep seprate from da whiteys.

"That's not right!!" said Grace in disgust.

"Grace, life ain't always right. Life ain't always fair. Y'all knowed dat. You have already did live dat." Grace nodded her head slightly in sad agreement. "But I always done reach down deep into here to find forgiveness." Danial patted his heart. "To liv with bitterness make fa a bitter life. I done have freedom and joy in's my life. Dose guys jus don know a whole much better . . . Well, maybes they done do deep down. Sides, they is all missin' out on knowsin' a great guy: Me!" Daniel flashed a big grin. His teeth were bright against his cocoa skin.

Grace noticed a railroad spike laying on the ground next to the fire. "Daniel, what is this railroad spike doing here?"

"Well, Grace, da spike real special to me."

"How so?"

"I carry dat thar spike wit me wherever I done go." A curious look washed over Grace's face. He continued, "I'm no real, church-like person, but I's keep it to remind me of da sumone who had hiz hans and feet spiked to da cross . . . for all of us. Any hurtin' I have ain't nothin' compared to wha he all done."

Grace smiled at Daniel. She liked this stranger. He was content with the simplicity in his life and found goodness in others. He was a good man. Darkness was being ushered in as the day slipped away. Grace hopped up and said, "I've got to get going. It's getting late. It was nice meeting you, Mr. Daniel."

From his sitting position, Daniel responded, "And it was real nice ta meet y'all as well, Miss Grace."

CHAPTER 32 - OH, MY

Jose's Landscaping trucks with large, industrialized trailers were parked on the street in front of the Cromwell estate. An army of laborers were scattered over the estate. Some were mounted on commercial lawnmowers. Others carried weed whackers or hedge clippers or hoes or rakes. They were efficient with each aware of their responsibilities and incredibly skilled at the job that they were assigned.

The trio was at the pool sipping on their wine or, in Alex's case, chugging a beer. Dolly wasn't in her usual sunning spot for she was out playing bridge with the girl friends at the country club. With a beer in hand, Norman was resting on a lounge chair checking out the "scenery" as Judy and Dora were nearly popping out of their skimpy, two piece bathing suits dangling their feet in the water. Nellie was mixing up a container of iced tea for the landscapers. She had a particular bond with them. They were dedicated, hard workers and good, family men. She respected them.

Judy, Alex, and Dora began their verbal assault on the Hispanic laborers mocking their heritage. "Como esta?" waved Judy in her bathing suit to the man on a mower. He grinned back at her. She continued waving and smiling saying, "What a dipshit," drowned out by the drone of the machine.

Dora picked up where Judy left off, "Aloha, Amigo!!" she yelled accompanied by a flirtatious wave.

"It's Hola," said Norman.

"What?" said Dora.

"It's Hola. Not Aloha. Aloha is Hawaiian for hello. Hola is Spanish for hello. These guys are all Mexicans," said Norman casually without looking at Dora.

"Oh! Thanks for the Spanish lesson," she giggled.

"It's gracias," Norman said.

"What?" Dora squawked.

"Never mind," said an exasperated Norman as he continued gazing out at the scenery by the pool.

Alex blurted, "They look like a bunch of locusts swarming around. I wouldn't do that work in a million years." Of course, he wouldn't. The dork hadn't had a job at any time in his life. He epitomized the word slacker. After all the landscaping had been completed, Alex yelled, "Who wants to play golf and go for a ride on the carts."

"I do," said Dora as she jumped up from her sitting position by the pool.

"I'm good here with my wine," said Judy as she glanced at Norman and shot him a sly grin. "Take it to the Limit" by the Eagles was playing on the radio.

Dora and Alex headed for the barn and picked up a set of clubs that were always available for guests. They jumped in their carts and took off like bats out of hell. Their impression of golf was not the traditional game. They threw out their golf balls and played it like polo using their carts as horses. Needless to say, they left divots and tracks all over the course. So much for all that landscaping.

. . . .

"Gracias, Senorita Nellie," said Jose as he and his men bowed in appreciation finishing up their iced tea. They smacked their lips, put their cups down, and all chimed, "Adios, Amiga."

"De Nada y adios, mis amigos," Nellie responded with a smile. Then she waved goodbye cheerfully but with a hint of sadness. The felt comfortable with them around: not so much being alone with the Cromwell family and, especially now, with the trio of visitors.

She grabbed the water jug turned tea jug and hauled it in the front door to the kitchen in the back of the house. She began cleaning it in the sink and looked out the window at the backyard. The boy and the girl, Nellie didn't know which girl, were riding their carts out on the golf course yelping, laughing and hollering.

Nellie shook her head, filled the jug with water and soap, and looked out the window again. The pool area was vacant of people. The chairs were empty and a little askew. The pool house door was closed, and the shades were drawn. A float in the shape of a horse and a few colorful balls floated harmlessly on top. All was quiet. A screaming "Wahoo" from one of the golf carts shook the air.

Well, almost quiet.

CHAPTER 33 - FIGURING IT OUT

Not hearing the occasional bark and seeing the empty dog house was difficult for all three living at the Keenan house. Lily was buried near the garden with a bed of flowers planted at her grave-sight. A stone marker with a picture of a dog that Grace had painted on it sat in the middle of the flowers. When they were in the back yard working or relaxing, each of the family members took time to walk over and pay their respects to Lily. Lily's death, as sad as it was, seemed to have created a temporary calm between Pam, Grace, and Billy.

That didn't last long. Charlie had come over to visit. He heard the voices in the back yard as he curled around the corner of the house. Pam and Grace were weeding the garden, and Billy was sitting on the backstops, beer in hand which now had become more common and reluctantly accepted by the girls.

Billy turned and sneered at Charlie. He didn't like him. Charlie had danced too closely with his wife and seemed a little too touchy with her trying to provide comfort when Lily had died. Although Billy and Grace had their problems, he wasn't going to let Charlie be one of them. "What the hell are you doing here?" Billy barked. The two girls angled around to see what was going on.

"Hey, Billy. How are you doin'?" Charlie replied harmlessly thinking that Billy was only kidding.

Pam and Grace got up to greet Charlie. Billy put his beer down, rose from his sitting position, and stepped between the girls and Charlie. Staring down at Charlie, he growled, "I said, 'What the hell are you doing here?'"

Charlie put his hands up in front of him in a protective stance. "Billy, I just came over to visit, to say hi. That's all."

Billy took a step forward toward Charlie. Grace skipped in between the two men, turned and snarled at Billy, "Stop it, Billy. Calm down. What are you doing?"

Billy backed off and sat down on the step, again, picked up his beer. Pam, Grace, and Charlie all stared at him suspiciously. Billy rested his elbows on his knees, caressed his beer, and focused on the can in his hands. Grace shook her head in disgust, took Charlie's hand, and guided him over the garden area. This did not sit well with Billy, but he also knew he had made a fool of himself and let it go.

. . . .

Again, tension gripped the Keenan home. They sat around the kitchen table stabbing at their food with their forks, occasionally, raising some bits of casserole to their mouths. The silence was finally broken when Grace said, "I'm going for a walk." She slid her chair away from the table and was heading out the door.

Pam said, "Be careful, and don't be late." My baby was all that Pam could think about at that moment.

Billy looked up from his food as the door closed. "I'm sorry," he whispered, but Grace had already left. The words only were received by Pam's ears. Pam reached her hand over to

Billy's and patted it gently. She stood up, went to the kitchen window and watched her baby walk away.

. . . .

Grace didn't take her time walking along the tracks: she marched; her arms were swinging in sync with her legs; her eyes glaring down the train tracks. She passed the memorial without as much as a glance. Grace stormed by the spot they found Lily, eyes fixated straight ahead. She reached the special place where her Pop and she would meditate. Grace climbed over the berm and spotted Daniel who was trying his luck with his trusty, fishing branch. She loudly strutted down to him. He turned as he heard her steps.

"I can't stand him," she snapped with tears welling in her eyes.

"Sweetheart. Y'all settle down, sit by da fire," said Daniel desperately trying to calm her; guiding her to a sitting position. Grace wiped her eyes as he sat down across from her. "Now, tell Daniel wha these here tears are all bout."

Grace told him about Billy's fray with Charlie and how his drinking was getting to be more and more of a problem. "He just cares about nothing but himself. He's just a spoiled rich kid," she whimpered. She paused and looked up across the fire at Daniel. Daniel was silent. "Well?" She was expecting an answer. Daniel still sat there looking back at Grace. "Aren't you going to say something? What should I do?" Grace's voice was bordering on frantic.

Daniel spoke, "Grace, dis here fella was da man y'all married?"

"Yes?" she responded quietly with surprise.

"And y'all loved him when y'all cepted his proposal?"

"I think so." Her eyes looked away as though searching for the right answer. "He was the first boy who took an interest in me." She lifted her head. "He noticed me. He seemed to care. We got married, and then I found out that he was the boy who my father had tried to save . . ."

"Wait! Y'all don't tell me dat your papa died tryins to save a youngin . . . a boy dat end up bein' yur husban."

"I didn't think to . . . "

"Grace," he paused. "Grace, dat boy, . . . or I should say "man" of y'all's, cares."

"But he married me out of sympathy not love."

"He done married y'all cuz he cared. He married y'all to try to make up fa y'all's loss."

"Well, he's not doing a very good job," she sobbed. "He's just a rich kid used to having everything he wanted."

Daniel's voice became softer, "No! No. Not everythin' he all wanted. You done give em somethin' in his life dat had nuttin' to do wit stuff." She turned her head and stared out onto the lake. "Be careful of bein' judgmental."

"I'm not!!!" she blurted.

"Grace, y'all jus said dat he was a spoiled, rich kid." He pointed to the fire of his coworkers, ". . . and they done think I's a dumb nigga." Grace's eyes widened. "People is always judgin' bout wha day don't know nuttin' bout, or bout folk dat is not what or who dey is. Good folk and bad folk comes in all shape, color, religion, rich or poor." He paused trying to find the right words. "Jus cuz sumone live in da big ole house or drives a big ole car don't mean dat dey is snobs. Dey have learned skills, been workin' hard, and, ins mos cases, have paid der dues." Grace listened. Her mind processing what he was saying. He continued, "No! Don't judge dem jus cuz day is cessful, jus as folk shun't judge dose who is poor. Many folk are jus an axdent, a fall away from losin' everythin'." He stopped and asked, "Are ya still wit me, Grace?"

She nodded and quietly said, "Yes, I'm thinking about what you've said." She leaned back, laid down on the ground and crossed hands like a pillow behind her head. She gazed up at the stars and said, "What should I do, Daniel?"

Daniel tossed some twigs onto the fire. Flames leaped up. He laid down on the ground as well. The two of them gazing up at the stars. He said in his deep baritone voice, "Forgibness, Grace. Forgibness." The moon reflected off the surface of the lake. A fish jumped making a tiny splash.

CHAPTER 34 - BLOOD

Grace made one more visit to see Daniel after an especially dark encounter with Billy. Her husband had become exceedingly belligerent after a few hours of heavy drinking; he had screamed and grabbed her by the arm. She had pulled away in fear that he might strike her. Grace was seeking out Daniel for consolation and guidance. The forgiveness piece did not work with Billy, . . . at least that time.

It was getting dark, but Grace had to get out of that madhouse. Her mother was visiting with Ashlie, so there was no one there to serve as a buffer between Billy and her. Daniel was the only one who seemed to understand, to empathize with her suffering.

Daniel was sitting by the fire cooking a fish that he had caught. When Grace's figure approached, he could read the sadness painted on her face. The tears, the frown, the slouched posture all screamed misery. He got up and walked toward Grace.

"Grace. My dear, Grace. Wha is wrong."

"Daniel, I don't think I can take it anymore." She gasped sucking in air. "The rejection, the cruelty is just too much for me to stand."

"Sit here, Grace, by da fire." Daniel escorted her to a sitting position. He sat beside her and tenderly patted her shoulder not saying anything.

Grace looked up at him with sad eyes. "What should I do, Daniel?" she said pleading for an answer.

Daniel looked into her eyes and smiled gently. "Grace, da more hard da times git , sum time da more precious da results."

"What do you mean by that?"

"I mean dat . . ." suddenly Daniels yes widened and became frantic. He quickly leaned toward Grace and coaxed her to a standing position. "Y'all got ta go. Now!"

"But why? I don't hear anything."

Daniel whispered in desperation, "Da's why." He looked in the direction of the other fire. "Dare ain't no noises. Quick, Grace, git in da water wit making no noise as y'all can."

Grace did what he said and slid quietly into the water. She made her way to the overextending brush. Her hair flared out like a fan floating on the water. She heard thrashing through the woods and hugged herself closer to the shoreline concealed by the vegetation.

Three men fumbled their way out of the woods. One was gigantic and dwarfed the other two. He had a scruffy beard, and his arms were the size of tree trunks. In his left hand, he was lugging around a large stick. His eyes were dark and angry. A scar ran across his right cheek. The other two shorter men were in sharp contrast: one was stout with a red face; he too had a beard, and his hair was longer and dangled recklessly around the collar of his shirt. The other man was thin, almost to the point of being gaunt. His shirt hung carelessly outside his pants, and he teetered as he walked. He had a shit eating grin with two teeth missing in the front. Those two had beers in their hands. All three of them wore shabby, dirty clothes that exposed the toil of their labor.

"So, what y'all goin' on here, Daniel," Scarface said gruffly.

"Na . . . Nut . . . tin'!" Daniel stuttered.

"Don't play wit me, boy. We heard a woman's voice, and it came from dis direction." The words spit out of his mouth. "Y'all hidin' a sweet, lil thang here?" He and his cohorts scanned the surroundings.

"No, sir. Is jus me singin' in a high voice," Daniel squeaked.

Pudgy said, "Y'all ain't got no high voice, boy."

"Yeah! Y'all got no high voice, boy," repeated toothless pleased with his input.

Grace watched from her watery concealment. She was shivering with fear. That fear intensified when she felt something long begin to slither under her hair and along her shoulders. Snake. She hated snakes, feared snakes, and now one was slithering along her back. She wanted to leap out of the water, but she knew she couldn't. She gasped and remained as still as she could. The snake ventured off. Grace breathed a sigh of relief.

The three men heard the slight gasp. "Wha was dat?" asked Pudgy as he made his way to the shoreline. Grace hugged the shore even tighter trying to make herself smaller. Pudgy looked around and then walked back to the group.

"Y'all see anythang?'" grunted scarface.

All three then glared at Daniel. Scarface suddenly raised the stick and whacked Daniel across his face. Blood spurted out of his nose. Pudgy then kicked him in the groin. Daniel fell back on his side. Toothless got into the act by kicking Daniel behind the head. Daniel's face lunged forward banging into the stones around the fire. He groaned in pain.

"Hey, y'all. Le's brand him," Toothless cried out with glee.

"You Jackass. We ain't goin' to brand him," said Scarface. "We could gets in a heap of trouble for dat."

Toothless looked disappointed. The coworkers looked down at the bloody heap by the fire. Scarface spoke up, "Well, we dun good here, boys. Le's let Daniel rest tonight so he cans work tomorra."

They turned and rambled off back to their campfire laughing about their deeds. "We done good, ah, boss," said Pudgy.

"Ya! We done good," replied Scarface.

Grace remained motionless in the water while Daniel remained motionless by the fire. She heard the voices trail off into the distance, and slowly, cautiously creeped out of the lake. Grace knelt down on the ground to allow the water to drain off her as quietly as possible. After a few moments, she crawled up to where Daniel was.

"Daniel, are you OK?" she whispered.

Daniel painstakingly turned his head toward her. Blood was splattered all over his face, his clothes dripped off of the rocks, and permeated the soil. Tears came to Grace's eyes. She took her wet blouse off and with it wiped his face as clean as she could. He looked into her eyes, reached up and gently touched her face. She leaned down, gently caressed him, and kissed him on the cheeks. She loved this man: this poor, beaten, downtrodden black man.

Grace tiptoed quietly up the back steps in her muddy, wet, bloody clothes. She didn't know what to expect when she entered the house. She hoped for the best but expected the worse. She delicately opened the door and peeked into the kitchen. Nothing. She nudged the door open and entered. When she looked into the living room, Billy was motionless on the sofa. Beer cans were strewn around on the floor. He was out: passed out. Billy wasn't about to wake up. Unfortunately, this had been a repeated scenario for several weeks. However, on this night, it was a blessing.

Grace wondered where her mom was. The house was silent except for the guttural noises coming from Billy. She swiveled her head around and scanning the downstairs and the kitchen. She then noticed a piece of paper with a scribbled message on the kitchen table. It was written by Billy and looked more like hieroglyphics than printing. She was able to make out the note; her mom had gone to stay with Ashlie for the night.

In most cases, Grace would have been disappointed being left alone with Billy. But, under the circumstances, she was relieved. She was now able to avoid explaining her condition and the events leading up to it to her mom. It was her little secret.

She quickly undressed in the kitchen, put her garments in a paper bag, and, although naked, creeped out into the back yard and put the items in the rubbish. She quickly but quietly reentered the house. Billy was still asleep. With the quick swipe of a paper towel, she cleaned up the wet, dirty remnants of her muddy clothing that were on the floor. She looked up again at Billy. Out like a light.

Grace softly sped by her husband, climbed the stairs, took a shallow bath, and went to bed. She had dodged a bullet, yet, guilt haunted her mind. Her little secret.

Downstairs, Billy stirred on the sofa with one eye open. His mind was foggy, and his vision was blurred. He rolled over on his side and thought: What the hell was that?

. . . .

Grace had gone back to see Daniel three more times. On her last visit, the work sign had been taken down. She trotted along the repaired tracks to where Daniel had been camping out. No one was there. His makeshift fishing pole was lying by the shoreline. The fire had been extinguished except for a few harmless coils of smoke reaching upward and dark ashes remaining with stones circling them. One of the rocks still had blood stains.

She stepped around the fire pit and on the other side she noticed a $10 bill with Daniel's spike weighing it down. Grace knelt and picked up the spike with her left hand and raised the money with the fingers on her right hand. Daniel had written something on the paper bill:

Grace,
Let forgibnes, undirstandin, an luv
gide you thru life.
C.M.

Grace looked sadly out onto the lake holding the spike and the $10 bill in her hand as a train rumbled by behind her.

CHAPTER 35 - JOY

About two months had transpired since Billy's face to face with Charlie and about a month since Daniel had been beaten up. The tension in the house mitigated. Grace's little secret guided her to be more tolerant and forgiving. She had been much kinder to Billy even though he still had some drinking episodes. But they were very few. He had begun to become a contributing member of the family by doing chores around the house; picking up items; cutting the lawn; taking out the trash. These acts did not go unnoticed by either Pam nor Grace.

While the three were sitting at the kitchen table eating pancakes, Billy spoke very quietly and awkwardly, "I've been a jerk."

The two women looked at each other and Pam said, "Excuse me?"

Billy raised his head and stared at Pam and Grace, "I said, 'I've been a jerk. I am truly sorry for the way I have behaved." He took a breath. "I am very sorry for my drinking and careless behavior." The two girls' eyes widened. He continued, "I am going to get my act together." His eyes looked down, "Please forgive me."

Grace reached over with both hands and held both of his hands. With deep emotion, she said, "Billy, We all make mistakes. We all make mistakes."

Pam got up, went over to Billy and softly patted him on the back. She whispered, "We forgive you, Billy."

The mood in the Keenan home brightened. The conversations at dinner time were pleasant, and Billy had stepped up helping around the house, even more; contributing rather than being a freeloader. Pam was grateful for this effort and slowly began to warm up to Billy.

One day, Grace became dizzy and nearly fainted while working in the garden.

Billy rushed to her side.

"Are you OK, Grace?

"Oh, sure. I'm just a little dizzy. It must be the heat."

Billy noticed that Grace was sweating bullets and breathing heavily. He didn't buy into her reasoning.

"Grace, we're going to the doctor. No way am I going to have you stay at home like this."

He gently helped her up, and they walked to the back steps. Pam was watching from the kitchen window and rushed to open the door. "What's wrong?" she asked.

Just by looking at Grace, she could tell something was off: really off.

Billy said, "Grace is not feeling well, and I'm not going to mess around. I'm going to take her to the doctor's."

"Well, I'm going, too," blurted Pam. She wasn't about to stay home with her little girl heading out for medical care.

Billy and Pam waited nervously in the reception room to hear from the doctor about Grace's condition. Billy's knees swung back and forth, and he tapped his fingers together. The door to the doctor's office opened, and Grace walked out. She was pale and appeared flustered. The doctor escorted her to meet with Billy and her mom. They both popped up from their seats. The doctor spoke first, "Bill . . . , Pam, . . . Grace is pregnant."

Billy staggered back a few steps, collected himself, and looked at Grace bug-eyed. "You're pregnant?" he said as though he didn't believe the doctor.

Grace nodded her head up and down. A grin the size of Tennessee stretched across her face. "Yes, YES! I AM!!" she sang.

Billy hugged her and then backed off. "I didn't hurt you, did I?" . . . And then he hugged the doctor, looked up and joyfully yelled to the ceiling, "My wife is PREGNANT. . . . I'm going to be a DAD." Then he picked up Pam and swung her around.

. . . .

The news of Grace's pregnancy spread quickly. That weekend, her girlfriends converged on her house to share in the excitement. Angie was beside herself. She loved children and was actually going to community college taking courses in early childhood education. Ninette and Stephanie peppered Grace with all sorts of questions; "When is the baby due? Do you want a boy or a girl? Where is the baby going to sleep?" and many more.

Enjoying this time with her friends, Grace answered each question. The answer to when is the baby due was easy: in less than nine months. Whether she wanted a boy or a girl was another easy one: just a healthy baby. However, where was the baby going to sleep was a little more perplexing. Grace turned to her mom and asked, "Where will the baby sleep?"

Pam smiled, "In your room, of course, with you and Billy."

"You're kidding? Right? Where would we put the crib?"

"I am kidding," grinned Mrs. Keenan. "I've been thinking about that. I thought we could convert the sewing room at the end of the hallway into the baby's room. I know it isn't that big, but by moving the sewing table and other small items out, it would make an ideal baby's bedroom."

The girls all nodded in agreement and turned to Grace to see how she felt. Grace said, "That's a great idea. Mom, you're the best."

. . . .

A week had passed when Billy drove home from work and parked his truck in front of the Keenan house. He hopped out of the truck, sprinted up onto the porch and partially opened the front door. He yelled into the house, "Hey, I need your help out here," and scramble back to the truck.

Pam and Grace hurried out to the porch. Grace asked concerned, "What's going on, Billy?"

"Come here! Y'all see!"

They approached the back of the Bronco where Billy was standing. He grinned from ear to ear and, like a magician, opened the trunk and waved his arm. Grace cupped her hands over her mouth and gasped, "Oh! Billy, it's beautiful."

And there it was. A pristine, cherry cradle that was so new, the sun glistened off the varnished wood. Grace wrapped her arms around Billy, gave him a kiss and said, "I love you, Billy." Pam soaked in the tender moment which seemed so rare in this household.

CHAPTER 36 - IT'S A . . .

Billy was transformed into a different person after learning that he was going to be a father. He became a whirlwind of assistance at home doing everything from washing the dishes to weeding the garden to cleaning the bathroom. No chore was off limits for him. He doted over Grace as though she were a queen. Billy was at her side to address any of her needs or even if she didn't need him. He brought her ice water, ironed her clothes, helped Grace up from her chair, opened doors. Name it: he did it. Billy was overjoyed with the thought of being a father.

Nine months seemed to whiz by. Maybe not for Grace, whose tiny frame struggled carrying her bundle of joy, but to everyone else, yes, it whizzed by. Billy paced back and forth in the waiting room with visions of his son or his daughter; one second he was throwing the ball to his son; the next, he was attending a ballet recital for his daughter; another time, the family was enjoying a cookout in the backyard as the baby crawled through the garden. The excitement was nearly uncontrollable.

Pam was more reserved as she watched Billy's movements. Though, she was excited as well. Being a grandmother warmed her heart. She couldn't wait to cradle and care for the newborn. She vowed to herself that she would be the best grandmother in the world and smiled.

The door swung open from the delivery room. The nurse walked in nestling a cute, sweet baby in her arms. Billy couldn't contain his curiosity, "Is it a boy or a girl?"

With a straight face, the nurse flatly said, "It's a boy."

He turned to Pam, and, with watery eyes, he grinned, "It's a boy." Then gave his mother-in-law a hug. He looked back at the nurse and, like a little kid wanting to open a present, he pleaded, "Can I see him?"

"Of course," the nurse dryly replied. She leaned over and held the little guy out for Billy to see his baby son for the first time.

Billy jumped back. His face contorted in anger and his body stiffened. He clenched his fists and yelled at the nurse, "That's not my baby. It's not..."

Pam looked over his shoulder at the newborn. Her head snapped back, and she stared at the nurse with a questioning look as Billy stormed out of the room and ran down the hall. She said acutely, "There must be some mistake?"

. . . .

Twenty minutes earlier in the delivery room, Grace gritted her teeth in pain. She responded to the doctor's orders, "Breath, deeply. Again. Now push. Push a little harder." Then there was a gushing sound and the pressure in her stomach dissipated. The nurses' and the doctor's eyes all looked at the newborn, their mouths concealed behind surgery masks. "It's a boy, Grace. It's a healthy, baby boy." The doctor said gently. "Would you like to hold your son, Grace."

"Yes," she said softly. All eyes were on her as the doctor handed Grace her son. Grace glowed and then her smile fell from her face. The boy was beautiful. The light brown, baby boy was beautiful.

. . . .

Billy jumped out of his Bronco, slammed the door shut, and scrambled up the stairs into the Keenan's house.

. . . .

Billy had abandoned Pam at the hospital without any comfort nor any support. He was consumed with anger, bitterness, and crushed emotionally. He was certainly not thinking. Grace held her newborn in her hospital room with mixed emotions: of joy with her beautiful baby and . . . of shame. Pam had to call Ashlie for a ride home. In the car, she shared the news with Ashlie about Grace's baby. Pam was crying. She was hurt and confused. The girl in the delivery room was not the Grace that she had raised. Questions banged around in her head, but no answers surfaced.

They arrived at the house in darkness. They parked behind Billy's Bronco.

"I'll go with you," Ashlie said.

"No, I'll be all right," whimpered Pam.

"You're not all right, Pam. I'm going with you." Ashlie was not taking no for an answer as she opened the driver's side door and shuffled around to be with Pam.

The two women walked gingerly to the house, Pam struggling with deep breaths. They opened the door with caution and stepped into the house. It was a mess. Beer cans were scattered on the floor, chairs were knocked over and in the living room the cradle, the brand new, cherry cradle, was smashed to bits with sharp, broken edges of wood extending out like spears. Billy was sitting in his chair with the erratic glow of the TV splashing on his face. He was in a trance just staring at nothing, and he was making strange, gargling sounds. Billy was not there. He was a boiling cauldron of rage and confusion.

CHAPTER 37 - SHAME

Grace stood in the kitchen cradling her newborn protectively. Determining a name for him was not as difficult as one would think for her. She searched for an enlightening title which would convey strength and hope. When she searched for a name, she was intrigued by Caleb. She found that Caleb meant "astute powers of observation and fearlessness in the face of overwhelming odds. His devotion to God was symbolized by the 'dog' in some traditions." So, Caleb, it was. As far as Billy was concerned, he could care less. He didn't want to have anything to do with the little bastard. In fact, Billy didn't want to have anything to do with Grace either. But she was home with the baby in their kitchen, and he had no alternative but to face them both.

Grace was coiled in shame and guilt like a boa constrictor was wrapped around her body. She was nearly suffocating in misery and, yet, the little boy in her arms provided her with a speck of peace. Her mother, although swimming in confusion, was drawn to the baby. Her motherly instincts rose above her doubts, apprehension, and concerns. She reached for the for the little guy, the cute, light brown baby boy, and gazed into his eyes. He smiled up at her.

"Oh! Look, mom. He's smiling at you."

"I think that's gas, Grace. But I'd like to think of it as a smile."

Pam had questioned Grace over and over in the previous

weeks, "How could this have happened?" Grace couldn't provide an answer of clarity for she didn't know how it had happened. She was blindsided with an emotional experience which overwhelmed her. She couldn't explain away her actions. Grace was ashamed for she knew she had done an incredibly horrible act. At the time, Grace was wrestling with a myriad of emotions. Her emotional lovemaking with Daniel was impulsive, reckless, and wrong. She knew it, but she couldn't explain it. She still couldn't understand how it happened.

However, over time, Pam just accepted the circumstances as they were. She engaged in the mantra "It is what it is." She didn't want to lose Grace nor the baby as bazaar as the little guy's coming to being was. She also didn't blame Billy for his outrage, but, by the same token, she was Grace's mother and wanted to protect her as best she could. Billy had gone over the deep end and was unpredictable. She had to protect her baby; and her baby's baby.

. . . .

Judy grinned at the thought of Billy's bastard baby. She couldn't believe that shit, and it fed her enough callousness to torment Billy and his whore wife and, now, that baby for eternity. Dora grinned in the back seat of the blue Cadillac. Both Judy and Dora had just finished up their second year in college and were anticipating a grand future. Even though they had attended different schools, they partied like animals. School was just an extension of summer with good times, drinking, and co-eds. Such a great life. They ridiculed Billy. He lived in a dump, was married to a whore, and he had a two-bit job. They loved it. And so did Alex, who lived at home, played video games, and studied online at a prestigious university. At least that's what he told his cohorts.

The weather had warmed up. The pool at Cromwell's was ready for use. They didn't even announce that they were coming over anymore because Norman didn't care. However, Nellie and Dolly did. Dolly's privacy was invaded without notice and Nellie had to run around getting food and beverages without advance notice for the "posse" as she called them. She also had to clean up the mess after they left. No! Nellie and Dolly were not happy.

This time it was even worse, for now, they had juicy, new material for their conversations. Judy snidely remarked to Dolly, "I hear Billy' wife had a baby boy."

Dolly moved the magazine that she was reading to the side and raised her sunglasses, "Yes. She did."

"You must be so thrilled. Your first grandchild," Judy said acting as if she didn't know the full story.

"I am," Dolly managed to respond.

Judy loved turning the screw. "Who does he look like? Billy or that girl . . ." Just then, Alex did a cannonball into the pool drenching Judy, Dora....and Dolly. Dolly had had enough. She got up and glared at the posse. "Get the hell out of my yard."

Judy began, "But we didn't . . ."

"I said LEAVE and don't come back!!!!" she blasted pointing to the way out.

"Well, that's not very nice," taunted Judy. Dora and Alex giggled behind her. Dolly's eyes flared with fire as she glared at them. Eventually, they got the message. They grabbed some beers and their stuff. They waddled their way to the gate. Every once in a while they looked back, laughed, poked each other and mocked Dolly, ". . . and don't come back." Like that's going to stop them.

. . . .

Billy had moved to the downstairs sofa for his sleeping purposes and to have a few drinks at night. Intimacy with Grace was now impossible for him. He was repulsed by her. When he was collecting some items from their bedroom, he searched the drawers for socks, a watch, underwear, and so on.

He decided to check the drawers Grace used to see if any essentials he might need were stored inside the dresser. There was nothing for him, but he did see a railroad spike and a ten dollar bill with something scrawled on it. Billy picked up the spike, examined it, and then put it back down. His fingers snatched up the ten dollar bill, and he held it up to his eyes to read the writing:

Grace,
Let forgibnes, undirstandin, an luv
gide you thru life.
C.M.

"What's this about?" he said to himself, "and who the hell is C.M." He thought it might be from Charlie. However, he couldn't remember Charlie's last name but didn't think it began with an M. He dropped the bill back in the drawer and dismissed both items. He wanted to get his stuff. He snatched his belongings, brought them downstairs and stored them behind the sofa. He then turned on the TV: *Charlie's Angels* appeared. He liked that Farrah Fawcett. He smiled . . . for her name always reminded him of a dripping faucet, but she was no drip. He flopped down and popped open a beer.

. . . .

A light knocking at the front door disrupted his peace. Billy put his beer down on the table and got up to answer it. When he opened the door, he was looking at the face of his mother, Dolly, with Nellie standing behind her. He was flustered and didn't know what to say. "Hi, mom. Come in. Hi, Nellie. Err, ahh. Nice to see you. What brings you here?"

"Billy, you know why we came . . . to see the baby," his mother snapped.

Billy looked down and turned to walk away, "Yeah, the baby." He simply pointed to the kitchen and said, "In the back yard, mom. Just go to the back yard." Then he grabbed his beer off the table and plopped himself back into his chair.

Dolly and Nellie looked at each other and Nellie said, "The back yard," and they marched off to, yep, the back yard.

Pam was cradling the baby while sitting in a lawn chair. Grace was weeding the garden near Lily's memorial when the back door opened and out came Dolly and Nellie.

"Hi, Pam. Hi, Grace," Dolly cheerfully said. "We hope that this isn't a bad time, but we wanted to see the baby."

Grace stood up from the garden and walked over to her mother-in-law. Dolly surprised her with a hug. This gesture immediately dissolved the mounting tension of the impromptu visit.

"Well, here he is," smiled Pam. She curled her body in a way where Dolly and Nellie could get a good peek at Caleb. Both women broadly smiled when seeing the sweet face looking up at them.

"Oh! He's so cute," cooed Dolly. Nellie's face also glowed with approval. Dolly looked up at Grace and repeated the praise: "Your baby is so cute, Grace."

"Thank you. Thank you so much," Mrs. Cromwell.

. . . .

They talked for over an hour in the backyard with everyone having a chance to hold Caleb and to do the "coochie coo" bit. It was a lovely visit. Even Caleb seemed to enjoy the attention smiling at each woman as she held him. He was gifting everyone, and they soaked it in.

Billy glared out of the kitchen window shaking his head: it wasn't his baby. He took a swig of his beer. His mom saw him in the window. She got up from her chair and headed in to see him as the rest of the crew played with the baby. When she stepped into the kitchen, Billy was still staring out the window.

"Billy, are you OK?"

"Yeah, sure. Why shouldn't I be?" Billy blurted sarcastically still staring out the window.

"Billy, I know this is incredibly difficult for you and . . . "

He pivoted toward her. "You know nothing," he blasted. "The pain I feel in here," pointing to his heart, "is beyond excruciating. I don't think I can take it living with that whore and that bastard."

Dolly grabbed him by the arm and pulled him down so that they were nose to nose. Billy had no idea that she was so strong. She said through gritted teach, "Don't ever use those two words again." She shook his arm, "Do you hear me!?!"

"Yes! I freakin' hear you," snapped Billy.

"This is your opportunity to make things better. Don't judge. Don't!!!!!" Her voice trailed off, ". . . Don't . . . judge." Dolly's face was etched with determination and pain. Her forehead gleamed with sweat.

When his mom and Nellie drove off, Billy watched the car get smaller as it glided down the road. He grabbed his beer, flopped down into his chair and muttered, "Who the hell does she think she is?"

CHAPTER 38 - BABYSITTERS

There was a rush of babysitters early in the mothering stages. Occasionally, Grace's friends would come over to help out; initially, out of curiosity to see the little guy; later, with reluctance. They felt that Grace had betrayed them with her little secret. Angie had become more distant as did some of the other girls. Fortunately, Ashlie would assist from time to time when she was feeling up to it, and even Nellie and Dolly would show up to lend a hand. This was more than just a good thing. It was essential. Billy's behavior necessitated someone being with the baby at all times for Billy was a "hands-off" dad in the most extreme way: he was dangerous.

Not only did Grace and Caleb receive criticism from her friends, but from her beloved community as well. It was like a switch had been turned. They were disgusted with Grace. In their minds, she had committed one of the most heinous crimes: sleeping with a black man. The "N" word was thrown about in many conversations as well as the words bastard and whore. When Grace would walk to the Donnelly's, she was hit with cruel stares and demeaning whispers. No! Life was not easy for Grace now in her surroundings and, especially, not at home.

Under the dark clouds of harsh disapproval, Caleb grew from a baby to a four year old sheltered and protected by the love of his mother and grandmother. He was always smiling and seemed to bring joy to everyone. Even some of Grace's friends seemed to be pulled in to Caleb's charm; everyone except Billy who was still engrossed in his anger. He remained distant, hollow, and trapped in rage.

They say time heals everything. Not with this guy. It almost seemed like he reveled in his own misery. He appeared to try to create even more angst for himself. Billy had lost his job because he was found not to be dependable. He came to work under the weather and smelling of booze. Isn't that amazing? Same thing at home. He had sunk to the depths of being a total waste.

By this stage in everyone's life, they had accepted Caleb. They expressed love and kindness for the little guy. Not Billy. The kid represented everything ugly and repulsive to him. Billy had become isolated in his house. He had grown thorns of repugnancy that nobody dared to approach. However, others didn't feel sorry for him. They thought he should just get over it. Easy for them to say. They didn't experience the pangs of betrayal and the daily reminder of her deception. With every cry, whimper, step that Caleb made, Billy seethed. The rage swelled inside of him.

However, not everyone felt this way. When the blue, now faded blue, Cadillac was parked in front of the Keenan home, it meant trouble. Judy and her posse always brought beer and wine to get Billy wound up. Grace would be home with Caleb usually escaping to the back yard while Billy got tanked with his "friends." Even from outside, through the screen door, she could hear them belittling her and making jokes about Caleb's brown skin. She wanted to go in and say get the hell out of here. She needed Dolly's assertiveness. But she was afraid; afraid of the gang mentality they had concocted; afraid of how Billy would react; and afraid for Caleb's safety. No! She best keep her mouth shut and out of sight while protecting her Caleb, her baby.

Little Tommy Dalton, from next door, and his friend, P. J. Feeney, who were the same age as Caleb, would wander over and play with him. Fortunately, they popped over on this day giving Grace a relief from the hostilities brewing inside of her house. Tommy's mother waved from her yard to make sure it was OK. It was definitely OK with Grace. She loved watching Caleb interact with his little buddies. They were always laughing, chasing each other around, and being boys. They liked to use Lily's dog house, still with her collar and rope hanging near the entrance, as their little clubhouse. Although, only one could fit in comfortably. Grace chuckled when all three tried to cram themselves into the structure with their little bottoms sticking out of the opening. Tommy was a regular character. He found joy in everything and was a significant influence on Caleb. P. J. was just funny and mischievous. He had a perpetual smile planted on his face which Caleb picked up on. They were a happy trio. That's for sure.

Grace heard the house grow quiet inside and then the purr of an engine. The posse had left, but the mess they made remained, and Billy was in no shape to clean it up. Not that he would if he was sober. Billy staggered to the back door and looked out at the kids playing. Grace could feel his eyes on her back like daggers but dared not turn around. Billy stared at the two white kids playing with the bastard. That black bastard.

. . . .

"It is a man's own mind, not his enemy or foe, that lures him to evil ways." Buddha

. . . .

Finding babysitters became more challenging to find as time progressed. Grace's friends had gone off to community college or found jobs, so they weren't available. Ashlie had had a knee operation, and Grace had to work. Her mom would have helped, but she had to stay with Ashlie providing her home care. Since Billy didn't have a job, he was the only one home consistently to watch Caleb during the day. This was not good, but it was the only formula that worked.

Billy didn't like Caleb. Not that Caleb ever did anything wrong, but for obvious reasons, Billy didn't like the wretched, despicable, little nigger. The first day that Grace went off to work, Billy and Caleb were in the kitchen waiting for Grace to depart. She had made a peanut butter and jelly sandwich for Caleb and showed him where in the refrigerator he could find it. Grace also pointed to a cup of milk she had left for him. She trusted Caleb to feed himself more than she did Billy taking care of it. She then hugged Caleb and said, "I love you, my little buddy. Now, you be good a boy for daddy while I'm at work." Caleb smiled back at her and nodded his head, yes. Billy cringed when she mentioned the title, daddy. Grace gave Billy a quick glance and was rewarded with a contemptuous glare.

Caleb reached up and held her hand. He then walked his mommy to the door and waved goodbye as she shuffled down the sidewalk turning to wave to him. Rain began to fall from the sky lightly. From the living room, Billy watched Caleb. The little guy turned around, smiled and said, "I'll be good, daddy."

"I'm not your daddy!" he growled through gritted teeth, "and I'll take care of you. Believe me!!! I'll take real good care of you!!" Billy leaped up the stairs, went into their bedroom, ripped open Grace's drawer and grabbed the spike.

. . . .

The rain was pouring down now. Billy was in the kitchen; the spike dangled out of his pants pocket. Caleb just looked up dismayed. Billy grabbed Caleb by one hand, whipped him out the back door, bounced him down the steps, and dragged him across the back yard. On his way by the garden, he grabbed a shovel. "What are you doing, daddy? You're hutting me." cried Caleb.

"Billy snapped, "I'm not your daddy." He let go of Caleb and he dropped like a wet sack of dead fish. He placed the spike into the ground and raised the shovel high above his head. He paused momentarily and glared at the little bastard. In one swift motion, the shovel slashed down wildly just missing Caleb's head. It hit the spike and drove it deep into the soggy ground. Water matted down Billy's hair and his clothes were soaked. He looked like a madman. He was a madman.

He snatched Lily's collar off of the dog house and quickly put it around Caleb's neck. He took the old rope that was used to tie up Lily and threaded it through the loop in the collar. Then he secured the line to the spike in the ground. Caleb looked up with sad eyes and moaned, "Daddy!??!"

Billy ignored him and abruptly turned; splashing his way through the mud up to the screen door. He stopped and looked back at Caleb: the little guy stood up and limply gazed back at Billy. Caleb's clothes were drenched. The mud, from being dragged, painted a sickening, filthy stain on his tiny pants and blotched his face. He was crying, but one could not tell with all the rain drenching him. Billy whispered, "I'm not your daddy." Caleb couldn't hear him but could read the anger, the rejection in his face. Sobbing, he dropped to his knees, turned, and crawled into the doghouse.

CHAPTER 39 - FEAR

When Grace had come home from work that evening, the house was quiet. Billy was sleeping or passed out on the sofa. Grace was cautious as she tiptoed around the house searching for Caleb, but she couldn't find him. She looked out the back door into the yard. The rain was still drowning everything. Water flowed rapidly out of the gutters. Flowers had been knocked over by the pounding of drops, and puddles were getting beaten with pellets of moisture. She didn't see Caleb. Where was he? Then her eyes caught a subtle movement in the doghouse. She noticed a rope leading into it. The rope was tied to a spike. Wait?! A railroad spike? Again, she saw movement. She flung open the door, leaped forward when suddenly she was jerked back. Billy was clutching her by the collar of her shirt and pulled her into the kitchen. Her heels were dragging on the floor.

"You go get that kid, and it will be the last thing you ever do?" he snarled. He let her go. She dropped to the floor; water dripped from her clothing and puddled around her. Billy hovered over her. His face was menacing and not a Billy she had ever seen. "DID YOU HEAR ME!?!?" he yelled. Too afraid to talk, to move, to breath, Grace nodded her head, gasping for breath.

The panic, the fear made her a prisoner in her own body. She wanted so badly to run out, grab Caleb, caress her son, and take him away from this monster. It was fear that trapped her; that made her blind to clear thinking, to alternatives, to a way out of this misery. It was not fear for her, but fear for Caleb. A wrong move, a misinterpreted comment, a questionable facial expression might set Billy off. No! Grace was not willing to risk that. She would wait for the right time: the safe time to make her move.

. . . .

Several days had passed. Four tiny eyes peered down at the dog house from the second floor of the neighboring house. It was early, very early in the morning when Tommy and P.J., who was sleeping over, noticed tiny feet wiggling out of the dog house. Then Caleb crawled out. He sat on the cold ground watching ants climb up small, still muddy mounds they had built just before the rainstorm. The sun slowly began to rise; sending long shadows across the lawn. Two of the shadows were moving. Caleb looked up. He had visitors.

"Hi Caleb," Tommy said. P. J. gave a little wave.

Caleb said with a smile, "Hi, Tommy. Hi, P.J. Whatcha got in your hand, Tommy?"

"Oh, I thought you'd like something to eat." Tommy extended his hands out. He was cupping a plastic bowl full of Cheerios.

Caleb, said, "Thanks." Grabbed the bowl and started eating. He then extended the bowl back to Tommy and P.J. "Want some?"

"We're good, Caleb, but thank you."

The boys played like nothing was out of order. For Caleb, this was his life. He just accepted it and was, well, Caleb: happy, friendly, and content. For Tommy and P. J., they found nothing wrong with it. They thought it was cool that Caleb could sleep out in the dog house and, actually, wished they could as well.

Meanwhile, Mrs. Dalton had been inside her house searching frantically for her son and P.J. Her heart was thumping wildly. When passing by a window, she noticed the activity of the kids playing in the Keenan's back yard. Tommy's mom decompressed and relaxed somewhat. She glared out of her window studying; analyzing the scene: the boys playing, the dog house, Caleb; the little, dirty, scruffy, black boy with a leash around his neck. WHAT . . . a leash around his neck.

During the days ahead, the boys would come over and play and talk with Caleb. Caleb would even chase them and being tied to the spike made for a fun game of catch me if you can. The boys would run by Caleb, and he would try to tag them. Because he was limited by the radius of the rope, Tommy and P. J. would run beyond that point of the arc. That was their safe spot. Sometimes they would play in the dog house or their fort as they called it. The innocence, creativity, and compatibility of little people made a situation that most would find horrifying, more than tolerable; even fun.

This did not go unnoticed. Grace found hints of comfort watching her son smiling, laughing and playing as a little boy should. She would bring him out spaghetti, apples, and ice cream. Grace also was able to convince Billy that Caleb needed to come into the house to go to the bathroom: number two. While he was there, she would give him a bath and have him brush his teeth. If he had to pee, he would take care of that business behind the dog house. This act of humanity, as small as it was, allowed her to live with the guilt she felt. When anybody came over, Caleb was freed from his chains, so to speak. As soon as any visitor left, Billy brought him back out, put the collar on and secured the rope.

Billy harbored some guilt about his cruelty as well. However, he also realized that the circumstances forced Grace to be more compliant. She deserved this for what she did to him. Even to the point where she would bring him his beer after work. He made some concessions by cleaning up occasionally, but not often. The yard, the house, their world became a mess. Fear, selfishness, and apathy all became the recipe for Billy's control over Grace.

CHAPTER 40 - SUSPICIONS

Angie sat in her living room at one end of the sofa. Stephanie was sitting at the opposite end. They spoke with hushed voices although it wasn't necessary for her mom and dad were working, and her little brother was outside playing. Nonetheless, the subject was too worrisome and needed to be approached gently to prevent any bits of the topic from leaking out; not yet; at least, until they had it figured out.

Angie felt betrayed by Grace. She thought it was awful that she had slept with a man, especially a black man. She felt that Grace cheating on Billy was terrible as well. Angie didn't like Billy, but, none-the-less, Grace was married to him. He was her husband, and she was his wife for better or for worse. Angie believed in the sanctity of marriage and that one should communicate with one's spouse: be open and honest and let the other know what is bothering you. Yes! She believed that couples should do everything possible to make the marriage work.

Stephanie tried to calm her down. "Angie, try being a little understanding. We don't know what Grace has been going through." Angie just stared at the wall. Stephanie continued. "Look how Billy is now. He's a monster. I'm even afraid of him. We don't know how he acted when Grace had. . . well, you know."

"Sex! Just say it," snapped Angie. "How could she do such a thing . . . and with a black man."

"Her dad was from the North. Some of those folks don't

got no sense. He probably is . . . I mean . . . was a real free-spirit and that rubbed off on Grace."

Angie looked dubiously at Stephanie. "Aah. That's a stretch, Steph." However, that point brought back the memory of Clark. Sadness ushered them away from their criticism for they remembered how kind Clark was to everyone. Stephanie even felt a sense of guilt for bringing up such a demeaning thought about him.

"Well, what about Caleb?" said Stephanie. "He's just an innocent baby thrust into that mess."

Stephanie must have hit a soft spot in Angie. "Poor, little Caleb," she said. "I wonder how he is doing." She turned to Stephanie and said, "Something is going on at Grace's house," Angie said. "Something not good." Stephanie nodded her head in agreement.

"I feel the same way, Angie. Billy has become crazy after Caleb was born. He drinks too much, and Grace is just not the same: she's jittery, emaciated, and the coloring in her face is almost grey."

"I wish she never married him. I just don't understand," said Angie.

"What about Caleb?" I hope he is OK.

Angie's eyebrows furrowed, and she cooed, "Oh, poor, sweet Caleb. He is just so cute. Although, any time I've stopped by to see them, his knees and hands were dirty." Angie's face turned serious. "Stephanie, I think Caleb might be in danger."

"What? How? Grace would never let anything bad happen to him."

"Maybe not Grace," said Angie in a hushed voice. "But

Billy, yes. He has just become so unhinged and unpredictable. It's obvious he doesn't like Caleb the way he scowls at him. He barely even acknowledges that he exists except for those beady eyes of his staring down at him and the gross contortions his face makes when Caleb is around."

"What should we do? We don't know what the hell is going on there." Stephanie was concerned and even afraid. The Keenan house was not a safe place.

"Well, let's find out," Angie said eagerly. She had a tendency to be judgmental at times, but she also liked to play detective. She wanted to know what was going on at the Keenan's household, and she was going to find out.

"How can we do that?" asked Stephanie with a glimmer of hope.

Just then her mother entered the house and greeted the girls. The conversation abruptly ended.

. . . .

The early evening was pleasant. It was a great night to be out for a walk; in Angie's and Stephanie's case, an excellent night for spying. Inside the Keenan house, Billy was in his usual spot in front of the T.V., beer in hand. *Happy Days*, the sitcom, was showing on the T.V. Grace had just walked in from a long day at work. When she passed by Billy, she managed to pry out a smile. He waved back listlessly. His eyes followed her into the kitchen. He saw her put the six-pack on the table which she had just purchased at Donnelly's and grabbed some food from the fridge for Caleb.

After Grace had entered the house, Angie and Stephanie

quietly crept up near the front porch. They could see Billy through the window. The glow of the T.V. lit up his face, and he was clutching a beer. They decided to go to the side windows to see if they could find Grace. They crouched down and shuffled past one side window and stopped by the second window when they could discreetly look into both the living room and the kitchen. There Grace was, in the kitchen. She was getting something from the refrigerator. She started walking toward the back door. They scrambled quietly to the back, rear corner of the house to see where she was going. They were giddy about their detective surveillance and tried to muffle their giggles with their hands as they peeked around the corner.

Grace walked out of the house with a bowl of baked beans mixed with sliced hotdogs. She could hear Caleb singing as he often did when he was alone. Discarded plastic cups, paper plates, and bottles littered the ground. Hearing the back door shut, Caleb scurried out from his dog house to greet her. "Hi, mom," he said with his usual, cheery voice." Grace couldn't help but put the bowl down and to grab his sweet, brown, rosy cheeks. He was a miracle. He was a joy. He was so much stronger in his demeanor than she was in hers. She not only loved this child. She admired him.

"Hi, my little buddy. Are you doing OK today?"

"I sure am. Tommy and P. J. came over and brought me some books and this stuffed bear." He held it up for Grace to see. It was furry, brown with a shiny nose and glistening eyes.

"That's great," she said with a broad smile.

He gave the fluffy, soft bear a hug and a kiss then placed it softly back into the dog house. He turned, smiled, and sat Indian style to eat his beans and hot dogs. "Thank you for bringing me this, mom." He lifted a spoonful of the food into his mouth. "Wow, it tastes great."

Grace couldn't help but to be amazed by his gratefulness, his goodness. Here he was, her little buddy, living in a dog house, rejected by his father and, yet, so thankful and kind. "I love you, too, Caleb. I love you so very much."

He looked up after scooping another spoonful of beans and hotdogs. With a mouth full of food, he garbled, "I love you, too, mommy." She couldn't resist and leaned over from her kneeling position and hugged him. She then let him continue with his meal. He held his spoon by his side and looked up into her eyes. "And I love daddy, too." Her heart sunk. She reached her arms around him again and held him even tighter.

. . . .

Angie and Stephanie watched intensely. There giggling was replaced with lumps in their throats. They couldn't believe what they were seeing. They crept away as carefully as they could, but Stephanie stumbled over a watering can. It didn't make a lot of noise, but enough. They panicked. When they got to the street, they ran back in the direction of Angie's house.

The Keenan's front door suddenly banged opened, and Billy yelled, "Who's there?" The girls stopped abruptly and huddled together behind a tree. Billy took a few steps from the door onto the porch and used his left hand to shield the light from the porch lantern. "I said, 'Who's there!!'" The girls were terrified.

They held each other closer to shrink themselves as much as they could trying not to be seen while muffling their heavy breathing.

Billy stood silently on the porch trying to take in the sounds of the night and, more importantly, any other noises that didn't belong. He stood there for about three minutes for what seemed more like an eternity to the girls. Billy took a swig of his beer and then backed his way into the house scanning out into the darkness and eventually shutting the door. The girls waited until they felt that it was safe. Then they turned and bolted as fast as they could back to Angie's house.

CHAPTER 41 - THE CARD

The mail dropped through the opening in the front door like a mini waterfall. Billy heard the letters cascading to the floor and got up to get them. He leaned over, raked them up with his fingers, and then shuffled through them like a deck of cards. One, in particular, caught his attention. It was to Caleb in beautiful handwriting which Billy recognized immediately. He disregarded the fact that it was for Caleb and brought it and the rest of the mail to the kitchen table. Billy fanned the letters to the side and pulled out Caleb's letter. He opened it and plucked out a card. A hundred dollar bill fell to the tabletop. It was a gift from his mom that always accompanied any letter that she sent to Caleb. His eyes glanced at the bill, and then he focused on the bright, cheery card with Mickey Mouse and Goofy frolicking on the front. The outside said, "Best Buddies." The inside read, "Through thick and thin" with Mickey holding a big, fat ice-cream cone and Goofy holding a skinny licorice stick. It sure was goofy. Billy read the message that Dolly wrote.

Dear Caleb,
Your smile, your goodness, your kindness are treats
to everyone you meet.
You are a gift to all of us and, especially, to me.
Love,
Grammy Dolly

Billy held the card in his hand and looked out into nothingness. He wasn't concentrating on anything; he wasn't even in the room. Billy was back in time with his mother as a young boy. He looked down at the signature: Love, Grammy Dolly. He reread the card several times and lingered on the words *your smile, your goodness, your kindness are treats to everyone.* Again his mom surprised him. And he thought, ... she is the one with goodness and kindness. Then he whispered to himself in tenderness as he had done once before, "Mom."

He then slipped back to his miserable self. Went into the living room, plopped on the sofa and grabbed his beer. He turned on the TV: breaking news interrupted the program; John Lennon had been shot. The news pried Billy away from his own world. He loved the Beatles. He wished that he was one of them even though his music skills were so limited he couldn't carry a note in a bucket.

After the shock of the news had eased, he realized he was still holding the Goofy card. All his memories of his mom rushed back: his mom pushing him on the swing in the back yard, her singing a lullaby when he was going to bed, their rides through the countryside after getting ice cream. He was distracted momentarily, but the emotions of his family weighed heavily on his mind, especially about his mom. The images on the TV now just appeared as a blur and the voices . . . just noise.

. . . .

Pam was sitting in Ashlie's living room happy that Ashlie was near a full recovery from her knee surgery and didn't need her much longer to help around the house and shop for her. Pam missed her home. She missed her daughter, and she especially longed for little Caleb. She shut her eyes and envisioned him running around the back yard with his little buddies, Tommy and P. J. The thoughts of his captivating grin, his rosy, light, brown cheeks, and his singing made her smile.

In complete contrast, she tried to block Billy out of her mind. She couldn't have been more disappointed with him, but she still had an inkling of understanding of why he was so upset all the time. Caleb wasn't his son. Also, it was a double whammy because Caleb wasn't white either. She, too, was so disappointed with Grace, but Grace was her daughter. Pam had to live with what Grace had done, and, besides, Caleb was her grandson no matter what the circumstance and no matter who the father was. She was going to be the best damn grandmother Caleb would ever have.

The phone rang on the table waking up Ashlie who was resting in her favorite chair. She tried to get her bearings and realized it was the phone that had awakened her. She picked it up and after a few words, handed the receiver over to Pam, "It's for you."

With a questioning look, Pam took the phone and answered, "Hello." And then listened intently. Her face began to sag with worry.

"Is everything OK?" asked Ashlie.

"I hope so. I certainly hope so."

. . . .

Stephanie and Angie were skipping rocks on the lake. Angie was pretty good at it as she was able to get six hops. Stephanie's effort only produced two hops at best. It was a relatively calm day with just enough breeze to usher the sailboats along in the distance. Serene would be the word to describe the setting. However, serene would not be the word to describe the conversation Stephanie and Ange were about to embark upon. "Hello!" a voice from behind startled them. They both jumped and turned around simultaneously.

"Oh, you scared us, Mrs. Keenan."

"I'm sorry! I just wanted to let you know that I was here. Angie, you're pretty good at skipping stones."

"Thank you. The secret is to find the flattest stones. They work the best," Angie said, trying to delay the purpose of the meeting. But Pam wanted to get right down to the point.

"Now, you said it was urgent that I meet with you. And why did you want to meet at such an isolated area? We could have met at Donnelly's."

Stephanie spoke first, "Because what we have to tell you is private. We didn't want others overhearing what we have to say to you."

"And what do you have to tell me?" Pam was more than curious. She was concerned. It was unusual for the girls to request a private meeting and more unusual to have such an isolated location for the talk.

Angie and Stephanie nervously told Pam about their spying activities at the her house. They told her about Billy's excessive drinking and Grace's despondency. The news about Billy's drinking and Grace's sadness brought tears to Pam's eyes. The girls looked at each other awkwardly.

"There's more!?! Please don't keep it from me!" urged Grace's mom. She didn't know what Grace's friends were about to divulge, but her concern had erupted into fear. The girls kept exchanging quick, jittery glances. Neither one of them was wanting to go any further with the discussion. "You must tell me!!" pleaded Pam. "Don't torture me by prolonging what you want to say. What you need to say!"

Angie finally mustered enough courage to speak. She took a deep breath, let it out slowly, and followed with, "Mrs. Keenan . . . ," she paused slightly. Pam's eye's coaxed her on. "Mrs. Keenan, Caleb isn't sleeping in the house any more . . ."

"What the hell do you mean, 'Caleb isn't sleeping in the house.'" Fury replaced fear. Pam's body began to tremble. The girls were shaking as well.

Angie put her hands up in front of her creating a physical barrier between Pam and herself. "Mrs. Keenan, please, let me continue." Pam tried to compose herself and backed off. Angie pressed on, "Caleb is outside living in Lily's doghouse."

Pam gasped, "What did you say?" not believing her ears. " . . . living in the doghouse?" She paused a few seconds mired in confusion. Then a moment of determination hammered her to respond. "I'm going over there right now," she snarled through gritted teeth.

"But, Mrs. Keenan," Angie blurted trying to hold her by the shoulder, "Let us just talk to you a little more."

"I've heard enough. That Billy is evil, and I'm going to put an end to it. And Grace . . . , she's evil too." Pam swung around, took a few steps away from the girls and then suddenly dropped to her knees, cupped her face into her hands and started crying uncontrollably.

Stephanie knelt down beside her as did Angie. They didn't say anything and just patted Pam and tried to comfort her allowing her to wallow in her grief. Eventually, the heavy sobs subsided, and Pam lifted her head. "I'm sorry. I'm . . . sorry . . . ," coughed Pam between spurts of breath.

"We understand," said Stephanie. "We didn't know what to do." Stephanie glanced at Angie seeking help in her messaging. Angie stood silent so Stephanie continued: "But we were thinking we all should have some idea of what to say, of how to help Grace and Caleb? We all love them. This is. . ."

"Right now. . . I am so mad at Grace for allowing this nightmare to happen that I don't need a plan," Pam interrupted. She leaped up and turned to rush off. She took about five quick steps and then suddenly stopped. Pam slowly pivoted around and looked at the girls. "You're right!" she said in between sobs. "You're absolutely right." Angie and Stephanie approached Pam and gave her a gentle hug. They all were crying now as they tried to support each other. They will all need a lot more than a gentle hug to navigate their way through this disaster.

CHAPTER 42 - SNAPPED

"It is during our darkest moments that we must focus to see the light." Aristotle

It was getting late, and Grace had not arrived home from work yet. Billy, amazingly, became concerned: this night he didn't drink; his emotions were pure; his hostilities did not need to be lubricated. Rain began falling from the sky, and an occasional bolt of lightning would light up the evening. Where the hell was she? The phone rang and jolted Billy from the sofa. He hustled to the kitchen and grabbed the phone, "Where the hell are you?"

The voice on the other end wasn't Grace. It was Nellie. "Billy, I have some sad news for you. Some very, very sad news for you." Billy took a deep breath trying to brace for whatever news Nellie had. Was Grace in an accident? Was she OK? It wasn't that, but it was terrible news. Billy could hear Nellie sobbing over the phone.

"Nellie, what is it?" he insisted.

"Billy, your mother has died. she ..." Billy dropped the phone, fell to his knees and began gasping for breath. The heartache was massive. He never realized until that very moment how much his mother meant to him. How much he loved her. Water filled his eyes.

Billy started to scream, "Noo.... Nooooo!!!!!"

Nellie's muffled voice on the other end could barely be heard, "Are you all right, Billy? . . . Billy? . . . Billy, are you there?"

Billy fell silent. He was stunned. His face became contorted with anger and frustration and a sense of helplessness. Nellie's voice was barely audible over the phone dangling precariously from its cord. Billy then started gasping for air as more tears flooded his face. He leaped to his feet, pulled the back door open. It slammed behind him as he ventured outside.

The rain was relentless. Billy leaped off the back steps almost falling as he landed on the soaking, muddy ground. He then slipped and slid recklessly as he headed toward the garden in the deluge. Sporadic bolts of lightning flashed nearby that lit up the yard followed by loud claps of thunder. Billy grabbed a shovel leaning on the fence surrounding the garden. He turned and shuffled his way to the dog house. Caleb peaked out. His eyes were bulging with fear. Billy raised the shovel high above his head. He swung it down as hard as he could sideways. Wham. He lifted it again and thrust it down again with even a mightier blow. He then dropped the shovel and let it splash in the mud. He looked to the sky as rain caressed his face. "Help me, momma. Please help me." He then plodded to the back steps. He sat in the wetness of the boards with rain drenching him and everything around him. He buried his face in his hands and sobbed.

For what seemed like an eternity, Billy wallowed in his despair. Then he felt something on his shoulder. He looked up. It was Caleb touching him with his tiny hand. The rope hung around his neck with the shredded end menacingly flopping in the wind and the rain. With a mountain of tenderness, Caleb softly said, "Are you OK, Daddy."

Billy gazed into Caleb's light, brown face as tiny streams of rainwater trickled down. Quietly, Billy said, "Yes. Yes, I am, . . . son." He then pulled Caleb close to his chest and hugged him. "Yes, I am, my son." The rain poured down, and a slight shadow moved behind them. Grace, stood at the back door, smiled and teared up as she looked at her son....and his father embracing each other.

. . . .

The loss of a loved one impacts people differently. Many go through several stages beginning with denial and isolation, onto anger, then bargaining, moving to depression, and, finally, acceptance. Others may be involved with some but not all of these stages. Some folks don't cope at all and fall into a deep depression to never get up again. Others, however, become tortured by their feelings of guilt that colors their whole life. With Billy, the guilt hit him as soon as he heard that his mother had died. It hit him like a Mack Truck. He had hurt his mother with his attitude, his actions, and his words. Dolly's death reminded Billy of those hurts and failings; of words, he immediately regretted saying; incidents he'd like to forget; that could never be erased.   He thought of her kindness and her caring for Caleb. Her goodness was a lesson he had dismissed but, with her death, those lessons rang loud and clear in his mind. Billy instantly sought to make amends. Caleb was loved by his own mother, and Billy's mother, and now it was Billy's need to love Caleb as well, to make amends for his horrible decisions. He just hoped that it wasn't too late.

That night Caleb slept in the house for the first time in

many months. He slept closely between his mother and his father. His mother and father had not been in the same bed in
years. It was not Caleb who needed to be comforted. It was
Billy, Caleb's father, who needed this time to heal the wounds
of bitterness and cruelty that he had imposed on his son and
on Grace. He had to cleanse himself somehow; to shake the
guilt. He needed to be loved by the ones he had hurt most. Billy
longed for their forgiveness to extinguish the guilt and the shame
that he suffered within himself.

Billy was fortunate to have married Grace who epitomized
goodness; to have Caleb whose innocence and kindness blos-
somed each day he matured. These two people in Billy's life were
the only ones that could make him whole and extend himself beyond what he used to be: a selfish, spoiled, cruel, manipulative
being. But could forgiveness be bestowed upon Billy by the two
whom he had harmed the most?

While Grace and Caleb slept on the same bed as him, Billy
leaned over to the nightstand and picked up the card his mother
had given to Caleb. In the moonlight cast through the window,
he reread his mother's words:

Dear Caleb,
Your smile, your goodness, your kindness
 are treats to everyone you meet.
You are a gift to all of us and especially to me.
Love,
Grammy Dolly

When he finished, he looked up and repeated a portion

of the note to himself: "Your goodness, your kindness." He held the card close to his heart, closed his eyes tightly and quietly murmured, "Mom, your goodness and kindness are a gift to me. I'm so sorry I never told you." He bowed his head, put the card back on the table and looked at Grace and Caleb sleeping and whispered, "And your goodness and kindness are a gift to me. I will not make the mistake of not telling you ever again." Caleb squirmed a little. Grace had her arm draped over him. Billy laid his head on the pillow, pulled the sheets up to his chin, and smiled as he closed his eyes.

. . . .

Pam was at Ashlie's gathering her belongings about to head back to her house when the phone rang. From a back room, Ashlie called out, "Could you get that, Pam?"

Pam picked it up and, to her surprise, it was Grace. She jumped into the conversation with the news of Billy's mom's death. She told her that Dolly had died of a heart attack and that it was extremely unusual for a woman her age. Apparently, Dolly had had a congenital heart problem as a child, and it had never been diagnosed. She had died of a congestive heart attack.

Pam was caught off guard by this news. She was saddened. Over the phone was not the time to talk about Grace's family issues. Though, tomorrow was. She said she'd like to see Grace in the morning and that she was moving back and that they had a lot to discuss. Grace was happy with the thought of having her mom at the house again even though the sadness of Billy's mom's death clouded the homecoming. She couldn't wait to have her mother back to share time together and to talk. However, Grace had no idea that her mom had more to talk to her about other than Mrs. Cromwell's death.

. . . .

Billy wasn't at home. He was at the mansion with Nellie who was quite shaken up about Mrs. Cromwell's passing. Mr. Cromwell was on his way back from a business trip and would meet up with Billy and Nellie as soon as possible. So it was just Grace and Pam.

Grace was so happy to see her mom: not so much Pam to see her. Grace gave her a hug when her mom walked into the home. Pam lightly hugged her back and then grabbed her by the shoulders, pushed her away at arm's length, and stared her in the face. "Pam, we've got to talk," she said sternly. Pam was a little shocked. She wasn't expecting that. Her mother took her by the arm and guided her to the sofa. They both sat down and angled to face each other.

Her mom wanted to get right to the point and didn't mix words. "Grace, I have heard about Caleb living in the dog house," she said trying to control her anger. "Billy's the one who should be out there in the dog house with his attitude and drinking. Why didn't you call me?" Her voice rose and became shrill. " Why would you let this happen?"

Grace leaned toward her mother seeking forgiveness. As she wrung her hands together tightly, Grace pleaded, "I'm sorry, mom! I'm so sorry! Please help me." Pam kept silent allowing Grace to tell her side. She wanted to scream at her daughter but contained her anger inside. "I wanted to do something, but I didn't know what to do. Billy was so...so mean and threatening. I didn't want him to hurt Caleb."

If Billy had been there, Pam would have attacked him with a butcher knife. Her anger now shifted to Billy, and she was livid. However, she still managed to keep up a thin veil of composure and let Grace continue. "But mom, Billy has changed," Grace said with earnest eyes. I know it has only been a few days, but he isn't drinking anymore. He is with Caleb every chance he has. And, mom," Grace paused and meekly smiled. "Caleb calls him daddy . . . and Billy calls him son."

Pam started to settle a bit, but she thought to herself: It's not that easy. She was disillusioned by her daughter. She couldn't believe how naive she was. But Grace was her daughter, her baby, and now Pam had to do everything that she could to right this horrible wrong. "Grace, he will have to prove it to me. Now that I'm back home, I will be watching every move Billy makes. If he says or does anything to you or Caleb that is hurtful, he's out of here. He can take his crappy Bronco and go back to his fucking mansion." That was the first time Grace had ever heard her mother use the "F" word. Hopefully, it would be that last.

. . . .

The funeral was short and lightly attended. Mr. Cromwell and Nellie sat in the front pew on the left side of the aisle. Billy, Grace, and Caleb were settled on the right side accompanied by Grace's mom and her good friend, Ashlie, who was on the tail end of her recovery. The seating arrangement reflected the hostility that Mr. Cromwell had toward Billy. He still wanted no part of his son, and, even in this most somber of occasions, distanced himself from Billy. While sitting, Billy felt this distance reverberate through his body. And then he thought about Caleb. Billy did not want ever to shun his son as he had done previously and how his father continues to do so toward Billy till this day: this very sad day.

Billy turned to look at the attendees. Among the scattered faces, he recognized some as friends of his father, and some were distant relatives he had only seen in pictures. However, he did recognize the three people in the pew directly behind his father and Nellie: Judy, Dora, and Alex who conveyed no expressions of sadness. They sat erect with an occasional smile. Alex would poke one of the girls now and then. His facial contortions reflected the humor he found in this. The girls would muffle their giggles with cupped hands as Billy's mother lay in her coffin in front of the altar. Billy contained the rage that was building up within him. Grace looked at him noticing his body stiffen and the tightness in his eyes. She reached down and put her hand on Billy's. He looked at her, and calm was restored.

The ingredients for a blowup in the church were all there: anger, despair, guilt, hatred, deception, avoidance. But nothing of extreme ever occurred. After the service, folks gathered in front of the church to pay their respects. Norman never even so much as peeked at his son. Billy had looked over at his father for some hint of recognition but never received any. Nellie greeted Billy, Grace, and Pam. She expressed her sorrow to Dolly's son. Billy reciprocated knowing that her heart was as heavy as his if not heavier in the loss of Dolly. Nellie and Dolly had become very close. Billy gave her a gentle hug. Judy, Dora, and Alex walked by Billy; shot him a glance, a quick smile; and departed the front of the church. Yes! It was awkward, but, in this case, that was good. Between Billy's coerced composure and Grace's gentle coaxing as well as being at the house of the lord, calamity had been averted. Hallelujah!

CHAPTER 43 - WICKED

Mr. Cromwell drove back home with Nellie after the funeral. The bucolic meadows, streams, forests they passed by mellowed the variety of sentiments they both felt. They harbored conflicting emotions. Norman's mind was swirling with . . . what the hell do I do now . . . thoughts. Whereas, Nellie was weighted down by sadness for the loss of Dolly who had become a dear friend in the large, lonely mansion. In many people's mind, the estate represented success, happiness, and fulfillment. Not for Nellie. Death has a way of stripping away the significance of "stuff." Even though it wasn't Nellie's "stuff," she had been a part of it. Lived it. With Dolly gone, a feeling of emptiness engulfed her.

Mr. Cromwell broke the silence, "What are you thinking, Nellie?"

Nellie continued looking out the window at the countryside. "I was thinking how much I will miss her, sir."

"So will I, Nellie. So will I."

On the remainder of the ride home, both were consumed with their thoughts. The countryside seemed to beckon to them with its beauty and tranquility: horses grazed in pastures, hawks flew in the blue sky above, hills with their majestic shadow variations appeared in the distance. But Norman and Nellie were blind to the natural beauty around them. Only silence, sadness and darkness occupied the shiny, black Mercedes.

When they arrived home, they saw the faded, blue Cadillac parked in the horseshoe driveway. Mr. Cromwell parked the car outside the four-car garage. As they got out, they could hear laughter and splashing coming from the pool area. Nellie simply said, "I'm going inside now, sir. Do you need me for anything?"

"No, Nellie. Thank you." He removed his suit jacket, swung it over his shoulder and walked to the back of the house toward the pool. Alex had just made a belly flop off the diving board landing next to Dora who was on a pony, blowup float. Judy was laying down on a chaise lounge where Dolly always had sunned herself. "Jessie's Girl" by Rick Springfield was blasting from the radio. Judy's back was cropped up so she could see the buffoonery taking place in the pool. She had a full glass of wine in her hand, and Dolly's sunglasses were resting on top of her head. Norman didn't seem to notice the sunglasses. He was too busy staring at Judy's assets.

In her room, Nellie had finished sobbing her eyes out. It would not be the same for her around the mansion without Dolly. She managed to make her way to the kitchen and glanced out the window. Dora and Alex were riding the golf carts off in the distance near the woods. The pool area was free of any activity. Judy and Mr. Cromwell were nowhere to be found. All the pool furniture were angled this way and that way. She saw Mrs. Cromwell's sunglasses resting on Dolly's favorite lounge and a half-empty bottle of wine sitting on the tile with a wine glass resting on its side. By the chair next to it, rested two empty cans of beer. Her eyes scanned the entire back area. Hooting and laughter from the cart riders filled the air. Nellie looked at the pool house. Its door was closed, the shades were shut. Nellie shook her head and went back to her room.

. . . .

The Keenan household was thriving. Pam had come back home to live, and Billy had gone back to the furniture store and somehow worked some magic to get his job back. Billy was a changed man: he felt productive; he was gainfully employed; he was being responsible. At home, Billy cleaned the gutters, cut the lawn, picked up the mess that he had created in the back yard. He would help out with the gardening, Grace by his side, and Caleb running around with Tommy and P.J. Tommy's mother, Mrs. Dalton, watched from her window with curious eyes.

This weekend day was no different. Billy, Grace, and Caleb were outside in the garden pulling weeds as Pam was preparing a large spaghetti dinner for them all. A vehicle screeched to a stop in front of the Keenan home. Car doors slammed followed by loud banging at the front door. Pam, startled, rushed to see what was going on.

"What the heck was that? Billy said to Grace. They both stood up from the garden when Pam opened the back door. Behind her was Judy glowing with excitement. Her smile was stretching from ear to ear. Alex and Dora were crammed behind her.

"Billy, you've got company . . ." Pam tried to say just as

Judy nudged her aside with her posse scooting after her. She was holding out her hand as she ran toward Billy.

"Look!! Look what your father gave me," she gushed. On her finger sparkled a huge diamond resting in a nest of gleaming, smaller diamonds. "Your father asked me to marry him, Billy . . . and I said, 'YES!!!'"

Billy was stunned to say the least. Grace couldn't believe it. And Pam, from her perch, shook her head.

"Billy, do you know what this means?" cackled Judy with Alex and Dora snickering behind her. Billy simply shook his head "no" in a perplexed manner. "It means I'm going to be your stepmom." She started jumping around staring at her ring. Billy wanted to throttle her. Grace was beside herself. Pam just bowed her head, and Caleb began dancing and clapping his hands.

CHAPTER 44 - SCHOOL

Caleb was going to go to kindergarten. For the first time, he was going to go to school and was excited, enormously excited. Pam had purchased brand new clothes for him and not the Goodwill items Grace had dressed him with. He had new sneakers which he kept peeking down at. This made it difficult for Grace to comb his hair with his little head bobbing up and down. "Come on, Caleb, hold still, little buddy."

He looked up with a huge smile and said, "I'm going to school." He had been on visitation trips to get used to his new "home" away from home. He also had been tested to see if he was at the correct developmental age. He was not. His knowledge, apparently, had been disrupted from his doghouse experience where learning did not take place.

Another revelation was that he could not run at full capacity. For the months, he had slept in the cramped conditions of the doghouse. As a result, his bone development in his right leg had been slightly impaired. Pointing to a bone diagram; the doctor described it this way to the distraught mom and the guilt-ridden dad: "The fibula, the long bone, the thinner of the two leg bones, is located lateral to the tibia. The proximal part of the fibula has an enlarged head that forms a joint with the tibia." Here he pointed and then continued. The shafts of the tibia and fibula are connected by an interosseous membrane. It's a sheet of connective tissue that fills most of the space between the two bones. The membrane has one opening at the top that allows for passage of blood vessels. . . "

Billy grew inpatient and broke in, "Doctor, I'm sorry. But I have no idea what you're saying."

The doctor looked at Billy and Grace apologetically and said, "Well, let's just say that the connective tissues growth had been weakened." He paused, "Caleb will have this impairment, slight as it is, for the rest of his life." Grace leaned forward in her seat and stared at the doctor. He noticed her frantic eyes and tried to assuage her fears as well as Billy's. "Let me just emphasize the word slight. Caleb will be able to function very well in life. Will he be a star quarterback? No! But will he have a full, mobile life? Absolutely!"

On the way home, Billy expressed his regret for what he had done to Caleb. His remorse was genuine and heartfelt. His eyes shifted to Grace, ". . . and I'm so sorry for what I put you through, too, Grace." She, as always, took the empathic road patting Billy on his thigh and then leaning her head on his shoulder as he drove.

Pam had been caring for Caleb. When they opened the front door of their home and walked inside, Caleb ran up to them and wrapped his arms around Billy' s legs.

"I love you, daddy," he said as he leaned his head back looking up at Billy.

"I love you, too, my little buddy."

Then Caleb hugged his mom in the same fashion. He took his mom's hand and then his daddy's and marched them into the kitchen where Pam had been seated with coloring books and crayons. "I'm going to school," he sang. "I'm going to school."

. . . .

Billy wasn't invited to the wedding nor did he want to attend anyway. He was baffled by his father's lapse in judgment. Norman was considered to be a no-nonsense man and, yet, he goes out and marries this ditz. He hated the idea of Judy living in his house, inviting her posse over, and getting slobbered by the pool. He thought of poor, sweet Nellie who had been nothing but dedicated and kind to him and especially to his mother. Now she had to deal with a manipulative, backstabbing bitch. He knew that Judy would play his dad like a puppet, pulling strings to make him jump, releasing them to make him fall until she got all the "stuff" that she could.

Billy and Grace were in the kitchen having a sandwich when the phone rang. Grace got up to answer it. "Hi, Nellie. It is nice to hear . . . Nellie is everything OK," She pauses and shrugs her shoulders looking at Billy. "No, no. That's OK. Just take a deep breath and then continue." Billy gives her a questioning, concerned look, Grace looks back and reaches the phone out to Billy. "It's Nellie. She wants to talk to you."

. . . .

Billy didn't know his old Bronco could travel that fast; trees, houses, fencing were all blurs as he sped by. He turned into his father's horseshoe driveway, the wheels screeching. Billy saw Nellie kneeling; bent over crying on the front entrance way.

He slammed on the breaks, leaped out of the car, and ran up to her.

"Mr. Billy, I'm so hap...happy to see you," she said between sobs as Billy tried to comfort her.

"Nellie, what's going on?" he asked, lifting Nellie and walking her inside to the kitchen. They sat down. Billy glanced outside while he was lowering Nellie into a chair. He noticed beer cans, wine bottles, trash strewn everywhere. A fleeting memory of his own back yard raced through his mind, and he quickly erased it.

Through sobs, Nellie explained how Judy had her posse over the previous night: they had invited other people over as well since Mr. Cromwell was away on business; the partying had gotten crazy; people had thrown beer bottles into the pool; guys had relieved themselves just outside the fence; celebrators had driven the golf carts wildly crashing them into shrubs. One of the carts ended up at the bottom of the pond, and there was heavy usage of the pool house. Some of the guests tried to move the party indoors. That was it for Nellie: she locked all the doors to protect the Cromwell's belongings and to protect herself.

"Oh, Mr. Billy! I was so...o sc..scared," she stuttered. "And that Ju...d Jud..y," she could hardly get the name out, "kep..t yell...ing at m..me and lau...gh..ing with h..er lou..d ca..ckle."

"Where is she, now?" inquired Billy. He was pissed.

Nellie gained a little more composure. "She, she, left this morn..ing to go for brea..k..fast with Dora, and A..lex."

"Why didn't they eat here?"

Nellie looked up and for the first time and entertained a smile, a sly one at that. "Because I never unlocked the doors. I wouldn't let them in, and I sure as heck wasn't going to make them breakfast."

Even Billy smiled, patted her on the back and said, "You done good, Nellie."

She looked at Billy and said, " There's more. Judy screamed at me, 'You better have this place cleaned up by the time we get back or you'll be sorry, bitch.' Oh, Mr. Billy, I don't know what to do. I'm afraid," as Nellie started to tear up again.

With that, Billy uttered, "Grab some clothing, Nellie. You're coming with me."

CHAPTER 45 - KNOCK AT THE DOOR

Nellie had taken up Billy's former spot for sleeping purposes: the sofa. She was happy to be with the people she loved and people who loved her. Nellie didn't need the big house and all the glitter and glitz that came with it. She was where she wanted to be. Caleb raised her spirits every day with his smile, his joy, and his energy. She also was cheered by the company of Pam, Grace, and the occasional visit from Ashlie. Billy had matured and assumed the responsibilities of being a husband and a father beyond what Nellie had ever anticipated. She was proud of Billy, and she admired Billy. Nellie only wished that Billy's father could see the young man his son had become and not let money be the determining factor in assessing a man's real worth. His loss, she thought.

Caleb had gone to school. Billy and Grace had headed off to work. Nellie and Pam had a chance to chat in the kitchen as they cleaned the dishes from an apple pancake feast Nellie had prepared for them all. As Pam washed the dishes, Nellie wiped them dry while talking about Caleb and how he was doing, and he was doing great.

Pam looked out the kitchen window over the sink and admired the manicured yard. Billy had devoted much time making it a useful, appealing play area for Caleb and a pleasant family retreat for everyone. He was able to purchase new outdoor furniture from his job. The picnic table had a bouquet of flowers sitting in the middle of it. The new chairs were spaced in perfect order around it. And a few extra chairs were situated next to outdoor side tables which also had small vases with an array of flowers from their garden. Billy had even painted the dog house a vibrant blue, Caleb's favorite color. Billy had hung up the collar on the side of the little house. Caleb wanted to keep it in case they ever got another dog. The railroad spike had been cleaned to the point of almost shining and placed back in Grace's drawer on top of the ten dollar bill that read:

Grace,
Let forgibnes, undirstandin, an luv
gide you thru life.
C.M.

Every now and then, Billy, in a weak moment, would open the drawer and read the message. He gained strength and direction from the words. Grace, too, would take time to pick up the bill and read the words that C.M. wrote. She would also think about how much of a blessing Caleb had been in their lives. Neither spouse was aware that the other had referred to the note on occasions. Nor did they realize that they each garnered such strength from the message.

. . . .

The woman walked up to the Keenan home and made some mental notes about its condition. Although Billy had worked diligently at restoring the back yard, the front had been denied such attention. It was next on Billy's list of things to do, but first things first. The porch swing had been secured with two chains, but other than that and the lawn having been cut, the house was still in disrepair. It needed painting and porch railings had to be nailed into place. No! The appearance of the Keenan home did not create a good image.

Pam and Nellie heard the light, but a deliberate knock at the door. They looked curiously at each other as Pam quickly dried her hands. She walked the front of the house to answer the door, reached for the handle and pulled. It groaned open. Standing in front of her was a professional looking woman with dark-rimmed glasses and light, brown hair scooped up in a bun. Her skirt settled just below the knees, and she wore a white blouse peeking out of the neck opening of a grey sweater. The fingers in her right hand were curled around the handle of a brown, leather briefcase.

"Hello?" said Pam tentatively.

"Hello," said the woman with a disarming smile. "I'm from the Child Protective Services and would like to talk to Mr. and Mrs. Cromwell. May I come in." Caught off guard, Pam hesitantly moved aside to allow the woman to enter. She escorted her to the sofa which had been tidied up from Nellie's bed.

"Have a seat," gestured Pam as Nellie walked to the entrance way of the living room from the kitchen. Pam sat down at the opposite end of the sofa.

"I'm sorry to bother you. My name is Mrs. Katie Hubbuch, and I am from the Child Protective Services." Pam and Nellie gave each other a puzzled look. "We investigate cases of abuse or neglect, and we have reason to believe that...," She looked at her folder, "...that little Caleb may have been the victim of abuse in your home."

Someone may have well taken a baseball bat and hit Pam over the head. The words "victim" and "abuse" slammed down hard. Mrs. Hubbuch continued, "We have received concern from a neighbor that Caleb was left outside for some time to fend for himself, alone and neglected." She waited and, again, took mental notes as she observed the two women. Shock was the only emotion that registered. "We also have medical records that indicate a physical impairment that may have originated from physical abuse." Again, she paused to observe the two women and, again, the read was shock. "Are you residents of the home and what are your relationships to Caleb?"

Pam tried to get herself together, "I'm Caleb's grand-mother."

Nellie was clueless about this entire revelation. She spoke up, "And I'm Nellie, a friend of the family."

"Are Mr. and/or Mrs. Cromwell at home?"

"No, they're not," said Pam.

"Well, we would like an at home visitation with them, and we would like to talk to Caleb .... alone," Mrs. Hubbuch reached into her briefcase and pulled out her business card. Please have either Mr. or Mrs. Cromwell give me a call to arrange a visitation at their earliest convenience and with Caleb home so we can talk to him as well."

Pam reached for the card, looked at it, and breathed deeply. Mrs. Hubbuch rose, extended her hand to shake Grace's who was still sitting. "Thank you for your time. If you or Mr. or Mrs. Cromwell have any questions, please don't hesitate to call." Nellie went into her maid mode and accompanied Mrs. Hubbuch to the door. She opened it to allow Mrs. Hubbuch to exit. Mrs. Hubbuch turned, "Thank you, Nellie," and proceeded down the walkway to her car. Nellie shut the door, looked back at Pam who was now a wreck on the sofa with her hands cupped over her eyes.

. . . .

The chime rang as Grace and Pam entered Donnelly's store after work. Their heads were swirling with concern over the Department of Child Protective Services accusations and the possible consequences. Mrs. Donnelly, who had become an expert at reading faces over the years, could see that they were both distraught. She prepared their favorites: a vanilla coke and chocolate chip ice cream, and quietly placed them in front of the two women. She didn't say anything, but presented a face of empathy, went on with her duties, and let the woman talk.

"Mom, I'm so worried something terrible may happen."

"Grace, all we can do is wait and see. Just hold on to optimism," said Pam trying to comfort her. Her daughter remained quiet. Mrs. Donnelly went about her business of clearing the counter from earlier customers.

"But, mom, what if they take Caleb away from us?" said a rattled Grace.

"That won't happen!" said Pam emphatically. But down deep inside, she doubted herself. Lynnda couldn't help but hear. She glanced up and then went back to her work.

"Now, how many days is it before Mrs. Hubbuch and the supervisor come for the visitation, mom?"

"It's five days before they come to the house."

The mother and daughter paused in thought when Grace's demeanor changed, and a crooked smile creased her face. "I've got an idea, mom. Let's go!" She grabbed her mother's hand, and they both slid off their stools. With renewed energy, Grace headed for the door gently pulling her mother along while licking her chocolate chip ice cream.

Mike had just slipped out of the back room when the door closed behind Grace and Pam ringing the chimes. Lynnda had come around next to Mike. They watched their friends through the store window walk on their way home. The Donnelly's shared a look of concern and Mike gave Lynnda a reassuring hug.

"Will everything be OK?" asked Mike.

Lynnda, not knowing fully about the trouble Pam and Grace faced, gave a disturbed response, "I hope so. I sure hope so."

CHAPTER 46 - A PLAN

The Keenan house was steaming with activity as it had been for three days straight. Ninette and Stephanie were inside mopping, vacuuming, washing away fingerprints, cleaning windows . . . the works. Angie and Grace were in the back yard sprucing up the garden, planting shrubs and laying down red, bark mulch consisting of a cedar/pine blend. Billy and Shaun were painting the back of the house. Shaun concentrated on the trim work because he was a little more meticulous than Billy. Billy was trying, but Billy still lacked the skill to do fine hand-eye coordinated tasks. He was slapping paint on the clapboard which didn't require the care that the trim work did.

In the front of the house, Nellie and Ashlie were trimming the shrubs, edging the garden areas, and spreading the same deep, red bark mulch as that of the back yard. Pam was painting the trim white and Chris, the clapboard, a soft grey. Jaybird, as everyone called him, was putting the final touches on the porch. They were like brothers joking, teasing, and having fun while they painted. It was a social event, not just for the three "brothers" but for everyone. It was that way from the first time they started the work; when the house was a mess and had to be prepped by scraping and sanding the old paint off. They had decided on grey clapboard, white trim, and black shutters. "Eye of the Tiger" by Survivor was blaring from the radio in the back yard and could be heard in the front as well.

However, on day three, it was almost done. The only

things left were to complete the final steps of touching up, hanging the shutters, spreading the rest of the mulch, and putting away all the ladders, paint cans, garden supplies, and anything else they could think of. It was just about four o'clock. The grill had been started, and the hotdogs and hamburgers were sizzling. The team of workers was washing out their buckets and cleaning their hands under the hose. Caleb with his buddies were running around the dog house shooting each other with water pistols.

Jaybird and Shaun had just finished putting up the last shutter. Shaun came around from the front of the house and called out, "OK, everyone. Come take a look." Caleb, Tommy, and P. J. scurried ahead of the group still squirting at each other, hands flapping, trying to deflect the streams of water. Everyone else moved a little more slowly carrying the aches and pains for all their labor. Pam stayed behind tending to the burgers and hotdogs. She turned down the volume of the radio as Eddie Rabbitt, and Crystal Gayle sang "You and I".

When they gathered in front of the home by the street, all of them were amazed at how beautiful the house appeared. It was a cozy cottage now. The landscaping was impeccable. All the shrubs were trimmed perfectly, and the fresh mulch was red and vibrant. Nellie's idea of transplanting flowers and placing them in strategic spots enhanced the look completely. The colorful marigolds and impatiens added the pop the front needed. The house stood out in a charming way. The combination of colors accented the architectural lines, and the white trim framed the windows and hi-lighted the porch. Bob Vila from This Old House would be impressed with this crew. What pleased Grace the most was the porch swing. The guys had replaced the chains holding it up with bright stainless steel ones. The swing had been restored to a glossy white piece of furniture. Instantly, visions of Grace and her dad ran through her mind. She thought of how happy he would be now . . . for she was ecstatic.

She turned and hugged Billy who was smiling from ear to ear. Then she turned to all her friends and said, "You guys are the best. I love you. Thank you, thank, thank you." They all moved in for a group hug. Between the forest of legs crawled Caleb only to pop up and give his mom and dad a big hug.

. . . .

The black Mercedes drove slowly down the street, past the grey house with the white trim. It then stopped, turned around and parked across the street from the Keenan home. The driver walked up slowly observing the condition of the home. Although the cottage was tiny, he was impressed with the landscaping, the colors of the house, and the charming appearance. The knock on the door was gentle but deliberate, reminding the residents of Mrs. Hubbuch's tapping.

Grace nervously got up from the kitchen chair where she, Pam, and Nellie were raving about how beautiful the house looked. She walked to the door smiling and pulled it open. Mr. Cromwell greeted her with, "Hello, Grace. May I come in." He was dressed more casually than the usual black suit. He had on new jeans, a white polo shirt, and white tennis sneakers.

Grace was dumbfounded. She and Mr. Cromwell had never talked, and the incident at Donnelly's still hung vividly in her mind with him standing over her. However, his appearance this time was less intimidating. "Yes, come in." The words tumbled out of her mouth.

"I know this is awkward, but I would like to talk with Nellie if I may."

His politeness was a side she had not seen before and especially from a no-nonsense businessman like Mr. Cromwell. "I'll get her. Please sit down." She began to walk to the kitchen then turned. "Would you like to see Billy?"

He assumed a pensive posture and said, "No. That will not be necessary."

She turned and went to get Nellie who was already aware of Mr. Cromwell's presence. She carried a worried expression and mouthed, "What does he want?"

Grace shrugged her shoulders. Nellie looked at Pam and Grace and then peeked out to the living room. She saw the white sneakers and dark jeans Mr. Cromwell was wearing but not his face. She slowly rose and shuffled out to the living room where Mr. Cromwell sat. He immediately got up, smiled, and, in a gentlemanly way, offered her the chair next to the sofa. She sat down nervously. *What the hell is he doing here?*

"Nellie, I miss you. Actually, it's more than that; I need you." She just stared back waiting. He continued, "I know why you left, and I don't blame you. I told Mrs. Cromwell ...." Nellie's body shuddered at hearing the title, Mrs. Cromwell. To her, there were only two Mrs. Cromwell's. One was her dear friend, Dolly, and the other was Billy's wife, Grace. No way in hell would or should that witch, Judy, ever get the distinction of being associated with those two, fine women. ". . . that her friends, Dora and Alex, are no longer welcomed to our estate." He waited for a reaction. None. He pressed on, "I would like you to come back with me today. I will make sure Judy treats you with respect and kindness..." Those were two words that Nellie had never heard Mr. Cromwell utter: respect and kindness. ". . . and I will make sure that in your retirement you will never ever have any financial concerns." He waited.

Just then, from the kitchen, Billy walked in. "Hi, dad." His dad simply stared at him. "It's nice to see you." Norman just continued to stare. Billy mustered up the courage to speak to his dad who had been an impenetrable fortress of stoicism to him all his life. "I couldn't help but overhear your conversation with Nellie." Then he looked at Nellie. "Nellie, you know you are part of this family, and we all love you." What Billy had to say next was difficult for him. He gulped and just threw the words out to get it over with. "But dad's offer is more than generous and provides security for you in the future. As hard as it is for me to say this: Nellie, take his offer." Norman smiled approvingly.

Hesitantly, Nellie responded, "Do you really I should, Mr. Billy."

"I do. You are always more than welcome here, but now you have to think of your future and your welfare."

Nellie sat in her seat quietly for a few minutes. In her head, she weighed the loss she would feel by leaving the family she loved and the horror she would have to face back at the mansion: Judy. She looked up at Billy. His gentle encouraging eyes seemed to plead with her to take care of herself, her future. Nellie looked around the room, then at Billy and Mr. Norman. "I will get my things, Mr. Cromwell." She smiled weakly, got up,

TRAIN TRACKS - 235

and walked out of the room to collect her items to leave the home, . . . the family that she loved.

Mr. Cromwell witnessed a different son before him than he had known in the past. A feeling shuddered through him, but he didn't know what it was. Hard to understand when a wall had been obstructing emotions all these years. "Thank you, Billy."

Billy looked at his dad, "You're welcome. I just want what's best for Nellie."

While Nellie gathered her belongings, Grace and Pam wandered into the living room. They had heard the conversation and Nellie's decision. Mr. Cromwell stood and spoke, "I almost didn't recognize the place when I drove up. You've done a terrific job with it." That was the closest that Billy had ever come to a compliment from his dad. He wrapped it up like a package in his mind and locked it in a vault.

"Thank you," Billy said. "But I can't take the credit. "It was Grace and all of her friends and Pam and her friend who deserve most of the kudos."

Mr. Cromwell looked at Grace and Pam, smiled and nodded his approval. Nellie entered the room, baggage in hand, "I'm ready, sir."

Just then the back door swung open, and Caleb ran into the house laughing, "I've got to fill my squirt...." He stopped abruptly and smiled up at the well-dressed man even though it was just jeans and a white polo shirt in front of him. "Hello, I'm Caleb," he said with his bubbly voice. "Who are you?"

Mr. Cromwell got down on one knee, eye level with Caleb, "Why, I'm Billy's daddy."

Caleb's eyes widened, and then he leaped forward and hugged Mr. Cromwell. He cooed, "Daddy's daddy."

. . . .

Mr. Cromwell put his vehicle into drive. Nellie leaned over and waved to her "family" who were gathered on the porch. They all waved back choking the emotions which stirred inside each and every one of them. Billy picked up Caleb. Grace put her arm around Billy's waist as they walked back into the house followed by Pam. The black Mercedes drove away with the afternoon sun reflecting off of it.

CHAPTER 47 - INNOCENCE

The large, black SUV pulled up to the Keenan home. Mrs. Hubbuch and the male driver got out, and both took a minute or two to check out the exterior of the house. In a home visitation, everything is taken into consideration. Examined would possibly be a better word to use. It was evident to Mrs. Hubbuch that the home had experienced an incredible transformation. It was not only improved. It was appealing. As they walked up to the door, her male companion commented on how nice everything looked. However, the focus is always on the child. Certainly, if a home is a dump with potential hazards existing, that would be a red flag. The Keenan house passed that "examination" with flying colors. Score one for the good guys. But there was more to a home visitation than landscaping and paint.

Earlier that day, Grace was frantic selecting just the right clothes, picking up breakfast dishes, fluffing pillows. Billy wasn't any better. He put a lot of thought into what he would wear as well. Initially, he picked out a gray suit and selected a conservative matching tie. When Grace walked into the room, she immediately shook her head "no."

"Billy, it's a nice thought, but we shouldn't overdo it."

"Well, what would you suggest?" he asked with a hint annoyance."

"Just something safe; like khaki pants and one of those polo shirts you have in the closet." He was satisfied and went for the change. He stared at Grace: she looked beautiful. She wore a simple white blouse ruffled at the sleeves and black pants. A delicate silver necklace curled around her neck. She had let her hair hang down but tied into a ponytail in back. She had a minimal amount of makeup on. In fact, you could hardly tell if she had any makeup on at all; a very natural look.

Caleb was up in Pam's bedroom with her. She was reading to him and sometimes he would start singing. Sometimes they sang together. He wanted to learn how to play Grampa Keenan's guitar which was leaning in the corner of the bedroom. "Another time," Pam suggested.

"OK," Caleb said, and they continued singing Old Mac-Donald for the third time. It was his favorite song. He loved making the animal sounds.

From outside the living room window, Grace saw the black vehicle parking in front of the house. She called up upstairs, "They're here, Billy." He quickly brushed his hair and hopped down the stairs, two steps at a time, to join her.

Grace opened the door with Billy rushing up to stand behind her.

Grace answered with her most charming voice, "Oh! Hi, Mrs. Hubbuch. I'm Grace, and this is my husband, Billy. Please come in." The gentleman followed her inside, and Grace greeted him as well, "Hello, Sir." He smiled back at her and said, "Hi," and nodded to Billy on the way by.

Grace hurried to catch up to Mrs. Hubbuch directing her and the gentleman to the sofa. They sat down, and Billy and Grace sat down as well. Mrs. Hubbuch spoke first, "It's so nice to meet you in person, Billy, and Grace. Thank you for calling so soon to set up the visitation." They both smiled back at her. "It was also nice to have met your mother, Grace. She is a lovely woman."

"She is wonderful. In fact, she is upstairs with Caleb reading to him. Should I get them?"

"No! Not now. I'd like to introduce you to Mr. Paul Sanguine. He is our supervisor at the Department of Child Protective Services." Billy and Grace rose instinctively to shake hands. He was dressed casually and didn't have the appearance of an official. If Billy had to guess, he would say the man was around fortyish. He wore a blue shirt and khaki pants with loafers on his feet. He smiled and leaned forward a bit from his sitting position to shake their hands. Caleb could be heard upstairs singing.

When everyone was settled, Mr. Sanguine spoke softly, "Mrs. Hubbuch has shared with me the background information as it relates to Caleb. The school has reported that he is a delightful child and gets along extremely well with his peers." Billy and Grace exchanged quick smiles. Score two for the good guys. "However, he does have some developmental issues. He is behind grade level and struggles to keep up with his classmates." Grace and Billy again look at each other but this time with concern. "But that is not the real problem."

Billy leaned forward, "The real problem, Mr. Sanguine?"

"Well, sir, there is concern about the mobility problem that he has with his leg."

"But the doctor said it was minimal and that he would have a full and happy life," Grace injected.

Mrs. Hubbuch responded, "Grace, it is not about his physical limitation." She paused . . . perhaps a bit too long. "It is
about how he suffered this malady." Another pause. This one
was more painful as Mrs. Hubbuch turned to look at Billy. "We
have received reports that Caleb was inhabiting a . . . a dog
house for long periods of time." Billy dropped his head as shame
throbbed throughout his body. "Is that true, Billy."

Billy raised his head and quietly replied, "That is true, Mrs.
Hubbuch." He looked at both Mrs. Hubbuch and Mr. Sanguine.
"It is with great shame that I admit this horrendous act. I was..."
He spoke candidly. He was not about to misrepresent or justify
his actions. He went for the truth as difficult as it was him. "As
you may not know, our son Caleb is black." Now it was Grace's
turn to feel the shame.

"We know that, Billy," said Mrs. Hubbuch.

Billy felt foolish. Of course, they would know that Caleb
was black. They checked everything related to Caleb, or they
would not be here in the first place. He continued awkwardly:
"When I found out that Caleb was not my son, I went off the
deep end. I...."

"That is our concern," interrupted Mr. Sanguine. "We
never want Caleb ever to experience anything that bad ever
again."

"And nor do we," snapped Billy. "I know that Caleb is not
my natural born son but, believe me . . . " Billy gripped his hands
together and pleaded, ". . . Caleb is my son now and forever. I
was wrong, and I regret what I did with all my heart." Tears now
were streaming down his face. "please know how..."

Mr. Sanguine raised his hand to stop him, "Billy, there's more."

"What do you mean there's more?" said Grace dumb-founded.

"Well, the doctor also reported that there was a permanent bruise around Caleb's neck." Billy and Grace both gasped. "He said it was caused by something that had been tied or placed there for a long time." Billy and Grace knew exactly what he was talking about. However, the discoloration from wearing the collar was so faint and blended with his light, brown skin that it was barely noticeable.

Mrs. Hubbuch spoke, "We have no choice but to place him in a temporary home while we assess his mental and physical state. The Child Welfare Services will oversee child custody arrangements and family support."

Grace and Billy melted into each other's arms. Grace said, "Please don't take.."

"There's more," Mr. Sanguine said reluctantly. Billy and Grace looked up from their embrace of torment. "If you want Caleb back . . ."

"Of course we want Caleb back!!!" cried Grace. Upstairs, the singing stopped.

"Do you want me?" Caleb called down as the patter of his feet could be heard as he descended the stairs. He was smiling and bubbly. He ran up to his mother and gave her a big hug. "Why are you crying, mommy?" He looked at his daddy, and he was crying, too. He shuffled over to Billy and gave him a hug as well.

"Don't cry, daddy. Don't cry, mommy. I'll take care of you."

Mrs. Hubbuch and Mr. Sanguine looked on in silence. Unfortunately, they had witnessed similar drama play out time and again in their line of work. Protecting kids is not easy; but measures, tough measures, often times had to be taken for the safety of the child. Sadness was part of the baggage that came with their job.

Pam had followed Caleb down the stairs and had overheard Caleb's concern's for his parents. Grace stood up and hugged her mother, "Mom, would you mind taking Caleb out back to play until we finish. Pam nodded with concern. She took Caleb's hand and walked out to the kitchen. As they were leaving, Caleb craned his head around and then waved bye-bye.

The room seemed as though the oxygen had been sucked out of it. The four adults remained silent until Billy said, "There's more . . ."

Mr. Sanguine said, "Billy . . . ," He hesitates and begins looking around the room as if searching for the right words. ". . . How can I put this gently? Billy, there is concern about your stability. The department would like you to meet with a psychiatrist to determine if you are . . . are qualified to be around Caleb."

Billy stood up in near rage. Grace jumped up beside him coaxed him back down with her gentle hands, "Billy, just listen. Just listen."

"I can't just listen." He looked at both of the Child Protection Services representatives in the eyes, "Caleb is my son. He is our son. I love him and will do anything to keep him with us." He began breathing heavily; holding back his emotions, "And even if it is to meet with your psychiatrist. Hell, I'll meet with thirty of them if you want me to. I just want Caleb in our lives, in our home, with us."

. . . .

Caleb's clothes, toothbrush, and his favorite toys were in his little backpack in the trunk of the SUV. He was sitting in the backseat gripping his stuffed Teddy bear looking out at his mother, his daddy and his grammy waving goodbye on the porch. He pressed his tiny nose against the glass fogging it up. As they drove off, he watched his parents and his grammy get smaller and smaller until they were out of sight. He stopped waving. His hand rested temporarily against the fogged window and slowly slid down leaving a trail of little fingers.

CHAPTER 48 - WORRY

Billy walked up to the standard, three-storied, brick building which housed the Department of Child Protective Services among other related government agencies that addressed community welfare issues. The front door opened to a broad entryway with four shiny, stainless steel, elevator doors. Between doors two and three there was a directory. Billy searched for Dr. Hodges, the psychiatrist that was assigned to him or for him or whatever they wanted. Dr. Hodges was on the third floor, suite 307. On the ride up, Billy took out the card from his jacket that his mother had given Caleb. He began to read it just as the doors opened. Billy stepped aside to allow an elderly woman to enter. He then walked out and down the hall. At the entrance to suite 307, he stopped and finished reading the card:

Dear Caleb,
Your smile, your goodness, your kindness
 are treats to everyone you meet.
You are a gift to all of us and especially to me.
Love,
Grammy Dolly

He continued walking until he reached the door to Suite 307. He stopped, took a deep breath, let it out slowly, and thought: Oh, shit! I'm a mess.

. . . .

Billy had met with Dr. Hodges on three separate occasions for three weeks. Caleb had been in the care of the Child Protective Services for about the same amount of time. Billy and Grace were able to visit Caleb on two occasions within that three-week time frame. Needless to say, it was very emotional for all of them. Caleb pleaded to come home. Billy and Grace explained that he would be coming back as soon as possible, but he had to be patient. However, being patient for a seven-year-old is the equivalent to having a puppy wait for his treat. For Caleb, this was not a happy time, and, yet, he always managed a smile with false understanding.

Grace and Billy wished that the people who assessed Caleb's well-being would see past the "abuse" he endured. Thousands upon thousands of children in each state are under the watchful of eyes of protective services. The amount of abuse is staggering, and the department is thin on manpower as well as finances. They do the best they can with what they have, but, in this case, Grace and Billy hoped that Caleb would not be a child considered in need of permanent foster care or any care. He should be at home with them.

. . . .

Judy sat by the pool looking through fashion and home improvement magazines: The Royal Wedding of Prince Charles and Lady Diana Spencer was displayed prominently on the cover of one of them. She flipped that one aside and picked out a beautiful home magazine. Judy was bored and needed to do something, and that was to create a project for the house. Heck, she lived in a mansion, had everything and more than anybody could want, why not spend more money to satisfy her whims. Norman wasn't home that much, and, besides, having some hunky carpenters around the house would provide some nice distractions for her. Speaking of distractions, Alex snuck into the pool area from the side of the house.

"Hey, beautiful," Alex grinned.

"What are you doing here?" Judy whispered glancing at the kitchen window to see if Nellie was looking out. No. She wasn't. "Quick! Come over here." She ushered Alex out of the pool area and toward the barn glancing back every now and then to make sure they were not being watched. When they got inside the barn, Judy said, "So what the heck are you doing here, Alex.

His eyes scanned her from the top of her head to her toes and then back again, "You're looking pretty good, Judy. This rich life is working for you."

"Shut up, stupid! What are you doing here?"

"Well, Dora and I thought we'd drive by the Keenan house just to see what was happening. We drove by a couple of days ago." Judy listened intently. "Judy, it wasn't the same place. It looked like something out of one of those cottage magazines."

"How's that?" she asked curiously.

"It was freshly painted, landscaped beautifully, good look-ing bark mulch, and..."

"Are they selling the place?" she interrupted.

"Well, no. We were so curious what was goin' on that we

decided to walk up to the door. Grace answered it. We asked her if Billy was there."

"....And?"

"And he wasn't. He was at an appointment of some kind."

"What kind?"

"She didn't say. I tried to peek around her to see who was there, but nobody was. Not her mother and not even Caleb, and it wasn't even a school day."

"So?"

"So, something is going on. I don't know what, but something."

"When you find out, tell me. In the meantime, I have something to show you in the pool house."

. . . .

Nellie was in the front of the house watering the plants. She hated being at the Cromwell's. Sure, it was beautiful, spacious, and had everything imaginable at her fingertips: her bedroom was as big as the Keenan's entire downstairs; the kitchen pantry was stocked with every kind of spice, soup, and delicacy. The refrigerator was full of vegetables, meats, juices, milk. You name it; it was there. The extra benefit was that Mr. Cromwell would let her use any of the amenities on the property; the pool, the carts, anything. She could cook anything she wanted. She was not limited to spaghetti dinners or stew or hotdogs like the limited menu that was available at the Keenan home. Even with all that, she hated it at the mansion. The building was void of tenderness and of goodness. If the walls could talk, they would spew out nothing but misery.

Nellie missed the simple meals at the Keenan's. She missed Pam who had become a friend. She missed Grace who almost seemed like a daughter to her. She yearned for the sense of family that was at the Keenan home. Most of all, Nellie missed Caleb, his bubbly, happy face glowing as he looked up at her. She craved for the laughter she heard when Caleb was outside playing with his friends; the pitter patter of his feet coming down the stairs to wake her up. Little did she know that the Keenan household missed all of that as well.

When she finished watering, she wrapped up the hose by the side of the house and noticed a car parked on the side of the road down the street. It looked familiar, but from this distance, she couldn't make it out.

She turned to go back inside which she hated because she didn't want to deal with Judy. Nellie couldn't stand it when Judy was home especially when Norman was not there. And he was not there this day. Not that Judy was mean. Well, yes. She was mean in a Judy sort of way. She was condescending and belittling. She did not look at Nellie as an equal, and Nellie understood that to a degree. Judy was now the boss, and Nellie was the employee. But Judy liked to emphasize Nellie's role as that of the maid, the servant. When she requested her wine, which Nellie would bring out to the pool for her, Judy would extend her hand out waiting for Nellie to place it between her fingers. No eye contact. Just a subtle thank you was all to indicate any appreciation. No. Nellie was not her equal nor did she want to be. But nor did Nellie want to be degraded each day with hurt-ful subtleties that made her feel less as a person.

Nellie picked up the brunch plates from the table and brought them to the sink to be rinsed. She looked out of the window. It was a gorgeous day. She splattered water over the plates and leaned down to put them in the dishwasher. When she rose up to the sink in front of the window, she caught a glimpse of a shadow that disappeared out the gate leading to the side of the house by the garage. She scanned back to the pool area and saw the shades in the pool house were being raised. Then Judy walked out and shut the door. She took a quick dip into the pool, climbed out, and returned to her chair. Nellie shook her head and closed the door to the dishwasher.

CHAPTER 49 - THE DECISION

Grace and Billy were asked to meet at Mr. Hodge's office at the beginning of the fourth week after Caleb had been taken away. When they got to Suite 307, Grace said to Billy, "I'm so nervous."

"Me, too, Grace." He reached down, held her hand and gave it a gentle squeeze.

When they entered the waiting room, the secretary said, "Hi, Mr. and Mrs. Cromwell. Mr. Hodges is waiting for you." She held the door open to his office to admit them. They walked into the room. Dr. Hodges was not alone. Mrs. Hubbuch and Mr. Sanguine were there as well.

Dr. Hodges smiled at them and gestured to two chairs that backed up to a wall. A coffee table with the most recent issues of Time, Newsweek, and Sports Illustrated stood between the three other chairs occupied by the representative and supervisor for the Department of Child Protective Services, and now Mr. Hodges, who took the third seat. "I wanted to have Mr. Sanguine and Mrs. Hubbuch here so I could share my report with them concerning Mr. Cromwell."

"Billy, please! Just call me Billy."

"Yes, Billy," and he continued. "First of all, I want to apologize for not telling you in advance that they would be attending, but it was a last minute decision on my part that I thought might expedite things." Grace and Billy nodded with acceptance at his reasoning as Mr. Sanguine, and Ms. Hubbuch studied their reactions. Their scrutiny was perpetual. "Billy and Grace. May I call you Grace?"

"Yes, Dr. Hodges. I am more than comfortable with that. In fact, I prefer that you do call me Grace," she said making sure she was as accommodating and compliant as possible.

"Thank you." He continued, "First of all, Mr. Cromwell. Excuse me. I mean Billy, initially, never revealed any hostility, anger, or regret about the circumstances relating to Caleb's birth. I found that highly unusual." The doctor paused. Grace squirmed in her seat, and Billy listened intently. "In our first appointment, Billy was pleasant but reticent to divulge his true feelings. He did tell me very candidly about finding out in the hospital that Caleb was not his son, but he did not express any anger or emotion. He delivered that information with complete control.

"But, Dr. Hodges..." Billy tried to say leaning forward in his chair.

"Billy, if I could continue please," the doctor politely said. Billy clamped his lips together and leaned back. "I let Billy talk about his placing Caleb in the dog house, and about the death of his mother which was very difficult for him and other details about the relationship with his dad and so on. Nothing significant to impact a decision about Caleb in that first session".

Mr. Sanguine asked, "Were the other two sessions different?"

"Yes, very different. Billy, in the second session, started talking about his anger toward Grace. How he hated her for what she had done and regretted even marrying her." Grace turned away from Billy. "He mentioned that he hated Caleb even more." The room hung in silence. Tension filled the air like deadly escaping gas.

Mrs. Hubbuch looked extremely disturbed and wanted to make a decision right then and there. Grace moved her chair further away. Mr. Hodges sat in contemplation while Billy didn't budge. His face was blank. "I think we can make a decision right now about Caleb's future." Mrs. Hubbuch said with exasperation.

"It would seem that way," said Dr. Hodges, "but the third session was the most telling." Grace returned her attention to the doctor as everyone leaned a little forward, toward him, so as not to miss a word. "Billy was very candid with me during this session and unleashed a multitude of emotions." That caught everyone's' attention. "Billy spoke about his love for his wife. How she changed him into being a better man; to being more understanding, forgiving, and nonjudgmental. Not by what she said, but by just being herself." Grace looked at Billy fondly and put her hand on top of his. "Billy talked about how he was the jerk and how, not only had Grace tolerated and accepted him, but how her mother and her friends did as well." Mrs. Hubbuch relaxed and leaned back. Mr. Sanguine seemed to depress as well.

"Dr. Hodges, I don't mean to interrupt, but what caused this transformation in Billy?" asked Mr. Sanguine.

"Well, there were a lot of variables that came into play; the death of Billy's mother was an awakening; the kindness of Grace and her mother; the acceptance of their friends; Billy's escaping a toxic home environment of his own which not only included family but former friends as well."

"Where does Caleb fit in there?" Mrs. Hubbuch said with concern.

"Interesting you should ask that. Caleb was the catalyst that made Billy aware of his failings, his weaknesses."

"And how could Caleb, a little boy, had such an influence on Billy?" questioned Mr. Sanguine.

"Caleb is innocent and a good little guy. He didn't judge Billy but just wanted Billy to love him. Caleb was just being Caleb. And Billy saw in him what he wasn't."

"And that is?" asked Mrs. Hubbuch.

"Innocent and good," replied Dr. Hodges. Billy dropped his head a bit and nodded in agreement. "Billy looked at Caleb as an example of what he wanted to be like, and that desire has changed Billy.

Mr. Sanguine looked at the young couple and said, "That's nice, but it still doesn't negate the fact that Billy had committed a horrendous act against Caleb."

Billy harshly whispered, "You mean my son."

Mr. Sanguine didn't acknowledge Billy's input and continued to speak, " Also, Billy's verbal abuse and threats toward Grace can't be dismissed."

"I have another concern," Mrs. Hubbuch interjected. All eyes shifted to her. "Grace, during Caleb's," she looked away searching for the right words. Grace wiggled in her seat in anticipation of Mrs. Hubbuch's "concern." "During Caleb's time of confinement by Billy, you did nothing. Is that correct?'

Grace regretfully answered, "Yes, mam." Then she seemed to get mildly offended and defensive. "Well, I did do something!: I gave Caleb meals; bathed him when I could; held him and told him constantly that I loved him." Her voice became a bit louder, and she began to shake, "I DID do something!"

"Grace, you never reached out to your mother, your friends or anybody." Mrs. Hubbuch challenged and then paused. "I know these truths are difficult for you to accept, but, Grace, your motherly instincts were casual at best."

Grace dropped her head into the palms of her hands, and a flood of tears came pouring out. She lifted her eyes and pleaded, "I love Caleb. I didn't know what to do. Please believe me! I love Caleb with all my heart!" Again, she buried her head into the palms of her hands in a vain attempt to stifle her sobs.

Mrs. Hubbuch got up from her seat and went to Grace's side. She placed her hand of Grace's shoulder and said, "Grace, I'm sorry. We have to ask difficult questions. Our concern is for Caleb's welfare." Billy glared at Mrs. Hubbuch restraining himself from exploding. Grace kept sobbing.

Dr. Hodges appeared frustrated. He knew he had made a difficult situation even more problematic. That was not his purpose. His intent of having a group session completely backfired. He had to say something to mitigate the pressure which occupied the office. Looking at Mrs. Hubbuch and Mr. Sanguine he said, "All the issues have now been addressed. Having Caleb back in his home is what I believe would be best for him. Mr. and Mrs. Cromwell have made a grave mistake of which they have been very candid and honest and for which they are incredibly remorseful. Mr. Cromwell profusely regrets his treatment of Caleb and of his wife. He has demonstrated that he has changed for the better, not only to be a better father but to be a better husband and to be a better man.

Mr. Sanguine got up as did Mrs. Hubbuch, and he addressed Dr. Hodges, "Thank you for your comments. I know you were hoping to come to a conclusion as to Caleb's placement with the revelations presented at this session. Although it is good to know that Billy has made strides, there are too many questions about both Mr. and Mrs. Cromwell that remain that do not allow us to make a determination about Caleb at this time." He turned to Grace and Billy who just looked back with stark expressions, "I'm sorry. Ms. Hubbuch, myself, and a team of experts will evaluate all the information we have and get back to you as soon as possible with our findings and our decision."

They then walked out the door, and it clicked shut behind them. The room felt like death. Grace and Billy and Dr. Hodges were speechless. The fate of Caleb hung in limbo. The shock of that tore at their hearts. The silence lasted for what seemed like hours. The pain seemed cemented in their hearts forever.

. . . .

The two Child Protective Service workers sat in Katie's car agonizing about what to do as they traveled back to their offices. They both were replaying the conversation in Dr. Hodges Office. Katie spoke first, "What do you think?"

"Katie, I don't know what to think," Paul said and paused. "I wish we could just decide to have Caleb returned to his home, but both parents have had questionable involvement in jeopardizing Caleb's welfare."

"I'm just out of sorts with Grace's lack of action to extract

Caleb from that imprisonment." Paul glanced at her upon hearing the word imprisonment. "I would have taken Caleb . . . "

"Grace is not you, Katie." He interrupted. "No one knows how one would react if threatened or in fear for the safety of their child. Maybe we should cut her a little slack."

Kate sighed, "We will look at all factors, Paul. But, as a mother, . . . that just bugs me. So many of these women we deal with don't put their children first."

"Katie, you know as well as me that in domestic violence abusive, forceful, or a threatening acts or words can stifle anyone." She stared at the road in front of them as they got closer to their destination and listened. "What concerns me is Billy's drinking. If he was able to stop, like he said, that may be OK. However, if there was even a remote chance he would engage in such reckless behavior, I would not let Caleb back into that home. All of Billy's rage erupted when he was boozing it up. I'm not about to subject little Caleb to that torment again."

"We've got to get it right, either way, Paul. Almost five children die every day from child abuse. Caleb can't be included in that statistic."

They finally reached the building that housed their offices. The number of referrals they had to evaluate and act upon was twirling around in their heads. Nationwide, four million child maltreatment referral reports are received. At their office, there were only a handful of folks attempting to do the right thing for all the kids in their jurisdiction. The monumental weight of their decisions was a strain on them. Caleb was just one of the many children that they were trying to protect. And they've got to get it right.

. . . .

Katie and Paul pulled up to the Nash's home. It was in a middle-class community, made of brick, and had a yard that was a little shabby in contrast to their neighbors'. The visitation was scheduled for a time when Caleb was home from school. The Nash's seemed like a friendly couple, but Katie was suspicious of their intentions for fostering a child. Sometimes money was the incentive for people to take a child in rather than concern for the child's welfare. For a child between the ages of five to eight, the board was $329 per month which the foster parents would receive. There was help for clothing at $56 a month and an allowance of $14 a month. The total take-in for them to care for Caleb was $409 per month. This was not a lot of money, but for some folks, it was good pocket change.

Mrs. Nash answered the door. She flashed a smile and said, "We were expecting you." She turned to the living room, "Right, Caleb?"

"Yes," said Caleb, as he ran up to meet Katie and Paul. He grabbed Paul by the finger and led him to the kitchen. The two women followed. "We were just having a treat," pointing to the apple pie on the table. "Would you like some?"

"Thank you, but we're all set," said Paul. Caleb seemed mildly disappointed but plopped himself down on a chair and started munching at his pie. The grownups chatted about idle matters until Caleb had finished his "treat." Mr. Sanguine picked up the conversation when the plate was empty, "Caleb, could we talk with you in the living room while Mrs. Nash does some work around the house?

"Sure," he blurted and hopped off his chair, ran to the living room and jumped onto the sofa. He looked up at Mrs. Hubbuch and patted the cushion to his right, "You sit here." Then he pointed to the left side, "You sit here, sir." The two grownups smiled and did as they were told.

"How do you like it here, Caleb?" asked Mrs. Hubbuch. Caleb squirmed in his seat, said nothing and just smiled back at her. "Do you like school?"

"Oh, yes. I get to be with all my friends, and my teacher, Ms. Linkas. She is the nicest."

"You seem to be eating well," Mr. Sanguine kidded poking him in the tummy.

"Oh, yes! Mr. and Mrs. Nash give me lots of treats, but they don't have a garden like mommy and daddy do."

Katie and Paul made eye contact, and then Mrs. Hubbuch asked, "Do you miss home, Caleb?" Caleb sat there smiling up at Mrs. Hubbuch. A tear trickled down his cheek.

CHAPTER 50 - NEW YORK

"It is greed to do all the talking but not to want to listen at all." Democritus

Norman Cromwell loved New York City. To him, the mansion was too isolated, too quiet. Others may call the setting where he lived bucolic or tranquil, but, to Norman, it was just plain dull. The city was vibrant, alive. He even liked the congestion, the honking of horns, and the people watching. And, holy cow, there were a lot of people. Dressed in his signature black suit with a green and white striped tie and gripping a briefcase in his right hand, he walked up 7th Ave heading toward Central Park. He passed Carnegie Hall, and two blocks later he was at 59th St. He then took a right. He arrived at 50 Central Park South. Not an extremely impressive entranceway, but across the street was the beautiful vegetation of Central Park.

The park looked spectacular with its waterway and forest setting seated in the middle of all the high-rises, asphalt roads, cement sidewalks, and people. He could never get over the fact that this space of green could exist amongst the towering buildings. Most people embraced this oasis of vegetation as an escape from city life. Not Norman. He thought about the money he could make if he could just develop a sliver of that greenery. The St. Moritz Hotel was situated ideally for him: adjacent to the park with close proximity to the theater district. Just awesome.

The gleaming noonday sun reflected off of the spotless

glass doors. The concierge approached him immediately. "Good afternoon, Mr. Cromwell."

"Good afternoon, James, and I hope it is a good one for you."

"Yes, sir, and for you as well. Can I carry your briefcase for you?"

"No, James. But thank you." Norman loved the attention to courtesy received when he came here. He loved the glitz and the glamor. Even more, he loved the money it all represented. Everybody in that building was of the elite. He felt at home. He was one of them. Even though it was an old building, it's location was central to everything. It was 38 stories high with a thousand rooms. Some were just one room, others were two rooms, and other spaces were large suites. Many opened up to terraces with incredible views of the city.

A dinner and dancing salon was on the 31st floor where Omar Khayyam murals painted by David Karfunkel provided an artistic venue. The panoramic views were breathtaking. To add to the ostentatious affluence was the Rumpelmayer pastry and tea shop and the Cafe de la Paix: both popular eating spots. Rumpelmayers was known as the most expensive ice cream parlor in New York City. Norman didn't mind shelling out the over-the-top money for the ice cream. He felt as though he was worth it; that he deserved it. He loved the hot chocolate that was served with melted Swill chocolate bars eased with hot milk in metal pitchers with a ramekin of whipped cream on the side. Yes! He deserved it.

He stepped into the elevator and pressed the bottom for the thirty-seventh floor. The elevator door opened to a large, luxury, two bedroom suite (1350 square feet by 1540 square feet). When he walked in, he let out a slight gasp as he viewed Central Park on the outside of the almost floor-to-ceiling windows. Even though he had seen it many times, he was always enthralled by its beauty and his dream of converting it to money. He loved this view.

The master bedroom featured a luxurious king-size bed and en-suite master bath. The guest bedroom offered a queen-size bed, a sitting area incredible view of the city and, through double doors, a full master bathroom with ornate lighting, a huge mirror and a tub that could fit four people The beautiful and spacious separate living room included a dining area with a dining table and chairs with a spectacular handcrafted Schonbek crystal chandelier hanging overhead, and a plush velvet over-sized sofa bed.

The two bedroom suite also featured a large TV, comfortable oversized stairs, a luxurious sofa, a glass coffee table tastefully decorated with plants, various pieces of silver trays, and recent editions of magazines. Exquisite end tables with Greek lamps balanced that side of the room. A fully equipped European-style kitchen with appliances occupied a full side of the spacious area. Everything one would need for a meeting and more was there.

Norman dropped his briefcase and sat down on the sofa. He leaned forward and leafed through the magazines. He picked up *The New York Times* which was among the reading material. He scanned the headlines: "Michael Jackson Releases *Thriller* Album," "First CD Player Sold in Japan," "Dutch Elm Disease Destroys Millions of Elm Trees," "Tylenol Capsules

Laced with Potassium Cyanide Kill 7 in Chicago," "Times Man of The Year is THE COMPUTER," "A Major Recession Hits the United States." He looked at the last headline, again and reread it: "A major recession hits the United States." Perfect, he thought to himself. The market was ripe for sweeping in to procure foreclosed properties. He saw dollar signs in other peoples' misfortune. He leaned back, closed his eyes and whispered, "Perfect."

. . . .

That evening three executives arrived at the suite. They were dressed similar to what Norman had on earlier in the day, but Norman had shed his suit jacket. Heck! He was paying for the room, and at nearly $1,000 per night, he could dress any way he wanted.

"Hi, Mr. Cromwell," said the first in a heavy Russian accent. The other two followed and nodded their heads seriously in recognition.

"Hi, Fyodor. Kazim. Hello, Fabrizio." It was like a meeting of the United Nations: a Russian, an Arab, and an Italian. Norman always thought of the beginning of a joke...were on this plane. But this was no laughing matter. Fyodor was an influential Russian financier who wore a huge, ruby ring. He was careful about where his money went and ruthless if it did not turn up profits. Kazim was a wealthy Arab who had real estate interests all over the world. And Fabrizio, the friendliest of the crew, was the enforcer. His smile, however, camouflaged the ruthlessness in the man.

They seated themselves around the glass dining room table. Norman had ordered room service earlier in the day: shrimp, caviar, a variety of crackers and a plate of sandwiches and another platter with broccoli, carrots, fruit, cheeses were there for the taking. He also made sure he had a bottle or two of vodka for Fyodor, the Russian, and several bottles of Sangiovese wine, the pride of Tuscany, for Fabrizio, the Italian. Kazim did not drink, so water was available for him. Fyodor spoke first: "Mr. Cromwell, how are the projects proceeding in Florida." He picked up a sandwich and took a bite.

"Very well. We have secured the purchase of a large piece of property in the panhandle. However, more than half of it is composed of wetlands."

"Then it is a waste of our money. Wetlands are protected. The EPA will stop our development," Kazim fretted.

"No, they won't," said a confident Cromwell as he turned and looked at the grinning Russian. "Fyodor wired me enough money to take care of any human obstacles that were in the way. The EPA, surveyors, and building inspectors are all happy not to mention a few local officials. It should be clear sailing."

They talked about several other projects that they had invested in throughout the world. Then the conversation came back to the real estate ventures in the United States. In fact, to Mr. Cromwell's community. Fabrizio stuffed a sandwich in his mouth, and Kazim took a sip of his water.

After swallowing, Kazim said, "How about that downtown reeestooration plan weee have goeeg on een your townnn?"

"We took care of most of the payoffs there, and development is off and running. However, we have one holdout. I have offered him a sweet deal, but they are obstinate. They don't want to sell," said Cromwell.

Fyodor rose from his seat and slammed his fist down on the glass table sending a crooked crack through the length of it. The rest of the men jumped. Fabrizio instinctively went for his weapon but didn't draw it. "Then offer the bastards a better deal. Get it done!" Fyodor bellowed.

Cromwell casually looked at him and then casually pointed to the table, "I'll put that on my tab."

Just then the intercom chimed with a delicate melody, and a calm voice said, "Mr. Cromwell, you have more guests who would like to come up." Giggling could be heard in the background.

Norman responded, "Send them up and thank you." Billy turned to the UN contingency. They were all grinning sheepishly. Your bonus has arrived. I'm going out to Carnegie Hall." He grabbed his jacket and left.

CHAPTER 51 - WITH FRIENDS LIKE THESE . . .

Alex and Dora missed their buddy, Judy, and she missed them as well. They decided to all get together at Alex's house just to catch up. Judy picked up Dora in front of her house, not a mansion like Judy was now living in but still quite an impressive home. Majestic Magnolia trees guarded the house in front, and the long driveway passed by the front door and led to a three car garage. The homes in the area, like Dora's, were nestled on about three acres of land. Some had more. None had less. It was a private community with signs signifying that the neighborhood watch was in full force. Hard to imagine since there was little activity in the area except for an occasional dog barking and some horses scattered around in pastures.

Dora had two four packs of wine in her left hand, and her purse was dangling from the other.

"Atta, girl," Judy yelled out of her window.

"Nice wheels, girl," grinned Dora as she checked out the shiny Mercedes. Dora was happy to see Judy, but inside she was envious. Judy was now living in a mansion, drove a slick car, and had money to burn. Not that Dora had anything to complain about, but measuring one's happiness by comparing what you have with others makes bitterness inevitable. Before Judy got married, she and Dora were material equals from basically the same type of neighborhoods with the same amount of stuff.

"Thanks! I'll have one of those cabernets on the way over to Alex's.

"Sure," said Dora as she unscrewed the top and handed it to Judy. "Have you seen Alex lately?"

"A few times, once he came over when Nellie was out shopping," Dora raised her eyebrows. "And another time when I ran into him at Macy's." Dora waited for more, but Judy just kept driving and sipped more of her wine.

The rest of the ride heading to Alex's house was filled with girl talk, movies, actresses, bands, and the like. They rolled up to Alex's house and parked in front. Alex's house was nice, but it was quite modest in contrast to their homes. That gave the girls a sense of superiority to Alex. But he was the one who used to drive them around all the time back in the day so they could use him. The old, now rusting, blue Cadillac was still around parked in the driveway. An oil stain underneath it marked its parking spot. The women giggled as they walked by it.

Alex looked out the window as Judy and Dora approached the front door. "Dip-shits," he muttered to himself and went to answer the door. Alex didn't have much fondness for the girls. He knew they used him, but he knew he used them as well. He liked his experience in the pool house, and he loved the experience he had had in his basement. Neither girl was the wiser so they could use him as much as they wanted.

Alex grabbed the doorknob and pulled it open. The girls smiled and in unison said, "Hi, Alex." Dora held up the wine.

"What? No beer??"

Judy said, "Alex, you always have beer."

He smirked, "You're right. I do. But I was hoping you would get me a house warming gift."

"Alex, it's your mother's house," Judy blurted.

He coyly smiled, and the three of them sat down in the living room. Alex had a beer already opened sitting on the coffee table in front of the sofa.

They talked about the old days when they would party at Billy's mansion, drive golf carts like race cars and go downtown across the tracks to make fun of the factory workers.

"I wonder how Billy is doing?" asked Judy.

"I don't know. I haven't seen Billy since your wedding," said Alex. They heard a car stop in front of the house.

"Are you expecting company, Alex?" Judy asked.

"Not that I know of." Alex got up to look out the window. "Who the hell are these stiffs?"

Judy got up to look out the window as a man and a woman opened the door to black SUV and got out. Alex turned to Judy, "You know them?"

"Never seen them in my life."

"Maybe they're candidates for the local government seeking our votes," laughed Dora from her chair.

A light knock could be heard from the front door. Alex opens it and with his usual poise said, "Yah! What do you want?"

Katie Hubbuch smiled and said, "My name is Mrs. Hubbuch, and this is Mr. Sanguine." Mr. Sanguine nodded. Katie continued. "We're from the Child Protective Services, and we'd like to ask you a few questions.

"I never abused any kid," Alex snapped.

"Sir, the questions aren't about you. We'd just like to get to know about Billy Cromwell and what he was like before he got married."

"In that case, come on in," said Alex. Dora stood up, and

Judy gathered her most gracious demeanor. "This is Dora, and this is Judy. They're also friends of Billy's who just happen to stop by for a visit." They nodded their heads in agreement. "You want something to drink?" Alex said holding up his beer.

"No thank you!" said Katie. Looking at the girls. "Do you mind if we ask you questions as well since you all are friends of Billy's?" Alex ran into the kitchen to fetch two more chairs.

"No, not at all," Judy said.

"Fine with me," Dora smiled.

Judy then said, "Do you mind if we sip on our drinks while we talk?"

"Not at all," said Mr. Sanguine. "We're the ones who came announced. We didn't mean to disrupt your gathering."

Judy responded, "Well, that's good. This could be fun."

For the next hour and a half, the trio answered the questions and did more than sip their drinks: guzzle would be the more accurate verb. Alex had to visit the bathroom three times, and the girls had to excuse themselves on more than one occasion. Their commentaries on Billy were often accompanied by group laughter and a few profanities; dip-shit being the most common. They talked about wild drinking, making fun of folks across the tracks, playing hide and seek in the mansion. The talk went on and on. Katie and Paul hardly had to ask any questions. Alex, Judy, and Dora were fountains of information with talk cascading out of their mouths. In fact, it was Katie and Paul who had to call an end to the festivities. They thanked them all and told them that they had been accommodating.

Judy glanced at Alex and snapped, "Go open the door for them."

"They know where the damn door is."

"Yeah! Come on, Alex. Be a gentleman," Dora slurred.

"That won't be necessary, but thank you," said Judy calmly.

"What? Don't you think I'm a gentleman?" Alex struggled to his feet and staggered over to the door. He fumbled with the knob but finally was able to swing the door open. It banged against his toe, and he started hopping around. The girls began cackling. Alex released a swarm of obscenities.

Katie was guided out the door by Mr. Sanguine. Paul said to Alex, "I hope you are alright." Alex said nothing and just glared at him. "Well, thank you for your time," Mr. Sanguine offered after he was once outside. The door then was slammed in his face.

. . . .

Katie and Paul once again found themselves in the SUV pondering the Cromwell family and the fate of little Caleb.

"What do you think?" said Mrs. Hubbuch.

"Do you really want to know?" asked Paul looking at her.

"Yes, I really want to know?" she steered to avoid a rabbit in the road.

"I think that the three of them, all three, are dip-shits." Katie rocked her head back with laughter. "Hey, keep your eyes on the road," pleaded Paul.

"OK," She paused slightly and then looked over to Paul, ". . . Dip-shit."

It was one of the few times that they had shared a laugh trying to determine what was best for Caleb. For the rest of the ride to the office, they both drifted back to their thoughts with the information about Billy's past and his friends whirling in their heads.

CHAPTER 52 - WHAT TO DO?

In their apartment above the store, Lynnda and Mike sat across from each other at the kitchen table. Mike was sipping on some homemade chicken soup that Lynnda had made. His wife stirred her bowl deep in thought looking up occasionally. The apartment, the store, and their lives had been wrapped within the walls of this old building for over thirty-five years. When they first purchased the dilapidated structure, they were young and ambitious. Much in the same way that Clark and Pam were when they first acquired their home. Both the Donnelly's and the Keenan's had devoted a great deal of time and effort into making their abodes unique, warm, and welcoming.

The expression 'blood, sweat, and tears' was more than a poignant part of Sir Winston Churchill's famous speech. Blood, sweat, and tears were the actual ingredients in making the Don-nelly's future. They experienced them literally. Hot summer days accounted for the beads of sweat when one of them was on a ladder painting or another on the floor sanding away the scuffs and scratches. When Mike cut his hand with a saw making the counter top and had to go to the hospital, that represented the blood. And when they were close to bankruptcy and about to lose what they had worked so hard for, that became the tears. Throughout years of tribulations, they were able to forge ahead, and become one of the cornerstones of the community, and peo-ple loved Lynnda and Mike.

This night, however, all those memories were impediments

to moving on to their future, to making a move for what would seem to be best for them. Second loans and equity loans, as well as rising taxes, were taking a massive bite out of their earnings. Selling vanilla cokes and chocolate chip ice cream were not going to address the financial demands. But letting go of all that they had worked for, for all that they had dreamed for, would be much more difficult than they ever could have imagined.

. . . .

Earlier that day, Lynnda and Mike were in their store. Lynnda was chatting with Mr. Jim who would routinely come in for his morning cup of coffee and donut. He was joined by his buddy, Griff, who used to shine shoes outside of Donnelly's. They loved coming in for the company but, maybe even more so, for the free coffee Lynnda gave them.

Mike was lubricating the hinges on the front door, so it wouldn't be so difficult to open. It was a quiet morning which was normal for a weekday when everyone had gone to work. "Mama He's Crazy" by the Judds played on the speakers. The rush had subsided about an hour earlier, and now they would be coasting until about noon when folks would come in for lunch or goodies. While Mike knelt down working on the door, he saw a pair of shiny black shoes walk by him. He looked up and saw a well-dressed man whom he had never seen before. Behind him walked another gentleman who was also dressed to the hilt. Michael continued his work and peeked up every now and then to check to see if anybody needed help.

The first man took the third remaining stool and folded

his hands as though in prayer and looked around the shop. The other man stood beside him and also scanned the store. "Can I help you?" Lynnda said with a cheery greeting.

"Yeh!" said the man sitting with a thick, foreign accent. "Is theere another stool for my freeend?"

Lynnda nodded pleasantly, "There sure is?" and she shuffled to get the stool reserved for special occasions. "Here you go," as she set it down. "Would you like something to eat."

"Yes," said the man for whom the stool was procured. "I'd like a ...."

The other man with the thick accent slammed his hand down on the counter, turned to him and said, "Weee deen't come heere to eeat. Just shu . . . keeeep quiet." Then he turned back to look at Lynnda. "So, do you work heere?"

Lynnda noticed the huge gem on his ring and then looked up, "Yes, I do." Mike didn't feel comfortable with the conversation, got up and walked near the counter appearing as though he was straightening out magazines.

"Weeell, who owns theese dive?"

Mike stepped toward them. "We do, sir. We own this shop." Mike emphasized the word shop in an attempt to push aside the dive insult. I am Mike Donnelly, and this is," gesturing, "my wife, Lynnda."

"Well, me name is Kazim and thees ees me asseeciate, Fabrizio." Fabrizio nodded and smiled. He liked being called an associate. Mr. Jim and Mr. Griff decided to get up and leave. They weren't getting good vibes and wanted to distance themselves from the two visitors. Kazim continued to talk, "You have worked heere for a long time. Yeess?"

Mike replied, "Yes."

"And you are geetting older. Yeess?"

Mike smiled and looked at Lynnda, "Well, yes, but we're young at heart."

"Someday that heart of yours will stop beeating and your wife will bee alone. Yeess?"

Mike became agitated. This line of questioning was beginning to get him unhinged. He didn't know if that was a threat or a stupid comment. "What are you getting at, Mr. Kazim," he asserted forcefully.

"My asseeciates and me are weelling to buy thees dump from you for big money. You and Leenda will have a great life. No worry about cleeaning this dump. No worree about moneee. No worree about nottin." He looked at Fabrizio who was still looking at the menu, "Right, Fabrizio?"

"Oh, yeah. Absolutely."

Lynnda and Mike exchanged looks, and Mike spoke, "We are not considering selling right now, Mr. Kazim, Mr. Fabrizio."

Kazim's face twisted and evil pulsated in his eyes, "You better conseeeeder it soon," he growled." He then slapped a stack full of $100 bills on the counter in front of Lynnda. "Heere is ten thousand dollars to heeelp you conseeeder it soon." He slid off his stool and walked out. Fabrizio followed grabbing a Snickers Bar on the way.

Mike and Lynnda exchanged puzzled looks. They were stunned and somewhat afraid. Lynnda then blurted out, "Michael, we don't want their money," and threw the bound stack of one hundred dollar bills across the counter. "Give it back to them!!!" she yelled.

Two men just entered the store as Kazim and Fabrizio pushed their way by them. "Get out of my way," Kazim. blurted.

The one with a scar on his face snarled back. "Fu..." Fabrizio turned and flashed a knife at the two men. They both shut up as Mike scooped up the money from the counter and ran out the door. A black Mercedes was driving by the store and stopped. Kazim and Fabrizio slid into the leather seats and glared at Mike who was yelling, "We don't want your money." The Mercedes then pulled away as Fabrizio smiled at him from the passenger side and took a bite from his Snickers Bar.

CHAPTER 53 - APPLE PIE

"Your pain is the breaking of the shell that encloses your understanding."
Khalil Gibran

It was a Saturday, and Ninette, Angie, and Stephanie had decided to go over to the Keenan's house to comfort Grace. She was upset worrying about what was going to happen with Caleb. She was fearing the worst. They were all sitting in the living room. Pam had cooked up a bowl of popcorn and brought them soft drinks. They were talking about neighborhood happenings until Ninette snuck the topic of Caleb into the conversation "Have you heard anything about Caleb?" Caleb had been away for over a month. The silence in the house was deafening, and the residents were going through the motions of life but not living it.

"No! We haven't," Grace forced out the answer. Pam's mother observed from the kitchen. Billy had just come down the stairs and squeezed into a small space beside Grace.

Billy said, "We did get a call from Ms. Hubbuch, the caseworker, and she said that a decision will be made soon. If it weren't for me, we wouldn't be worried about Caleb." All eyes shifted to Billy as he spoke. He faced Grace, "I am such a jerk..."

Grace looked at him sincerely and said, "Were a jerk. You are a different person now, Billy."

He turned to the others, "I messed up real bad. I was a jerk to Grace and a real jerk to Caleb." As he looked out to the kitchen where Pam was standing, he raised his voice a little louder, "and a real jerk to you, Mrs. Keenan." She nodded back acknowledging his admission.

Grace patted his knee gently. "What's been done has been done, Billy."

"I'm not finished." Everyone perked up with curiosity. "You girls, Stephanie, Ninette, and Angie have been great as well as Chris, Shaun, Jaybird, and Charlie. You never questioned me or attacked me, and you had every right to do so." The girls were all thinking the same thing: They wanted to . . . big time. "I'm sorry to y'all as well."

Pam entered the room. "Thank you, Billy, but this isn't about you now. Sorry to be so blunt, but let's focus on Caleb and what..."

The phone rang. A hush smothered the room. Pam answered it. "It's for you, Grace," said Pam with a worried look.

Grace got up with a perplexed face and shuffled to her mom. She mouthed the words, "Who is it?" before taking the receiver from her mom's outstretched hand. Pam just shrugged her shoulders.

Grace listened carefully to the voice at the other end. She then hung the phone up and looked at all the faces staring at her: "He's coming home."

. . . .

They couldn't believe that it would be so soon. Later, that same Saturday, Katie's SUV pulled up in front of the Keenan's house. Pam, Grace, and Billy ran out to greet Caleb who was in the car and smiling from ear to ear. Mrs. Hubbuch got out and was unhitching Caleb from his seat belt. Mr. Sanguine stepped aside to allow the family to get close to their little buddy. When Caleb was finally unharnessed, he hopped into his mommy's arms and gave her big, tight, pulsating hugs. He then reached out for Billy, and Grace transferred Caleb into his arms. Pam was the recipient of the final, handoff. Caleb looked up at her sweetly and said, softly, "I missed you, Grammy, soooo much and your cookouts."

Billy turned to Mrs. Hubbuch and Mr. Sanguine and said, "Thank you! Words can't express how grateful we are."

Grace chimed in as well, "Yes, thank you sooo much," echoing Caleb's comment."

They both smiled back and then Mr. Sanguine said, "We still have to talk to you, Grace and Billy. There are some conditions we have to spell out for you. Can we come in and talk for a bit?"

"Why, yes, of course," said Grace.

They all walked up onto the porch. Pam held the door as Grace carried Caleb in and the rest followed. Grace took a quick peek at the picture of her mom and dad on the swing as she passed by it.

Pam reached out to Caleb and said, "Do you want to come with grammy and see the garden?"

"Yes," he responded with a giant smile, so glad to be home again. They then walked out to the kitchen to the back yard leaving the others behind in the house.

Mrs. Hubbuch and Mr. Sanguine sat in the chairs opposite the couch. Billy and Grace sat down on the sofa and waited intently for either one of the guests to speak. Mrs. Hubbuch spoke first, "We are happy that you are reunited with Caleb. He couldn't wait to come home."

"We're sooo glad to have him back as well," Grace said joyfully gripping a smiling Billy's arm.

"Well, there are a few conditions on having him home with you," Mr. Sanguine said in a very professional manner. The parents just listened. "As you know there were some real concerns about having him come back into your home." He looked at Billy. "Your past behavior was very questionable as we have discussed before, Billy. However, it seems as though you have expressed great remorse and have become a different person. It was also made obvious in our foster home visitation that Caleb missed you both tremendously. He loves you both and talked about the happy times he had at his home especially after the . . ." He paused searching for the right words. ". . . the incident."

Also, Billy, we expanded our assessment to include your past friendships." Billy looked curiously at him, "and one of the conditions we would like you to adhere to is to distance yourself from your former friends. We realize that it will be difficult in that Judy is married to your dad. We expect some interaction is inevitable in that case. However, Alex and Dora, although they are probably very nice people, aren't a good influence on you and their group dynamics, in our opinion, is very toxic to you and your family.

Grace couldn't help but say, "You're not kidding."

Billy smiled in agreement and said, "We feel the same way and would be more than willing to distance, as you say, ourselves from them. In fact, we avoid them as much as possible as it is.

Our contact with them is only when they force themselves into our lives."

"Good!" said Mr. Sanguine. "Another condition is for you, Billy." Billy perked up in his seat as Mr. Sanguine locked eyes with him. "You have got to stop drinking. Your behavior and decision making are altered when you are under the influence." Billy bowed his head in agreement. "We know you have not had anything to drink since the incident and, frankly, we are very proud of you for that. Your concerted effort to correct that problem was one of the factors in our decision to send Caleb back home to you and to Pam.

"I don't miss the drinking," Billy said sincerely. "I did miss Caleb, and won't take any chances of losing him again."

Mrs. Hubbuch entered into the conversation, "Nice to hear that, Billy. However, just to let you know, that any missteps in your drinking could result in our reversing our decision at some time in the future."

"I understand, Mrs. Hubbuch. And I assure you, it won't happen again."

"Nice to hear you say that, Billy. The final condition is that we would like to arrange monthly visitations for six months at your convenience. If everything looks good after that, we'd want to check in twice over the following year.

Grace and Billy looked at each other. Then Grace said, "That would be great. Would you mind making some of those visitations when we're having a cookout? Mom makes super hamburgers.

. . . .

The home visitations by the Children's Protective Services had gone well. There was only one incident, but that one was a doozy. It was after a full year since the conditions had been set. Mr. Sanguine and Mrs. Hubbuch conducted the visitations together for they had a soft spot in their hearts for Caleb and for the parents who had unveiled themselves as being good people and loving parents. Not many of the outcomes in their work turned out to be this satisfying. The other reason they both wanted to do the visitations together was that Pam made great hamburgers in which she mixed diced onions and green peppers topped with a hint of her secret flavoring, Italian salad dressing. Yummmm!

Everyone was gathered in the back yard on this particular occasion. As usual, music from the radio drifted throughout the yard. "Tennessee Homesick Blues" by Dolly Parton was playing. Pam, Mrs. Hubbuch, and Mr. Sanguine were gathered around the grill. Caleb was playing tag with Tommy and P. J. and some of Grace's friends, Ninette and Jaybird. Pam, Billy, and Grace were seated with Katie and Paul. Shaun and Chris were throwing the ball around. A new one. The ball they had used to tease Lily with had seen better days.

Amongst all the noise in the back, the screeching of brakes could be heard as multiple cars doors opened and slammed. The front door slamming open could be heard and then a cluster of feet stomping through the house. The back door flung open, and there they were: Billy's old gang with Judy leading the charge.

Judy poked her head from behind the door and stomped

onto the landing followed by her posse. Looking at Billy, she blurts out, "Hey, son. Where have ya been?

Billy stood up and said, "Please don't call me that. I'm not your son."

Behind Judy, Alex and Dora were giggling. Then Judy says, "Yes, you are. You're my stepson. I married your daaadeeee." She hung on to the title much too long.

Billy made a step toward her and Paul stood between them, and said, "Hi, Judy, Alex, Dora. Remember me."

Alex slurs, "Yah, you're the guy who came to my house and asked us a bunch of questions."

"Yes, I was that guy, and this is the gal." Paul pointed to Katie. Katie stood and offered a smile and a slight wave. "You all were a great help. Again, thank you."

The posse was caught somewhat off guard by his kindness. Alex, not knowing what to say, stuttered, "Th. .th .thanks." They all stepped down onto the backyard, when Alex says, "Hey, I brought some beer. What's left of it. Anybody want one?"

Everyone politely said, "No," either that or just shook their heads. Dora reached out and grabbed one, popped it open and took a swig.

Then Judy started up again, "So son, what have you been doing? Where's my grandson?" She started to cackle and then spotted Caleb. She started to run after him. "Oh, baby. Come to grandma." Caleb thought she was playing tag with the rest of them. He hurried around the back yard with his slight limp and was able to avoid her. She almost grabbed him when Paul stepped between them. Katie was close by.

"Judy, it's time for you to leave," he said calmly but firmly.

"Who are you to tell me to . . . " The entire family and friends gather around. "Oh, I get it," Judy snapped. "Mob rule. Well, all right. We're going to go, but we'll remember this." She glared at Billy, "Goodbye, . . . son." Then she looked at Caleb who was standing with his two friends wondering who this "grandma" was and what the heck was going on. She took a step toward Caleb and said, "Bye, grandson."

Caleb looked back, and with a crooked smiled said, "Bye, gran....., well, bye."

CHAPTER 54 - THAT'S JUST WRONG

"At the innermost core of all loneliness is a deep and powerful
yearning for union with one's lost self." Brendan Behan

It had been five years since Judy and Norman had married. Both were miserable. Norman was gone quite frequently on business which left Judy home alone and lonely. She made up for that to some extent with off and on trips to the pool house with Alex or some handyman who would be working on the house.

Nellie hated the environment she was working in now. Dolly had been a friend, and they would often talk while Nellie cooked breakfasts and dinners. In fact, often times Dolly would ask Nellie to join her. One conversation, in particular, struck Nellie. Dolly was a little more withdrawn at the time but wanted to share some very personal events in her life with Nellie.

"Nellie, what type of a person do you think I am," Dolly asked fragilely.

"Why would you ask me that type of a question, Mrs. Cromwell."

"Because I just want to know. Am I a good person or am I a bad person..."

"Why, Mrs. Cromwell, you know the answer to that. You're a good person."

"Sometimes I don't think so," said Dolly sadly. Nellie just listened. "I've been married twice before I met Norman." Nellie simply nodded. She had known that. "I thought I was truly in love with my first husband but that love faded. Oh, he left me well off, but I was still missing something." She looked upward as though searching for more thoughts to pluck out of the air. She then continued, "My second marriage was bad from the start. That guy was overbearing and controlling. He wouldn't let me go anywhere without knowing all the details; Who was I going to be with? Where I was going? When would I be home? He was suffocating. I felt like a prisoner being married to him. I had to get out of that marriage because I couldn't be myself, . . . whatever that is."

Nellie's expression was sympathetic, "Miss Dolly, why are you telling me all this?"

"Nellie, I don't know. I just want to someone to talk to . . . release my thoughts, my feelings. Please, just let me go on." Nellie smiled and gently nodded her head in agreement. "When I first met Norman, he was different. That man was in control but not controlling. He was decisive, strong, and caring. He gave me my freedom to play bridge with my friends, to go where I wanted to go. He bought me gifts, surprised me with flowers, and he was pleasant. Then I . . ." She rested her head on the table and started crying.

"Miss Dolly, are you OK?" Nellie asked patting her elbow. Mrs. Cromwell then got up and left for her bedroom, but the conversation never drifted from Nellie's mind. Miss Dolly wanted to share something with her but couldn't find the strength. That something that burdened Mrs. Cromwell also overwhelmed Nellie for Nellie thought of her as more than a friend, much more.

· · · · · · · · · ·

Mr. Cromwell had come home early from a business trip. He had stopped by the florist's to pick up some flowers for Judy and Nellie. He had been buried with work but finally was able to come up for air. This momentary freedom relaxed him and also gave him time to realize that he wasn't as attentive at home as he should have been. The flowers were a kind gesture that he wanted both of the women to experience. In the back of his mind, he was really thinking of it as a peace offering. Hoping to snatch a sense of family back into his life.

He was actually pretty pleased with himself. For once he thought of someone else rather than just himself. He was looking forward to seeing the expressions on Judy's and Nellie's faces. He chuckled with self-satisfaction as he pulled into the horseshoe driveway, thinking that they may faint when they see the flowers. It was a happy image for him. He went all the way to the garage. Quietly got of his Mercedes with the two bouquets of flowers. He decided to slip into the back yard where Judy was often sunbathing by the pool to surprise her.

He looked over at the chair which was Judy's bathing spot. A towel hung over it haphazardly and a glass of wine, half full, rested on the tile. Norman scanned the area, but there was no sign of anybody. They must be inside he thought to himself. Still giddy with the prospects of surprising the two women, he almost skipped up to the back door and opened it. Nellie was in the refrigerator foraging for dinner items. She pivoted when she heard the door open.

"Oh, Mr. Cromwell. I wasn't expecting you until later."

"I know, Nellie, but I was able to finish up with the meetings and came home early." With a big smile, he handed her one of the bouquets. "This is for you, Nellie. Just a little thank you for all you do for us."

"Oh, thank you, Mr. Cromwell," she said as she gazed at the flowers that she cradled in her arms.

"Where's Mrs. Cromwell?"

Nellie gave a nervous look. "I'm not sure."

Then suddenly voices and laughter could be heard from outside. Norman's attention was drawn to the kitchen window just as Judy and Alex were shuffling out of the pool house: Alex was pulling up his pants while poking her in the back. Judy was dodging his advances and laughing. Mr. Cromwell was NOT laughing; he threw the bouquet aside and rushed for the back door. Nellie's eyes widened. She was engulfed in fear as much as Norman was engulfed in anger.

Judy and Alex looked up at the back door as it slammed shut behind Norman. Judy yelled out, "It's not what you think, Norman."

Norman was hopping down the stairs and made a beeline for Alex who had already turned to run. "You bastard," Norman yelled after Alex. "You better run." Norman knew Alex was much younger and faster. He stopped and turned to glare at Judy.

"Norman, it's not what you think," she pleaded with empty words.

"It's exactly what I think. Go get your things and get the hell out of my life," he growled. Norman was just as much crushed as he was angry. The contrast of the two emotions clashed like cymbals. He went from being happy with a bouquet of flowers to being slapped unconscious by infidelity. Something he knew a little bit about.

That night, Nellie and Mr. Cromwell had a quiet dinner together in the kitchen. Nothing fancy: a little pasta, some salad, and tiramisu for dessert. Norman pretty much kept to himself deep in thought. Judy had done what she had been told. She grabbed her things which consisted of jewelry, much of it being Dolly's, and her garments. She had shoved them into a large suitcase which she had to lug downstairs by herself and out to her car, another shiny Mercedes. Norman wouldn't help nor would he let Nellie lift a finger to aid Judy.

Toward the end of the meal, Norman lifted his head to look at Nellie and asked, "Am I a good man, Nellie, or am I a bad man?"

CHAPTER 55 - NOTHING LASTS FOREVER

"Hate is a bottomless; I will pour and our." Euripides, *Media*

The Keenan home was bubbling with happiness. Caleb's presence filled the once empty, sad spaces with joy. He bounced around the home laughing, singing and smiling. He helped his mommy and grammy out in the garden, kicked the ball with his father, and snuggled with them at night. Yes! Joy had engulfed their home now that Caleb had returned.

Grace had just put Caleb in his bed still in the sewing room at the end of the hallway. Billy was changing into his night clothes, and Pam was in her bed reading a book. All was quiet. Grace had decided to take a bubble bath. The warm water relaxed her body. She sunk down in the tub with just her head and her knees poking out from the shimmering bubbles.

Her mind drifted off thinking about how their lives had turned around; Billy had become the husband, the father that she had hoped for; Caleb was back in their lives, and the posse had been contained. It was perfect now. She sighed with joy. Just then the sound of breaking glass crashed her serenity followed by screaming: Caleb screaming.

Grace jumped out of the tub nearly slipping on the soapy water and quickly wrapped a towel around herself. Billy had just popped out of the bedroom, and Pam had dropped her book and shuffled out into the hallway as well.

Caleb was on the floor beside his bed. The window above

where he slept was broken and the night air flowed in freely. Pieces of glass were scattered everywhere. Blood was dripping down various parts of Caleb's body. Shards of glass could be seen poking out here and there as tears poured down his face. A brick rested on his bed among a nest of broken glass.

Earlier that evening, Caleb smiled after just hugging his mother good night. He was in the happiest world he could be in: reunited with his parents, in his home, and surrounded by love.

As he rested, he looked up out the window and gazed at the stars. So many shiny, sparkling stars. Such a beautiful night. He even started to hum to himself. Then he heard something outside near the street. It was a shuffling sound that tugged at his curiosity. He scrambled to his knees on the bed and looked out the window. He saw nothing. Wait! There was some movement across the street. The front porch light wasn't on, so it was hard to see. Caleb squinted his eyes hoping to get a better view. He could see something move behind the tall tree on the other side of the road. Holy catfish! It's a man or a woman coming to the front of the house. Caleb was peeking with curiosity of who was visiting. The figure scrambled to the front steps, he/she stopped, swung their arm back and flung an object toward Caleb's window. Caleb's eyes widened as he saw the brick heading right for his face. He leaned back, fell out of the bed as glass rained down on him.

Grace ran to Caleb. She wanted to hold him but dared not to for fear of pushing some of the glass deeper into his skin.

"Are you OK, buddy?" she blurted frantically.

Caleb sobbed, "Yes.'

Billy hurriedly walked up behind her, pulled off his shirt and used it to gently brush the glass to the side to create a path for Caleb to walk, afraid to pick him out fear of shoving protruding glass deeper into his skin.

"Take Caleb to the bathroom and make sure he is OK," he said firmly.

Grace and Caleb followed by Pam walked into the bathroom to care for their little buddy. Billy stayed behind and stared at the wreckage. The window had been shattered, glass was strewn everywhere, and a red, worn brick lay menacingly on the bed. Billy leaned over and picked it up. Something was scribbled on it that was hardly legible. Billy tried to make it out. He was able to figure out the first letter: an N and then an I and then a G. It was sloppy, but he didn't need to go any further to know the rest of the letters. Billy was furious. He glared out the window down below at the path leading up to the house. Caleb's father was near his melting point. He wasn't even close.

. . . .

Billy reported the incident immediately to the Cauldron Police Department Shortly after the call, an officer had driven over to check out the damage and to make a report. The squad car pulled up with its blue lights flashing in front of their home. A short, plump officer with a scrubby mustache got out, slammed the door, paused, looked around, and then strutted up to the house of the crime scene. He stopped just before climbing the steps to the porch. He looked up at the broken window and then continued up to the front door.

When Billy opened the door, the officer smiled and said with a voice of authority, "Hi, y'all. I'm Officer George Gordon, and I'm here responding to a complaint concerning property damage."

"Yes, Officer. Thank you for coming so soon." Grace was huddled behind Billy. Caleb was upstairs with Pam in her bedroom still being treated for his wounds.

"Tell me what happened."

"Sure. Would you like to come in?" Billy swayed his hand gesturing for the officer to enter. Officer Gordon walked in, and Billy offered him a seat in the living room and explained to him everything that had occurred: the brick being thrown, the breaking of the window, Caleb being injured with glass.

Officer Gordon seemed very concerned and said, "May I go upstairs to assess the damage?"

"Absolutely," said Billy.

The two men followed by Grace climbed the steps to the upstairs hallway. Officer Gordon looked at the damage: the broken window, the shattered glass.

"Y'all had quite a wake-up call. How badly was your boy hurt?" asked Officer Gordon with a sympathetic smile.

"Caleb had shards of glass in various parts of his body. His grandmother is taking care of him right now in that bedroom." Billy pointed in the direction.

"Can I see him?"

Grace spoke for the first time, "Yes, I'll get him."

Grace went into her mother's bedroom and then emerged with Caleb holding her hand. Pam followed.

"Oh! So this is Caleb?" The policeman said.

"Yes," said Grace with pride. "This is our baby."

The officer's demeanor changed completely. He went from caring to being apathetic, even annoyed. "OK. I'm done here. Let us know if it happens again."

"Is that it?" Billy asked.

"Yeah, that's it. What do you want me to do?" The question irked Billy and Grace, but they didn't know how to respond.

The Officer gave them an empty wave and marched down the stairs. Billy began to lunge after him, but Grace grabbed him by the arm. "No, Billy!!!"

They watched the back of Officer Gordon from the top of the stairs as he descended the steps. He opened the front door and made his way to the squad car.

Officer George Gordon got into his vehicle and turned off the flashing blue lights. "No emergency here," he muttered to himself and cruised off down the street.

Billy was pissed with the officer for brushing aside the incident, the terrible assault. This was about their son, his wife, and his family. He wanted action. If he wasn't going to get it at his home, he was going to go where he would get some action.

Grace and Billy sat impatiently in the lobby of the police

station. They had been waiting there for more than fifteen minutes. Billy's knees were bouncing up and down as he gripped the brick with both hands; His sweat painted smudges on it. Grace patted Billy's arm. She was afraid. She was fearful of what Billy might do. She was worried for their family, but she was terrified for Caleb's safety.

The door from the captain's office opened and a large man, maybe 6'4" emerged. His face was serious. He marched up to them and extended his hand to Billy.

"Hello, I'm Captain LoPiccolo." He didn't mix words. "So what's the story here?"

Billy talked, for the most part, telling his version of the incident. The captain looked over at Grace every once in a while and smiled at her reassuringly. Then the captain looked down at the brick on Billy's lap.

"What's that?"

"It's the brick that they threw through the window," said Billy.

"Let me see it." Billy handed Captain LoPiccolo the brick. The Captain held it in his hand, turned it over, and paused to read the scribbling. He then looked at the married couple in front of him. "I don't get it. You're both white.?"

"Grace spoke up, "But our son is black."

"Oh, so you adopted a negro?"

This interview was getting awkward. Neither Grace nor Billy wanted to get into the details of Caleb's origin. Not at the police station; not with this man.

"Sir," said Billy, "we just want to be protected. We want to make sure our son and our family are safe. What can you do for us? How can you help us?

Captain LoPiccolo responded, "Grace, Billy, we will send patrol cars by every once in a while to make sure whoever did this is aware that they're being watched. If anything unusual happens, you give us a call immediately." Billy and Grace just sighed. "I know it doesn't seem like much, but, for now, we can't do anything until we have some clues; something tangible to go on."

Grace and Billy got up. Disappointed and still rattled by the attack on their home, the injuries to their son, they limply thanked Captain LoPiccolo.

"Could you please the brick here, Mr. Cromwell."

Billy looked down at the brick in his hand. "Yes, sir."

The captain reach over and grabbed the brick from Billy. "This is something tangible. We'll keep in touch, sir."

Billy just nodded reluctant to give up the brick, but he did.

On the short drive home, Billy said, "They won't do anything."

Grace tended to agree, but held out hope, "They may, Billy. They just may."

Captain LoPiccolo sat in his worn, leather chair in his office. He stared at the brick, studied the scribblings, and got up. He walked to the door and looked out at Officer Gordon who was yucking it up with some police buddies.

"George," the captain said strongly. "Would you please step into my office?"

"Sure," George said perplexed, looking at his fellow officers.

He walked into the Captain's office with questions written all over his face.

Captain LoPiccolo spoke, "George, what is the story with this window incident?"

"Captain, it ain't nothing. Just some kids who threw a rock through a window. That's all."

"You mean, brick."

"OK. Brick. Rock. What does it matter?"

"It matters. A little boy got injured."

George tossed the comment aside, "Oh, it's no big deal: a scratch here and a scratch there. That was it. The window will get fixed, and they all can get back to whatever."

"Tell me about the boy," said the Captain. His eyes were more curious.

"He was just a little, negro kid. No big deal."

Captain LoPiccolo took a step forward. The short officer backed up a bit. "Do you have children, George?"

"You know I do, Captain."

"Would it be 'no big deal' if a brick was thrown into your kids' room?"

Officer Gordon squirmed a little. "Well, of course. But that's different."

"Different?" The captain paused and stared Gordon in the eyes. "Did you know that I was in Vietnam?"

"Yeah, I did, sir."

"Did you know that a bomb exploded ten feet from where I was standing?" Officer Gordon shook his head no. "Well, a piece of shrapnel sliced open my gut. Blood was flowing every-where." Gordon's eyes widened at the visual. The Captain con-tinued, "I was bleeding to death. Then a medic appeared from nowhere, dropped to his knees beside me, stopped the bleeding, bandaged what he could, and waited until help arrived as bullets whizzed by our heads."

"Were you scared, Captain?"

"I was more than scared. I truly thought I was going to meet my maker. The medic was calm and encouraged me to hang on; that I was going to make it. He told me where he was from and that his name was James Jr., but folks called him J. J."

LoPiccolo paused for a long time. Then he spoke again, " The bullets seemed to be getting closer. J. J. laid his body over mine to shield me from the oncoming fire." Another pause. "The medic took a bullet to the head. It ripped through his hel-met and blew his skull into bits. He died instantly."

"Wow! And you made it, Captain."

"I made it, Officer Gordon, and do you know what else?" The Captain took two steps toward him. They were inches apart. The captain's glare seemed to sear into the officer's eyes.

"No, I don't, sir," said George nervously.

Captain LoPiccolo took one step closer. He was nose to nose with the officer. "That medic was black."

. . . .

Weeks had passed since the window incident. A large piece of plywood covered the opening which was a reminder of that night. Caleb had seemed to shake it off, although he was reluctant to sleep in his own bed for several days. Caleb didn't know it, but his parents felt the same way. At night they found themselves staring out the windows into the darkness trying to detect any kind of movement, a shadow. They had a fear for whom may be lurking amongst the trees wanting to do harm to their little boy. They couldn't shake it off.

However, the time allowed them to heal but not forget. The scar still remained. Billy, Grace, and Pam were much more alert now and cautious. Everything seemed to gravitate toward normalcy: cookouts with their friends; Grace off to work at the factory; Billy hustling around the house after his job keeping things clean; Caleb smiling and running around.

At bed this night, Caleb's mom gave her son an extra, huge hug and looked down into his big, brown eyes.

"Caleb, do you know that I love you?"

"Yes, Mom, up to the sky and back again."

". . . and around the moon three times."

They both looked out the window as glass had now replaced the plywood. The moon was bright and even though it was night, it made everything appear as a dull gray as opposed to black and concealed. Grace gave Caleb another tight hug and went to her bedroom. She looked back at her son one more time before she entered. Caleb gave her a wave with his fingers, rested his head on his pillow, and smiled.

Grace entered the bedroom. Billy was turning back the sheets on the bed.

"How's he doin'?" asked Billy.

"He's doing fine. He is such a good, little guy." She got into bed, shut off the light, and gave Billy a peck on the cheek.

"What's that for?"

"Oh, I don't know. You just make me feel good.

". . . And you make me feel good, Grace. Sweet, sweet Grace."

CHAPTER 56 - GIVE ME A BREAK?

Grace, Billy, Pam, and Caleb seemed to melt into their beds: carefree and relaxed. They were finally able to put the brick incident behind them. Time has a way of healing; ushering pain and misery to the past. It had been weeks since they experienced such serenity. It was about two in the morning when Billy was stirred from his sleep. He forced his eyes open which were still under the spell of the Sandman. A vibrating, red and yellow glow shimmered outside their bedroom window. Billy rubbed his eyes to make sure that he was awake as the brightness magnified. "What the hell is that?" he said out loud.

Billy jumped out of bed and ran to the window. Then he pivoted quickly and shook Grace from her deep sleep. "FIRE!!! Get up, Pam. NOWWWW!"

Pam was still half asleep but quickly interpreted the panic in Billy. He grabbed her, pulled her out of bed, and nearly dragged out into the hall. Caleb was awake sitting up staring out the window. They ran up to Caleb to grab him. When they got to their son, they saw what Caleb was looking at: a large, wooden cross in their front yard consumed in flames.

Pam emerged from her bedroom seeing the three of them staring out the window silhouetted by the glow of the fire. "What's going on?" she screamed. None of them turned around and just stared out the window. Pam approached them, looked out the window, and saw the burning cross.

"What's that?" asked Caleb, his face brightened by the

blaze outside. Grace whose arms were already secured around him didn't answer. Nor did his father. Nor did his grand-mother. Anger, fear, helplessness, and despair suppressed their voices, but it was anger that throbbed within them more than anything. However, Caleb was just enthralled with the flames. His innocence allowed him to take in the fire display only with wonderment.

The firemen were dousing the remains of the charred cross and glowing coals as the family stood on their porch out of harm's way. The cross had been placed there and stabilized with wooden supports similar to what holds up a giant Christmas tree.

Billy stepped down from the porch and talked to one of the firemen in a heated tone, "What the hell do you think is going on here?"

"What do you mean?" he said removing his helmet and fanning his face.

"I mean, what is going on with this cross burning?"

The fireman looked at Billy. "Every once in a while we get a call for something like this, but usually, it's related to a black family." Billy looks up at the porch with Caleb looking back at him. The fireman sees Caleb. "Oh, . . . he could be the reason," as he gestures with his hand toward Caleb."

Billy was about to explode. Seeing anger like this before, Grace quickly descended the stairs and trotted up to Billy patting his arm. The firemen sensing the growing hostility began to work on extinguishing another alarm: Billy. "There are still, unfortunately, some strange folks in these parts who don't take to black folks."

"And this is how they show their dislike?" Grace asks.

"And you are?" asks the fireman.

"I'm Billy's wife, Grace," She grabs Billy's arm and pulls him close to her.

"Well, Mr. Billy, Miss Pam, it could have been worse. Be thankful that you are all alive. I wish I could provide more comforting words, but please know that all of us here in town are not like the ones who did this." The fireman looks at the smoldering ashes and then glances back up at the troubled couple. "My name is Will McGrath. If there is anything I can do to help you, don't hesitate to call the fire station and ask for me." He then turned and walked toward his men and check up on the cleanup.

Grace's mother nervously retreated to her room. Billy was walking back and forth in their bedroom scowling and muttering profanities. Grace couldn't help them, but she could help Caleb. Caleb's mom tucked her little guy back into bed and patted his forehead. Smiling down at him, she said, "Well, buddy, I think the excitement is all over. You can sleep peacefully now." The words rung hollow with her. She was petrified. However, the police car parked across the street from their home gave her some temporary comfort.

She stroked Caleb's hair and forced a smile. Caleb looked up at his mom and said, "He wasn't very big."

Pam's head popped up, and she stared into her sons face, "Who, Caleb?"

"The man who lit the fire." From the embers, smoke curled up past their window.

. . . .

A week after the blaze, the phone rang in the kitchen. Pam quickly grabbed it. "Hello!"

"Hello. This is Captain LoPiccolo from the Caldron Police Department. May I please speak with either Mr. or Mrs. Cromwell."

. . . .

Billy, Grace, and Caleb huddled in the darkened room at the police station. Captain LoPiccolo walked in the door. "Why don't you all have a seat. Let me go over again what is going to happen." They all sat down in the chairs scattered around the tiny room. Caleb scramble over to one closest to his mom. When they seemed relatively comfortable, the Captain addressed little Caleb. "Hi, Caleb. How are you doin'?"

"I'm doin' good, sir. How Y'all doin'?"

The Captain smiled, "I'm doin' real good, Caleb. Thank you for asking." Caleb smiled back at him. "Now, Caleb, let me just go over what we discussed earlier." Caleb nodded his head. "You said that you saw the person who lit the cross on fire. Is that right?"

"Yes, Mr. Picola."

The captained grinned. "And you think you can identify that person if you saw him. Is that correct?"

"Oh, yeah, Mr. Picola."

"Now, the other thing is that you weren't sure if it was a boy or a girl. Correct?"

"Correct," repeated Caleb, pleased with himself for answering all the questions.

"Well, this is what we're going to do." Captain addressed all three of them. "We are going to have what is called a lineup."

Caleb furrowed his eyebrows. "What's that?"

"Well, Caleb, that's what I was talking about earlier. We're going to have people walk out onto a platform, and they will face us. There will be lines on a white wall behind them to show how tall they of are. Do you understand so far?"

"I think so?"

"So, now, when they walk out, you will tell us if any of them look like the person who lit the fire. They will not be able to see you, but you can see them."

"How can that happen? If I look out a window, people can see me from the other side."

Captain LoPiccolo tries to answer his question, "It's called a trick mirror." Caleb seemed by buy into that explanation. He liked tricks.

The Captain then picks up a phone, "OK. You can have them enter the lineup room."

After a few moments, the motley group walks onto the brightly lit stage in single file and turn to face the two-way mirror. Captain LoPiccolo, Billy, and Grace looked at the lineup and looked back at Caleb to see his reaction. Caleb's eyes widen as he looked over the suspects.

They were surprised by the seven people standing in front

of them; they knew four of them: Officer Gordon, Dora, Charlie, Alex, and Angie. There were two other men: a worker from the factory that Grace hardly knew and a man with a scar on his face. He sent shivers down Grace's spine.

Caleb spotted Charlie and Angie. He started waving: "Hi Charlie! Hi Angie!"

Grace leaned over to try to silence Caleb. Officer Lopiccolo assured them that the folks on the other side of the mirror could not hear them as well as not see them. Inwardly, he scolded himself for not mentioning that fact earlier.

Billy and Grace were shocked at the lineup. Without talking to each other, they both toyed with the possibility of who the arsonist could be. Officer Gordon already divulged himself as a racist by his reaction to Caleb being black; Dora and Alex both harbored animosity toward Billy and Grace; Charlie and Angie were friends of Grace's so they were unlikely suspects; the factory worker was an unknown; so was the man with the scar. At least to Billy he was, but not to Grace. She kept that to herself. The couple were baffled and waited anxiously for Caleb's reaction.

"Do you recognize anybody, Caleb?" Asked the Captain.

"Oh, yeah. I see Angie and Charlie. Also, there's that mean policeman who came to our house, and there are those friends of Billy's. I forget their names." Billy squirmed. Caleb started to wave and then remembered they couldn't see him.

"OK. Do you recognize the person who lit the fire at your house?"

"Now I do. I wasn't real, real sure before, but, yeah, I do

now," said Caleb with a smiling face. "Right there!" he pointed to the person."

"Are you sure?" inquired Captain LoPiccolo.

"Oh, yeah. Yes, sir! I am really sure."

Members of the lineup were led out of the room. The police then escorted the person Caleb had picked out to another room used for interrogation. Billy and Grace were also escorted to another room that was adjacent to the interrogation room and sat down. They looked through the two way mirror into the room where the person who had lit the cross on fire sat. Their face was buried in their folded arms on the table. Captain LoPiccolo was seated across the table.

The captain began the questioning: "We have solid evidence that you were the arsonist who lit the cross on fire at Grace's and Billy's house." No answer. "We have a gasoline container with your fingerprints, and you have no clear alibi of where you were on that night." Silence. "We also have you positively identified as the person who lit the cross on fire. My only question is why?"

The head peeked up from their folded arms: "Because I loved her."

Billy and Grace couldn't believe their eyes.

"Who did you love?"

"I loved Grace." The head flopped back down into his folded arms. Muffled sobs could be heard.

"But that doesn't make sense," said Captain LoPiccolo. "If you love someone, why would you do such a thing?"

The head popped back up. "Because she married that

jerk." His eyes became steely and intense. ". . . And because she had sex with a black man. Ain't no one good who mixes the races. They are impure."

"I don't care about your philosophies. What I do care about is that you put that family in harm's way."

"I don't give a shi . . ."

"OK! That does it. You are now under arrest for arson. Come with me while we read you your rights and do the paperwork." Charlie stood up and raked his hair back with his hand.

Grace and Billy gazed at the scene in the interrogation room frozen in disbelief.

. . . .

Two days later, Pam, Grace, Ashlie, and Billy sat in chairs in the living room while Ninette, Angie, Stephanie, Jaybird, Chris and Shaun all sat on the floor Indian style near them. Caleb was outside playing with his friends, Tommy, and P. J.

"So Charlie was the one who lit the fire?" asked Shaun. "How did he get the wooden cross there? The thing was pretty big even in its charred form."

Billy answered, "Charlie wasn't alone."

A chorus of "You're kidding," mixed with "what the...?" and other responses filled the living room.

"He had help from two of his fellow KKK friends," Grace said.

Stephanie interrupted, "You mean he was a member of the KKK?"

"Apparently so," said Grace. "And they were the ones who

helped him make and deliver the cross. They were in the shadows when Charlie had come up to light the cross that they had doused with gasoline When it burst into flames, Caleb was able to see who it was."

"Why would he join the KKK?" asked Ninette.

Ashlie fielded this question, "Because everyone needs to feel a part of something even if it is something bad. Another thing. There are some folks who like to dehumanize others. They like to have power over others. They get a sense of superiority."

Billy thought to himself: I've been there.

"That's sad," said Jaybird. "It's amazing Charlie veered off into that direction."

"I can't believe it," said Angie. "I was surprised that they asked me to be in the lineup and when I saw Charlie, we just talked like old times; wondering why we were there."

"Did anyone ever guess that it might be Charlie?" asked Grace.

"Never had a clue," said Angie. Others shook their heads in agreement.

"Come to think of it, he did become more distant after Caleb was born," said Shaun.

"You're right!" Chris jumped in. "He never came over to help when we all spruced up your house, Grace."

Grace presented a blank look pondering the fact. "That's right. And he stopped coming by the house."

"I feel sorry for him," said Ashlie. All the eyes gravitated toward her.

"Why would you feel sorry for him?" pressed Billy.

"Because he has to live within a dark place to do such a thing. That's just a miserable way to live your life."

Caleb burst into the living room from outside full of giggles, "Hey, what's going on in here? Looks like you're having a party."

CHAPTER 57 - HERTZ DONUT

Five years had seemed to fly by quickly. Caleb was not a little kid anymore and now was trying to settle into middle school. It was during the year that the US stock market crashed with a 508 point drop. *Three Men and a Baby*, *Fatal Attraction*, *Dirty Dancing* were just some of the movies that splashed on the screens across America. Los Lobos' "La Bamba" album along with Fleetwood Mac's "Tangle in the Night" album were climbing to the top of the record charts.

However, little Caleb was wrestling with school. All that other stuff didn't matter to him except for the singing of "La Bamba" all the time. He liked his teachers, but, as expected, struggled in school except for the chorus. He loved to sing. He couldn't read music, but he could mimic the songs perfectly.

The teachers were patient with him. One teacher, in particular, made sure that he felt comfortable in school. Mr. Sousa was pleasant, funny and a character. But, more importantly, he cared about those who struggled. Caleb was one of those students. Teachers were drawn to Caleb because of his cheerfulness. Even when he was having difficulty with his classes, he always tried his hardest and entertained that incessant smile of his.

But school was not always pretty. Primarily because some kids would pick on him for a combination of reasons. Some ridiculed Caleb because he was a little slower than his classmates. Some made fun of the way he limped slightly and would walk down the hall beside him with a similar stride. Others were just prejudice and because he was light brown: they would taunt him and call him racist names. And finally, some knew about his birth situation and not only made fun of him but ridiculed his family to his face. Middle school can be a hell hole for some kids. It was that way to some degree for Caleb.

There were many times Caleb did not smile. On this day in the lunch room, there were a group of kids who thought a lot about themselves and didn't think a lot about others. Caleb was sitting alone singing to himself when one of the bullies sat down beside him. Caleb looked at him curiously. He looked back at his lunch plate trying to ignore his new seat mate. Then three others joined him. One sat on the other side of Caleb, and the other two sat across from him. Caleb continued to be lured to his food attempting to shield himself from the intruders.

"So, what's y'all singin' about, kid?" said the boy who first sat down beside him. Caleb just looked at him with his signature smile. "What's the matter. Don't y'all know how to talk." The others started to giggle. Caleb looked down at his pizza and took a bite. "Hey, I'm talking to ya," sneered the boy. Caleb just glanced at him and smiled. The boy asked, "Does ya want a hertz donut?"

Caleb said through his smile, "Sure! That would be nice."

"Wow! The kid does talk," the bully jeered looking at the others. They all chuckled. Then the bully turned and hit Caleb on the upper arm and laughed loudly, "Hurts! Don't it."

Caleb tucked down in pain momentarily. He grimaced and then suddenly swung around. With all his might, he unleashed a punch to the kid's arm knocking him off his seat and

312 - PETER ALDERMAN

onto the cafeteria floor. Caleb looked down at him and smiled, "Hurts! Don't it," and casually took another bite of his pizza.

. . . .

Caleb sat alone outside of the principal's office. He was nervous. Students and teachers would walk by and give him curious stares as if to say, "What the heck did that kid do?" Well, that kid did what any other kid would do. Unfortunately, all that anyone had seen was Caleb hitting the ring leader. It was similar to a football player throwing a punch and the referee turning around to see the other player retaliate only to get the penalty. Caleb got the penalty.

Mr. McConchie, the principal, came out of his office surprised to see Caleb sitting waiting for him. Caleb was regarded as a good kid. He had his learning problems, sure, but he was considered to be a good person. Mrs. Robidoux, the school secretary, approached Mr. McConchie and told him what happened. When Mrs. Robidoux mentioned the name of the boy Caleb hit to the principal, he smiled and said quietly to her, "Caleb should get a medal for that." Apparently the bully had some notoriety in the office.

Mr. Mac, as the students affectionately called him, escorted Caleb into his office and directed him to a chair in front of his desk.

"Have a seat right here, Caleb." Caleb did as he was told. He wiggled in his seat and looked around the office. He saw pictures of what he assumed were Mr. Mac's children and several framed papers with fancy writing. Most people would recognize them as diplomas. One was from the University of Tennessee. Another, bigger one, was from Vanderbilt, and the third one from Duke. Caleb wasn't impressed. He didn't know what that all meant. And he was more concerned about what might happen to him for hitting the bully. His visual tour of the office scanned pencil holders, staplers, and a red, scratched, toy truck on a shelf. Caleb really liked that.

"What is the toy truck for, Mr. Mac."

Mr. Mac turned to look at the truck and said, "That, Caleb, is a truck I had when I was a young boy. I used to play with it all the time. That is why it is a little beat up. That red truck reminds me of the joy I had as a youngster." He gets lost in thought then resumes speaking. "Being young is a time of innocence and of dreaming."

"I like to dream," said Caleb. "I dream that someday I'll meet my real daddy. Have him tell me stories when he was young like you just did. But I guess I'm not that innocent. " Caleb begins to smirk. "I slugged that kid in the arm, but he deserved it. He gave me a 'Hertz Donut' and I...."

"A what?" Mr. Mac interrupts.

"A Hertz Donut."

"What's that?"

"I'll show you." Caleb got out of his seat and circled around the table to Mr. Mac's chair.

"What are you doing, Caleb?"

"I'm going to give you a Hertz Donut." He gave Mr. Mac a little punch on the upper arm and smiled, "Hurts. Don't it? But he punched a lot harder than I just did."

Mr. Mac smiled back. The punch was light, but he got the idea as Caleb went back to nestle into his seat. "Caleb, you are young, and you are full of innocence. However, we can't have kids punching each other, so I am going to have to do something."

. . . .

The next day, Caleb was in the secretary's closet reorganizing all the files and such that had been disrupted over the last few months. He was sitting down on the floor putting documents away in alphabetical order. From his seat, he had a perfect view of the office and all the goings on there. Parents came in dropping off school lunches or lunch money. Some of them were picking up their kids from the nurse's clinic. Others were there to drop off homework that their son or daughter had forgotten to take back to school with them. Then there was the occasional distraught parent who came in to see the principal about a concern they had about their child.

To Caleb, it was like being at the movie theatre with all sorts of drama and activity happening. His parents had been notified about what he had done and had talked to him about consequences and punishment. He apologized and was ready for his discipline. But this was great. He had to receive his lumps, but he was not expecting a ringside seat to office activity. The bonus was when the bully and his buddies walked into the office ushered in by the gym teacher, Mr. Von Euw.

"I didn't do anything," yelled the ring leader. His comrades followed in sulking silence. "You can't do anything to me."

The gym teacher guided them to three chairs outside the

principal's office and then handed a note to Mrs. Robodeux. She looked at him and said, "So, they were punching other kids and screaming? ... What's this, 'hertz donut?'"

"That's it. I've got to get back to my class."

Caleb snickered to himself and went back to his chore. About a half hour later a man and two women stormed into the office. The man blurted, "What's this all about? I had to leave work for this crap." The two women had the same body language: irritated, aggressive.

Mr. Mac heard the commotion and came out immediately and herded the fuming parents into his office. The door was closed, but the fireworks could be heard through the walls; the kids were screaming at their parents; the parents were yelling at the kids. Then the noise died down. Only the level, calm voice of Mr. McConchie could be heard. After a brief silence, the door swung open, and the three boys shuffled out of the office. Their heads were down followed by their parents. Their faces were red with anger.

As they stomped out of the office, Mr. Mac turned to the secretary. "They all will be suspended for three days for fighting. Please notify their teachers to forward them their work for that number of days." He hesitated, shook his head, and then said, "I hate these type of episodes."

Mrs. Robodeux looked up and smiled, "Hurts. Don't it."

CHAPTER 58 - LONELY

"The truth is rarely pure and never simple." Oscar Wilde

Mr. Cromwell always considered himself a decisive, hard-nosed man with an emotional barrier thicker than steel. He could manipulate business deals to the tune of millions of dollars while unsuspecting sellers were drained of their life savings. He would play his three goons like puppets so they would do his dirty work while he never even got a smudge on his slick outfits.

Nothing seemed to faze him, until now. He sat in the back of his mansion looking out at his estate wrapped in a somber mood. He had so much: his mini golf course was pristine; the pool sparkled in the noonday sun; he could see a family of deer grazing at the edge of the forest; his glass of Barbaresco wine was among the very finest in the world and also one of the most expensive. He had it all. At least one would think so.

Norman missed Dolly much more than he thought he would: she was steady, pleasant, predictable, and, basically, a good person. Oh, sure, she liked to spend money and buy all sorts of things, but that did not make her a bad person. He wished that she was right there in the chaise lounge beside him talking about bridge or their vacation trips or her favorite wine. Like lyrics in a song: "You don't know how much you miss someone until they're gone."

Judy, however, was a different story: she fiddled with him like an old violin. Why in the world did he make such a mistake? She was too young and was a vulture looking for nothing more than what she could take from him. He thought he still had it at the time. Money? Yes. Electric charm? No. He took another sip of his wine and couldn't help to think but what a fool he was.

Nellie looked at Mr. Cromwell from the kitchen window. The house was dead. The large spaces, the quiet, the gloom made it seem like a massive mausoleum. Nellie didn't want to stay, but she had a fondness or was it sympathy, for Mr. Cromwell. She did not want to abandon him nor did she want to jeopardize her future. After all, his guarantee of a retirement free of financial burden was not only appealing; it was necessary. She wasn't getting any younger.

Suddenly, she heard the front door open and then it swished closed. A shadow lurched into the living room. Nellie wasn't expecting anyone.

A voice she recognized called out, "Hello! Nellie, are you here? . . . Dad?"

Nellie couldn't help herself. She rushed out of the kitchen into the living room and hugged Billy. "Oh, Billy, I'm so glad to see you."

"I'm so glad to see you too, Nellie. How have you been?"

"Oh, Billy. It's quiet around here. Just so quiet. I miss the days your mom was here, and you were here as well," she looked up at him, "but I don't miss Judy and your old friends."

Billy wasn't shocked. He didn't miss them either. "I don't blame you, Nellie." He looked around, "Where's dad?"

"He's out by the pool."

Billy gave Nellie a pat on the shoulder and said, "Thank

you," and went out the back door. Mr. Cromwell instinctively turned around. "Hi, dad. How are you doing?"

"Good!" he said trying to conceal his darkness. "What brings you here."

"Well, actually, I just wanted to see how you were doing. I know that the situation with Judy was not easy. She can be....."

" . . . A bitch," his father finished the sentence for him. "Yes, she can be and is. I'm glad she's gone." He looked at Billy in the eyes. "I don't say this too often, but I made a mistake." Norman then tightened his lips together and gazed out over the estate. The deer disappeared into the forest.

"I'm sorry, dad."

His father turned, looked at him, and forced a whisper, "Thanks."

Nellie was out by the grill cooking up steaks for dinner. Norman asked Billy to stay if he could, and he did. They talked about a myriad of things: how they missed Dolly, the messiness of the marriage to Judy, how great Nellie was, playing golf in the back yard, and how business was going.

When dinner was ready, they gathered around the table by the pool. They asked Nellie to join them. She was thrilled and sat down with them at the table. Norman talked about funny stories on his business trips, Nellie spoke about her favorite dish, and Billy just listened and commented every once in a while. It was nice. It was the first time that Billy had spent any chunk of time with his father. The company of Nellie just added that element of family and humanity to cushion any friction between the two men that may surface. None ever did and the evening was extraordinary for all three of them.

Nellie cleaned off the table and went back into the kitchen to clean the dishes. Norman and Billy remained by the pool. Nellie had offered Billy a beer or wine before she left, but keeping to the conditions set forth by Child Protective Services, he abstained. He had grown sick and tired of drinking anyway, so it wasn't like he was struggling not to accept the gesture.

Norman had another glass of wine while Billy sipped on a bottle of water. The deer began to emerge from the woods again as the sun crept behind the woods. Billy put his water down and focused on his father. He spoke softly but firmly, "Dad, why didn't you ever say you loved me? In all these years, you never once said that you loved me." His father looked away as though observing the forest. "Dad, why?"

"Well, Billy,. . ." he sucked in a deep breath, let it out slowly, "I...I do.."

"Dad, just tell me," Billy pleaded.

"Billy," he locked eyes with him. "I never said I loved you . . . ." another deep breath, "because I don't." He gazed off at the forest again.

Billy's jaw dropped. His heart sunk. His eyes began to pool with water, but he managed to choke out the words, "Why not? I'm your SON."

His father looked back at him and blurted, "Because you are NOT MY SON, and I am NOT your father."

Billy was stunned. He stood up and walked toward the

fence facing the woods, pivoted and almost screamed, "What are you saying?" through a flood of tears.

Norman looked at him casually. "Billy, I am saying that I am not your father." Billy grimaced as he listened; Nellie looked out from the kitchen window; the last deer had faded into the forest. "Your mother had a relationship before we were married. I knew she had a boyfriend, but I did not know that she was pregnant with you. Eight months after your mother and I were married, you were born."

Billy scanned the sky as if searching for an explanation. He choked, ". . . So you don't love me...because..."

"Billy, I don't love you, and certainly not like a son. But I do admire you; you have grown up to be a man; you take responsibility for your actions; you have a wonderful wife and family and . . . "

Billy abruptly strutted to the gate leading to the garage, turned to Norman and said, "Thanks for dinner, Mr. Cromwell."

. . . .

During the drive home, a myriad of thoughts and emotions were swirling through Billy's mind. He couldn't believe the news his father had hurled at him about not being his son. It hit him like a boulder falling from the sky. For the first time, Billy realized that he didn't know his real dad and that the man whom he had been raised by was not his father. The real issue that tortured him was that his mother was not alive to give him answers and, quite honestly, to love him, to hug him. He also felt betrayed, in some remote way, by Nellie. Why didn't she tell him about his father? However, the more he thought about that, he came to the conclusion that it was possible that Nellie did not even know. For much of the ride home, he dwelled on the fact that he didn't know his real father. He had no clue.

Then the correlation of Billy and his son came to life. He started to search for answers to questions he should have examined years ago; Did Caleb feel the same void deep down inside? . . . that he didn't know his father? Did he treat Caleb in the same way that his father, . . . Mr. Cromwell, . . . had treated him: with tolerance but not acceptance? A pang of guilt dug into Billy's chest. He realized that he had acted horribly; much worse than Mr. Cromwell had ever treated him. Visions of Caleb crawling around in the dog house wormed into his mind; the little guy, muddy and lonely, tied up to a railroad spike with just a limited leash for movement. He saw his wife, Grace, walking out in the rain to feed Caleb, to comfort Caleb while he watched from the kitchen guzzling beer.

He was turning the corner onto the street where his home was. He couldn't remember anything about the ride. If he passed by horses or barns or people, he had no memory of them. He had been consumed with the revelations that were poured out at the mansion by Norman and reflections about his own family.

Billy applied the brakes, put the car into park, and gazed at the cottage he now called home. The lights were on, and shadows of images walking around inside could be seen through the windows. He jumped out of the car and hopped the stairs to the porch thumping on the landing. He pushed open the door and called out, "Caleb, where are you? Caleb?"

"Here I am, daddy," Caleb said running around the corner.

Billy opened his arms to hoist up the not so little guy now. He hugged him and said, "I love you, son. I love you."

Caleb replied, "I love you, too, daddy."

Grace and Pam came from the kitchen to greet Billy. They both stopped to soak in the tender moment wondering what was the reason for such an embrace. Then Grace said, "How'd it go?"

Billy gazed back and said almost in a whisper said, "Great!" and gave Caleb another big hug.

"I'm too old for hugs, daddy."

"You're never too old, Caleb. You're never too old, son."

CHAPTER 59 - WAG

It was Saturday morning and absolutely beautiful. The blue sky had a few puffy clouds floating high above. The family was inside the kitchen chowing down blueberry pancakes, Caleb's favorite. "So, what are you going to do today, Caleb?" asked his mother.

"I'm not sure, but I was thinking . . . "

"Oh, were you now?" smiled Grace.

"Yes! I was thinking we should get a dog." Everyone's ears perked up. Caleb sensed all eyes on him. "I mean, we have that great dog house, and we don't have a dog. I think..."

"I do as well," injected Pam.

"Mom, a dog would be another thing we'd have to take care of," said Grace. Billy just watched and scooped up a forkful of pancake sitting on his plate.

"I suppose you're right, Grace," her mom replied. Billy seemed to sigh in relief.

"So, what are you going to do today, Caleb," said Grace going back to her original question.

"I'm going to the lake. It is a beautiful day."

"Who are you going with?" asked Pam as Billy munched on a forkful of pancakes.

"Well, I was thinking we all could go." The family exchanged glances. We haven't been down the tracks in like forever." Heads started nodding in agreement.

"We could actually go soon after breakfast," Billy said.

"When we've completed our walk, and I could do some work around the house."

"That sounds like a good idea," agreed Grace. "I can garden when we return. Are you going to come, mom?"

"Sounds like a fun time, but I have some things to do around the house. Y'all go and have a good time together.

After everyone helped with the dishes and got their bedrooms shipshape, they headed out the backdoor. As they walked by the doghouse, Caleb kicked a ball into the opening.

. . . .

Caleb had had a great suggestion. It was the first time in a long time that the three of them had walked along the tracks together. Caleb ran ahead and tried walking on one of the tracks as though it were a balance beam. Billy tried it, slipped and was caught by Grace who laughed at his antics.

Many things have changed in their world: their house had been restored with the help of friends and family; the downtown area was being renewed and looking real nice with trees being planted on the new brick sidewalks; telephone poles had been replaced with black street lamps fed by underground wires. They sprung up in an orderly fashion along the storefronts illuminating them with a soft glow at night. The buildings had all been restored back to their historic charm except for the Donnelly's who did not have the money to renovate but still were the heart of the community.

All that change, and, yet, the tracks remained the same with the woods on one side clutching onto preserving the natural setting, and the same houses nestled behind the berm on the other. A sign indicating track work was going to be performed soon was the only detachment from the norm.

It was as peaceful now as it was back in the day when Grace used to take walks with her father. She looked up at Billy and took hold of his hand. "Billy, we've come a long way."

"We're not even at the lake yet."

"You, goof. You know what I mean."

"Yes, I do," said Billy as he squeezed her hand.

Only a small mound of pebbles remained where the memorial for Grace's dad had been built. The wooden cross had been long gone thanks to the elements of nature and the natural aging of time. Caleb had gotten to the lake before them and was skimming rocks along the surface of the water. As his parents neared him, Caleb had gotten six skips.

"Did you see that!" he howled.

"Sure did, Caleb.," said Billy. He leaned down and picked up a rock. "Let me try my luck." He flung it sideways, and it hopped four times across the water."

"That was pretty good, dad," gleamed Caleb happy to be at the lake with his parents.

Grace leaned over, examined the rocks on the ground, and picked one up. "OK, guys. Mom's going to give it a try. I'll show you how it's done." They moved out of her way to give her plenty of room, and she let the rock fly. Billy and Caleb counted the skips all the way to seven, eight, nine, ten.

"Holy cow, mom. You're the winner."

They sat by the lake's edge looking at the fish swimming in the clear water. An eagle soared high above, and a deer bent her head down a little further away from them and lapped water up from the lake. A fisherman's lure could be heard dropping into the water. For a time they didn't even talk to each other. They all seemed to slide back into their place of tranquility and had it melt into their being. Then Billy broke the silence and said, "Do you know why fish are so smart?"

Grace and Caleb replied sarcastically in unison, "Because they're in schools."

As they headed home, a pair of eyes behind the brush followed them walking down the tracks.

. . . .

The walk back to the house was just as peaceful. Again Caleb tried his skill in walking on the track. Still, Billy decided to do the same and, again, he slid off clumsily.

Pam was sitting in a chair next to the back steps. "How was your walk?"

"Great!" came a chorus of replies. "Did you get all your work done?" asked Grace.

With a smirk, "I sure did."

Then a scratching from inside the house could be heard. They all exchanged curious glances, and Billy said, "What the heck is that?"

Pam got up, climbed the stairs, and opened the back door. A fluffy, little, black and brown mutt flopped out onto the landing, rolled down the steps and landed at their feet. He got back on all fours and began jumping around them, his tail wagging as if to say "pick me up." Caleb did just that, snuggled the little ball of fur, and smiled at his grammy.

CHAPTER 60 - TIN BOX

"There is no love without forgiveness, and there is no forgiveness without love."
Bryant H. McGill

The ball of fur was now three years old, and Caleb was going to be entering high school. Fluffy didn't seem to act the same as most dogs did. She would try to run and trip over her paws, get up, tail wagging, and chase after Caleb again. Fluffy also didn't reside in the dog house. She had been too spoiled for that and had taken residence in the house. Her sleeping quarters were in Caleb's little room on his bed.

Even though Tommy, P. J., and Caleb were going into high school, they still liked the games they played as kids. They would play tag, throw the ball around, and have Fluffy chase them the entire time.

Grace loved watching them from the kitchen window when she wasn't vacuuming the house or doing laundry, which was often. With a house full of people and a dog that shed hair like snow falling from the sky, she was always busy. It was worth it. She wouldn't trade any of it for anything.

There was a light knocking at the front door. Grace heard her mother's steps heading to the front foyer and the swishing of the front door opening. After a few moments, Pam walked into the kitchen. She was holding a small box in her hand.

"What's that?" said Grace.

"I don't know. When I got to the front door, no one was there. I found this box on the front porch."

Grace looked at it curiously. "It seems like it is made of tin. Have you opened it?"

"Not yet."

"Well, open it, mom," Grace said excitedly.

Pam pried the lid off the tin box with her fingers. It resisted a little bit, but, eventually, flipped open. Inside, there was a note addressed to Caleb with a cluster of pebbles on top. The two women looked at each other. Pam pulled the letter out delicately. Some of the small stones that were on top slid off.

"Are you going to read it? mom."

"It's not addressed to me. It is for Caleb."

Grace reached over and said, "May I?" Pam released the note as Grace plucked it out of her fingers. Grace held it up and silently read the letter. She gasped and let her hand with the note in it drop to her side.

"What is it?" her mom questioned with concern.

Grace gazed at her. "It's from him."

"Who?" Pam said. Grace handed her the note and sat down by the kitchen table lost in thought. The paper was a bit soiled, and the handwriting was a little awkward. Her mother sat down as well and read the note:

Dear Caleb,
I have thot bout y'all for manny years an of
Yur mom who is a very good woman.
I hope dat dis note finds y'all well an happy.
I know you mus be wondrin bout me I wonder bout y'all.

Caleb, I am your poppa, and
even dou I's not wit y'all,
I luv y'all very much.
Thru y'all, I live on cuz you is my son.
I hav not always been the bes person I culd hav been,
but my hope is dat y'all will be wha I am not.
Incide dis here tin box y'all will find 10 lil stones.
Each pebble bein' a qwality
for y'all to reach for as y'all liv yur life . . .
Goodnes, kindnes, thotfulnes, diligenc,
compashion, empathee, genirosity, helpfulnes, understandin',
and, most empotantlee - - luv.
Y'all will alwayz be in my thots.
Luv,
Dad (M.C.)

. . . .

That night Billy sat at the kitchen table with Grace. Pam had taken Caleb for a walk along the tracks with Fluffy to give mom and dad some time to sort things out. Billy reread the note for about the fifth time. Grace just watched him trying to read the emotion written on his face. It unveiled nothing. He was tranquil, calm and stoic considering whom the letter was from.

He put the note down on the kitchen table and looked across at Grace. He was not mad, upset, nor distraught. He was just pensive; staring at Grace. Finally, he spoke, "Grace, so this was the man you...."

"Yes, Billy. This is Caleb's biological father," she spilled it out with emotion and shame.

Billy looked down at the letter again; his finger scrolling along the words. Then he peeked up at Grace. "He was a good man, Grace?" he said more as a question than a statement.

"Yes," she whispered.

"There was a time when I would be angry," he looked away, got up and stared out the window at the dog house. "But now, knowing Caleb... No! Not that. Loving Caleb as I do. I am not angry." Grace remained seated and silent. "I want to be a better man than I am." He bowed his head toward the sink. "Does every man think about that as they get older? Do other men think of the mistakes they made: the people they've hurt; the misery they've caused." Billy felt a hand on his shoulder as Grace gently pivoted him toward her. She saw tears in his eyes.

"Not every man does, Billy. Only good men who see the mistakes they've made and want to make amends." Billy listened. "A man with apathy doesn't care about those who he has hurt. That man just becomes bitter and alone. A man with empathy feels the pain of those he has hurt. We both feel pain, Billy. We also feel compassion and love."

Billy put his arms around Grace, said nothing, and held her tightly.

. . . .

That night Caleb sat between his mom and dad on the sofa. The tin box with the pebbles rested on the coffee table. He read the note and reread it again and said, "So I have two daddies?"

"Yes! You do, Caleb," said Billy. "You have two daddies who love you."

"Two daddies," whispered Caleb. He paused, looked up at Billy and his mom and smiled: "Cool."

He then looked back at the note and pointed to it. "I don't mean to be mean, but this daddy has got to work on his spelling."

Grace patted him gently on his back, "Well, that daddy never got a chance to go to school. But he is a good, kind man which is a whole lot more important."

Caleb thought about what his mom just said. He then reached down into the tin box and circled his index finger through the ten pebbles. He picked up one of them: "I wonder which this one is? . . . Goodness?" He rested it in the palm of his hand. "And this one? . . . Kindness?" His parents just watched him as he dropped the pebble into his hand along with the other one. "And this one?" He swiveled his head to look at both of his parents. "Love?"

CHAPTER 61 - THE NEWS

The rain hammered the ground. It beat against the window panes and rumbled on the roof. Streams could be seen meandering through the backyard as water rushed out of the downspouts. Grace and Billy were glued to the TV: reports of the torrential downpours were being covered by every station. Pam was in the kitchen preparing a special meal for the family. Well, more for Caleb than the family. He loved spaghetti and meatballs, so that was the meal for this night as well as a house salad. Caleb was cutting up tomatoes and cucumbers, and Fluffy was resting nervously by their feet; a little disturbed by the weather outside.

Billy and Grace talked between commercials that promoted the movie *Jurassic Park* and the new toy craze, Beanie Babies. They both were interested in Chris and Angie who had gotten married four years ago and were going to have their first baby. They were excited for them. Jason and Ninette had gone off to South Africa to visit Ninette's grandparents, so the conversation steered in their direction.

"How long will Jason and Ninette be gone?" asked Billy.

"Well, they left for South Africa about a month ago. I would think that they would be back shortly."

"Do you think they will get married?"

Billy, not waiting for an answer, switched couples. "I think that it is a hoot that Chris and Angie had gotten married and now...wow...they're having a kid." Grace smiled back in approval.

"Yes. That was a surprise when they got married. Angie loved her girl trips to Florida and going to concerts with her buddies She gave that up to be with Chris who always wanted a family, and you never know about Ninette and Jaybird. It could happen," she responded.

The local news came on again. Pictures of flooded streets and rising rivers dominated the footage. Then local news broke away to cover a Texas conflict. The reporter spoke in a smooth voice of authority: "A religious group known as the Branch Davidians in Waco, Texas are under siege in their compound by American and federal and Texas state law enforcement. The US military are believed to provide support at some time shortly."

The couple listened with interest until the news transitioned for some sports talk. Neither Billy nor Grace cared for tennis, which was being reported, so they continued their conversation. "What is Shaun up to?" asked Billy.

"I hear he is in Nashville working for some country act," said Grace. "He tours all over the place."

"What does he do?"

"Heck if I know. But it sounds like he's having fun. You know that Stephanie got a promotion as a public defender in the county."

"She'd be good at that," said Billy. "She's a stickler for details and also for doing the right thing."

The sports had finished, and the newscast segued back to local flooding news. Pam called the family in for dinner. Billy and Grace hoisted themselves up from their seats and headed to the kitchen leaving the news commentary behind addressing an empty room: "Breaking Now! There has been an accident on Old Hickory road. A late year, blue Cadillac has crashed into a stone wall. A male driver has died at the scene, and a female passenger is clinging to life and being transported to the nearest hospital.

There is an ongoing investigation to determine the cause of the accident, but initial findings seem to rule it a combination of torrential rains and drinking. Several beer cans and wine bottles were found in and around the scene of the accident. We will get back to you when more of the story unfolds."

Pam and the Keenan family held hands and went around the table saying their thank you's. They all liked to acknowledge what was right in their lives. They have certainly come a long way.

Caleb went first as always: "I'm thankful for my mommy, daddy, and grammy." That was his usual contribution.

Pam went next: "I'm thankful for this meal." She paused. They looked at Pam, "And I'm thankful we're all here together on this rainy night."

"And I'm thankful the roof doesn't leak," smiled Billy.

Grace finished the thank you prayer: "I am thankful for us; all of us."

As they were eating, the conversation covered a lot of ground; to how Caleb's chorus was doing; what songs they were singing; to Pam's work at the factory; to the weather that they were now experiencing. Grace finally changed the subject and looked at her husband, "Have you heard anything about what Judy is up to, Billy?"

"Funny you should ask. She's still doing the real estate thing and is getting married to ...," he sighed, "...another rich guy. The poor fella doesn't know what he's getting into."

"Actually, they're getting married tonight." Pam chimed in, grinning, knowing she was the bearer of new news.

"How did you know that?" Grace asked in astonishment.

"I read in the papers a few weeks ago that they were getting married tonight. Too bad it's raining," Pam said genuinely.

The TV was still on in the background, but they weren't listening. If they were, they would have heard the most recent report on the accident: "Here is the latest update on that accident on Old Hickory Road. It has been determined that the primary cause of the crash was due to drinking although the wet roads may have had a roll in the event. Apparently, they were returning from a wedding since invitations dated for today were found on the floorboards among the beer bottles and other debris. The names of the victims are being withheld until members of the family have been notified."

CHAPTER 62 - SAD...SADDER

"Death is not the greatest loss in life. The greatest loss is what dies inside us while we live." Norman Cousins

Billy had gone to both funerals of his previous friends. Dora's funeral was reasonably well attended with family and friends. Judy was there with her husband sitting close to Dora's family. She looked broken, sad as did Dora's family. Dora's little brother, who wasn't quite that little standing at six feet four inches behind the lecture, gave a brief description of growing up with his sister. Dora was about six years older than her brother so their bonding was limited. The age gap and the brother-sister thing didn't allow for commonality in their sibling relationship, but he did an admirable job depicting Dora in a good light.

After the funeral, Judy got up and exited down the aisle with her new husband. He was about twenty years older than she was. He was balding, pot-bellied and about an inch taller than she. Judy caught Billy's eyes as she passed by and quickly looked the other way. The gesture could have several meanings. One could have been that she didn't want to see Billy after his father "dumped" her as she would put it. The other could have been that she felt the Billy had abandoned her and her friends for the girl across the tracks. The third could have been because she was embarrassed to be seen with her new catch; who wasn't exactly a candidate for a GQ cover.

To Billy, it didn't matter. He didn't care and sincerely hoped nothing but the best for her. Hardship is a difficult thing to endure, and even though Judy seemed to be oblivious to other's during their down times, Billy wasn't like that anymore. Other people's misery now touched his heart.

Billy later attended the funeral for Alex which was, ironically, held the same day but at a later time; different church. This was in stark contrast to the other funeral for it was very lightly attended with no one speaking to represent the family. Alex's mother was huddled in the pew close to the center isle being comforted by an older woman. A friend? A family member?

When the minister asked if anyone from the family would like to say a few words about Alex, no one budged. He paused to see if anybody would respond, but everyone remained glued to their seats. He, again, asked if anyone would like to say a few words on behalf of Alex. Again, awkward silence.

It was Billy who got up without even realizing it and walked to the front of the church. During his steps to the podium, he questioned himself about what he was doing or what he was going to say. When he reached the pulpit and turned to face the audience, curious eyes stared back at him. The only person he recognized was Judy and her husband, who, this time, were seated at the back of the church. He searched his mind for the right words to say, and then he spoke.

"Hello. My name is Billy Cromwell, and I was a friend of Alex's." He drew a breath and continued, "Alex and I lived in the same town; went to the same high school; had some of the same friends; and had many good times together. He liked to have fun. We raced golf carts together; dove off the diving board into the pool making cannon balls. Alex was really good at it. Water would splash over everybody relaxing in their lounge chairs." The crowd smiled with a few giggles mixed in as well. "Yes, Alex liked to have fun, but he was also a good person." Billy paused. He didn't want to blow Alex's image up to the point that it burst the truth. "I am glad that I had the privilege of knowing Alex. He will be missed."

Billy separated himself from the podium and walked back to his seat. Alex's mother reached out from her pew and grabbed Billy's arm; a tear beading down her cheek: "Thank you, Billy. Thank you so much." Billy smiled back in a comforting manner, and she let his arm go. When he walking back to his seat, he saw the backs of Judy and her husband leaving the church.

. . . .

When Billy got home later that day, he saw Pam and Grace sitting at the kitchen table entrenched in serious conversation. Caleb was upstairs singing and doing homework.

"Hey, girls. What's up?"

"Not much. How were the funeral services?" asked Grace.

"Sad, which was to be expected. I saw Judy." Pam cast a questioning glance. "She was with her husband. An older gentleman with very nice threads. We didn't talk, and that's about it for my day. Now, again, what's up? You two look serious."

Pam spoke first, "Well, I was coming back from the factory, and I was going to stop in, grab a vanilla coke, and say hi to the Donnelly's." She paused...a little too long for Billy's satisfaction."

"And...?" he tried coaxing her along.

"And it was closed. Not only was it closed, but the windows were also boarded up, and workers were all over the front doing all sorts of renovations."

"You're kidding?" said a disappointed Billy.

"I wish I were kidding, Billy," responded Pam. Grace watched in silence observing Billy's reaction. He was clearly stunned with the news and saddened.

"Were Lynnda or Mike around? Did you see them?"

"They may have been around. If Mike and Lynnda were, I didn't see them."

Grace decided to speak, "We don't know what is happening. None of the neighbors seem to know either. The only thing we heard was that there were two well-dressed men on the sidewalk standing by a big black Mercedes watching the work."

"Was one of them my father?" asked Billy, a little heated.

"No! For sure neither one was your father nor was he there. The only other thing I heard was that the two gentlemen were grinning ear to ear and that they had heavy accents when speaking with each other." Billy soaked in the information. "Oh, one more thing." Billy perked up. "One of the guys had a ring with a huge gem on his finger."

CHAPTER 63 - MOVING ON

Billy decided to take a ride out to the mansion to see his father. He wanted to know if he had anything to do with the Donnelly's leaving and the renovations. Grace had joined him. Caleb, now smothered with high school obligations, was at home, his face buried in a book determined to get better grades in his subjects.

Billy loved the ride out to his house. It brought back memories when he and his mother would go strawberry picking as a kid and when he would go to the local farm and ride horses. He shared these memories with Grace who loved hearing the stories and actually seeing the settings of these moments took place.

As they approached the mansion, Billy's eyes nearly popped out of their sockets. The "For Sale" sign on the front lawn just as well could have said "Screw You." He had lost his mother; didn't know who his birth father was, and now the home he grew up in was being sold. The tattered red Bronco, still hanging on by a thread and too fond for Billy to let go, pulled into the horseshoe driveway, parked, and the passengers exited the car. Billy walked up to the front door with Grace following behind and rang the doorbell. He usually would have stepped right in but was intimidated by the sign menacingly sticking up in his front lawn...if it was still his.

. . . .

Norman walked around the massive apartment. It's floor to ceiling windows giving way to majestic views of New York City. The stately, young women said, "And this is the kitchen. As you can see, it also has the floor to ceiling windows giving you visual access to the beauty of our city." She beckoned him to the left where a double door waited. She opened them, "And this is your master bath complete with a double sink, separate bath, and shower. Again, there is a floor to ceiling window to allow you to bring the outside in." She smiled. Her black skirt fitted tightly and displayed just enough of her legs to make one notice. She had a light, blue blouse on with a dark blue, sports jacket finishing off her apparel. She was dressed professionally and acted in the same way: confident, informed, and eager to make a sale, especially this sale which would put approximately two hundred thousand dollars into the pocket of that sports jacket of hers. "And this is your master closet." Norman peeked in. It stretched for fifteen feet with built-in dressers of light brown oak and a separate area for hanging suits and arranging shoes. "What do you think?"

Norman wasn't impressed. Compared to his mansion, this was the equivalent to an outhouse. However, he didn't want the overwhelming space that attributed to his loneliness back home. This was good. They walked into the kitchen that opened up to the dining/living room which epitomized the concept of open space. Miss Laper, the real estate agent, walked into the living room with the background of the city displayed behind her. "Is there anything else I can show you, Mr. Cromwell?" She started taking off her sports jacket.

"Miss Laper, I've seen enough. I'm here to buy a luxury condominium in the city. This will do. Put your jacket back on."

"Please, call me Natalie."

"Put your jacket back on, . . . Natalie."

. . . .

Billy and Grace were happy and relieved when Nellie answered the door. She smiled and gave Billy a hug. "Oh, Billy. I'm so happy to see you and you too Grace." She gave her a hug as well. "Come in. Can I get you something to eat? We have sandwiches and drinks left over from the open house."

"No thank you, Nellie," Billy paused and looked around: the pictures of his mother and him by the pool were taken down; the vacation images that adorned various shelves and tables were missing; objects that represented events in his life weren't there anymore. Even with the existing furniture, the rooms seemed empty to him. "I was not expecting to find that sign on the front lawn. What's going on?"

"Your father decided to sell the estate, Billy," she said sadly seeing Billy's eyes moisten. "It was just too big for him and, for that fact, me as well."

Grace just listened, understanding that this was an exclusive conversation for only Billy and Nellie. "So what's he going to do?"

"He's moving to New York City where he conducts most of his business?"

"And what's going to happen to you, Nellie?" Billy asked with concern.

"Your dad is true to his word, Billy. He has left me with a retirement account and enough money for me to buy a small condo in which to live."

Billy thought about what she said. He looked around bathing in the memories of his former house and then locked eyes with Nellie, "I'm glad he is taking care of you, Nellie. You have been great to all of us, and you deserve to be taken care of. But one thing."

Nellie cocked her head: "What's that?"

"He's not my dad."

. . . .

On the ride back home, Billy gathered in all the sights of the countryside, realizing that it was not a portion of his life anymore, but just a batch of memories. Some good. Some bad. It was hard for him. Similar to when his mother died. A part of him was about to fall into the past. Grace sensed his loss, his sadness and placed her hand on his thigh not saying anything. He looked at her and smiled. "Thank God for you, Grace. Thank God." She smiled back at him.

They didn't talk for the rest of the ride. Billy and Grace didn't need to.

CHAPTER 64 - RENOVATIONS

Grace and Pam strolled downtown to check out the work being done at the former Donnelly Mom and Pop store. The entire block had been restored tastefully embracing the architecture of the past and blending it with ambiances of the present. The telephone poles which stood like stiff soldiers, wires stretching from one to the other, were no longer there. Underground electrical systems replaced the webbing that once was strung from pole to pole. Black, carriage lampposts now sprung from the sidewalks complimenting the storefronts and providing soft lighting in the evening. A parking garage had been erected to accommodate the increase in traffic that had been drawn to the quaint shopping area which once was deemed as "the wrong side of the tracks."

People were bustling along the sidewalks and darting in and out of the now upscale shops that lined Main Street. Window boxes with an array Coleus, frosted curls, Blazin Rose Irisine, white licorice plant, sweet potato vine, dracaena, and other plants overflowing their sides welcomed shoppers inside. Some of the shops even had crape myrtles adorned with bright red blossoms or mountain laurels with brilliant pink flowers or a collection of hibiscus plants wound together like a rope with a colorful mixture of red, yellow, and white flowers guarding their entryways. Grace and Pam were in awe of the incredible, the beautiful transformation of their once downtrodden Main Street.

When they approached the sight of Donnelly's, the renovations had been completed except for the sign. The outside maintained the original appearance to some degree, but, like many of the other shops, was very tastefully adorned with lanterns, outdoor benches, and appealing window boxes; the flowers arranged just perfectly. They had no idea what would replace their beloved neighborhood haunt, but, one thing was for sure, whatever was sold in there would cost a lot more than a vanilla coke or a chocolate chip ice cream cone.

. . . .

Billy had gotten a promotion as manager of the furniture store. Grace was able to go back to the factory to work, and Pam was able to join her now that Caleb was consumed with his senior year responsibilities in high school. Caleb had struggled in school. His developmental issues, although addressed, never propelled him any further than being a less than an average student. Even at that, he had to work his hardest. Fortunately, his buddies, Tommy, and P. J. were there to help him. But those weren't the only friends he had. Caleb's happy, positive demeanor attracted people to him like a magnet. When someone was down, Caleb was there to lift them up. To say Caleb was well liked is an understatement. Even the middle school bully now gave a nod and a grin to Caleb as they passed in the halls.

Although Caleb had his struggles in school, he did have a talent which elevated him above his peers. The kid could sing and sing well. Billy couldn't carry a note in a bucket, and Grace had trouble keeping the tune to Happy Birthday, but Caleb was blessed with this ability, and he loved to sing. One time his buddies, Tommy, and P. J. were in the back yard throwing a football around. Fluffy was having a blast running after the football as it spiraled in the air, and, as typical, Pam was cooking up some burgers. Caleb caught a pass from Tommy, held on to the ball and said, "I have an idea."

"What's that?" said Tommy. As Pam watched from her position near the grill.

"Well, I thought we could start a singing trio."

"What? Are you nuts?" laughed P. J.

"No. I'm serious," Caleb said.

"What do you have in mind?" questioned Tommy.

"I thought we could try singing a song today just to see how it works out. Something like . . . Kumbaya. Everybody knows that."

"Yeah, I know it, but I can't sing it," snickered P. J.

"Let's just give it a try. It will be fun," pleaded Caleb. His buddies reluctantly agreed, and they gave it a whirl. After a few attempts, it became painfully evident that this trio would quickly dissolve into a solo act. The three of them trying to sing together was comical. Billy would have been a better replacement for either Tommy or P. J. Poor Fluffy was even tormented as she looked up briefly at them; her head tilted slightly to the side; her ears were flopping; dashed to her dog house. She swiveled around facing them and put her paws over her head. No! This trio was never going to make it. Pam even stopped her cooking and went to retrieve the ball and handed it over to P. J.

"I'd stick with throwing the football around if I were y'all."

Billy then popped open the backdoor and yelled, "Hey, Caleb. There's a phone call for you.

CHAPTER 65 - JUST BUSINESS

"There is no class so pitiably wretched as that which possesses money and nothing else." Andrew Carnegie

Norman Cromwell sat on his luxurious sofa, a glass of wine in hand, looking out at the New York skyline. It was too early for wine being 3:00 PM, but Norman was feeling good. He was planning his evening for listening to the concert at Carnegie Hall. He questioned himself about his addiction to the attending performances; Was it for the incredible talent? Was it for the magnificent architecture? Or was it a tribute to the man he admired so much, Andrew Carnegie, a self-made steel tycoon and one of the wealthiest businessmen of the 19th century? Most likely a combination of all three. However, Carnegie's business success, drive, intelligence and complete ownership of every facet of his company from raw materials, ships, railroads, to even coal fields and steel furnaces made him Norman's idol. By 1889, the Carnegie Steel Corporation was the largest of its kind in the world. Norman didn't have expectations of that type of success for himself, but he did try to model himself after Carnegie's financial success . . . at least incrementally.

There was a ring from the intercom. Norman knew who it was and pressed the access button for the visitor. He drank the rest of his wine and put it in the sink. The elevator slid open, and an attractive woman said, "Hi Norman. Are you excited about this evening?"

To Norman that could have several meanings, but he interpreted in its purest form. "Yes, I'm looking forward to the concert."

The attractive woman moved closer to Norman and draped her arms around him. "How do you know I'm talking about the concert, Mr. Cromwell?"

Norman ignored the question and gave her a quick peck on the cheek. "Do you feel like Italian tonight?"

"No! I'd prefer an English man."

"Come on, Natalie. Focus on music, please. You're degrading the evening," said Norman, a little amused but a little frustrated as well. He loved Carnegie Hall for so many reasons; the Italian Renaissance design of the exterior reflected the eclectic architectural tastes of the period, which look to European models of earlier centuries for inspiration. Tuthill, the architect, deliberately chose to keep the styling and decorative elements simple, elegant, and functional, focusing his energies on designing an excellent acoustic environment. To Norman, Carnegie hall represented style, wealth, history, and he didn't want to taint its sanctity with questionable commentaries. At least, not before the main event.

"Music. Yes! I love music," answered Natalie with a flirtatious grin.

Miss Naper and Cromwell dined at Trattoria Dell'Arte which was a step away from the Hall as Norman often affectionately referred to it. They decided to share a Lasagna dinner. Christian, the manager, was like a friend to Norman and would create any meal at his request. The 101 layer lasagna hit the spot. The noodles were thin with a perfect ratio of meat to sauce to pasta with a hint of cheese. Not too much. Not too little. And the red, Italian wine was an enhancement to a splendid dinner.

"Are you looking forward to the concert, Natalie?"

She finished swallowing her sip of wine and said, "Very much so. I love all those performers."

"It is a great line up: Paul Simon, Jon Bon Jovi, Billy Joel, and Elton John. Which one is your favorite?"

"I think Bon Jovi. He's adorable."

"I meant music-wise."

"I'd have to go with Elton John then. Why are they all at Carnegie Hall tonight?"

"It's the sixth Annual Rainforest Foundation International Benefit." Norman nearly gagged on his lasagna just saying that. He was thinking that the rainforest would be a great place for development, but it was a great concert, so he set aside his personal opinions about development. However, he did segue to another topic. "Did you know that Carnegie decided to spend the rest of his days helping others after selling his company."

"I heard something about his philanthropic work but not al...."

An excited Norman interrupted, "While he had begun his benevolent work years earlier by building libraries and making donations, Carnegie expanded his efforts in the early 20th century. He was an avid reader for much of his life and donated approximately $5 million to the New York Public Library so that the library could open several branches. Andrew," as Norman addressed him as if he was an old friend, ". . . was devoted to learning. He established the Carnegie Institute of Technology in Pittsburgh, which is now known as Carnegie-Mellon University in 1904. The next year, he created the Carnegie Foundation for the Advancement of Teaching in 1905."

Natalie chewing on a morsel of Lasagna politely responded, "Oh, really?" She could care less. However, seeing Bon Jovi was a different story.

Norman noticed the detachment she had for his fountain of information and decided to get to the point, "Natalie, I really feel good about what I've done for that couple in my hometown."

Miss Naper looked at him like she had just choked on an olive. "What are you talking about?"

"Natalie, I have not been the best man I could have been." She just kept chomping and thinking . . . Oh, no. I hope this guy doesn't get maudlin on me. "Carnegie had been a philanthropist in the later years of his life. I had ignored that fact because I was so intrigued by his financial successes." Natalie reached for her wine and nodded as if in agreement. In reality, she didn't know what the hell he was talking about. He continued, oblivious to her presence and even to where he was, "He choose to do good for others; to help humanity. I am glad that I've done a little in terms of philanthro..."

"Do you think we'll be late for our concert Norman?" interrupted Miss Naper who was now totally bored with the sermon about Andrew Carnegie.

He stopped his commentary, smiled at his date or more so to himself and said, "We'll be fine, Natalie."

. . . .

"No man can become rich without himself enriching others."
Andrew Carnegie

Lynnda and Mike were putting up the last decor for the shop. It wasn't the same as the old shop with its weathered, wide board floors that endured the soles of thousands of shoes over the years. However, it was the same floor which had been sanded and stained to look brand new. The dented counter had been replaced with a sharp, shiny, quartz one and its length could accommodate up to as many as six customers. There were two booths now instead of one. They were made of distressed, varnished pine. All the shelving was new and well positioned with merchandising that reflected not only a soda fountain but also a grocery store with knickknacks for sale.

Behind the counter, was a soda dispenser system complete with everything one would need: self-contained soda syrup refrigeration unit with carbonator, Wunder Bar soda gun, Catalina five pound CO_2 tank, Flojet soda syrup pumps, quick connects for Coca-Cola and Pepsi Bag-In-Box soda syrup products, syrup brix cup, soda syrup separator, and high and low-pressure CO_2 regulator and supply lines. But the items that pleased Mike and Lynnda the most we're the espresso grinders, coffee maker, pastry case, blender, ice maker, oven, panini grill, and the three compartment sink all conveniently located with enough room to swivel, pivot, and turn to address all the customers' needs. Lynnda was in heaven.

The old oak door had been refurbished as well. It opened and closed easily with a swish sound followed by the ringing of chimes. Yes, the chimes that Mike had put up years ago to signal the entering and exiting of customers was still a part of the new shop. Mike was working checking out its mobility when a voice from the back called him, "Where do you want these, Mr. Donnelly?" He was holding a handful of straws.

"Put them in the glass jar on top of the counter."

"Yes, sir!"

"Thank you. And thank you for being our first employee at our new store."

"Yes, sir!"

. . . .

Pam, Grace, Billy, and Nellie sat at the quartz counter on the new vintage stools. Billy was slurping on her strawberry milkshake, Grace was licking a chocolate chip cone, Pam was sipping on a vanilla coke through a straw while Nellie was indulging in a slice of apple pie with a mound of vanilla ice cream on top. "This is the best service I've ever had," Grace said.

Hey," snapped Lynnda. "I give good service too," she said as she walked in front of the counter by her dear customers.

"You sure do, Lynnda, but this new guy is the best." Caleb smiled from ear to ear from behind the counter. He proudly wore a white apron. His name was monogrammed on the front in bright red letters. He loved working at Donnelly's. He loved seeing his family. He loved seeing his friends, and he was exceptionally good at his job. Greeting customers and making them happy was natural for him, and his parents were proud of him.

"I understand where you're coming from," Lynnda said as

she curled behind the counter and gave Caleb a pat on the back. "He's the best."

CHAPTER 66 - THE GATHERING

"Do not dwell in the past, do not dream of the future, concentrate the mind on the present moment." Buddha

The Keenan house was packed with friends and family. This time, instead of a cookout, everyone brought something for a buffet consisting of a smorgasbord of foods. Pulled pork sandwiches, homemade sweet rolls, sausage biscuits, homemade chicken and dumplings, trays of fresh fruit, muffins, assorted pastries and more were available on tables throughout the house. Even Grace's friends were there. Chris, Shaun, and Jason huddled in the corner of the kitchen rehashing old times. The girls, Angie, Ninette, Stephanie, and Grace, were seated in the living room, chairs were drawn close to share recent events in their lives. Pam was happy to see Ashlie and Nellie. They drove to the Keenan's together since Nellie had purchased a condo in the same complex as Ashlie's.

Billy stood to the side observing everyone engaged in conversation thinking about how far they all have traveled in life and the history of their past. "Only Wanna Be With You" by Hootie and the Blowfish played softly on the radio. Billy was happy, actually, beyond glad to be standing at that living room seeing all the smiles and laughter. He also thought of his own past: the mistakes he had made; the forgiveness Grace and her mother had shown; and the acceptance of him by their friends. He was grateful, but he also harbored a shade of sadness for Alex and Dora, who never were able to navigate to calmer waters and drowned too soon in their bitterness toward others who had more than they did.

He also felt sadness for Judy. She was locked in a tomb of misery which she created. Loneliness, bitterness, and despair just seemed to be her preference in life. Billy understood that. He was once there, but incredibly fortunate that, somehow, he turned a new page in his life.

Billy thought most about his dad, at least the only one who had served as some kind of a father figure. Yes, Billy now realized that even Mr. Cromwell deserved his gratefulness. Billy wondered how Norman was doing. Was he happy? Billy hoped so for Norman was the only father he had known. Billy sure hoped so.

. . . .

The auditorium was packed. Families had gathered together, members saving seats for late arrivals with coats draped over them. Students were greeting their friends, and moms and dads were happy to see old friends. The arca that the Keenan entourage occupied was large. Linda and Mike responded to Pam's hand waving wildly in the air beckoning them in her direction to take the two remaining seats that awaited them. The Donnelly's couldn't make the buffet because they had no one to watch the shop. However, they shuttered the store early so that they could at least join them all in the auditorium.

"So glad you could make it," Grace said as she held their hands.

"We're excited. Thank you for saving our seats," said Lynnda. Mike was beaming behind her.

"Glad to do it. Lynn ... ," Grace stopped. Something caught her eye tucked way back at the rear of the auditorium. Then she dismissed it and continued, "... I am so glad that you're here."

The lights flickered off and on. Everyone made their way to their seats and, after a few moments, they were settled waiting for the show to begin. Music from the high school band played a prelude to the production. The curtains opened, and there were Tommy and P. J. with a group of other students dressed in outfits reflecting the early, riverboat days. The setting was made to appear like a riverboat adjacent to a pier active with slaves hauling supplies here and there. The music was incredible, especially considering that they were just high school kids. After each performer sang their song, the crowd applauded in approval.

At intermission, the lights came on, and the auditorium erupted with chatter. Grace swiveled in her seat and looked back to see whatever it was that caught her attention earlier in the evening. Even though the lights were on, it was still dark way in the back. She then returned to the ongoing conversations. Everyone was relaxed and enjoying the play, *Showboat*. It was a beautiful musical with extremely challenging but alluring songs and harmonies. The lights flickered again, and the curtains were drawn open once more.

It was a bit later in the program when Caleb made his appearance. He shuffled out onto the stage looking weary and downtrodden. However, he was neither. He was consumed with excitement and joy. He made his way to the pier and set himself

down on a bale of cotton. The music gently provided the intro-
duction for Caleb's song. When he started singing, the auditorium froze in amazement. His deep baritone wrapped around
everyone and gathered them into the moment. It exceeded being
beautiful for it was heartfelt and wracked with emotion. And
from his bale of cotton, Caleb rose and walked to the center
of the stage. The spotlight glowed around him and caught his
every gesture. His hands were gripped in prayer revealing his
pure passion. His eyes were emotional; imploring for the essence
of life. He looked at everybody as though he was singing to each
and every one of them.

In the darkness at the rear of the auditorium, in the last
row, aisle seat, a black man sat. His face glowed with pride, and
his white teeth stretched from ear to ear. He watched Caleb
as he sang and delivered his performance to perfection. And
Daniel, C. M., sang along as well. Daniel and his son were in harmony for the first time. "He just keeps rollin', he keeps on rollin'
along."

When Caleb had finished with his smooth, baritone delivery, the last note hovered in the air, and his hands stretched
out as if embracing everyone there. The audience rose from their
seats and exploded with applause. Caleb reacted with his signature smile, took a bow, and paused for a few seconds. He waved
casually as he scanned the audience. In the rear of the auditorium, a figure waved back, and everyone turned to see who Caleb
was gesturing to. All they saw was the back door to the auditorium closing.

The black man was walking to the lobby when he bumped
into a man dressed in a slick, black suit. "Oh, cuse me, sah."

"Actually, it was my fault," said the well-dressed man. "Incredible performance by that last young man, wouldn't you say?"

"I's sures would. Yes! I's sures would," smiled Daniel dressed in his dirty jeans and stained, work shirt.

"Well, I have to go." The man began to leave and then stopped and turned to the black man. "Are you on your way somewhere?"

"I is, sah."

"Do you need a ride?"

Surprised at the offer, Daniel thought about it briefly and then replied gratefully, "If y'all don't mind."

"Not a bit. Not one bit," the well-dressed man said. "Where are you going?"

"Downs by da train tracks."

The man paused and smiled, "I know it well. Let's go." They walked and talked about the show as they went to the well-dressed man's dark Mercedes, got in and drove off to the . . . train tracks.

THE END

AUTHOR'S NOTE

Although this story is fiction, it was created with threads of truth that were sewn together from the misery and the sorrow of children from every walk of life.

Caleb was fortunate. His life, miraculously, was not tarnished to the extent that his innocence was robbed entirely from him.

Billy was also a victim of abuse. He had to deal with the effects of neglect and the things money couldn't buy. Love, understanding, and hope saved both Billy and Caleb from becoming two more victims to be added to the Child Abuse Statistics.

However, some scars will always remain.

. . . .

My very special thanks to my wife, Pam,
who always epitomizes love, understanding, and hope.

CHILD ABUSE

Child abuse knows no boundaries, no restrictions, no one culture. Unfortunately, neglect, harm, and mistreatment of all kinds plague households throughout the world.

"Over the past 10 years, more than 20,000 American children are believed to have been killed in their own homes by family members. That is nearly four times the number of US soldiers killed in Iraq and Afghanistan. . . . Millions of children are reported as abused and neglected every year."
http://www.bbc.co.uk/news/magazine-15193530.

. . . .

NATIONAL CHILD ABUSE STATISTICS

- 4 million child maltreatment referral reports received.

- Child abuse reports involved 7.2 million children.

- 4 million children received prevention & post-response services.

- 207,000 children received foster care services.

- 3% of victims are neglected.

- 2% of the victims are physically abused.

- 4% of victims are sexually abused.

- 9% of the victims are psychologically maltreated.

- The highest rate of child abuse in children under one (24.2% per 1,000).

- Over one-quarter (27.%) of victims are younger than 3 years.

- Annual estimate: 1,670 to 1740 children died from abuse and neglect.

- Almost five children die every day from child abuse.

- 80% of child fatalities involve at least one parent.

- 8% of child fatalities are under the age of 3.

About the Author

Peter Alderman was an educator for thirty seven years in Natick, Ma. He had an annual scholarship established in his name. He has written children's book. *The Rockets' Red Glare*, an historical account of the origin of our national anthem and accompanied by a CD by Platinum Award winning artist JoDee Messina, is his most notable creation to this point. *Train Tracks* has emerged as his first novel and is certainly not a children's book as it explores the darker side of life in a quick moving, riveting style.

Acknowledgments

Behind every production, accomplishment, or work of literature, there are people who serve as the inspirations and architects of the eventual outcome. I would like to express my sincerest gratitude to the people who provided that foundation for me.

First and foremost, I would like to thank my wife, Pam, who has been a model of stability and goodness. Her patience, diligence, advice, and encouragement in my writing efforts and, more importantly, in my life, have provided the impetus needed to complete my project and to be a better man. I could have not done it without you, Pam. Love ya.

To my publisher and friend, Pat Hayes of Flowerpot Press, who has always been there for me in and believed in my literary efforts.

To Barbara McGrath, prolific children's author, who launched me into my writing career and recognized skills in me that I never realized.

To Howie Klausner, screenwriter of six movies, who took the time to read my initial manuscript and gave me the confidence to forge ahead to complete my story.

To H.T Manogue, award winning author, who guided me in my efforts a provided suggestions in shaping my novel.

To my sisters, Susan and Marianne (Pinky), for being the best sisters in every conceivable way.

To my brother-in-law, John McConchie, whose intelligence, humor, and creativity filled my life with a myriad of examples on how to live life.

To all those who provided examples from which to model my characters: Mike and Lynnda Donnelly, the best neighbors a person could have; Mark and Ashlie Freeman who epitomize goodness and kindness; Jon LoPiccolo, who served our country both in the military and now as a firefighter captain; Katie Hubbuch, whose calm and virtue serve as guidance for everyone; my childhood friends who were there to pick me up when I was down: Dan Cashman, Tom Dalton, Clarke Keenan, and the late P.J. Feeney.

To Khaki Bedford, incredible photographer, who snapped the shot for the cover of *Train Tracks*.

To Brian Gates and his daughter, Aubrey, for posing for the cover of *Train Tracks*.

To the educators who earned characters spots in my novel;

Dr. John Buckley, Peter Souza, Danielle Linkas, Pam Robidoux, Jim Von Euw.

To the following people who elevate others with their kindness and goodness and served as examples for me to be a better person: Steve and Marijean Green, JoDee Messina, Ricky Heller, Steve and Eileen Samuels, Amanda Savo, Nanette and Jeff Avery, Devin Belle, Eric and Krissy Nordhoff, Johanna Zettersten, Wendy and Ryan Thomas, Courtney Hawksley, The Senquist family, Brian and Traci Seeliger, Christy Steinfeld, Allison Fernandez, Finlay and Kristin Long, The Lohrding family, Olympia Lamuno, Katherine and Steve Hodges, Jim Dunn, Griffin Bland, The Aker family, Nick and Karen Shuford, Don Muzquiz, The Gates family, The Milewski family, Sharon Femia, Doug and Bradley McLaughlin, Flip and Erin Porter, Dr. Jim and Sarah McGinley, Dr. Tad Yoneyama, Jennifer Haskett, Maureen ONeill, Barbara Doherty, Ted and Kathy Hobein, Kirk and Sue Patee, Jack and Bonnie Olson, and John and Susan Shannahan, Nate Hilliard, and Chris Wormer, who also plays a mean guitar.

To our grandsons who epitomize innocence, joy, and love: Brody, Branson, Quinn, Vaughn, River, Maxwell, and Xavior.

And finally, to our three sons, Chris, Shaun and Jason, who have given me enough experiences to fill twenty volumes of stories and who have become men of integrity and goodness. Fortunately, they absorbed their mother's qualities.